DEMONS OF DIVINITY

BOOK TWO OF THE ENOCHIAN WAR

LUKE MITCHELL

Thank you for reading.

1

INTERRUPTED

"**B**reathe," I sent softly, just as the thin band of my palmlight buzzed against my wrist again. The third incessant buzz in as many minutes. *"Just breathe,"* I repeated, possibly more to myself than to Elise. *"Let your senses flow."*

I closed my eyes. Tried for my own deep breath. It came like sucking air from a vacuum. A remnant of the punctured lung that'd already had two cycles to heal? Sure. Maybe. Definitely not apprehension over my buzzing palmlight and all the unwelcome scud it no doubt heralded—scud I was in no mood to think about right now.

So I sank into my extended senses instead, doing my best to breathe. I focused on Elise. Felt the tendrils of her presence unwrapping from her physical form, stretching out slowly, tentatively.

"The stone," I sent. *"Focus on the st—"*

My wrist buzzed again.

Alpha be damned.

I opened my eyes to find Elise watching me, concern evident in the depths of her startlingly blue eyes.

Had I said that out loud?

I tilted my head toward the pebble on the floor between us. "Aren't you supposed to be focusing?"

"Kinda hard with..." She bit her lip, rethinking whatever she'd been about to say. "I can feel you too, you know."

I dropped her gaze, focusing on the pebble. "Let's just try again."

"It might be important, Hal," she said slowly. "Maybe you should—"

"Later." I forced myself to meet her eyes, softening my tone. "This is more important, Lise. Let's try again. Please."

A small grin tugged at her lovely lips. "Well, since you asked so nicely…"

She was so gorgeous when she smiled like that. So gorgeous all the time, really, with her regal cheekbones and her vibrant blue eyes and her raven hair, pulled into a tight ponytail. But it was the smile that killed me—sweet, gentle, and just a touch hesitant, like she was awaiting my signal to go ahead and let me have it in full.

I wanted to give that signal—to beam it like an exploding star. Alpha save me, I wanted more than anything to forget the stupid stone and throw myself at her like any reasonable teenage guy would have. But I didn't do any of those things. Couldn't bring myself to rise to the heavenly invitation.

That was what really killed me.

Elise let out a breath as I looked away and gestured at the stone.

A dejected sigh? A calming breath of focus?

Maybe both.

I felt her in my senses, closing her eyes, settling hands to knees. Breathing, breathing. Dark eyebrows knitted together, her forehead creased with concentration. She extended herself more smoothly this time. Found the stone with only a slight waver. From there, I did my best to wait patiently as the seconds ticked by. And by. And—

The stone twitched on the rug. It wasn't much. I might not have even noticed had I not been monitoring with my extended senses. But it was something. And before I could point that out, she was already trying again.

This time it wasn't just a twitch. The stone visibly moved—rising up on its edge, slowly, slowly. It was like watching a tingler bug ascend the Auborean Mountains. But I waited, breath held… until the stone turned its edge, lost its balance, and keeled back to the rug on its other side.

I consciously refrained from sighing.

"What?" Elise asked anyway.

"What, nothing. That was great, Lise. You're right there. All you need to do now is control it."

Her eyebrow took on the arch that said I was barking for a beating in our next sparring match. I held up my hands in surrender, a genuine smile threatening to spill over. Then my palmlight buzzed for the fifth time, killing that smile right where it stood.

"Why don't you just turn it off?" she asked.

"Just... Look, let me help this time. You lift, I'll stabilize?"

Elise frowned at my palmlight a moment longer, then nodded and settled back into her focus. I reached out as I had ten-thousand times before, not bothering to close my eyes as I fixed my mind on the stone. Elise's brow furrowed, and a second later, there she was, her mind brushing lightly against mine.

"Easy," I sent. *"Control."*

The crease in her forehead lessened, and the stone began to slowly stand once more. I drew the faintest trickle of energy from my own body heat to keep it stable, fixing it on a steady track in my mind that would only allow it to move up or down.

Up or down.

Slowly, slowly, the stone rose from the rug.

Up or—

Buzz.

"Gropping scudbuckets!" I cried, slamming my fists to the rug as the stone flew across the room and buried itself in the pale yellow wall with a *thwap* and a small puff of plastwall debris.

Elise opened her eyes and looked meaningfully between the wall and me. "You were saying? About control?"

I clenched my jaw, biting back the thoughtless retorts fighting to escape. "I know, I know. If Johnny would just stop—"

"If you wanted it to stop," she said, giving me a look usually reserved for unruly toddlers, "you'd turn the damn thing off."

"Well, I..."

Scud.

I what? Wanted to know that Johnny was trying to reach me just so I could throw a tantrum about it? Maybe I deserved that look. I shook my head and turned toward the display on the wall.

There must be some reason he was being so tenacious today.

At a wave of my hand, the display came to life with a list of recent newsreel stories. It didn't take long to figure out what I was looking for—or for my stomach to turn to ice.

Headline after headline, all basically the same, the first ones from a couple hours ago, when Elise and I had been tangled in our morning spar.

Oasis Under Attack by Foreign Forces.

Alpha be good and gropped.

Elise sucked in a sharp breath when she saw it. I was already on my feet somehow, looking around the room like there might be something to explain how the scud this was happening. Because foreign forces could only mean one thing.

The raknoth.

I waved the first story to full screen, pretty sure I knew what was coming, but not quite able to believe it until the display filled with a distant shot of Oasis.

It didn't look good.

Black smoke drifted lazily up in the morning sun, tiny figures converging on the standing defenses with inhuman leaps and bounds—too far away to make out the details, but I knew if I could've, it would've been the scaly green hides of raknoth hybrids I saw. Nothing else could move like that.

My palmlight was open and at the ready before my brain could even register what I needed to do. Instead, I just stared dumbly at the azure light in my palm. My hand was trembling.

How was this happening?

We'd warned them. Alpha damn them, after everything we'd gone through to warn them…

Too late, I tried to pull away from the memories.

Hybrids tearing through the crowd, madness in their pale red eyes, crimson blood rolling down their stubby snouts. Bodies. Civilians and legionnaires and hybrids alike. Hundreds of them. The dark stone of the Great Hall thick with their blood.

And Carlisle…

Something slid around my chest from behind. Elise's arms, I vaguely noted. She might've whispered something too, but I was too lost in my thoughts to hear.

The White Tower Massacre, the newsreels had dubbed it. My very own Sanctum execution ceremony turned nightmare bloodbath. The same night Carlisle had blown the entire Great Hall and every enemy in it to dust right along with himself and his old mentor. In one stroke, he'd destroyed two of the raknoth and severed their control over The Sanctum and the Legion.

And yet here the raknoth forces were, right on the reels, attacking the third-largest Legion base on the planet. Because the world had been too frightened to listen to us. Because the wise clerics of the Sanctum and the hardened generals of the Legion couldn't bring themselves to believe Enochia could actually be under invasion by bloodsucking aliens. Because—

"Hal," Elise said, squeezing me tight enough to tell me it wasn't the first time she'd said my name.

The contact pulled me back to our dull living quarters. Back to my racing pulse and painfully clenched fists. I disentangled myself from her arms, wiping off sweaty palms before remembering my palmlight.

Johnny's messages. That's what I'd been trying to check. I pulled them up. Eight of them, six from the past ten minutes, and two from a few hours earlier, when I'd been sparring with Elise.

<Your favorite lizards are back in town. Could be bad.>

<It's bad. Real bad.>

<Check the reels.>

<Unless you're either 1) actively swiving our favorite raven-haired staff twirler or 2) suffering honest-to-Alpha rage-induced heart failure at all this contact from the outside world, check the reels.>

<In which case, still check the reels.>

<Also, FEEL FREE TO REPLY ANYTIME, you ass. Alpha's wrinklies, man, it's not like I'm asking you to come to couples' therapy with me...>

<Hal, I think we should consider couples' therapy. Love, Johnny>

<P.S. THIS IS NOT A GROPPING DRILL. Check the reels.>

I stared at the messages, wanting to think his light tone meant things couldn't actually be that bad. Definitely not *the-raknoth-just-destroyed-Oasis* bad. But I knew better.

If the day ever came when Johnny Wingard didn't try to crack a joke, it probably meant we were already dead.

I swiped with shaky fingers at the translucent azure holo of my palmlight. *<Saw the news. Big five there?>*

Johnny's reply came back with startling rapidity. *<Only a threesome as far as we can tell. You around this afternoon?>* Moments later, another message followed. *<See, it's funny because you haven't seen the sun in over a cycle. Seriously, though. Stay put. Please.>*

"What do we do?" Elise asked softly when I looked up.

"Stay put, apparently." I looked numbly from my palmlight to the smoking outline of Oasis on the display. "They'll route the hybrids at Oasis, and then..."

But I didn't know what else to say. Because what if they didn't route the hybrids? I didn't even want to think about it. Almost before I knew it, I found myself wrapping Elise into a tight hug. After her own flicker of surprise, she returned it readily.

"It's okay, love," she said softly, her breath warm against the side of my neck. "We're okay." She didn't ask why my heart was hammering like I'd just escaped a roomful of hungry haga beasts. She just held me tight, cradling the back of my head, whispering comforting words.

Eventually, she pulled back to meet my eyes. "Maybe you should call Johnny. Get more details."

"Maybe." I kissed her forehead and glanced at my palmlight, rereading his last message. *Stay put. Please.* "Something tells me we'll be talking soon anyway, whether I like it or not."

Elise gave me one last squeeze before pulling away. "I'm gonna call my dad, make sure they're safe."

I didn't argue. It wasn't like we were going to be able to return to our training session. But before she'd even unlocked her palmlight, a soft tone chimed through the small living space.

Someone was here. One flamboyantly red-headed legionnaire, if I had to guess. I met Elise's curious look with my grim one and gestured the wall display over to the door camera feeds.

Not one, but six men stood in the cramped hallway outside our modest Legion-sponsored living quarters. We'd been hesitant to take their off-base amenities. Almost as hesitant as they'd been to let us nominally pardoned terrorists wander off without a handy way to keep an eye on us. They'd insisted our staying here would be safer—though for them or for us, they didn't specify. Either way, as Franco put it, if we ended up needing to disappear, better they feel overconfident rather than wary from the start.

Except now, staring at the armed men outside, I couldn't help but think I might've rather taken them on edge at a distance than comfortable on our doorstep.

Of the two men who stepped forward, I was a bit surprised to see Docere Mathis, my old instructor. His ebony brow was scrunched into its perpetual scowl, and right beside him—surprise, surprise—was Johnny, who hardly looked light-of-spirit himself. That didn't bode well.

"Should I put on tea or something?" Elise said.

Something between a sigh and derisive laugh blew out of me. "I dunno, are you feeling particularly hospitable toward the people who blew your real house to shreds last season?"

Elise frowned. "Fair point."

I unlocked the door with my palmlight. I suppose I could've gotten it by hand—it wasn't like the apartment was very big. Mathis, though, seemed to be in a hurry. He was striding in almost before I could blink, the fiery red fuzz that was Johnny's hair marching along at his heels. Even buzzed to Legion regulations, you couldn't miss that hair.

The other four legionnaires posted up outside to wait.

Part of me wished Franco was there. He was a good man to have around when it came to sensitive conversations, which was exactly what I was guessing we were about to have. But he was off with Phineas and James, tracking down a lead—a farmer who claimed he'd sighted the raknoth ship landing on Enochia twelve years ago.

Of course, since the raknoth had been at least unofficially outed to the public, there'd been about as many of those stories as I had hairs on my body, but we had to start somewhere if we wanted to find that ship. And we wanted to find that damn ship.

At any rate, it'd probably be another day or two before Franco returned, which unfortunately meant it was down to Elise and I to make sure this didn't blow up.

Maybe I should have hid in the tiny pantry. But it was too late now.

I forced myself to meet Johnny's blue-green eyes, guilt curling through me. He went straight for the throat.

"So all it takes is a major raknoth attack to get a reply these days, huh buddy?"

I opened my mouth to spit back some retort, then decided to leave it to Mathis, who was favoring Johnny with a perfectly unamused scowl.

"What?" Johnny said, spreading his hands. "You heard High General Glenbark, sir. 'You will lubricate negotiations as you deem fit, Legionnaire Wingard.' That was the order." He went distant for a moment, then blinked, remembering himself. "Uh, sir."

Mathis' jaw was pure adamantus. "Legionnaire Wingard, you will mind your tongue or I will leave it nailed to the door right alongside you and your lubricant for the duration of this meeting. Understood?"

Johnny looked like he was waging war with his lips for a moment, but he settled and gave a passable, "Sir, yes sir."

I watched them, caught between my desire to maintain stubborn silence and to launch into a thousand questions about what was happening and what the scud they were here for. Luckily, Elise had no such hang-ups.

"How major is major?" she asked. "What's happening over there, and what does it have to do with us?"

Johnny opened his mouth but fell silent at Mathis' glare. Satisfied, Mathis considered Elise warily before fixing his gaze on me.

"Citizen Raish, your presence has been requested at Haven."

The formality of his address was a hot knife in the side—a deliberate reminder of the fact that I'd made no effort to return to Legion service once my name had been at least nominally cleared where the Legion—if not the Sanctum—was concerned.

I couldn't even conjure a bitter smile in response. "Good to see you too, sir. Might you be able to tell me what the Legion wants with me?"

Any petty judgment he felt toward me vanished behind his professional mask. "You saw the news?"

I nodded. "Oasis is under attack. But you have the numbers ten times over. I assume it's under control."

Mathis traded a look with Johnny. "It is indeed."

"And?"

"And it's not our control it's under," Johnny said, all traces of humor gone now.

Dread crept in—the same dread I felt at nighttime when memories of red eyes and my bloody parents came to visit me in the darkness.

"You're saying…"

Mathis gave a reluctant nod, looking more tired than I'd ever seen.

"The raknoth have taken Oasis."

2

TROUBLE IN PARADISE

"Well look at us," Johnny said, rapping his knuckles on our shoddy kitchen table. "The gang, all back together again."

Elise shot him a half-hearted frown. Johnny gave her his most disarming grin, but there were traces of pain behind the look. I was just busy trying to ignore the part of me wanting to point out that the gang was decidedly not all back together.

Not my parents. Not Carlisle. Not the hundreds of civilians and legionnaires who'd died at the White Tower because I'd been stupid enough to think I could beat the raknoth at their own game.

"Any word on Anna?" I asked quietly, maybe because I wasn't already feeling enough pain, or maybe because some twisted part of me wanted Johnny to share in some of it.

His sister, Annabelle, had gone missing just a few days after he'd started his new post at Haven, when his family had been in transit to join him there. Dozens of transports had made the flight that day. One—the one Anna had boarded to ride with her best friend, Liza—had gone mysteriously dark mid-flight, and hadn't been heard from since.

That'd been nearly a cycle ago. Long enough that I wasn't expecting good news so much as praying for it. But the look on his face told me all I needed to know before he worked up the will to give a weak shake of his head.

No. The gang was most certainly not all back together.

I wished I would've been there for him like I should've. I wished a lot of things about these past twelve days. But here we were, reunited by the blunt force of disaster.

I looked from Mathis to Johnny and back again. "How the scud did this happen?"

Mathis was still busy on his palmlight, as he had been for minutes now. It kind of made me want to blow the thing's electronics with my mind after the way they'd just barged in unannounced. Johnny leaned forward and began his disgorge before temptation got the better of me.

"Sounds like the attacking force was way bigger than anything they'd projected from what little intel we have. They must be making new hybrids somewhere, because, well..." He dropped my gaze, like he was almost embarrassed by what came next.

"How many?" I asked.

"Estimates put their numbers over two thousand," Mathis said, closing his palmlight.

"What?" Elise said, her hand clamping onto mine underneath the table. I couldn't say if I squeezed back or not. I was too busy trying to process.

The hybrids were savage creatures—humans who'd been, for lack of a better word, infected with raknoth genetic material. Part human, part raknoth. Although from what I'd seen, I was pretty sure that balance tipped more to the scaly side with each passing day. The true raknoth, like Alton Parker, could telepathically control the creatures, but without that input, I'd never seen anything but mindless violence from them. They were as terrifying as they were strong.

And apparently there were still more than enough out there to take down a major Legion base.

"Was Parker there?" I asked.

"Alton Parker has not been seen since the night of the White Tower Massacre," Mathis said. He tried to keep it mechanical as usual, but I saw the waver in his face. He'd been there too, after all, and even a hardsteel chomper like Mathis couldn't live through something like that without carrying away a few scars, inside and out.

At the moment, though, I was more worried about where that slimy bastard Parker might've slithered off to now that his imploding Vantage Corp had publicly given him the boot in wake of the horrific blood farming and hybrid production operation we'd unmasked. The Legion hadn't shared all of the gritty details with the public, but it'd been more than enough.

Alpha only knew what Alton Parker was up to now.

"We think there were at least a couple of the raknoth present, though," Johnny added. "And there were a few humans, too. Civilian clothes. Odd reports."

"Seekers?" Elise asked.

Johnny shrugged as if to say *what else?*

Mathis looked like he wanted to point out that, officially, there was no such thing as Seekers.

I was about to ask why the Legion had seen fit to share even this much information with a pair of civilians when a buzz from Mathis' palmlight stole our attention.

"She's ready," the docere told Johnny, sliding a holodisk onto the table with authoritative weight and fixing me with a *you'd better behave* scowl. "The High General wished to speak with you herself."

That was unexpected.

What the scud was going on here?

Elise and I barely had time to trade a surprised look before the disk lit and a holo of Freya Glenbark from the shoulders up appeared beside Mathis. Even at half size and in the pale, translucent tones of holo, the new High General exerted an intimidating aura—like a lioness with her strong brow and her mane of straight, golden hair that looked as if it would stop softsteel slugs in their tracks. We all sat a little straighter. Especially Johnny.

"Citizen Raish," she said in her precise tone, studying us with eyes that were piercing if not quite unkind. "Citizen Fields. The Legion appreciates your time in this matter."

My fist was halfway to my chest in a reflexive salute when I caught myself. "High General Glenbark," I said. "It's an honor to meet you."

A minor pain in the ass too, maybe. But an honor all the same.

I'd never met Freya Glenbark, but from what I'd heard from my dad and others, she was unquestionably one of the good guys—or good ladies, as it were. The fact that she'd managed to become the second female ever to ascend to High General—and to do it before the age of forty and in such a time of crisis—spoke volumes of her ability.

Elise echoed my sentiment with genuine respect.

"Not to be rude, sir," I added, "but what matter is it, exactly, that the Legion appreciates our time in?"

"Have you been briefed?"

"Basics only."

"Then I understand your confusion," she said. "You are no doubt wondering why we haven't simply retaken Oasis by force."

"You have the numbers," I said. "The hybrids don't even know how to use weapons, as far as I've seen. And the raknoth aren't invulnerable. It should be a stroll in the flowers."

"But you're here, talking to us," Elise said. "Which means—"

"That it's not as simple as throwing numbers at the problem," I finished.

"Or that you've already tried," Elise added, shooting me a frown at having been cut off, "and something went wrong."

Glenbark studied Elise, her expression unreadable.

My stomach fell as the silence stretched. Too long.

"Citizen Fields is correct," Glenbark finally said. "Our attempt to reclaim Oasis failed an hour ago."

I looked at Mathis and Johnny, searching for some reaction—some sign of shock or acknowledgment.

They just looked grim.

"I was getting to that part," Johnny murmured.

"How?" was all I could manage.

"I don't know," Glenbark said, looking none too pleased about it. "But, given the unprecedented nature of what these raknoth did to our forces, it was brought to my attention that you might be able to offer some explanation."

So that's what this was about.

They'd hunted me. Called me terrorist, heretic, and enemy of Enochia. And now they wanted to pick my brain about the very thing I'd been trying to tell them all along.

"What happened?" I asked, keeping my voice as neutral as I could.

"It's as you said. We had the numbers, the superior firepower. We had everything, and, by all conventional reasoning, every reason to move before they could dig in."

"But?"

Her composure held, but it was the first time in the conversation that she dropped her gaze. "But all of that ceased to matter when our legionnaires inexplicably broke command and turned their weapons on one another. There was no warning."

"Sweet Alpha," Elise murmured.

"It was bad," Mathis agreed, his hard edges gone for the moment. "Real bad."

Glenbark's gaze flicked toward Johnny before returning to skewer me. "Can you tell me what happened to my people out there, Haldin?"

"I…"

… was still trying to figure that out myself. The raknoth were powerful telepaths. They'd be able to mind-snatch most humans in seconds and bend them to their will as they pleased. Scud, I could do that—*had* done that once, I was less than proud to say. But how many men might one raknoth be able to control at once if they pushed themselves?

I had no idea.

"How many legionnaires turned?"

Glenbark studied me like she was trying to ascertain whether I might really have any idea what was happening. "Difficult to say. Things got messy quite quickly."

That was probably an understatement. I couldn't even imagine the chaos —the way it would feel to watch your own squad mates turning to end the life you'd trusted them with.

"At a guess," Glenbark continued, "at least three hundred. Those who made it back reported a state of helpless paralysis. They saw events unfolding but were unable to prevent it, or control their own bodies. We're holding them for evaluation now."

I felt Elise's questioning look beside me. "Could they control that many at once?"

"I don't know." I considered how easy it had been for me to breach an unprotected human mind. Weighed that against my memory of Al'Kunde-sha's strength when we'd telepathically battled back at the Sanctuary brig. Made some laughably vague estimations. "It's possible, I guess. Especially if they had help from a few Seekers."

Mathis cleared his throat as if to say *Great, now share with the whole class.* A faint frown touched Glenbark's brow, but she said nothing, waiting for my explanation.

Glossing over the weirder points and the fact that I too possessed these abilities, I explained the raknoth's telepathy and the threat it posed as concisely as I could. I couldn't help but notice the way Johnny watched me, as if he were remembering all over again that I wasn't the tyro he'd grown up with—that I'd become something else. Something irrefutably *different.*

Mathis didn't hide his skepticism as I spoke. Glenbark, for her part, listened with rapt attention. If she found any of it hard to believe, she kept it to herself.

"Fine," she said when I'd finished. "Thank you for your candor. I only have one question left."

"How do you protect your legionnaires?" I asked.

She nodded, betraying none of the desperation I could only imagine she might be feeling right now. I was starting to see why her fellow officers sang her praises.

"You need to get your people cloaked," Elise said.

"Cloaked," Glenbark repeated. "How?"

A quick mental probe toward Johnny confirmed he was still wearing the cloak Carlisle had given him. The guilt on his face as he touched the spot where it must be resting beneath his uniform suggested he was just now realizing he should have brought this up sooner.

I held up my own pendant so Glenbark could see its rune-etched surface. "This keeps my mind safe from other telepaths."

Mathis looked like he wanted to slap the table and call bullscud but couldn't bring himself to break discipline in front of the High General. Glenbark's stare was intent until something interrupted her on her end. She looked off for a second, gave a curt nod, and returned her attention to me. "How does it work?"

"I'm pretty sure the only two people who knew that were…"

The words stuck in my throat, and just like that, I was back in the White Tower—howling winds whipping at me, Carlisle ahead, dying, clutching his old mentor's face, both of them wrapped in the violet storm consuming the—

A sharp squeeze on my leg brought me back to the tiny kitchen, where Elise was watching me with that look again.

Consciously, I relaxed tight shoulders. "I think the secret was lost at the White Tower. Have you talked to the Sanctum? By all rights, their Seekers should know more about this than I do."

A hint of disdain crept over Glenbark's features. "The Sanctum has been… unhistorically uncommunicative since the White Tower incident. Suffice it to say, even if they were willing to admit to the existence of these fabled Seekers—which they most certainly are not—I'm left with the sinking impression that their people lack the knowledge to fix this problem."

"And that's supposed to make it my job?"

The words left my mouth before I gave them leave.

Mathis tensed. I half-expected him to lunge across the table. Maybe I even wanted him to.

Grop it. I wasn't a soldier anymore, right?

Not according to official records, where I'd been dishonorably discharged somewhere right between being declared dead, being revived and branded a terrorist, and finally being sentenced to hang as a heretic.

By all rights, I was pretty sure I had good reason to be pissed right then. But somehow, all I seemed to feel was shame under Glenbark's steady stare.

"People are dying, Citizen Raish," she said. "And you might be able to do something about it. I pray that alone is enough that you'll consider it." She glanced off at another distraction and nodded at someone. "Now, I have other matters to tend to. Good day Citizen Fields, Citizen Raish."

Her holo died before either of us could say a thing. Somehow, her disappearance only increased the weight of the shame. It sank over me like molten softsteel, bowing my head under its weight.

Johnny was the first to break the silence.

"We really do need you, broto. We're out of our depths with this stuff, and this new High Cleric is playing coy with whatever Seekers he's hiding." He held his hands up, empty. "I know it sucks, but there's no one else."

I said nothing—didn't know where to start.

So Mathis took his turn, speaking as if he were actually reading straight from the field orders. "High General Glenbark has instructed us to extend her invitation to join us at Haven in a special consultant capacity. By extension, Citizen Fields and her family will also be entitled to civilian quarters on base. In return, we ask that you—"

"Why'd they send you, Mathis?"

He paused from his highly official invitation.

Anger rippled somewhere deep beneath the indignation and the shame, bright and sudden. Anger at what exactly, I couldn't say. But here was Mathis, watching me with inscrutable dark eyes.

"Why you? They just wanna remind me?"

All the times this man had called me silver spoon... Daddy's tyro... All the times he'd reminded me just how pathetically I measured up next to Captain Martin Raish, honored hero of Sanctuary...

Elise's hand tightened on mine, a silent reminder to keep it together. At Mathis, she forced a smile that said *kindly get the scud out of here.* "I think we could use a couple days to think about it, if you goodfellows wouldn't mind..."

Johnny nodded and started to stand.

Mathis didn't budge. "We can't afford days, Citizen Fields. Would that we could all bury our heads in the flowers and try to forget our—"

"Get out."

I only whispered the words, but they gave Mathis pause all the same.

Maybe he could hear what was bubbling beneath the surface. Maybe he even understood it. I sure as scud didn't. All I knew was that I needed them to stop telling me what I owed to the Legion. To Enochia.

As if I hadn't paid enough already.

Mathis took a deep breath. "Raish, I need you to—"

I didn't consciously think about channeling the energy, or focusing the will. Almost before I knew it, I was telekinetically hauling Mathis to his feet, half-tossing him out of the tiny kitchen space and toward the door.

He kept his wits enough to catch his balance, but it was the first time I'd ever seen him look surprised.

"I think you two should go," Elise said, her hand like a hardsteel turngrip on mine.

Mathis turned those wide eyes to Johnny, designated meeting lubricant, who was frozen halfway out of his chair. Johnny looked a question at Elise, touching a finger to his own chest as if to say, *Me too?*

"You shouldn't have brought backup if you wanted to talk," Elise said.

Johnny scowled, standing the rest of the way. "I didn't—" He glanced at Mathis. "That's not what this was." He focused on me, his eyes pleading. "Hal..."

I dropped his gaze. Focused on the table. I couldn't handle this. Not now.

"Fine." He spread his hands. "Fine. I'll go. But I'm not done with your stubborn ass, broto."

I kept my eyes on the table.

"Be careful out there, Johnny," Elise said.

"You be careful in here." He went to join Mathis. Paused at the doorway. "It doesn't matter whose gropping job it is, Hal. Just... remember what it was all for."

His words hit me like physical blows. My best friend, the king of cavalier lightheartedness, resorting to that tone with me. I forced myself to meet his eyes—just long enough to take in the judgment. The disappointment. Instead, all I saw in his eyes was worry, and maybe a hint of fear.

He gave me a somber nod. "Take care, buddy."

My stomach tightened, and I looked away.

Scud, what was wrong with me? Why couldn't I open my mouth and say something? Explain myself?

"We'll talk about it," Elise said, seemingly to Mathis, as she rose to show them to the door.

When they were gone, I buried my face in my hands, squeezing at my temples until the pain was sufficient to distract from my suddenly racing heart and frenetic breathing.

How in demon's depths could they do this?

How could they be so damn incompetent as to lose Oasis and then turn around and somehow make me feel like it was my fault? Like I should be doing their job for them barely two cycles after they'd been trying to kill me and my friends?

It wasn't fair.

I'd fought my fight. I'd bled for Enochia. Gotten good people killed.

I'd lost everything. Everything except Elise, I reminded myself as she walked back into the room. She sat beside me. Rested her head on my shoulder. For a long while, we sat there, lost in our own thoughts.

Eventually, she stirred and went to the kitchen cooler.

"You must be hungry," she said, rummaging around. "I'll make us something."

I watched her through a haze of loud, guilty thoughts, all warring for position until I thought my head might simply burst.

"Lise," I heard myself say.

She turned, still holding the cooler door open. Our eyes met and, for a moment, I lost myself in those royal blue depths. In that moment, the world condensed between us. Something snapped into focus. Something that'd been lost these past cycles.

My chair clattered to the floor behind me.

I didn't stop when I reached her—just pinned her to the cooler door, one hand to her hip, the other cradling her cheek. Her eyes were wide at the sudden burst of life, her mouth half open in surprise.

I kissed her before either of us could think about it.

Her lips were stiff at first, hesitant, but I pushed on, driven by some wild thing inside of me whose awakening had surprised me just as much as it had clearly surprised her. We hung there for a moment, teetering awkwardly on the edge. Then she let out a delicious little sigh, and her lips grew about twenty degrees warmer as they gave way to mine.

The kiss deepened, stirring that frantic apparition inside me, crying for release. I reached for the hem of her shirt and started to pull it up. She drew a sharp breath and put a hand to my chest.

"Hal," she said softly, searching my face. "I don't really understand where this is coming from. Not that I'm complaining. I just need to—"

I slid a hand behind her neck and pulled her lips back to mine.

I didn't want to talk. Didn't want to think. But a few seconds into the kiss, Elise pulled back again. "Talk to me, love. Please."

Something flashed inside me—red-hot and wild and ugly.

I didn't mean to do it. I might as well have been watching a vid from behind someone else's eyes as my fist slammed to the counter top and I heard myself growl, "I don't wanna talk, dammit!"

Then the scuddy bastard who'd just taken me for a rage-ride bailed from the driver's seat and left me standing there, mouth agape. Elise was watching me with shocked eyes, searching my face as if it belonged to a stranger.

A thousand apologies raced through my mind, vying for control of my tongue. Somehow, none of them got it. We just stared at each other, shocked silence stretching the moment.

Then my stomach let forth a low, mournful rumble, and Elise's expression shifted. For a moment, I thought we might both burst out laughing.

The moment passed.

I dropped my gaze to the floor, ashamed to meet her eyes. Ashamed of everything.

"I'm sorry, Lise."

She found my hand silently. Gave it a squeeze.

I swallowed, fighting tears, muttered another apology, and turned to leave, unsure where it was I was even going.

She didn't try to stop me.

3

DIRT

It was several Divinity blocks before I was capable of enough coherent thought to realize where my feet were carrying me. Much of a relief as it was to escape the confines of our tiny quarters and lose myself in the bustling crowd of the city, the experience quickly soured when I started noticing the looks.

They were little more than furtive glances, most of them, but they only seemed to increase in frequency the further I went. When I heard a mother whisper something about the Demon of Divinity to her child, that was enough. I woke my palmlight, flagged down an autoskimmer, and gladly took to the skies in the blessed quiet of the empty cab.

My mind flitted aimlessly from one inconsequential thought to another as the city swept by below, every citizen I saw going about their business as if it were any other day. As if the world weren't in danger of collapsing right around them.

The lucky bastards.

When we reached the southernmost edge of Divinity, the autoskimmer gave a light chirp, as if in indignation at having been forced it to leave the city limits. I pointedly ignored the inanimate console and stared instead at the rippling surface of the Red River below. It was only another ten minutes or so before my indignant autoskimmer and I were closing on the destination.

Bittersweet nostalgia crept in at the sight of the two great oaks atop the gentle hill where I'd spent so many evenings practicing with my abilities and contemplating the scudstorm that'd swept my life up whole. Beyond that were the crumbling ruins of the old temple hideout—the place Carlisle had sheltered me after I'd lost my parents to the raknoth. The place he'd trained me in the art of Shaping and helped me to find purpose again.

But where had that purpose gone?

We'd stood against the unfathomable odds. We'd done our best to stop the raknoth. And it had cost us everything.

All at once, I regretted having come here.

But the autoskimmer was already banking down for a landing in the tall grass not far from the ruins. I lingered in the cab and debated abandoning this mindless wandering and returning to Elise. Talking this thing out like a reasonable human being. She was there for me, I knew. Just like Johnny was. And Franco.

They were all there for me. And I couldn't gropping stand it.

I couldn't stand the way they looked at me, like some wounded animal who couldn't take care of itself, who surely couldn't do anything but lie around waiting to die. I couldn't stand the thought that maybe they were right.

A pair of abrasive chirps from the console startled me from my ruminations. I looked around at our woodland surroundings, muttered a dark curse at the console, and climbed out of the autoskimmer. Probably, I should have set the vehicle on standby and eaten the extra fee to secure my return trip home. But I couldn't seem to bring myself to do more than watch, almost daring the autoskimmer to follow its programming and return to the city for its next fare, leaving me to fend for myself with its perfectly robotic apathy.

It did.

I couldn't really say why, but it felt good, watching that autoskimmer fly away, relishing the silence that fell in its absence. Right then, I couldn't be troubled to care how I'd get back. Scud, maybe I'd just stay out here until someone came looking. I'd come out here to be alone. And alone, I was.

But for what?

I eyed the temple ruins for several minutes before finally deciding I wasn't quite ready for those memories yet. Instead, I strolled aimlessly into the forest.

It was a cool afternoon. Not quite cold, but crisp. Refreshing. For a while, I tried my best to not think and simply enjoy it. After everything I'd been through, I probably should've been ecstatic just to be able to walk.

Somehow, though, I didn't feel the need to throw myself to my knees and shout praises and thanks be to Alpha. No. All I felt was guilt, out there on my sunlit stroll while Oasis was burning.

Slowly though, the woods drew me in, soothing me with the soft give of dirt beneath my boots—the crack of the occasional twig underfoot, adding its short-lived voice to the peaceful chorus of forest life around me. A faint breeze tickled my cheeks, tinged with the scent of dirt and bark. Above all, I basked in the absence of people, and the absence of their demands and their problems.

What if I did just stay out here?

It was a ridiculous thought.

But what if I did?

Carlisle had been out here for years on his own. Of course, with the raknoth hunting him for his meddling and the Sanctum hunting him as they'd covertly hunted every Shaper alive for centuries, he'd had good reason to stay holed up out here, away from civilization. But my situation wasn't so different, was it?

The raknoth wanted me dead. I had no doubt of that. Whether or not I was still in the Sanctum's sights following my botched execution and my pardon from the Legion was less clear. My existence was almost certainly a thorn in their side, what with the wild rumors spreading about how the Demon of Divinity had defied gravity at the gallows and escaped death from right under the Sanctum's righteous fist.

Unsurprisingly, the Sanctum and their new High Cleric had yet to apologize for trying to hang me—yet to make any official statement at all, for that matter. I couldn't imagine it would be good news when they did.

Public opinion, in the meanwhile, seemed about as mixed as it was incendiary. Despite our mutual agreement that no good could come of it, Elise and I hadn't been able to completely ignore the flood of newsreel articles and vids touting me as everything from a Saint of Alpha himself, to a simple freak of nature, to a malicious shape-shifting alien, and finally to a nether-hopping Being of True Evil who required immediate and judicious execution. Again.

Suffice it to say, there were several good reasons I'd refrained from leaving the dull safety of our living quarters.

And now, in the midst of that scudstorm, the Legion decided to show up on my doorstep, asking me to dive back into their mess? Because it *was* their mess, wasn't it?

I'd fought my best to stop the raknoth, even when the Legion had tried to stop me. I'd since told them everything I could about the raknoth—glossing over some of the weirder details, maybe, like Urth, the planet of humans I'd glimpsed in Al'Kundesha's memories, and the borderline mystic origin of the sickness those humans had somehow wrought upon the raknoth, necessitating their need for human blood to survive. But I'd told the Legion everything I thought they'd believe. Certainly everything I thought could help them win the fight. And now I couldn't even walk the streets without causing minor panic.

At what point did I get to say I'd done my job?

Once I'd lost the few people I had left?

Once I was dead?

"I didn't ask for this," I muttered at a particularly knobby tree.

The tree stared back in stoic silence, and I continued on.

I'd done my best, and it hadn't been good enough. Not by a long shot. That's all there was to it.

My dad, he'd been a hero.

Carlisle had been a hero.

Me? I was a seventeen year old kid who'd tried to beat the raknoth at their own game, and I'd gotten hundreds of good men and women killed. I wasn't the man my dad had been. Couldn't do the things Carlisle had been capable of. They were the ones Enochia needed. Not me.

But they were dead. And, by some sick joke of fate, I was alive.

Lost as I was in my thoughts, I was surprised to notice my wandering feet had brought me back around to the maze of ruins in front of the temple entrance. I sank to the smooth remains of some long-forgotten monument and must've spent a good half hour just sitting there, lost in memories of the place, good and bad. Dreading what painful recollections might await if I were to go inside.

I hadn't been back here since before the White Tower—at first because the Legion had been holding us as polite prisoners at a remote outpost, then, I suppose, because I was scared to face the place when we'd been loosely cleared to resume our freedom. Of course, saying we were cleared might've been an overstatement.

Considering the targets on my head and the aid they'd just requested of me, I doubted whatever Legion eyes had been tasked with watching my movements would be receiving warm thanks when they reported I'd come out here without any discernible protection.

But grop them.

I looked back and forth between the gloomy, crumbling entrance of the temple and the warm, inviting swell of my old hilltop lookout, where I'd spent dozens of evenings contemplating the regal blaze of the Divinity skyline at sunset. It was the place where Elise had first told me she loved me.

Guilt poured into me, hot and sudden.

How in demon's depths had I snapped at her like that?

Elise was the best part of my life—kind and loving, not to mention perfectly capable of crushing my danglers for treating her that way. I kind of wished she had.

What had I been thinking?

No matter how many ways I approached the question, I kept coming to the same embarrassing answer. I'd yelled at her because I was afraid. Afraid of what, I could barely say, but the fear was there—a cold, bottomless pit in my stomach, waiting for me to wander too close so it could trip me up and consume me whole.

I felt it coming again—the trill of incoherent panic sliding down my spine, disrupting thought and control, quickening my breath, crushing my blurry world down to a cage where I couldn't seem to do anything but wring my sweaty hands. Even out in the open air, it was suffocating.

I closed my eyes, sinking into my extended senses. Other than Elise's touch, it was the one thing I'd found to help. Retreating into the world around me.

Only I didn't make it that far before a pair of terrible crimson eyes flared to life in the darkness of my mind, waiting for me.

"You have failed, Haldin," an airy voice whispered. *"You have saved nothing."*

I snapped my eyes open with a gasp, panting, heart thundering.

Around me, the ruins were serene—smooth stone baking in the gentle afternoon sun, soft breeze drifting in, pleasantly cool on my sweat-streaked back and forehead.

I checked the cloaking pendant at my chest, just to be sure.

Active.

Which meant that couldn't have been a real projection just now—unless I happened to be missing a telepath sitting within ten yards of me.

Which also meant that it had all been in my head.

I buried my face in my hands, leaving my eyes open this time as I moved through a deep breathing exercise.

What the hell was happening to me?

I pushed the question away, focusing on the breathing. When things felt sufficiently under control, I stood, eager to busy myself with something. Anything other than sitting here, thinking myself into oblivion.

I considered calling a ride or starting the trek back to Divinity. Considered the temple entrance again. Something weighed at the back of my mind. Some sense of lingering importance, pulling me toward the temple like the faintest tug of gravity.

Had I come here for a reason? Something beyond my conscious awareness?

Probably not. Probably, I'd come here out of some desperate hope that I'd find Carlisle and my parents and everyone else, somehow miraculously alive and well, ready to all band together and save Enochia, praise be to Alpha.

Probably, I was wasting my time.

But here I was.

So I stood, brushed myself off, and headed for the temple to find out.

4

____

GHOSTS

Whatever I'd been hoping to find in our old hideout, the dark, dusty silence quickly convinced me it wasn't there. No Carlisle, waiting for me with a masterly smile and a dazzling story of how he'd escaped the blast after all. No bright display messages declaring, *Attention: answers RIGHT HERE.*

Nothing but the barebones accommodations that had served as both home and operations room for the better part of mine and Carlisle's stint as the premiere enemies of Enochia.

I wandered about the room, aimlessly picking at this and that. I checked the node at Carlisle's desk and found nothing of obvious interest. Thinking about my talk with Glenbark, I begrudgingly perused the trinkets on Carlisle's workbench and was surprised to come up with a pair of cloaking pendants. Extras, I assumed, from the batch he'd made to cloak our band of merry terrorists before the White Tower.

I tucked the pendants into a pocket. They weren't much—certainly not enough to counter the telepathic threat the raknoth posed to the Legion— but I was sure they'd be helpful. More helpful than anything else I was going to find here, it seemed.

After a few more minutes of absentminded searching, I sank to the edge of my old cot, once again feeling foolish for having come here at all. For having allowed myself to hope for anything other than an empty nest, stale fab mix, and nostalgic memories of my first days with Carlisle.

How was it that I felt wistful for the days when it had only been my parents' murders I had to mourn?

I flopped down on the cot with a heavy sigh, feeling guilty for even thinking it, and frowned when something hard and flat dug into the back of my head through the pillow linen. I started to shift the pillow, and froze, sudden, desperate hope flooding back in.

I sat back up, heart thumping in my throat, and ripped off the pillow linen. A small lightsteel disk fell into my palm, plain and seemingly benign.

A holodisk.

For a long moment, all I could do was stare at the tiny object.

It could be nothing. Probably was. I activated it anyway, and felt my insides leap at the sight of the single file waiting there—audio only. I thumbed the translucent icon… and gasped at the sound of Carlisle's voice.

"Hal…"

HAL…

I'm afraid I don't quite know where to begin—nor, I suppose, where it is I'm headed with this message. Suffice it to say, if you're hearing this, there's a strong chance I'm either dead or irrevocably indisposed. Of course, it's also possible we both make it through what's about to happen and you find this disk before I have a chance to grab it. What an embarrassment that would be.

The truth is, I'm recording this because I suspect my time on Enochia is drawing to an end.

Make no mistake, I do not say this with any intention of going gently to the pyre tonight. I will fight to the ends of my power to see the raknoth foiled and all of us home safely. But there's a feeling I can't escape. Something... transcendent. Ineffable.

It's always been there—or so I've convinced myself—as elusive as it was inevitable. And when we spoke in our respective slumbers this morning... I don't know how to explain it. You confirmed what I can't help but feel I've somehow always known, and the shroud is truly falling now.

Cassius—my master, my oldest and dearest friend—desecrated by the raknoth, Zar'Faenor... It's a thing of beauty and some terror, the way the smallest discovery can shift the foundations of one's world so.

I set out twelve years ago to find my friend, to save him, knowing full well it was a fool's errand. Just as I know now that I will see it through. Tonight, I will finish my mission. I feel it beyond my bones, as if my senses have stretched forward through time itself, and I have but to follow the path to what's already happened.

It sounds as if I speak of fate, though I tell myself I believe in no such force. Perhaps it's plain hypocrisy or simple delusion for me to hold to this belief when it so clearly contradicts what I feel with such certainty. I won't claim to have the truth of the matter. I will, however, continue to take heart for the one miraculous exception.

You.

I did not expect you in my life, Haldin Raish. Not in the least. But I am immeasurably glad I've found you.

After everything... After Cassius and Liandra...

Melodramatic as it will no doubt sound, I truly believe you might've been the one thing in this world that could have given me new purpose after all these years. And so you have.

I do not expect you to understand in full—certainly not now. Perhaps never.

Even now, I hope that I might someday explain this to you in person rather than through this message. I hope that we'll have many years to live and train and do good for this world. Perhaps we might even convince Enochia that we are in fact not terrorists, and that the Emmútari, majestic peacekeepers of yore, should rise again. Hmm-hmm.

I hope all of these things, some more realistically than others.

But, if my suspicions should come to pass, I leave this message with the more important hope that it will help you to live on knowing that I do not regret a single decision that has led us here. I have lived most of my life for Cassius—to learn from him, to be with him, to free him from torment. I never expected anything more. And yet along you came.

As... closed off as I can be at times, I wouldn't be at all surprised if you haven't realized the impact you've had. Astute as you can be from time to time, I fear you will struggle to see what I see when I look at you. So, allow me to put it plainly.

You are the best I have to offer this world.

Do not scoff at these words, Haldin. Do not dismiss them as idle praise. They are as much the selfish plea of a broken man as they are a compliment—more so, if I'm to be honest with the both of us. But, selfish or not, I hope you will remember this when the way is dark and your path uncertain.

I have faith in you, Haldin. More, I fear, than you have in yourself.

This is the only gift I have left to give. If you are hearing this, if I've indeed perished, then know that I will have done so gladly if it meant life for you and peace for Cassius. Know that it is not your fault. Mourn if you will, but do not for a second give in to despair.

You are the best I have to offer this world, Hal.
I couldn't have asked for more.

I SAT in silence for a long time after the recording ended, trying to process everything he'd said. Trying to process anything. It was like my brain had shut down. There was nothing. No thought or feeling. I just stared at the stone floor for what might've been minutes or hours. At some point, maybe more than once, my palmlight buzzed against my wrist. I only distantly noticed.

I wanted to cry. Wanted to feel something—anything other than the crushing emptiness pressing in on me from inside and out. Anything at all.

Eventually, it came—the slow, simmering heat of anger, bubbling closer and closer to the surface. Anger at the Legion for having pushed me out here, for having been too stupid to see what was right before their eyes in time to stop Al'Kundesha and everything that was happening now. Anger at the raknoth for all that they'd done—for taking my parents and Carlisle, for treating this entire world like an open storage depot of spare parts and human blood.

Anger at myself for having failed to do a damn thing about any of it.

I'd tried, people had died, and I'd shut down like an overloaded skimmer engine. I could see that now—see it with embarrassing clarity.

Recovering? Laying low? Training Elise?

I'd damn near convinced myself I'd been doing the right thing, hiding in my little hole like the wounded animal everyone thought I was. Without knowing it, I'd been doing exactly what Carlisle's ghost had been silently begging me not to.

I'd given up. Given into despair.

I could almost feel him hanging over me, could only imagine what he would've thought watching earlier today as I'd shut down an honest request for help, watching now with soft disappointment as I stewed here in a steaming pile of self-indulgence, cowering from the mission he'd given his life to give me another shot at.

Anger flashed like lightning, and a chair exploded into wooden splinters against the stone wall almost before I realized I'd lashed out with telekinesis.

Carlisle had given his life for mine. Made me his legacy to Enochia. And so far, I'd used that time to waste away in our dingy Legion living quarters.

Grop that.

How had I ever deluded myself so far? So quickly forgotten the silent promise I'd made at Carlisle's pyre?

Finishing what the two of us had started—that had always been the plan. I hadn't known then how the nightmares would only get worse and worse with each passing day. Hadn't known how the sleepless nights would degrade me, how the smallest things would trigger cold sweats and heart-pounding bursts of panic.

I hadn't known then how badly I was broken. But I'd made a promise. And if I hadn't found this holodisk…

It's a thing of beauty and some terror, the way the smallest discovery can shift the foundations of one's world so.

Yes, I'd been wronged. I'd been hunted by the very people who were asking for my help. I'd been through too much—had gropped up too completely to ever be forgiven.

But the raknoth were still out there. Good people were still dying. And Carlisle had left me here to do something about it.

The only question was where to start. The hybrids? The cloaks?

Alton Parker.

I was already reaching to call Johnny when my palmlight started buzzing. Speak of the demon.

I jabbed the connect button.

"Oh, scud," Johnny's voice crackled, "I didn't really think you'd… Never mind. Listen, I just wanted to—"

"Why haven't you found Alton Parker?"

"Oh. Well, uh, first off, hello. Secondly, they're trying their little wrin-klies off around here. You might've already heard something about it on the reels, but they cleaned the whole Vantage facility out. It's a shell out there. I'm sure they'll find Parker soon enough."

Soon enough.

Yesterday wouldn't have been soon enough.

"We need to go back and burn that place to the ground."

"I don't think there's really much left to burn, man. They swept through the place with… Wait, we?"

"I'm coming." It barely even sounded like I was making this up as I went. "And unless the team that went out there was cloaked, which I'm assuming they weren't, you probably can't trust their operation wasn't tampered with. They could still be making hybrids down there."

"I… You really think so?"

"It'd hardly be the most insidious trick the raknoth had ever pulled. Call it a strong hunch. Ask if there was anything odd in the reports. Any gaps or disorientation. Maybe an accidental weapon discharge. That kind of thing."

Johnny chewed that over in silence for a long second.

"Scud. Okay. I'll run it up the chain, see if we can get a second look in there."

"I need to be there."

Hesitation. Then, "Is everything okay, buddy? Did something happen to change your mind?"

My insides tightened at the change in his voice, like he'd just remembered it was a wounded animal he was talking to, and not his old tyro broto. Had Elise messaged him when I'd stepped out?

"It's kind of a long story," I said slowly.

"I saw you four hours ago."

"It's been a long four hours."

"Okay, broto. I just… Don't get me wrong, Glenbark's probably gonna be rolling on sunshine if I tell her you're in. She wants those cloaks, man, and sweet Alpha do I wanna give that woman what she wants. It's just that I'm not sure she's gonna love the idea of you in the field."

"That's why you explain to her that anyone else she sends in is going to be vulnerable to telepathic manipulation. Unless you wanna point out that there may already be a certain red-headed legionnaire equipped for the task."

Silence.

"I need to see it with my own eyes, Johnny. It's important to me."

I didn't realize how much I meant it until the words were out of my mouth. Even before the White Tower, my dreams had been haunted by the memory of the dozens of helpless victims we'd been forced to leave bleeding out on the racks beneath Vantage when Alton Parker had set his hybrids loose on us. I owed it to those people to make sure the job was done.

"Okay," Johnny said finally. "Okay, buddy. I'll see what I can do."

"Thank you."

"Hey, what's a broto for if they can't even convince their superiors to pull you into a potential combat situation?"

The first hint of a smile tugged my lips. "I'm sorry about earlier, Johnny."

"Forget about it. It was a scuddy move for us to show up like that. But you know, Vantage might be an easier sell if I could bring Glenbark the news she really wants to hear."

"I don't know how to make the cloaks, man. I wish I did. It was something Carlisle and Cassius figured out. It might've been common knowledge a thousand years ago, before Sarentus had the Emmútari slaughtered, but now…"

Johnny waited a few seconds to see if I'd finish the thought. "So, glossing past that stuff about our holy prophet slaughtering people…"

"Well, I found a couple extra working pendants." I studied the runes on mine, thinking about everything Carlisle had taught me on the branch of Shaping he'd called Expression. "And I might have an idea where to start on trying to make more. That's about all I've got."

I could almost see Johnny perking up on the other side of the call. "Well that's a scudload better than we had five minutes ago." He hesitated. "Look, Glenbark would probably have me skinned alive for saying this, but… you don't have to do this, Hal. I'm honestly not sure how this plays out if we don't get our people cloaked. Alpha, you should hear the conversations going on over here. It's chaos for the history stacks. But I know how much scud you've been through."

Maybe Elise *had* messaged him. Scud, maybe she'd been keeping him updated all along about my… what? Behavior? Condition?

Did I have a condition now?

Maybe, I decided, as I realized I hadn't checked the messages I'd received since coming here. Elise was probably worried sick about me.

"I appreciate the concern, buddy," I said, "but Glenbark was right. You both were. I have to stop these bastards."

"Don't get me wrong, I appreciate the spirit, but I don't think either of us was suggesting you do it with your own mystical hands."

"No?" I wanted to argue, to dig in and insist it was all or nothing, but now probably wasn't the time. "Sounds like you've been spending a lot of time with the High General."

"Perks of being the one guy in the Legion they think you might talk to. She basically appointed me envoy to The Solemn Nation of Hal."

"Guess that might be better than getting brigged, right?"

"Ehh," Johnny said. "I'll get back to you on that one in a few cycles. Preferably when this is all over and we can have a good laugh about the time the Legion put it on a scraggly-faced tyro to protect them from an army of telepathic alien invaders."

"I'm not a tyro anymore. I have the dishonorable discharge to prove it."

"You're not exactly a civie either, broto."

I gave a noncommittal grunt, scratching at my two cycles' worth of uneven stubble. "So… you're saying you don't like the beard?"

"Let's be honest, beard is probably a strong word."

I smiled, a flicker of excitement touching my chest. For the first time since the White Tower, I was moving again, even if I didn't quite know where yet. I hadn't even realized how trapped I'd felt these past cycles. All I knew was that Carlisle was counting on me.

"Not to pry," Johnny said slowly, "but you should probably talk to Elise about all this, right?"

That killed the smile nice and quick.

Of course I should talk to Elise about this. I never should have stormed out on her at all. But now that I was moving…

"I'll call her on the way. Speaking of which, I might need a ride. I kinda… stranded myself."

"A ride, we can handle. But she deserves a sit-down, man."

"I know that," I snapped. "I just…"

"You know she can take it," he said quietly.

Of course I knew.

It wasn't a question of fortitude. Elise was as strong as they came. Stronger than me, if my behavior over the past couple cycles was any indication. And after everything I'd put her through…

I couldn't lie to Elise. She deserved so much more than that.

"I'll talk to her." I stood, looking around the room. My gaze settled on a pair of Carlisle's old daggers. "Just send a ride who can swing me by our place before they bring me in. I'm assuming you already have my location?"

"I can pretend I don't know what you're talking about if that would be less awkward."

I traced my fingers over the daggers, imagining their slender lengths piercing the crimson fire of raknoth eyes. "I'll see you soon, buddy."

"Good luck, broto," Johnny said. "Just, uh… Yeah. Talk soon."

I ended the call and closed the palmlight with a pinch and a curl of my fingers. I tucked Carlisle's holodisk gently in my pocket, looking around the room one last time in what felt like a goodbye. Then I sheathed his daggers, strapped them to my belt, and turned for the door.

I wasn't the best Carlisle had had to offer this world. I was damn sure about that. As sure as I was that Mathis would safely get to go to his stiff-backed pyre proclaiming that I'd never even measured up to my dad's polished boots, much less his heroism. But, like it or not, I was what they'd left behind. Which all amounted to one thing.

I had work to do.

5

CIVIE

"Well isn't this just a sunny trip down memory lane," I muttered, leaning back from the small duraglass port and the view of the sprawling countryside flying by below.

"What's that?" Johnny asked beside me.

"Nothing," I said. Then, nodding to the wide viewport at the head of the transport, I added. "Vantage, I mean."

The complex was easily visible a few miles ahead now. The primary research facility of Vantage Corp, alone out here, nothing but open fields all around. The place was the size of a small city and looked from the outside more like a military installment than a biological research compound—complete with perimeter wall and everything.

It was here Carlisle and I had first discovered the raknoth plot to construct an army of hybrids and assembly line style human blood farms to keep that army fed. And it was here I had a feeling they were still doing just that, though I had to admit now that it did look quite abandoned.

The fact didn't go unnoticed.

"Someone remind me why we're sweeping out Viper's sloppy seconds," someone grumbled back in the main hold.

"I think it's 'cause your mom was all booked, Jensen," another called.

There was a round of chuckles and guffaws from the first squad of the 51st Hound Company. I wanted to roll my eyes but couldn't help smiling at the feeling of being back around legionnaires.

Ordo Dillard, on the other hand, regarded his squad with a stern frown as he descended the stairs from the upper cabin. "We're out here because the civie here says Viper Company couldn't find a bova's teet with both hands."

Another round of chuckles, along with a few hearty agreements.

Dillard met my eyes as he continued. "Personally, I don't give a scud what Citizen Raish thinks, but the High General says sweep, we sweep. For ours is not to ask…"

"But to serve," the men barked back.

I did my best not to squirm beneath Dillard's stare before he finally broke off and began issuing fireteam orders.

A trip down memory lane indeed.

"Uh, buddy?" Johnny said quietly beside me.

I looked at him, expecting a word of comfort or caution. Instead, I saw his palmlight, lit with a long, mint green message from Elise.

"Care to explain why your lady love is threatening violence to my wrinklies and asking what we're up to?"

I opened my mouth. Closed it. Opened again, and let out a heavy sigh.

"You didn't talk to her."

I looked down at my hands.

"I know you stopped to see her. The eyes in the sky told me."

I just nodded, not overly keen on sharing that I'd simply stood outside our building for fifteen minutes before finally resorting to a string of short, vague messages explaining that I'd reconsidered the Legion's offer and that we'd talk about it soon.

I fully intended to have that talk. But I needed to do this first—to keep moving until I was sure I had enough momentum to avoid falling back into the pit of my own pathetic wallowing. I also needed to make damn sure that, if I was going to step back on the board and paint a bright red target on my chest, Elise wasn't anywhere near me when the slugs started flying.

I'd lost enough loved ones.

"She knows what she needs to."

"I don't know, broto." Johnny pointedly waved his palmlight. "The not-so-subtle threats of testicular peril kinda suggests otherwise."

"I didn't say she was happy about—"

"Citizen Raish," Dillard called, snapping me back to the transport cabin, where everyone was suddenly watching me with eager intent. Dillard stepped up and offered me a civilian issue handgun to go with the bulky yellow armor that marked me as a civilian should any enemy combatants care to take pity and honor the rules of war. "Your armament, citizen. Now if you and Legionnaire Wingard could stow the storyvid drama and prepare for landing, we'd all appreciate it."

Another round of chuckles, all directed at me.

Heat rushed to my cheeks—embarrassment, anger, and an urge to telekinetically pin Ordo Dillard to the wall all warring for dominance. The weapon was an insult more than a tool.

I should have taken it anyway.

Instead, I patted the pommel of one Carlisle's daggers. "All set, sir."

Dillard scowled and thrust the handgun at Johnny, grip first. "See to it your friend doesn't die and embarrass the company, Wingard. You two are with Fireteam E."

"Yes, sir," Johnny said, taking the gun without hesitation and handing it to me with a *what were you thinking?* look as Dillard moved on.

I shrugged and wordlessly tucked the handgun into my gear vest.

I'd known I wasn't going to make many friends, muscling my way into an operation that just about everyone besides me—and *maybe* Johnny and General Glenbark—thought was a goat-gropping waste of time and resources. That said, butting heads with the ordo wasn't going to do me or anyone else any favors.

Of course, Glenbark could've given her ordos instructions to operate on the assumption that I wasn't just a softsteel-sipping civie, but I got the impression she wasn't too happy about my maneuvering either. And even if she wasn't miffed, she didn't strike me as the type to tell her people what to think or who to respect—only what to get done.

Which meant I'd just have to compose myself and act like someone these legionnaires might actually take seriously.

The transport slowed, veering downward as we approached the perimeter wall and the large, rectangular main building at the front of the complex. It was stout in the back half and ten floors high in the front—the same ten floor rooftop where I'd fought my first raknoth, Alton Parker, ex-CEO of Vantage.

Hopefully, today would go more smoothly.

As we cleared the wall and the transport began to descend, I brought my palmlight to life, thinking to swipe a quick message to Elise. After a moment's hesitation, I closed it again.

We'd talk soon enough.

Telling her the details probably wouldn't worry her less anyway, nor would revealing operation details to another civilian be likely to impress anyone who might find out. Then again, if Alton Parker actually had uprooted his operation from the lab beneath Vantage, I was probably going to lose whatever credibility I might have with Glenbark anyway.

An unexplained weapon discharge. That was what had gotten under Glenbark's skin just enough for her to humor my wild suspicions. No injuries, no other mishaps. Just a single weapon that shouldn't have been fired, and not a single recollection as to why it had been.

Perhaps this had been a stupid move. But what else could that forgetful legionnaire have shot at?

The complex certainly looked dead out there. But these were the same raknoth who'd infiltrated the highest offices of both the Legion and the Sanctum. How hard would it have been to confound one search party?

Probably a lot less hard than moving all the equipment. Alton Parker or any other raknoth could've easily hopped into as many minds as need be and convinced them they'd seen nothing but an empty room where it counted.

The transport jostled to a landing.

Time to go find out, one way or another.

"You're sure about this?" Johnny said.

I stood and patted my sad civie armor. "Just like old times."

One of the nearby legionnaires turned a skeptical glance my way.

"Yeah," Johnny said. "That's kinda what I'm afraid of."

The twenty legionnaires of first squad were already sweeping neatly and quietly down the ramp to the Vantage yard.

Johnny picked up his rifle and gave me a look. "Just don't try to be a hero in there, okay?"

I frowned. "When did you become the worrier?"

"Right about the time it somehow became my wrinklies on Elise's chopping block if anything happens to you."

"So not fair," I said, trying to grin.

I don't think I managed more than a grimace as my mind turned to what it would do to Elise if something actually did happen to me after I'd run off like this.

At least I was more durable than normal, all bundled in fiber weave and unwieldy plate armor. A little *too* durable, I decided as I tromped through the main cabin on Johnny's heels, feeling clunky. Alpha forbid I ended up needing to move fast enough to fight a raknoth.

If anyone was still listening to a word I said after this operation, I was going to have to see if the powers that be could rustle me up a good armor skin.

Ordo Dillard's squad formed a perimeter as the other transport landed to divulge the second squad of Hound Company. For the most part, everyone pretended like Johnny and I weren't there as they went about their business and moved in on the main entrance. Everyone, that was, except for our compatriots in Fireteam E, who eyed us—or me, at least—with skepticism, distrust, and irritation as we approached.

I eyed them back, two solid-looking men, one slender steel whip of a woman, and a heavy gunner whose burly proportions reminded me of Phineas—if Phineas had grown twenty years younger, leaned out, and then eaten another Phineas.

I considered introducing myself—unnecessary as it was—but the woman pointedly ignored my attempt at eye contact and waved the fireteam forward with a silent hand signal. Johnny and I traded a shrug and fell in with them.

Whatever they may or may not have missed, Viper Company had left the main doors unlocked.

When I'd first infiltrated Vantage, the halls inside had been sterile, all spotless glass panels and immaculately organized lab equipment. Now, the powerless facility was barren under the beams of Hound Company's lanterns. The floors, once pristinely scrubbed, were dirty and heavily scuffed.

The place was dead. But that didn't stop the cool tingle whispering at my back.

Someone was watching us.

Or maybe that was just the feeling of desperation creeping down my spine—some baseless hope that I hadn't been wrong to push for this operation. I found my pendant and dialed my cloak out as far as it'd go, casting my extended senses into our surroundings, taking care not to fall behind or get in anyone's way.

It was hard, picking out anything meaningful through the considerable interference of the thirty-plus soldiers moving through the building all around us. Scanning large areas with my extended senses wasn't something I'd had much practice at. It was a problem not unlike dilution. The wider I threw my net, the vaguer the details got, as if I only had a finite amount of mental presence and I had to choose where to spend it.

Even so, I caught flickers here and there. Tiny life forms—rodents, maybe?—flitting about. And in the walls and the foundations, the subtlest of vibrations, so weak I was sure they'd be imperceptible to my flesh.

And there.

Power. Electricity.

It was faint—not the direct, crackling buzz of power lines or running machinery, but the tingling whisper of distant electromagnetism.

"You got something?" Johnny asked quietly.

I opened my eyes—hadn't even realized I'd closed them. Johnny was gently guiding me with a hand on the shoulder, having apparently noticed me leaving the driver's seat, so to speak. And so had our friendly fireteam, I surmised by their suspicious stares.

"Electronics below, I think," I muttered to Johnny, dialing my cloak in and withdrawing my extended senses.

That didn't ease the stares.

"What's the holdup?" Dillard asked, appearing beside us seemingly out of thin air, watching me with evident distrust. "Edwards?"

"Civie says electronics below, Ordo," rumbled the heavy gunner—Edwards, apparently.

"However the scud he arrived at that mystical observation," muttered one of the others.

Dillard eyed me warily, waiting for me to explain myself.

"Nothing certain yet, sir," I said slowly. "But it feels like something's still down there."

That earned a round of mutters and a dark frown from Dillard.

"Let's get to the central lifts," he finally said.

No one argued.

BY THE TIME we reached our destination, one of Hound's fireteams had succeeded at restoring the facility's powers. We arrived at the fully lit atrium with the five mag lifts that had almost cost me and Carlisle our lives last time we'd been here.

Had they been repaired since then?

It seemed so. Though I doubted that meant they'd be willingly taking us all the way down to the cavernous hybrid breeding facility that was marked neither on the lift controls nor in the Vantage building plans. Still, I held my tongue as Ordo Dillard discussed the plan with Ordo Carter, his counterpart from Second Squad.

Armored as we were—and armed as they were—it was an uncomfortable squeeze to fit even five legionnaires per lift car, so we split up, one squad descending to the lowest floor to work our way up while the other squad worked their way down on the stairs, one sublevel at a time.

The Legion inspector's passes happily granted us lift access to the "lowest" level, S5. A few moments of stomach wobbling descent later, we drew up a floor short of the *actual* lowest level and piled out at S5. I didn't mind the momentary stop, though. It gave me time to process what I felt when I clicked my cloak off to enable me to reach far enough below.

Hybrids.

Dozens just in the first few columns of breeding cylinders alone, none of them moving save for... were those humans I felt walking around down there? Yes. Three humans, and at least a couple hybrids patrolling the—

I nearly cried out as one of the hybrids' minds quivered at my probe. I tore my senses back, flipping my cloak on and dialing it just far enough to leave our squad covered from prying minds.

Had that thing felt me?

I waited for a painfully long handful of seconds, too tense to breathe.

No alarms. No distant battle roar.

I was about ready to sigh in relief when I noticed Dillard marching my way with a look that said it was time for my next public humiliation. Instead, though, he pulled me aside and spoke in a low voice.

"Look, kid, I don't know what your deal is or why Glenbark decided to trust you at all, but—Hey, what's wrong with you? You need a sugar lick or something?"

I must've looked as shaken as I felt. "No, sir. I'm... fine."

Dillard was less than convinced. "Kid, whatever the scud you're playing at, if you actually have intel, now's the time."

Hybrids. Humans. Blood racks. Breeding chambers. All still active.

Alpha, did I have intel. I just wasn't sure I could lay it all out without them crying demon and clapping me in restraints right there.

But grop it.

"We need to be careful," I said, quietly enough that only he and Johnny would hear. "This facility's live, but it feels like most of the hybrids are still in stasis down there. I pick up at least two patrolling. Three conscious humans, too. I'm not sure what they're doing down there, but given that the raknoth could've bent their minds, it's probably safest to assume they won't be glad to see us."

To his credit, Dillard managed to maintain a straight face throughout. No slack jaw. No laughing at me outright. He just waited until I'd finished, then looked questioningly at Johnny, who nodded almost apologetically.

Maybe Glenbark actually had told him to listen to me.

Dillard turned back to me, frown darkening. "You… feel all of this?"

I nodded, not really sure what I could say to make it sound less strange. Even more quietly, lest any of the dagger-staring squad overhear, I added, "Sir, if I might make a recommendation. I think we're going to be wanting Ordo Carter's squad down here sooner than later."

Dillard studied me for a long moment, betraying nothing.

"How do we access this alleged facility?" he finally asked.

I inclined my head in the direction of the lifts. "May I?"

Dillard watched me a second longer, then nodded, looking about as happy as a wet haga beast. I reached out and telekinetically thumbed the S4 button in one of the empty lifts. The doors slid shut, drawing several startled looks and a few half-raised weapons.

"It's okay guys," Johnny said.

I waited until I felt the lift stop at the floor above, then I reached for the doors ahead, disconnected their catches, and slid them apart with telekinesis, revealing the open lift shaft.

"Ta-da," Johnny said to the silent room, where several legionnaires were now staring at me like… well, like I truly was the Demon of Divinity.

There were mumbles and whispers. Beside me, Dillard gave a quiet command into his earpiece then held up a closed fist for silence. It fell like a heavy blanket, thick enough that Dillard's boot falls seemed painfully loud as he walked over and leaned in to look down the open shaft.

He looked for longer than seemed necessary, then finally turned and spoke quietly to the closest fireteam, who quickly began pulling rappelling gear from their packs. Half the men tensed as I padded over to join them.

Dillard only gave me a raised finger to wait before striding over to the nearby stairwell. I could feel the first of Carter's crew descending a floor above. When they reached the door, Dillard met Ordo Carter and pulled him aside. He talked too quietly for anyone to hear. Gestured toward the open lift shaft then to me.

Look what Raish found.

Carter looked at me like I was a bothersome piece of refuse he'd only just noticed before turning back to Dillard.

Who put the apostate civie in charge?

The look quickened my pulse, but I held my tongue and stood still until Dillard and Carter broke apart and started moving about, issuing quiet orders. At that point, I couldn't contain myself any longer.

"Permission to go down first, sir. I can keep things under control if it gets ugly."

Dillard pegged me with a look that was serious if not quite reprimanding. "I appreciate your showing us the way, Raish, but please, step aside and let us do our job."

Anger stirred in my chest.

I'd faced more hybrids than all of Hound Company combined—here at Vantage alone, for starters, but also at Sanctuary, and then again at the White Tower.

As quick as the thought came, I flashed back to the heart of the battle in the Great Hall. Inhuman roars. Corpses piling around me, civilians and legionnaires alike. Some fighting, some running for their lives. All of them dying. Dying because of me. Dying because—

"It's okay, Hal," Johnny's voice snapped me back to the lift lobby.

My hands were shaking on the pommels of Carlisle's daggers. I squeezed to steady them.

"These guys know what they're doing," Johnny added, laying a hand on my shoulder.

Did he see how close I'd just come? Did he feel me shaking now?

I didn't need extended senses to feel the dozens of eyes watching me.

I nodded to Dillard. "Yes, sir."

The room itself seemed to let out a relieved breath as Dillard made to move on. In a quieter voice, just for the three of us, I added, "I just assumed you'd want me protecting your people from what happened at the Oasis counterstrike."

Dillard froze. "Are you playing games with me, Raish?"

I held his merciless stare without flinching. "You want me at the front of your squad, Ordo. No games."

Our staring contest stretched until I thought Johnny might burst beside me. Then Dillard swept on, gesturing to his men. "Fireteam E. Suppressors on. Down the shaft. Mara and Davis on point. Lock it down, Hounds."

It took me a second to register that Fireteam E meant us.

Carter's squad was already in motion, a couple legionnaires taking another lift up a floor while others pried open the shaft door and prepared more lines to climb down. I scooted forward with Johnny, who looked as surprised as I felt, while two of our team, the steel whip of a woman and one of the smaller guys—Mara and Davis, I guessed—clipped onto their lines and disappeared into the lift shaft. Heavy gunner Edwards and our remaining team member went next.

Which left me and Johnny.

I'd telekinetically caught myself from enough falls by now that I was halfway into the open shaft before Johnny caught me, clipped on to his line, and pointedly indicated I should do the same. I took the cue and went through the unnecessary tedium of hooking in and rappelling down the shaft beside him.

"Waste of time," I muttered when it was just the two of us.

"You're already freaking people out enough, buddy. Would it kill you to keep your head down?"

"Maybe not. Might kill them, though."

He gave a noncommittal harrumph. We touched down and unclipped from the line.

I made quick work of the door mechanisms barring our way into the lab and reached out further to give the lab another quick sweep, trying to avoid touching the hybrid minds enough to risk another reaction.

"Scud," I mumbled, pulling back. "Three hybrids now. Two on our level to the right and left, one down below, by the humans." I looked at Johnny. "We need a third shooter."

He took a step toward the door and froze at a look from our steely-eyed lioness.

"Edwards," she said, quiet and calm. "Look sharp."

Edwards shot Johnny a kindly wink. "Yes, Ordo Mara."

"Cut the scud," she hissed, then muttered something under her breath about gropping children.

It seemed less than wise to press the issue.

"I've got the door when you're ready," I said.

Mara, Davis, and Edwards lined up and called their targets, only partially letting on how ridiculous they felt taking targets from a kid acting like he could see through walls. I voiced a quiet reminder to shoot for the head, earning myself a couple glares, then I gave them a countdown and pushed the doors apart with telekinesis.

The hum of running machinery poured into the shaft from the vast lab space. Three suppressors coughed. Mara's and Davis' hybrids dropped to the left and right. Below, Edwards' mark didn't.

Not that it was Edwards' fault.

The creature had thrown itself behind cover as if it'd been expecting us. I reached out and yanked it into the air with telekinesis. It took more energy than I'd expected—maybe because working over distance degraded my efficiency, or maybe because the thing was heavier than most of its kind.

Johnny's rifle coughed twice, and the hybrid went slack in my long-range grip, two neat holes in its head.

I lowered the hybrid. In addition to being rather heavy, it looked different than the other two—it's hide darker, thicker-looking. And maybe it was my imagination, but I thought its eyes had glowed more deeply crimson than its brethren as well. It probably didn't matter right now.

"Hostiles down," Mara murmured into her earpiece.

Below, the three humans hadn't even bothered looking up from their work consoles when the shooting had started. That couldn't be good.

"We need to stop whatever those people are doing," I said, starting forward.

Mara reached back and planted a hand on my chest without turning.

"Do it," Dillard's voice came through the comms.

Above, two more fireteams were already descending to join us.

Mara withdrew her hand with a scowl. "Affirmative, Ordo."

"You guys have restraints?" I asked.

Edwards nodded.

"Good." I squeezed around Edwards and into cavernous room that had haunted my nightmares ever since my first visit. "Because I think we might need them."

6

———

SPRUNG

If the hybrid breeding facility beneath Vantage was every bit as disturbing as I remembered, then the blood racks were almost certainly worse.

"Holy scud," Johnny murmured beside me.

I knew what he meant.

The room was enormous—so enormous that most of its extent was lost to darkness outside the lighting near the lifts. The faint green glow coming from the rows of large cylindrical tanks along the walls, though, showed that the room stretched on for at least a couple hundred yards. But no one seemed to be noticing that.

Their attention was fixed firmly on the ground floor below, where rows and rows of cold gray blood racks were stretched out like some sick collection of pristine trophies—each one affixed to an array of tubes and connectors. Each one occupied by a pale, unmoving body.

"Holy scud," Johnny repeated, his voice weaker this time.

The air reeked of pungent chemicals, underlaid by the sweet, sickly smell of decay. I shifted my gaze to the rows of tanks on the walls. Hundreds upon hundreds of them. And inside each of those tanks, a fledgling hybrid in the making.

"Sweet Alpha," someone whispered behind us.

Edwards. He'd gone pale and looked like he might throw up. Beside him, Mara's face had finally given in to open shock as she took in the horrors.

I felt for them. They'd probably be having nightmares tonight. Long after that, as well, if they were anything like me. But right now, we needed to know what the people below were doing at their respective consoles.

The three workers wore identical blue gowns. Two women and a man. None of them had so much as shot us a curious glance yet.

"Hey," I called, hurrying down the mesh metal steps to the ground floor.

No response.

"We're here to help," I called, drawing past the first row of blood racks. "But whatever you're doing, you need to stop for a minute."

One of the women paused momentarily, her hands curling into tense claws over her workstation. She started to glance my way as I neared, then thought better of it and resumed her work.

"Stop!" I said.

No response.

Gently as I could, I pulled her away from her console. She reached for the console, but the attempt was only half-hearted, like she didn't intend to fight me so much as she'd simply forgotten she was obstructed.

"A little help, guys?" I called.

Johnny and the rest of our fireteam had frozen at the blood racks, their faces all shades of ghostly white as they stared mesmerized at pale bodies and the blood lines slowly draining them dry. On the catwalk above, legionnaires were filing into the room from the lift shaft, many of them having similar reactions.

"Johnny," I called.

He snapped to, as did Mara, and Edwards a second later. They hurried over, preparing restraints for our three… rescues? Hostiles?

I wasn't sure yet.

"Help… me," mumbled the woman I was holding, still reaching for her console.

Rescues, then.

"You're okay," I said, holding fast against her weak struggles. "You're safe now."

"What in demons' depths is this place?" Dillard's voice crackled over the comms.

I glanced at my palmlight to see he'd opened a private line with me.

"This is where they've been building their army this whole time, sir," I said quietly. "And harvesting the blood supply to feed them. We take this place down and we might be able to keep Oasis under siege. Starve them out."

"A valiant proposition," called a voice from above. "Though I'm afraid you'd be disappointed were you to try it."

That voice curled my stomach into knots. I'd heard it before, in this very room. I followed the sound to the second level of catwalks, back where the cavernous room was still engulfed in shadow. I was squinting at a faint silhouette when one of Dillard's men found the lighting controls.

Floodlights snapped on throughout the gigantic room with a series of cracking pops, and there he was, nearly fifty feet above.

Alton Parker, the suave demon in a charcoal business suit.

Only he didn't look so suave now, I realized at a second glance. He looked ragged. Wild. His hair was disheveled, his sleeves balled up to the elbows, the lightsteel of the catwalk railing bent where he gripped onto it.

Somehow, it was far more terrifying than the composed monster I'd expected.

Johnny and Mara already had their rifles trained on him, Edwards easily holding the other two floundering rescues away from their consoles in his burly arms. Behind and above, boots were pounding down the steps and along the catwalks—more legionnaires getting into position.

Alton Parker hardly seemed to notice any of it. He just continued kneading the metal railing like a piece of dough, rambling to himself in apparent agitation. I could only pick out a few phrases—something about too many moving pieces and sticking to the plan.

"Idiots," he growled at the end of his stream, snapping the railing clean in two. "Cursed void, you mangy idiots!"

"Fireteams B and C," Dillard's voice crackled through the battle channel, "seize that maniac, and be careful about it."

"No!" I called. Or started to, before the trembling woman in my arms bucked against my hold, jolting my attention back to the ground floor. She began whimpering like a desperate pup, her struggles growing more urgent.

"You really should let those poor people get back to work, Raish," Alton called, suddenly seeming to remember we were there. "I was quite thorough in my instructions. I imagine they'll be ready to chew their own hands off soon if they think it'll help."

As if in response to his words, the woman struggled even harder against my arms. Beside us, Edwards nearly lost his balance as his two charges likewise struggled.

Something was wrong.

I looked around and saw a few legionnaires sweeping in to help us with our unruly workers, and several more fireteams already hastily planting explosives among the rows of hybrid cylinders as Fireteams B and C moved into position to come at Parker from both sides.

None of it eased the dread in my gut. Something was wrong. I felt it in my pounding heart and in the struggles of the blond worker gnashing her teeth and trying to catch me with a wild elbow.

"Parker!" I yelled, not really knowing what the plan was, only that I had to stop him.

But it was already too late. I saw it in the way he stood to his full height above, his eyes blazing to life with crimson demon fire. "Do you remember your last visit, Haldin?"

Horrible understanding hit me. I whipped around to the closest work-station just as it chimed with an alert.

<Rows B, C - Reanimation Complete. Drainage Commencing.>

"Scud," I heard myself whisper. Then, at a yell, "Dillard! He's waking the—"

But my voice was lost to the rapid-fire series of sharp clacks sounding down the lines of chambers on either side of the room. A choir of rumbling motors filled the air. Fluid levels began draining.

A few feet away, another console gave an identical chime.

Gropping scudbuckets.

"Fall back!" I looked wildly around for Dillard, panic gripping my chest. "Get them back to the lifts, Dillard! He's waking them all up!"

His voice sounded in my ear. "Control yourself, Raish. The explosives are almos—"

"We've got live civilians hooked up down here!" I snapped. "We need to come back with more men."

In the darkness above, Alton Parker began to laugh.

"Shoot that son of a bitch!" I cried.

But I wasn't in charge. No one did a damn thing. Not until Parker cocked back and hurled a piece of the broken railing at the approaching Fireteam B. That was all Mara needed.

She opened fire, followed almost immediately by Johnny and Davis, their rifles all coughing tight bursts. Above, B and C teams added their own fire, but Alton was already in motion. He covered a good forty feet of catwalk in one leap, nearly landing on Fireteam C, then he grabbed one of the shocked legionnaires by the armored utility vest and jumped again.

The gunfire died down through the room as Alton sailed another fifty yards, slammed down to ground floor permacrete, and took off at an inhuman sprint with his legionnaire human shield bouncing wildly over his shoulder.

Then the first hybrid chambers popped opened, and things got messy fast.

Eager howls filled the chemical-stained air. I dragged the frantic blond woman along, crying for everyone to fall back and rally at the lifts. I wasn't sure anyone was listening. Hybrids dropped from catwalks on both sides, a few at first, then more. And more.

I was drawing my paltry excuse for a handgun when one landed right in front of me. Johnny put two sofsteel slugs in its head. Another dropped from above, straight for Edwards and his struggling lab worker. I threw my senses out and yanked them both several feet backward with telekinesis.

Edwards landed on wobbly feet after the surprise ride, then got his heavy rifle under control enough to fire a burst from the hip. It punched a gory hole straight through the hybrid's bare chest, and the creature collapsed with a wet gurgle.

"Heads!" I snapped over the battle comms. "Shoot the heads!"

Johnny scooted to my side, picking off one hybrid after another. I took a medium range shot at one emerging from its chamber, but my blonde cargo bucked at the wrong moment and threw my aim.

Around us, legionnaires were falling back to the tune of Dillard's orders barked over the comms—keeping their scud together to an admirable degree, considering the situation.

We moved with the flow, Edwards dishing off his wily lab worker to Davis so he could better hold point beside Mara.

"Hal, above!" Johnny cried.

I followed his aim in time to see three hybrids leap from the upper catwalk for Mara and Edwards.

No time to warn them.

I cast my will like a fisherman's net and opened myself to the energy cells in my pack. The three hybrids yanked to a halt in midair. Liquid lightning crackled through my body, driving out my breath and spotting my vision, but I held on.

Mara, wide-eyed, caught on faster than slack-jawed Edwards. She darted backward, barking at him to do the same, and opened fire. Edwards unfroze, and when I released my hold a second later, the three hybrids were dead before they hit the ground.

As intense as the channeling had been, the sudden drop back to nothing hit me even harder. My head swam, my vision dipping darker before starting to recover. I was out of shape. Catching eight hundred pounds of hybrid wasn't an easy feat by any stretch, but it'd clearly been too long since I'd pushed myself.

Something smacked my back. I turned to see Johnny saying something and frantically waving. My ears were rushing. He was trying to get me moving.

A hybrid was closing on his turned back.

I twisted, pulling my unwilling blond passenger into Johnny and releasing her to draw one of Carlisle's daggers. The hybrid was almost on him, arms outstretched, eyes shimmering red—far too occupied to react when I stepped past Johnny and buried my blade in its left eye.

The hybrid fell.

We pushed on for the steps, Johnny handing back our passenger so he could take up his rifle again.

Most of the legionnaires had already made it to the lifts. I reached out to telekinetically hurl a few more hybrids away from Mara and Edwards. We reached the top of the stairs, and one of the legionnaires relieved me of my blonde charge, freeing me up to move to the railing and cover the few legionnaires still retreating.

The outpouring of waking hybrids seemed to be stabilizing, if not quite slowing. At least half of the chambers remained closed, holding their occupants in stasis, which seemed a small miracle.

But that still left more than enough coming for us.

Several dozen of the growling creatures pushed after us, some leaping up from the ground floor, others dropping down from upper catwalk, all driving us toward the lift doors, where our escape was critically bottlenecked.

No, I realized. Not just bottlenecked. Simply not happening.

At a second glance, I understood why.

Only two of the five lift cars stood open and waiting, the ones from the shafts we'd rappelled down apparently inoperable thanks to their breached shaft doors or maybe some collision detection sensors picking up our lines. Either way, Dillard and Carter had arrived at the same conclusion I promptly drew.

Retreat wasn't happening.

Not without heavy casualties.

We'd already lost a few legionnaires to the hybrids, but that still left far too many to fit into two lift cars. There was also the two open shafts, but ascending those manually would be a single-file bloodbath with a couple companies' worth of hybrids at our backs. There were less than a hundred hybrids still standing, and under Dillard's command, Hound Company was quickly organizing into a strong defensive formation—funneling the bulk of the hybrids into multiple lines of overlapping fire, two fireteams working to the catwalk above to provide additional cover.

Holding the line was our best bet of getting everyone out of here alive. Assuming the rest of the hybrids didn't start waking up from stasis, at least. So I followed Johnny in rallying with our fireteam and settled in for the fight.

Fireteam E had already dropped an additional four hybrids—one by Edwards' heavy rifle, two by Mara's sharpshooting, and one by my telekinetically-propelled dagger—when the ceiling amps clicked to life and Alton Parker's voice boomed down.

"Much as I've enjoyed reliving old memories, I have facilities to run, and imbeciles to manage." At the far end of the room, I could just make out his tiny shape, red eyes aglow, his legionnaire hostage still draped over one shoulder. "Best of luck protecting your own monkeys, Haldin."

With that, he gave a wave and disappeared into a mag lift.

I rounded on the lifts behind us, mind racing. If Alton was running... if there was a chance I could catch him alone... I looked and found Dillard already glancing my way, along with the couple legionnaires around him who weren't actively gunning down hybrids.

"He's headed for the roof," I called.

"Don't think about it, Raish," he snapped as I pushed my way over to him.

"I can stop him, Ordo."

I wasn't all that confident about that—or even about the *headed for the roof* part, really—but I must've at least sounded the part, because Dillard actually hesitated. He took the time to add a few bursts to Hound Company's thunderous kill zone before turning a troubled scowl back on me.

"No. Too dangerous." He turned away to fire again and bark a few commands to his squad. I thought about doing the same.

Maybe he was right. I couldn't leave Hound Company down here. Not when they were only here because I'd driven for it.

But I also couldn't let Alton Parker get away, and down here, with Hound Company firmly dug in and the hybrid tide slowing... would I even make much difference? I wasn't sure, about that or about what I should do.

So instead I asked myself: what would Carlisle do? He'd left me in his place, right? So what would he do if it were him here?

I was already turning for the lifts when Dillard rounded back on me.

"You want to help, Raish? Get your ass back in line and—Hey!"

I was almost as surprised as Dillard sounded to find myself dodging past his reach and darting for one of the open lifts. They had it under control down here. I believed that. But up there, Parker was getting away.

I couldn't let that happen.

One legionnaire tried to stop me at the lift doors, but I twisted outside his grab with the help of a light telekinetic nudge. As an afterthought, I tugged off my cloaking pendant and tossed it at him when he turned to give chase. "Tell Dillard to keep that with him."

His moment of surprised indecision was all I needed to slip into the lift car and jab the door controls. The door started sliding shut, and I was about to let out a tense breath when something slammed into it, halting its progress.

Johnny appeared a second later, prying his way into the lift car with red cheeks to match his hair. "What the scud are you thinking, Hal?"

"What are *you* thinking?" I shot back, jamming the button for the tenth floor button as soon as he scooted through and hoping my rooftop getaway assumption wasn't faulty.

The lift's rapid upward acceleration didn't settle my churning stomach any more than did the open defiance twisting across Johnny's face.

"I'm thinking you're not going alone, you crazy bastard."

"You're also defying orders."

"What orders?" A very Johnny grin split his face. "Dillard told you to stop, not me. The way I see it, I'm pursuing a rogue civie." The grin died. "And a dangerous softsteel sipping one at that."

He looked upward as if he could see through the steel, straight up to the fight we might be walking into, then he busied himself with reloading his rifle and sidearm. I followed his lead.

"So," he said, slamming a fresh feeder home, "did you have a plan, orrr…?"

I paused mid-reload to look at him, and suddenly all I could see was Alton Parker standing over his broken body, sneering at me with those glowing red eyes. Just as Al'Kundesha had done when he'd murdered my parents. Just as Zar'Faenor had looked at me when he'd plunged his scaly fist through Carlisle's intestines.

Cold dread quenched hot, tingling nerves, filling me with an equally cold certainty. I slid a fresh slug feeder into my handgun.

"Hal?"

The lift began to slow.

"Hal..."

I'm pretty sure he saw what I was about to do, but it didn't matter. I couldn't face Alton with Johnny at my side.

"Stay safe, buddy," I said. Then I darted out of the lift car and into the richly adorned executive floor.

Johnny lunged for the door after me, but I caught him with telekinesis and pinned him to the back of the lift.

He struggled as I reached in and pressed every button from the fifth floor down. "Dammit, man, don't do this! Hal... Hal!"

I let the lift doors close, listening to Johnny cursing my name until he disappeared from view. He was going to be furious with me. But at least he'd be alive. It was enough for now.

I drew my mental defenses tighter, sweeping out with my senses.

I didn't have to look far. The presence of a raknoth mind was unmistakable, like a roaring bonfire in the dead of night. I withdrew, tightening my defenses further before he could try to get in my head. I'd forgotten just how damned powerful the raknoth felt in my senses—how powerful they *were* in mind and body. It was more than a little terrifying.

But Alton Parker had to be stopped.

For Enochia. For Elise.

My fingers clenched, the crack of knuckles crisp in the eerie silence.

For Carlisle. For my parents.

Holding that thought firmly in mind, I started for the stairwell that would take me to the monster.

7

PAYBACK

Alton Parker watched me with the air of a bored wolf as I emerged onto the rooftop. He wasn't surprised to see me. But why would he be? I wasn't a raknoth, but my uncloaked telepathic presence would've been hard for him to miss approaching. And he'd clearly been waiting for me.

"I was hoping you might join me," he called. "I suppose it's the least you could do after bringing your meddlesome humans to wreck my facility."

It chilled me, the way he kept addressing me as if I weren't one of them. I thought about telling him to grop himself—that this facility was only the beginning and that I was going to dismantle his entire world piece by piece. Instead, I raised my gun and put three slugs in his chest.

He didn't even try to move. Just took the three rounds to the chest and staggered back a step. It was only then I noticed the legionnaire lying further back on the rooftop, neatly tied up beside a sleek black skimmer that must've been Alton's. I didn't have time to worry about it as Alton calmly straightened out his perforated jacket, patches of scaly green creeping out from under his collar and sleeves—the beginnings of the reactive shift into his true monstrous form.

"Are you done?" he asked.

"I'll be done when I put one of these slugs through your eye and into that slimy brain-jacking blob you call a body."

He arched a suave dark eyebrow, crimson eyes pulsing brighter as if daring me to try. In truth, I had no idea if his eyes were any more vulnerable to small arms fire than the rest of his body, but in the considerable time I'd spent thinking about how to kill a raknoth, it always seemed the best place to start.

I was thinking about giving it a try when Alton broke the silence.

"I was sorry to see your late friend go, Haldin. He was… interesting." He frowned. "Far more interesting than that lot downstairs."

It was all I needed. I took aim at the son of a bitch and kept pulling the trigger until the sidearm was empty. Alton kept his face covered throughout the assault, then threw his hands wide with an aggravated growl when I was empty, flexing freshly-sprouted claws, his eyes burning with crimson rage.

I was already hurling my empty sidearm at his scaly green face and drawing my second dagger to charge.

I expected him to lunge straight for me in kind. Instead, he plunged a hand into his pocket and yanked out a small cylindrical device. I faltered, uncertain. Then, with a clawed thumb, he flicked the cap aside to reveal a tiny red button. The kind that looked like it was meant for nothing good.

A detonator.

"Did you say goodbye to them, Haldin?"

I squeezed Carlisle's daggers, tensed to the exploding point. He was baiting me. He had to be. It's what Alton Parker did.

He cocked his reptilian head, like he could smell my uncertainty. "Did you not stop to wonder why I fled an engagement I easily could have won beside my children?"

That was exactly what I'd wondered, and he knew it.

"I was wondering if you'd come out of your shell long enough to catch my trickery here with those Viper Company fools." He bared glistening fangs. "And now that you have though, well…" He waved a hand as if to convey the obvious. "This facility has expired its usefulness. Time to deconstruct and move on."

"Bullscud. You'd never…"

He gave a humorless chuckle. "Do you know how obscenely *easy* it is to build places like this when we can bend their wills like copper wire? Defending a known location isn't worth the effort." He waved the detonator. "Which is why I had the lab rigged with explosives, for exactly this contingency. So nice of you to bring a full company for the occasion."

My mouth was too dry to swallow. "You're lying."

Thirty-some legionnaires down there, fighting for their lives. Johnny headed there right this moment. All because of me. All about to die because of me. I couldn't breathe. Couldn't process the next steam of words I vaguely noticed growling out of Alton's mouth.

All I could see was the legionnaire tied up behind him, wild-eyed, kicking and screaming through his gag for his brothers and sisters below.

I was springing forward before I knew it, throwing my mind out, latching onto the detonator to yank it free. I had to stop him. Couldn't let them die. Not again. But Alton's grip was raknoth strong, and he was ready for my trick.

"Stop!" he snapped, holding the detonator firm.

I threw a dagger, using telekinesis to propel it like a pulse gun, straight for one of his glowing eyes, at the same time reaching for the detonator button, desperate to lock it in place against his falling finger.

Too late.

I'm not sure how it happened. Maybe it was a flick of Alton's focus. Maybe it was the back of my brain catching up on exactly where the gagged soldier's wide eyes had been fixed.

Time slowed.

My senses brushed against the blinding-bright brick of chemical energy a few yards to my right, and I had just enough time to understand that Alton Parker had tricked me again. Just enough time to throw out a helpless hand in defense. Then his thumb hit the switch.

It was like Alpha himself had reached down to smack me with a fiery hand.

Flames everywhere, then I was rocketing through a wild blur of pain and motion, too fast to comprehend. I must've passed out momentarily, because next I knew, I wasn't looking at the rooftop, but at Vantage's high perimeter wall.

Plummeting straight for it like a human rocket.

Some blessed part of my mind managed to get a grip and pull up on my flight with telekinesis. Someone was screaming. Me, I realized. I cleared the top of the wall by bare inches, almost flying level, and my control slipped. The ground leapt up far too quickly. I channeled off one more hard pull of deadly velocity.

Then I hit.

I lost count of revolutions and bounces, skipping across grass and dirt like a pebble on water. There was no controlling it. When the world finally stopped spinning, a weak turn of my ringing head showed I lay a good thirty yards outside the perimeter wall I'd narrowly avoided becoming a permanent piece of.

For a few seconds, I was too overloaded to register anything more than that and the fact that I was still alive. Then the pain washed in past the shock, flowing through my body like liquid to a mold. Everything hurt. Everything. And the high, flat tone ringing through my head made me wonder if maybe my brain hadn't been liquefied on impact.

Impact?

Maybe it had, because I couldn't quite seem to string together what the scud had just happened.

Impact. Hot, flaming, hand-of-Alpha impact.

A bomb.

Alton Parker's bomb. I'd been charging at him, and then...

The detonator.

I tried to sit up and groaned at the effort.

"Johnny..." The word came out as a raw croak.

Sweet Alpha, the entire team. Hound Company.

Had they all gone up in flames with the press of that button?

I rolled over and vomited into the scraggly yellow grass, the convulsions sending fresh waves of agony through my everything. My heart was hammering, each beat setting the right side of my head awash with fire. Burns? Wouldn't exactly be a surprise.

When I was sure I wouldn't asphyxiate, I rolled back over—just in time to see Alton Parker's sleek black skimmer sailing by overhead, bound in the rough direction of Divinity.

The treacherous son of a bitch.

I wasn't sure how long I laid there staring numbly at the sky, the right side of my head steadily burning like it was still caught back in the blast. My body sneered at the thought of moving, whispering to me of the ground's soft comfort and how the pain would only double—quadruple even—if I worked up the audacity to try to move again.

But I needed to get up. Needed to see what had happened. I wasn't sure I wanted to, or that I was ready to handle what I might find. But I needed to know.

Had it happened again?

Had I led them all straight to death at the hands of the raknoth?

I closed my eyes, and Johnny's face was waiting in the darkness, etched with the anger and the betrayal of that final moment before the mag lift door had snapped shut to send him back below. Back to where...

"Alpha please, no," I whispered.

I couldn't push the thought away. Couldn't stop seeing that moment. Then something gave, and it was the entirety of Hound Company in my head, bravely fighting one moment only to die screaming, consumed by fire, the next.

"No," I groaned, jerkily shaking my head.

I couldn't believe it. It was too much.

Alton Parker might have blown my ass halfway to Alpha's waiting arms, but he was also a liar. Johnny and the others could still be all right. They had to be.

I gritted my teeth and sat up through a fresh wave of pain.

"No," I repeated, my voice stronger this time.

I got my legs under me, moving through the pain as best I could.

They were going to be all right. Had to be.

I nearly fell my first couple tries, but eventually I made it back to my feet. I appeared to be on the eastern side of the facility, so I turned left for the front gate and slowly, painstakingly, sidled forward.

I'd made it about twenty feet when my palmlight buzzed. My left leg buckled at the surprise, and I went down to a knee. I was too occupied with my palmlight to care.

Please. Please.

Over my shaking fingers, the display lit with a new message. I read the name on the message three times, just to be sure.

Johnathan Wingard.

I puffed out a jubilant gust of air and gestured the message open.

<Hope you had a fun ride, you ass.>

I looked around stupidly for a second. Just as my explosion-addled brain caught on, my earpiece crackled with Johnny's voice.

"Up here, steel sipper."

And there he was, a tiny figure peering down from the rooftop I'd been violently ejected from. Another legionnaire was beside him—maybe the one I hoped to Alpha Alton had left safely bound up there. My head spun a little as I processed just how damn far I'd flown.

"Johnny…" My voice almost failed me. "Thank Alpha." I pulled myself back to my feet. "The others—"

"They're fine," Johnny said, sounding a lot less touched than I felt. "They did their jobs and watched each other's backs."

I was opening my mouth to explain what I'd been afraid had happened to them when his words properly clicked in my mind.

I paused. "Johnny, I—"

"Are you badly hurt down there?"

"I've been better. Feels like I've got some burns and all, bu—"

"Are you able to make it to the main gate?"

"Yeah, I think—"

"Then have a nice walk, buddy."

I checked my palmlight to confirm what the click in my earpiece had already told me. He'd killed the line. And when I looked up, Johnny's distant figure had disappeared from the rooftop edge.

As quickly as my elation had come, it was gone. Had I messed up that badly? In all the years I'd known him, I could probably count on my fingers alone the number of times I'd seen Johnny properly pissed. He'd never just stormed off. Until now, at least.

I stood there in the dying grass, head burning, shaking with the pain and the residual shock, staring numbly at the empty rooftop.

At least Johnny was still alive. If he'd been up there with me when Parker had sprung his trap… There was no way I could've kept us both alive, was there? I'd barely managed for myself.

But that wasn't what he was upset about, was it? He was pissed I hadn't trusted him to hold his own and watch my back up there. But what was I supposed to do, let him die so he could feel like a valued member of the team?

I couldn't say why, but in that moment, I missed Carlisle more than I had since I'd lost him. The grief crashed down on me with violent force, a deep, longing ache in my chest that nearly drove me to my knees. The ache ascended to the back of my throat, bringing tears I didn't bother fighting. I trudged on, letting them stream freely down my cheeks, until the first heaving sob took hold of my body and dropped me to my knees. I reveled in the pain each movement jolted through my body. Cried until my eyes ran dry and my sobs went hoarse.

Then I blew out a long sigh and pulled myself to my feet. The burning on my head was getting worse. I probably needed to have it looked at—not to mention to find out what was happening inside. It was only then my mind caught up enough to remind me that Dillard was probably going to have my crispy skin on a platter for the way I'd run off.

All in all, it had been a pretty scuddy day, I decided. But I began my slow, limping plod to the main gate, holding three positive thoughts firmly in mind.

Johnny was alive.

Hound Company hadn't died horribly in an underground explosion.

And when I found Alton Parker, raknoth hide be damned, I was going to beat him bloody.

8

LOST & FOUND

By the time I reached the front gate of the Vantage compound, the burning on the side of my head had grown to severely aggravating. At least the reinforcements had begun arriving—four more Legion transports followed shortly by four bulky white skimmers bearing the open red hand insignia of the medica. They all landed in the perimeter yard near our transports and disembarked straight to work.

A quiver of trepidation passed through my gut when I spotted Dillard emerging from the main building, but I started limping his way, sure it was better to face any repercussions head on. It wasn't like he could discharge me for insubordination down there, seeing as I was already a civie, but I doubted he was going to be happy.

He either ignored my approach or didn't notice it, busy as he was speaking with the ordos of the new arrivals—Boar and Bear Company of the fifty-first legion, I gathered from their transports. Most of the fresh legionnaires began hustling into the facility, trailed closely by all the medics, who were heavily armed with first aid kits and compact stretchers.

All the medics, that was, except for one.

The young brunette woman stepped in front of me before I could reach Dillard, holding her first aid kit between us with a tentative expression. Her eyes traced the right side of my pale yellow civilian armor, which was admittedly a bit crispy, scanned the burning side of my head more carefully, and finally settled on my face before that flicker of recognition touched her eyes. "You're..." She seemed to catch herself, professionalism returning. "Are you okay, sir?"

"I'm fine."

I almost meant it. I was tired to the bones, but now that the shock of being blown off a ten-floor building was wearing off, I didn't feel all that much worse than if I'd taken a particularly savage beating, of which I'd had my fair share in the past cycles. The burning on the side of my head was getting pretty bad, but I could cope another few minutes, at least.

I moved to step around her.

She mirrored the motion almost apologetically, just enough to bar my path, watching me with worried eyes. "I think I should have a look anyway.

"I'm fine," I repeated. "I mean, my head burns, but—look, I just need to talk to someone real quick and then—"

"Please," she said, barring my way again with a raised hand when I tried to step around her. "I'm sorry, it just really looks like—"

"Looks like you were launched from the tenth floor by an explosive device," Dillard said, cutting around the medic to join us. "Minutes after disobeying a direct order, I might add. What the scud were you thinking, soldi—" He cut himself off, gnashing his teeth as he apparently remembered I wasn't a soldier at all. Not anymore.

"I apologize for my behavior, sir," I forced myself to say. "I thought I could stop him."

The medic was looking between us as if trying to decide whether she'd heard all that right and whether she should scurry out of the picture. Her sense of duty, it seemed, won out.

"Sir?" she said. "Might I have permission to administer care to this, um, patient while you two..." She looked between us, clearly uncertain what it was the two of us would be doing.

Dillard saved her from any additional floundering with a curt nod, some of the anger dimming in his eyes as they traced over my crispy right side. Curious, I glanced in the faded reflection of the medica skimmer's window and—

Sweet Alpha, my head.

I reached for it impulsively, but the medic darted forward and caught my arm, gently guiding it back to my side. I didn't resist.

Most of the hair on the right side of my head was gone.

The skin didn't look too happy, either, though it was hard to make out colors in the reflection of the dark window. Even so, the burning pain sizzled to new heights at the sight, like it had been waiting for visual confirmation before revealing its true intensity. But pain from a burned area was a good sign, right? I couldn't remember.

"I thought I'd misheard Wingard's report," Dillard said quietly, looking at me like he was only then seeing me properly. "Then when he repeated it, I thought he must've lost it. I don't understand how…" He seemed to remember himself then, and some of the stern anger crept back in. "What happened up there, Citizen Raish?"

The medic stiffened at the sound of my name, but quickly went back to her inspection.

"I gropped up," I said, still staring at the reflection. "I let Parker get to me, fell right into his trap. He told me the detonator was set to blow the lab, and… Well, I guess it doesn't matter anymore."

"I'll be the judge of what matters," Dillard said, resuming his stern ordo air in full. "I'm going to be needing a full report—complete with how the scud you survived that blast… Once we've returned to Haven and you've been cleared by the medica, of course," he added at my medic's indignant frown.

I clenched my jaw against my own indignant anger and nodded. "Yes, sir. But for now, the people in the blood racks—"

"It's under control. We'll get them out, then we'll blow everything else." He glanced between me and the medic. "Just make sure he doesn't bleed out internally before we get back."

"Affirmative, sir," she said.

Dillard shot me one last frown, started to turn for the facility, then paused, turning back. "I served under your father in the Dorrin Uprising."

He said it like he shouldn't need to explain what it meant—and he didn't need to. My dad had only been an ordo himself back then. If Dillard had served under him, then he must've been one of the legionnaires my dad had saved in the battle that'd cost him his leg. The battle where he'd ended up saving multiple companies and breaking through the enemy line in a turn that led to the final downfall of the rebellion only days later—all because he'd disobeyed a direct order to storm an enemy entrenchment he knew was a trap.

Dillard watched this all sink in on my face, his expression intense. "If you ever find yourself tempted to buck the reins again, you'd better be damn sure you have no other choice, Citizen."

I licked my lips, indignant anger giving way to something of far greater weight. "Yes, sir."

He held my gaze for a long moment, then reached in a pocket and produced my cloaking pendant. "I believe this belongs to you."

I took it, and he turned to go without another word.

"Sir?"

He paused, but didn't turn.

I cursed myself for having opened my mouth, wanting to ask if he was going to tell High General Glenbark what had happened here. But that question was beyond stupid. Of course he'd tell her. He couldn't not. And nothing I said would change that. So instead I muttered weak thanks and watched him leave with a sinking feeling in my gut.

I'd taken a gutsy risk, and now I had nothing but a steaming bucket of scud to show for it. Well, that, a furious best friend, and soon-to-be livid girlfriend.

The medic cleared her throat from the back of her heavy skimmer, and I turned to find her sliding the stretcher out of the rear hatch. "May I?" she asked, nodding to the padded stretcher.

I shrugged and followed her around the vehicle. Laying down for a minute suddenly didn't sound so bad. And if it happened to be on the medic's stretcher, what difference did it make?

The medic—Melanie, according to the tag on her white tunic—hovered beside me as I lowered my painful way onto the stretcher. She thrummed with a kind of nervous energy that made me wonder if she wasn't a little frightened to be left alone with the Demon of Divinity. Maybe she was just new to the job. She was barely older than me—and also rather cute, I couldn't help but notice as she leaned over me to begin a quick series of physical exams.

Once it became clear I was going to be compliant, Melanie's nervous energy dissipated, and her words took on a soothing tone as she talked me through the exams.

"How's the pain on your head?" she asked, leaning closer to inspect the burns.

"Insistent," I said. Then, not even sure I wanted to hear the answer, I added, "How bad does it look?"

"Really not that bad, considering... Well, I'll definitely get you set up with some salve strips after the scan, but I think it's safe to say it should heal nicely."

She showed me a friendly enough smile as she wrapped up and slid me into the skimmer to start some scans. She didn't directly ask about what had happened inside or how in demons' depths I'd managed to survive a bomb and a ten floor fall, but I could tell she wanted to. I might've told her had I not been so exhausted. It was enough effort to mumble bleary acknowledgments to her updates on the scanning process.

I don't know how long she was at it, but I must've nodded off, because next I knew, I was jolting upright at her light touch on my shoulder, and I wasn't in the scanner anymore. She tensed as if to catch me, apparently worried I'd fall off the stretcher, which she'd slid back out of the rear hatch.

"I'm good," I mumbled, swinging my legs to the ground.

Her hands stayed where they were until I was steadily on my feet. Then slowly, cautiously, she released me and stepped back.

I was starting to give her a thumbs-up when it occurred to me that the right half of my face felt oddly tight and gooey.

"Careful," Melanie said as I started to reach for it. "I went ahead and put those salve strips on while you were out." She smiled shyly. "I was going to wake you, but you kinda looked like you needed a few minutes' rest."

I touched lightly at the edge of the salve-smeared bandages. "I, uh, yeah… Thank you." I pointed to the tablet in the front pocket of her coat. "Any other news I should know about?"

She looked me over as if trying to make sense of something before answering. "Did you really get blasted off that roof?" she finally asked.

I held up my charred arm demonstratively, then gestured at the eastern wall. "Damn near became one with that wall on the way down."

She looked between the wall and me, forehead wrinkled. "Well, then aside from the fact that you apparently have the protection of Alpha himself, you should know that you do appear to have a mild concussion and a pretty astounding amount of internal bruising."

I couldn't help but smile a little at that. "Is that your professional opinion?"

Her smile looked tired and forced. "My professional opinion is that it's miraculous you're alive, much less walking and talking. And that you should get to the medica for a follow up as soon as you return to base."

I touched a casual salute to my chest. "Affirmative, goodlady. Thank you." For some reason, the impulse struck me then to introduce myself properly. Not that it was necessary. Very few people failed to recognize me these days. Still, I found myself wanting to.

Before I could, though, a few legionnaires exited the main building across the yard and turned to hold the doors while Melanie's colleagues carted several wounded legionnaires out on stretchers.

I traded a look with Melanie. "I'd better get in there and see what's going on. Guess I'll see you around."

She gave me a concerned look. "Let's hope you won't have to."

<hr>

INSIDE, the cavernous underground lab was awash with activity—some helping evacuate the wounded, some rigging the breeding facility to blow, most of the rest trying to help revive the dozens of pale victims strapped to those barbaric blood racks. I drew plenty of curious looks in my charred civie armor and my half-mask of salve strips. Many darkened when they made it to the rest of my face and recognition set in. Others looked surprised. But no one said anything, save for Edwards, who looked me up and down, clapped a beefy hand on my unburnt shoulder, and kindly—albeit grimly—answered my most pressing question.

Ten of Hound Company's forty-two legionnaires had been killed, another thirteen wounded—three critically. I couldn't help but notice Mara watching me with cold, unreadable eyes while Edwards filled me in.

It could have been worse, I told myself. If Alton Parker hadn't been bluffing about those explosives, all of Hound Company would be dead now, along with the blood rack victims. But legionnaires were still dead, and Alton Parker had escaped. Somehow, it was hard to call that a victory.

Down on the ground floor, some of the victims were coming off their blood racks now, at least somewhat awake. They sat in the aisles, pale-faced and draped in whatever the soldiers had been able to find—mostly more of the blue lab gowns. Some looked frantically around the room, tense and terrified. Others sat in languid dazes, still heavily under the influence of the sedatives that had kept them under for Alpha knew how many cycles now.

I spotted a fiery red buzzed head among the helpers and headed down the stairs toward Johnny. He was knelt down with his arms around a slender brunette woman who might've been in her early forties. As I approached, it was hard to tell if he was comforting or restraining her.

Then I came close enough to hear her, and I froze.

"I could care less about a gown!" she was saying, wriggling against Johnny's arms. "I need to talk to your commanding officer! Now!"

I knew that voice.

"All right," Johnny said, slowly releasing her and holding his hands up peacefully. "All right, it's okay."

She tried to rise, but her legs buckled beneath her. Johnny was there to catch her before she hit the ground.

She looked up at him, frustration and embarrassment evident in her eyes. "Okay. Maybe I could use that hand, then."

The more she spoke, the more I was sure of it. This was the woman who'd unknowingly helped us expose the raknoth to the world.

"Therese?"

She turned to me with a deep furrow in her brow.

Johnny looked around too, his expression flat and defensive. Then understanding dawned in his eyes, and he turned back to her. "Wait. You're Therese Brown?"

Therese looked back and forth between us, mouth slightly agape. Then she closed her mouth, took a closer look at the Legion activity around the lab, and nodded to herself. "Someone got my audio logs?"

I crouched down beside her and Johnny, who seemed to have forgotten for the moment that he was angry with me. "I did. I broke in here almost four cycles ago with my... with my old partner. We tried to get you out then, but there were only two of us. Alton Parker set his hybrids loose, and we had to run."

She gave a visible shudder at the sound of Alton's name, her eyes somewhere far off. "Hybrids..." Her eyes snapped up from wherever they'd been and locked onto mine. "So you already know about them?" She looked at Johnny's legionnaire armor. "The Legion knows about the raknoth?"

"Thanks to Hal here," Johnny said, tilting his head but not looking my way. "You can breathe easy, Therese. We've got them on the run. Sort of."

A few racks down the aisle, a sallow, middle-aged man shifted against his rack restraints, soft whimpers escaping his mouth as he began to surface from his drug-induced hibernation.

Johnny finally met my eyes, his gaze lingering on the mask of salve strips covering the burnt side of my face. "You have her?"

I nodded.

He gave Therese's shoulder a gentle pat and rose to go help the other guy. Next to me, Therese was beginning to shiver. I looked around and spotted a few shelves under the lift platform stocked full of the blue gowns that seemed to be the only clothing we were going to find. "Let me get you something to wear. Wait right here."

I hurried over, grabbed several gowns, and handed a few out on the way back, saving two for Therese. She accepted my hand up, and I hovered beside her as she slipped on the first gown, buttoned it, and slipped on the second. That done, she rubbed at her arms, trying to get warm as she looked around.

When her gaze fell on the soldiers prowling the catwalks, planting explosives, she froze. "What are they doing?"

"Shutting this facility down for good."

Her expression melted into one of horror.

"We can't let the raknoth keep building their army down here," I said. "We can't risk this equipment falling back into their hands."

"Those are people in those tubes," she said, her voice weak. "Human beings. They're every bit as much victims as I was."

I'd wondered about that more than a few times in the past cycles. Somehow, it was a bit easier to forget those things had started as humans once you'd seen them ripping innocent people to shreds, indiscriminately killing helpless men, women, and children.

Therese wasn't wrong, but still…

"Do you know how to stop them from turning into one of those things?" I asked, pointing at a hybrid that lay dead further down the aisle, snouted mouth open in an eternal roar.

She didn't cringe away from the sight like I'd expected. "No. Not yet." She waved a hand at the racks. "But we have most of the premier experts on raknoth physiology right here. Maybe with some time, we could—"

"We don't have time." It came out harsher than I'd intended. "There are only five raknoth left as far as we know, but they have an entire army of these creatures, and they can manipulate humans as easy as breathing. They took Oasis yesterday."

That gave her pause.

"We can't afford mercy here. Not if we want Enochia to survive." I looked back to where the soldiers were wrapping up with their demolition prep, feeling uneasy.

Since when had I become the one who'd argue for the big picture over the preciousness of each individual life?

Therese was right. These people were far from harmless. But they were also innocent. Through no fault of their own, they'd been touched by the savage nature of the raknoth. Everything I'd seen and heard suggested we couldn't save them—that there was nothing we could do but watch their metamorphosis progress until they were every bit the vicious, mindless killing machines the raknoth wanted them to be. But maybe that was just the story I was telling myself.

What about the hybrid who'd evaded Edwards' first shot when we'd breached the lab? The one who'd seemed to respond to my mental presence when I'd reached out. What if the people *were* still in there somewhere?

"What would you need to get to work on a… I don't know, a treatment for the hybrids?"

Therese didn't look away from the hybrid chambers. "I don't know. Hybrid samples and a lab to start with." She glanced at the slowly growing pool of awoken blood rack victims. "As many of these researchers as are willing to chip in." She pursed her lips then shook her head. "And even then, I don't know. There's no sure thing. Something like that would probably take years, if it's possible at all."

I looked around at the hundreds of hybrid breeding cylinders, each another human life all but lost. "Seems like it's worth a try. Guess you'll be needing a new job anyway right?"

I regretted the words as soon as they left my mouth, but to my surprise, the corners of Therese's mouth turned up in a gentle smile. "I suppose I will be. My mother's been telling me for years I should leave Vantage. Find a man, start a family, all those fun things. She'll be thrilled. Although I might've missed the train on the whole *starting a family* thing."

She'd started rubbing at her arms again, and it occurred to me she might simply be talking to avoid the silence now—to hold at bay the thoughts of what she'd been through and what was about to happen.

"You know, you might have been responsible for saving Enochia."

She gave me a skeptical look.

I shrugged. "I'm not sure the Legion or anyone else would've listened to us about the raknoth without the information in your logs. I probably would've died up in the White Tower like I was supposed to."

Her eyebrows shot up. "The Sanctum tried to execute you?"

"That's the short version of things, yeah. Mostly, I think the raknoth wanted a bloody show to throw Enochia into chaos for the taking." I took in all the pain and damage around us, feeling a familiar dark weight descending. "I guess it kind of worked for them in the end, even if that night didn't go as they'd planned."

"What happened?"

"My mentor stopped them."

"Oh." She seemed to grasp the gravity in those four words. "But… why the Sanctum?"

"The short version? Because the High Cleric was a raknoth."

"Oh, my…" Her eyes were wide. "I think I'm going to need to catch up on the longer version."

"I'll be happy to fill you in, assuming the raknoth or the new High Cleric don't catch up with me first. And I'll try to talk to High General Glenbark about getting you the resources you need. Not that I have all that much clout."

Especially after my actions today.

Therese was frowning. "Glenbark?"

"New High General," I said. "Adrian Kublich was a raknoth too. He's dead now."

Therese studied me as if only then seeing me for the first time, taking in my civilian armor and the burns along my right side. "How old are you?"

I blew out a laugh, feeling some mixture of bitter and embarrassed. "Guess I'll be eighteen next Willowsday. Almost forgot."

She didn't say anything. For a while, we stood in silence, watching the legionnaires move about, pulling more and more of the waking victims from their racks.

"I should go help them," I finally said. "Are you gonna be okay?"

"Nothing a few gallons of juice and a couple days of drug-free sleep won't fix," she said, her tone surprisingly chipper despite her harrowed raggedness. She started toward a pair of awakening victims, then turned back when I didn't immediately follow. "Let's go. I might not be able to help *them* right now"—she glanced at the hybrid chambers—"but I'll be damned if I'm just going to stand around and twiddle my thumbs while my colleagues wake up from the worst nightmare of their lives."

I was going to like Therese Brown, I decided.

9

FRAYED

In the history of our friendship, I—and anyone else, for that matter—never would have described Johnny Wingard as a man of few words. On the flight back, though, he seemed to have spontaneously discovered the discipline of the Sanctum's fabled Silent Clerics. The grand total of his involvement in our conversation consisted of one grunt, one, "Whatever," and several long, brooding silences before he finally stood and climbed to the transport's upper cabin on the grounds of needing to run something by Dillard.

"Lover's quarrel?" someone asked quietly.

I turned to find Mara watching me with those cold, precise eyes—not quite hostile, but certainly not friendly or trusting either.

Beside her, Edwards frowned. "Give the kid a break, Evie."

She looked at him with a kind of calm fury that made certain parts of me shrivel. "I told you not to call me that, you oversized ape."

Edwards grinned and winked at me. "Yeah, but how else am I supposed to bring out those cold hard bitch eyes? You know how they get me all —Hnghhh!"

Whatever Edwards was getting at ended in a violent rush of air as Mara drove her elbow straight into his diaphragm.

The big guy just chuckled and wheezed on. "See? That's what I'm talking about, baby."

They went on like that for a little while, but I soon decided it was none of my business and turned back toward the front. I was too occupied with being irritated at Johnny anyway. I wanted to grab him, shake him, and ask him what the scud he'd wanted me to do. What would he have done if he'd been up there when the bomb had gone off? Would that have made him feel better? Would he have rather died on that rooftop than swallow his pride and admit that maybe some fights weren't for him?

It continued like that for the rest of the hour-long flight, a vicious cycle of frustration, deepening until I wanted to scream at the top of my lungs. I wished I'd had the good sense to ride back to Haven in one of the survivor transports. I could've been talking with Therese instead of stuck in this ridiculous standoff with Johnny.

At least we'd be in Haven soon. Not that that was a wholly relieving thought either. Aside from having stayed there last night, I hadn't been to Haven in years, and never for more than day trip tours during our tyro years. Still, having spent almost all my life in Sanctuary, Haven should have seemed closer to home than most other places, but I couldn't ignore the uneasy feeling in my stomach as it came into view.

Maybe the sight of the dark perimeter walls and the sprawling permacrete compound beyond reminded me too much of my parents, and the time I'd spent hunted by the Legion after losing them. Maybe it was simply that I longed for the home I'd been starting to find with Carlisle.

If I still had a home now, it was with Elise—provided she'd still talk to me when I showed up with a side of charred Hal.

But, I lamented as the transport dipped to an easy landing, here I was for now. And until the raknoth threat was under control, here I was likely to stay. At least until Sanctuary's repairs were complete enough for the base to resume its role as Legion headquarters.

Johnny appeared at the steps from the upper cabin and gave me a second's consideration before wordlessly grabbing his gear and vacating the transport with the flow of legionnaires. I sat there until the transport emptied, in no rush to push my battered body to its feet and through the crowded compartment.

When I finally made it down the ramp, I saw High General Glenbark herself had come to greet us, along with a small gathering of curious legionnaires and what looked like a couple companies' worth of medics, sweeping in to grab our rescues and our wounded and whisk them away with military efficiency. I caught Therese's eye across the landing pad and gave her what I hoped was a reassuring nod.

I thought about scurrying off to hide in my quarters after that, but when

Glenbark looked up from her discussion with Dillard, Carter, and Johnny and caught my eye, there was no walking away.

Growing up on a Legion base, there'd been no shortage of officers who knew how to exude commanding presence. Freya Glenbark put them all to shame—though I couldn't have said exactly what it was about her that made everyone in her vicinity stand a little straighter, listen closer, try harder.

She was attractive in a way that reminded me of a finely tuned weapon —beautiful to behold with all its hard precise edges, until it was you the sights were fixed on. But it was more than just that. An air of discipline that radiated from every crisp line of her uniform and every strand of her golden hair. A vibrancy in her sky blue eyes that pierced through anything they fell on.

Talking to her via holodisk had been one thing. She'd been half-sized, paled out, and I'd been in a different place, both physically and mentally. Marching across the permacrete now, though, I was embarrassed at the way my stomach fluttered and my head spun. Like I was just a chubby-cheeked tyro again, meeting the grand leader of the entire Legion for the first time in my subservient life.

I wasn't a tyro, I reminded myself, resisting the reflex to salute as I drew up to Glenbark's circle with Johnny and the two ordos.

I was a civilian. And they were supposed to be at my service as much as I was at theirs. More so, even. But that didn't stop the stomach flutters as Glenbark gave me a once-over, taking in my crispy right side and the half-mask of salve strips on my burning head.

"I hear you're lucky to be alive," she said.

I glanced at Johnny and Dillard, wondering exactly how they'd chosen to spin the rooftop incident. "I'm not sure I'd call any of us lucky right now. Alton Parker got away, and I'm pretty sure that means our hybrid problem isn't even close to over."

"Ordo Dillard informed me of your concern. And you don't think Mister Parker could be lying about the existence of these additional facilities?"

"I don't know."

He could've been lying, of course. Lying was what Alton Parker did.

"But if they don't have other installments," I added, "I don't see why he would've run when he probably could have stopped us."

Glenbark's frown was barely perceptible—the slightest crinkling around her measuring eyes. "You don't think you could have stopped him?"

I looked at Dillard and Carter before answering, not overly eager to tread on any more toes. "Maybe." I indicated my scorched right side. "But Alton Parker doesn't make a habit of fighting fair."

Then again, neither had Carlisle and I when we'd last faced Parker on that rooftop, keeping him distracted until Phineas could ram him off the building with a skimmer. Maybe that was poetic justice for me.

Glenbark studied me for another long moment, her pale eyes unreadable. "I'll take your concern under advisement, Citizen Raish. If there are more facilities out there, we'll find them. In the meanwhile, I'd like you to focus on solutions for protecting our people, as we agreed."

That earned me a curious look from Dillard and Carter, but if they had questions, they held them. Personally, I just wanted to roll my eyes. I'd just been blown off a building trying to wrangle down one of the Legion's most potent threats, and now they were wondering if I could get around to fixing the rest of their problems?

I looked to Johnny for a little sympathy, but he was avoiding my gaze, focused on Glenbark.

"We'll discuss the matter later," Glenbark said, "once you've seen the medics and had food and rest. For now, consider yourself grounded from further operations."

"I—What?"

I'd been ready for stern words and a severe warning. But grounded? I wasn't even a damned soldier. What did she mean, grounded?

"You took down a major hybrid facility today because of me. I didn't sign up to—"

"Follow orders?" she asked, one eyebrow slightly arched. "If not, then you had better get off my base before you get someone else hurt or killed. I appreciate what you're doing here, Citizen Raish, especially considering the events of the past few cycles, but you know better than most how quickly this all falls down if discipline fails. No one gets a free pass, no matter what they can do."

I didn't bother trying to hide my anger. It was preposterous. Insulting. And yet, for some damned reason, I felt my cheeks warming, embarrassment seeping in at her calm chastising. Was that just some conditioned response from my tyro years, or was she actually right? I didn't know right then, and she seemed to read it on my tense face.

"See the medics, Haldin," she said, not unkindly. "Get some rest. We need to talk soon about what comes next."

I was far from happy about being told to shove off and sit in my corner after everything, but I could see arguing wasn't going to get me anywhere right now. Besides, she was right about one thing, at least. I needed food and rest. And picking up more regenerative salve from the medica wasn't a bad idea either, seeing as Melanie had been too busy—or, I suspected, too worried I wouldn't otherwise come for a checkup—to give me more back at Vantage.

So, I turned to leave, not bothering to salute Glenbark or the others. I wasn't a soldier, no matter what they wanted to pretend, and I wasn't feeling especially respectful of my would-be commanders right then, either.

Glenbark watched me go with calm appraisal. Carter was looking at me like he was sure I must be hiding something. Dillard didn't speak, but he did give me a fractional nod. Maybe at least one person saw that I'd been trying to do the right thing today.

Johnny certainly didn't seem to.

My friend barely met my eyes before I set off. It irritated me as much as it worried me, the silent brooding treatment. It wasn't Johnny's style. I'd have to talk to him after I got myself sorted out.

I set course for the medica first. Explaining what had happened to my face to Elise was already going to be bad enough. At least this way I could say I'd handled it responsibly after the fact.

"Hey, kid!" a deep voice called after me at the edge of the landing pad. "Haldin."

I turned to find big burly Edwards tromping toward me. He winced a little as he took in my crispy side.

Yep. Elise was going to be thrilled.

"It's not *that* bad, is it?"

He shot me a friendly grin. "Nah, the whole mummy mask thing really suits ya. I'm sure the burnt bacon below is perfectly lovely too. You're tough, kid, I'll give you that."

The way he said the word, *kid*, kind of made me want to do something very kid-like, but I did my best to listen politely as he continued.

"Just wanted to say thanks. For earlier, I mean. Pulling my ass out, catching those, uh, hybrids." He shook his head. "Didn't understand what the scud had even happened until after the fight." He smiled sheepishly. "Mara caught on a lot faster. Filled me in. Guess I'll give you her thanks too since you probably won't be hearing it from her."

I glanced over and spotted Mara watching me from beside a few of the Hound fireteams. I nodded. She rolled her eyes and looked away, looking frustrated.

Edwards chuckled. "I'm gonna pay for this. But I appreciate... uh, you know, whatever it was you did."

"No problem," I said. Then, feeling like I had to say something else, I added, "You guys held it together really well out there today. I'm sorry about the Hounds we lost."

It probably all sounded condescending coming from a kid who was still a cycle too young to even be a legionnaire, but Edwards didn't seem to have a problem with it.

He clapped my unburnt shoulder with a meaty hand. "I really don't see how that's any of your fault. You just get yourself taken care of, huh?"

I nodded dumbly, and with that, Edwards went to rejoin his pack, leaving me to wonder why in demons' depths he didn't despise me like the rest of them seemed to.

As busy as the stale, chemically-clean-smelling halls of the medica were, the medics seemed rather averse to the notion of simply handing me a salve and sending me on my way. Something about needing to have a closer look. Especially what with all the extensive crispiness and the wild rumors already circulating about the yellow-armored civie who'd been blown from clear atop a ten floor building and lived to tell about it. Or had it been fifteen floors? Maybe twenty.

Rumor had it that civie might've even been the Demon of Divinity.

I'd have thought the story would be less shocking after the tales of the Demon of Divinity's fall from the White Tower two cycles ago, but apparently weird was still weird. Suffice it to say, I wasn't getting out of there in a flash.

Thankfully, Melanie happened by and was able to help me out of a full workup with the scans she'd taken back at Vantage. She still insisted on pulling me aside for a quick checkup, though, and on properly cleaning and reapplying salve to my burns.

"You wouldn't believe the damage you stubborn warrior types do when you're left alone with a wound and a bottle of salve," she said as she worked.

Her voice was soft, and as close as she was, I could smell the fruity sweetness of whatever lip balm she was wearing. Goja fruit, maybe.

It was kind of nice, just sitting here, letting her gentle hands—

"Are you still with me, sir?"

I straightened back to attention. "I, uh... Yeah. No, I..."

She leaned back, considering me thoughtfully, and I swear I could almost hear the thought touching down in her mind.

"This isn't…" I said quickly, shaking my head. "I mean, this isn't—I'm not concussed. I mean, I am, but I'm not disoriented. Because of the concussion, I mean."

She was warring to keep a smile from her lips, but it danced in her golden brown eyes anyway.

"I'm fine," I said.

She just gave me a noncommittal nod, still stifling her smile, and raised her salved hand, silently asking to resume her duty.

I sighed and leaned in to let her. "So you were saying? About the stubborn warrior types? Which I'm totally not, by the way."

"Stubborn? Or a warrior?"

I tapped at the pale yellow armor I was still hauling around. "I'm a civilian, didn't you hear?"

She just smiled, traced her salved thumb over my temple one last time, and turned me by the chin to inspect her work before reaching for the bandages.

"My name's Haldin, by the way," I said as she began wrapping.

"I know. Came straight up in the scans. Plus…" Her eyes widened a touch, as if she'd just realized what she'd been about to say.

"It's hard to miss the Demon of Divinity?"

It was her turn to sigh. "I'm sorry, I didn't mean to… I'm Melanie."

"I know," I said, smiling. "Came straight up in the scans."

She followed my gaze down to the tag on her coat and breathed a light laugh at herself. "Right. Well"—she put the finishing touch on the bandage wrap and leaned back, satisfied—"I think we're all done, Haldin the unbreakable civilian."

"I'll take unbreakable over Demon, I guess," I said, gathering my gear and standing. "Thank you, Melanie."

She stood too, pulling off her gloves and looking like she still had consternations about letting me walk out of the medica.

"So," I said slowly, feeling like I had to say something, "is this the part where we hope you won't have cause to see me again?"

She considered that, then busied herself cleaning up the supplies she'd used. "I think it might be." She paused to shoot me a knowing smile. "But if that stubborn itch gets you in trouble again…"

She extended her left hand, palmlight waiting. I woke my palmlight and held my extended fingers over hers, our palms barely an inch apart. Somehow, it felt more intimate than actually touching. But maybe that had more to do with the golden brown depths of those eyes I couldn't seem to look away from.

After too long, her gaze ticked to the bandaged side of my face, breaking the spell. We broke our palmlight link.

"… just call," she concluded, moving back to her cleanup as I mumbled another thanks and turned for the door wondering what the scud I was doing.

I LEFT the medica with a salve-covered face, another full tube of the miraculous stuff, a bottle of painkillers I'd repeatedly told Melanie I didn't need, and a sharp dose of *what the scud was I thinking in there?*

Had I been flirting?

Had she?

No. It had just been friendly banter—medic and patient, passing the awkward silence. And the thing with the palmlights… it was an everyday act, swapping personal IDs like that. Right. An everyday act that'd felt so intimate that I'd forgotten to breathe in the moment.

Guilt crept through my excuses like the acrid bite of the salve, which the makers had only partially succeeded in hiding under a pungent mask of minty aromas. I inspected the tube and almost laughed. There, right on the corner of the salve container, was the inverted pyramid logo that formed the V in Vantage Corp.

As quickly as bitter amusement came, it was swept out by cold alarm at the thought that the raknoth could've put anything into any of Vantage's drugs. But that was paranoid, right? Alton Parker had used Vantage as a front for some truly horrible things, but he'd also needed to keep a legitimate company running on the surface all those years, hadn't he?

Sure. But that didn't really calm the itch to find a mirror and check that I wasn't already sprouting green scales.

Outside the medica, I deliberated for a few seconds then turned for the block of civilian barracks where they'd given me quarters. The fab in my tiny kitchen unit was paltry compared to the selection in the mess halls, but I suddenly wasn't feeling all that hungry anyway. All I really wanted to do was stash this ridiculous civie armor, clean off the rest of the grime of battle, and crawl into bed for a good day or two.

Briefly, I thought about adding Johnny to that list, seeing if we could talk about what'd happened today, but that was probably a conversation best left for after I'd slept. Which made it all the more startling when I walked in to find Johnny waiting for me in my small living room.

And he wasn't alone.

Elise turned from the wide window slowly, like she was afraid at what she might find. Scud, after the past week, maybe she was genuinely scared I'd spook and run if she moved too fast.

"Lise…"

I don't know why I expected to find her face livid as she turned. I'm sure there was anger bubbling in her somewhere, but for the most part, her blue eyes just looked tired and worried as they met mine. It only tripled the guilt tightening around my chest.

I stared, searching for something to say, hoping she'd beat me to it. Instead, she crossed the room, holding my gaze until she was close enough to wrap me in a tight hug. I wanted to return the hug, to melt into her, but I was too shocked, too off balance.

Behind Elise, Johnny let out a heavy sigh and dropped down on the bland gray couch. Elise's embrace was warm and caring, but their silence, their demeanors…

"What's going on?" I finally found my voice to ask.

I was pretty sure I knew the answer.

Elise pulled back. Looked up at me with those startling blue eyes I'd been too self-absorbed to tell her were beautiful for too long now.

"He's worried about you, love," she whispered in my mind. *"He told me what you did to try to protect him."* Her eyes drifted across the bandaged half of my face. *"And what happened on the rooftop."*

I tensed, anger flickering at the thought of Johnny running to Elise like a tail-tucked hound.

"Hal, don't."

The apprehension in her thoughts snapped me back to her. She'd stiffened against me, her eyes… what? Wary? Afraid? Since when had Elise been afraid of me?

I turned to Johnny, trying to keep calm. "You called her to pout? Seriously?"

Johnny exploded to his feet like he'd been waiting for it. "Great. You guys are doing that thing. Good, yeah. Go, team telepath. Hey, here's one for you." He stuck two fingers to the side of his head. "Are you getting it? Spoiler alert—I'm thinking you're an asshole."

"Johnny…" Elise said.

"Yeah," I said, pulling away from Elise. "An alive asshole. Just like you, buddy."

"You're so full of scud."

"What do you want me to do?" I shouted. "Huh? What? You want me to let you tag along next time so we can die together?"

"Let me?" He shook his head, his mouth pulling into a bitter, humorless smile. "You're really buying it aren't you? All in. The mighty Haldin Raish. Shaper. Raknoth slayer. Invincible hero of the—"

"Grop you, you—"

"Boys!" Elise's voice cut through the air like igniting scorch dust, snapping us both to attention.

Johnny spoke quietly now, head hung, refusing to meet my eyes. "You're not even considering for a second that things might've turned out differently if I'd had your back. That maybe one of us would've noticed the damn bomb before you charged in, or that maybe you wouldn't have done it at all. Can't you see that?"

I opened my mouth, certain that I had a good point to make yet curiously absent any of its details.

"You can do things I can't, Hal. Amazing things. You're better than me, I know that. But you're not invincible. You can't do it all on your own."

"I'm not..." I took a breath. "You think I don't know that? You think I went up there planning to just round up a raknoth and bring him down in a nice little bag for you guys? Do you know what I've watched those things do to people?"

I was trembling.

Tears were going to spill over any moment if I didn't keep talking. So I did.

"I watched Al'Kundesha suck the life from my mom's throat. Watched him break my dad's neck like a twig. Do you think I forgot watching Zar'-Faenor rip Carlisle's insides out?" My voice cracked, my lips trembling. "He was twice the fighter I'll ever be, and you think I don't know I can die out there?"

Elise reached for my arm. I jerked away before I could think about it and slid past her, my feet carrying me past the waist-high divider between entryway and living room. Toward the bedroom door. Around in inconclusive circles. I was breathing heavily. Couldn't think straight.

"Let me help you, man." Johnny glanced at Elise as she moved to join him. "Let *us* help you. You don't have to take this thing on by yourself."

Something bristled inside me at the sight of them side-by-side, arrayed against me. Some part of me knew they didn't mean it like that—them versus me—but my heart was racing, the walls pressing in on me. It was hard to see anything else.

Elise took a slow step toward me. "I know how much you've lost, love. But we're here for you."

My head was spinning, split down the center. I felt like I was caught between two hulking behemoths trying to tear me apart.

I wanted to go to Elise. Wanted to run my hands through her raven hair, so striking in the sunlit room, framing her beautiful face. Wanted to wrap her in my arms and kiss her. Fall to her feet, bury my face against her, and never, never let her go.

But when she reached for my face, that other behemoth roared, ripping me away. I recoiled from her touch, not knowing why.

We stayed frozen like that, Johnny and Elise watching me with surprise or sadness or I don't know what, me teetering between throwing myself at them and wanting to run the other direction.

Alpha, I missed Elise's smile. When had she started looking so tired? Had I done that to her?

And what about Johnny?

Every time I'd seen him, my ever-energetic friend had only been looking more and more like he'd just watched his pup die. And why? I'd agreed to come back. He'd gotten what he'd wanted, hadn't he?

Johnny held my gaze for only a few seconds before dropping his eyes to the floor. He looked like he wanted to hit something. But not me. And that's when it hit me.

My coming back to help stop the raknoth wasn't what Johnny had wanted at all. It was the Legion that had wanted it. The Legion which Johnny believed in with all his heart, even when he didn't see eye to eye with their methods. He'd acted as their instrument because he believed it was for the greater good. And now he hated himself for it.

We'd all been silent for minutes now.

Elise swallowed, like she was afraid to let go of the words hanging on her tongue.

"Carlisle gave his life for yours, Hal. He gave it so you could live, not so you could kill yourself trying to live up to him or whatever you think he wanted."

She was wrong.

My mind couldn't seem to find the pieces to tell her how and why—it was like she'd hit my brain with a raw bolt of electricity—but I was sure she was wrong.

You are the best I have to offer this world, he'd said.

She was wrong.

I was doing exactly what I had to.

Hot tears traced down my cheeks, past my nose. I refused to wipe them off.

"You've both said what you had to." My voice sounded thick, far away. "So thanks. You're off the hook now."

I turned and walked into the bedroom, away from the two people I loved most in the world, wanting to scream with each step. Wanting to lash out—put my fist through the wall. I kept walking until I crossed the threshold.

"I'm not leaving," Elise said behind me.

I closed the gray bedroom door and leaned heavily against the wall.

Elise and Johnny stood there on the other side, unmoving. I couldn't directly feel them in my extended senses—Carlisle's pendants saw to that. But I felt them there anyway by the absence of sensation—the faintest whispers of emptiness that shouldn't have been. Voids without explanation.

I fell to the bed, weeping silently.

10

DELIVERY

That I slept fitfully wasn't overly surprising. Not anymore, and especially not after the day I'd had. Peaceful sleep was a long forgotten memory, bordering on the mythical. But at least Alton Parker kept things original in my nightmares, each time finding new and horrible ways to torture me or make me watch as he hurt Elise and Johnny.

So no, I wasn't surprised to wake a dozen times through the night, covered in cold sweat. But I was surprised when I later woke to a familiar weight settling on the bed beside me and a soft touch on the shoulder.

Judging from the light pouring into the room, I'd slept clear through the evening, the night, and well into the next morning.

"Lise?" I mumbled, blinking sleep from my eyes.

Her face came into focus above me, soft and caring, if a bit guarded.

I sat up, wincing at my body's immediate and extensive reminders of yesterday's violent flight.

"I'm sorry," I groaned. "About yesterday. About everything, I guess."

She searched my face, weighing my words, and finally gave me a small smile.

It made me sick how much that smile didn't spread to her eyes.

She tilted her head at the bedside table, where she'd set a tray of food, and it hit me that I'd forgotten to eat yesterday. The rank smell of blood and sweat and explosive residue reminded me I'd forgotten to clean up too.

Elise wrinkled her nose a little, letting me know the fact wasn't lost on her. Then my stomach informed us with a mighty growl that there was far more pressing business to attend, and, for a moment, we shared a genuine smile.

She stood and went to the window as I pulled the tray onto my lap and began shoveling down fresh eggs and bacon like my life depended on it.

"Breakfast in bed," I said quietly after I'd gotten enough down to momentarily appease the hungry monster in my belly. I stared at her profile for a long moment. "You ever think maybe I don't deserve you?"

She turned slowly, her forehead crinkled, just enough sadness beneath her smile to tell me the thought must've occurred to her at least once in the past season, even if she didn't want to believe it herself.

"Hal…" She hesitated, then came to sit on the bed and take my hand in hers. "I love you."

It wasn't an answer, but the words warmed me nonetheless.

"Not as much as I love you."

She smiled at that but looked down, and I could tell she was weighing the validity of the statement.

Collecting herself, she met my eyes and shrugged. "Either way, my teacher needs to eat if he's ever gonna teach me how to put this thing"—she tapped the side of her head—"to good use."

I cupped her cheek, relishing the smooth softness. "Fair enough."

I took a few more bites and started to move the tray to the bedside table so I could get up.

Elise stopped me. "Eat more."

She rose from the bed with fluid grace, and for a second, I wanted to reach out and yank her back—to throw her down on the bed and lose myself in her.

"Eat," she repeated, gliding to the doorway. "I'll be meditating."

I ate until I was pleasantly stuffed, then I pulled myself out of bed and went to the shower the unholy mess from my body. When I was carefully patted dry and preparing to apply another helping of the salve, I nearly laughed at my reflection. The skin was already looking better thanks to the salve. The hair—or lack thereof—on the other hand…

I reached out and found that Elise had dropped her cloak to practice.

"I look ridiculous," I sent, reaching for the tube of salve that wasn't going to improve matters.

"Reasons to avoid getting bombed in the future," came Elise's voice. *"Also, you could get a hat. Like, a really big hat."*

I smiled, grabbed the trimmer that was standard issue in all Legion quarters, and took the rest of my hair down to a short buzz in quick order. It wasn't perfect, but at least it looked a bit less ridiculous with things closer to even on both sides.

It felt good to smile, to hear Elise joking. I doubted any of us were happy about how yesterday's little intervention had turned out, but maybe it had at least pushed us all over the hump of the tension I'd been feeling with Elise and with Johnny. Maybe things would get better from here.

I was nearly done applying new salve when I got a little too eager with my thumb. I winced at the burning pain, mind immediately flashing to what Melanie had said about stubborn warrior types, and to everything else.

Guilt crept in. Pushing the thought firmly from my mind, I closed the tube and reached for a fresh bandage.

When I finally emerged from the bedroom, dressed and freshly bandaged, Elise was sitting in the center of the living room, cross-legged, eyes closed. I reached out and felt her presence slowly sweeping here and there throughout the room.

"You're beautiful." I sent without thinking, meaning it with all my heart.

Her blue eyes snapped open, then she narrowed them at me. "Now you're just digging for extra points."

"You're so pretty when you're suspicious."

She made an unflattering face.

I smiled. "Yep. There's the face I fell in love with."

She arched a brow. "You take one too many of those pain meds from Medic Melanie Mills?"

An icy jolt slid through me. I hadn't even noticed Melanie's name on the container. But that was fine, right? Because there was no reason it shouldn't be.

"That's a mouthful, isn't it?" Elise was saying. "Johnny would probably… Hal?"

Fine. It was fine.

I sighed. "I didn't take any of those pills. I just… wanted you to know that I still feel the same way about you." I dropped her gaze. "Even when I'm… not myself." Feeling uncomfortably vulnerable, I quickly added, "Let's just train."

I looked up to find her wiping at her eyes. She sniffled once.

It only made me feel worse.

"I'm sorry," I said. "I shouldn't have thrown off your focus."

"No." She shook her head, sniffling again. "I think I kinda needed to hear that. Besides, if I can't focus past some standard teenage drama, how am I supposed to do it with a hungry raknoth coming at me?"

"Hopefully not at all," I said. "And I'm not sure I'd call anything about us *standard*."

Her lip twitched. "Oh, Alpha no. How could anything be standard about the mighty Haldin Raish?"

"Yeah, yeah." Drawing thermal energy from the air, I telekinetically plucked the two glassy decorative orbs from the table by the couch and brought them to hover in front of her. "How about you focus up and try to wrap your mind around my balls?"

"I need to find a new teacher," she grumbled.

I don't know exactly what had changed, but we went on for a while, joking like we'd done before I'd gone sullen and distant. Because I had to admit that now. I *had* been sullen. And distant. And unworthy of her love. But today was a new day, and for the first time in weeks, I felt properly awake. Focused. Ready to be there for her.

And ready to make Alton Parker and his kin pay in whatever way I could.

So, while Elise set to work practicing her telekinesis, I sat down on the other side of the room to begin teasing at the mystery of how to protect a mind from telepathy.

AFTER THINKING FOR A WHILE, I decided to start by deactivating my cloaking pendant and simply trying to create a similar effect for myself, no runes or devices involved. Whether it was the right place to start on the path to producing new cloaking pendants, I had no idea. I wished I'd asked Carlisle more about his rune system when I'd had the chance. What little he had told me was that the runes were essentially vessels which could be made to hold a Shaper's will even after he or she had ceased to exert it.

It wasn't much to go by, but it at least convinced me I should try to understand how to create the effect I wanted before trying to decipher how his runes were doing it. Not that the first part was necessarily going to be any easier.

I meditated quietly for a good while, thinking back to how I'd felt the first time I'd tapped into what Carlisle had called Expression and grown a stone flower for Elise straight from the floor of Franco's old home. I had a feeling Expression was the answer to what I was about to try, though I was still admittedly unclear on exactly what Expression was.

In the beginning, when I'd been learning to use my abilities, it had required painstaking specificity and focus. I'd needed a plan for each action. Tap energy from point A, channel it into my body, focus on how and where I wanted to apply it to point B, and let loose.

Expression, in my mind, was kind of like doing the same thing when there was a complicated process between points A and B that I only vaguely understood in the most abstract of terms. I hadn't understood the micromechanics of how I'd influenced each atom of that stone floor to swell and form into a new shape, nor had I possessed the mental control to organize that many moving pieces so neatly all at once.

What I'd had was Elise's blue eyes watching me, a stallion's kick of feelings in my chest for her, and an untamable desire to please her. I'd pictured the thing. Believed with all my heart and mind that it was possible, that is was right. That it simply was. Then I'd let the energy flow.

What I'd lacked in control and understanding, I'd made up for with a sheer force of will and, unless I was mistaken, a significantly higher amount of channeled energy than what was actually required by the physical act. Almost like I'd offered the universe a side payment of energy to do the thinking for me.

At the time, Expression had seemed like a wild beast of its own. But the more I practiced—and the less I found myself thinking about the details of where and how I was channeling energy to do things like yank Edwards away from a lunging hybrid—the more I was starting to think Expression might not be so different from "normal" Shaping. Really, they might be one and the same, outside the lens of the Shaper's perspective.

I wasn't sure the distinction even mattered. But it made me feel a bit more confident as I started clearing my mind, holding only to the idea that my mind was an island, at rest and perfectly alone in the world. Eyes closed. Breathing deep, easy breaths. I drew a bubble in my mind's eye. Inside, I was on the island. Outside, there was nothing. Silence. The world was gone.

Electric tingles spread up my torso. Across my shoulders. Into my head. I'd opened myself to the energy cell in my hand—started the channeling. I'd barely even noticed.

But was it working?

"Elise," I whispered. "Can you still feel me?"

It was no good.

As soon as I said the words—as soon as I acknowledged that something else existed outside my little island bubble—I knew I'd broken the sanctity of the illusion. A moment later, the light, curious brush of Elise's mind confirmed as much.

"I'm assuming this is a bad sign," came her voice.

"This might take some practice," I sent back. *"And if I'm doing it right, I don't think I'll be able to ask you to check again without breaking my focus."*

"You want me to give you a poke every few minutes?"

I smiled. *"You bet I do."*

A flicker of amusement.

"What would you do without me?" she asked.

"Guess I'd just be poking myself all day."

"You think you're sooo clever." She began to withdraw, returning to her own practice. *"I'll talk to you in a few."*

"Not if I do my job right."

I didn't do my job right.

Not on the second try, and not on the third. Time and time again, I pictured my bubble, retreated to my island. And each time, Elise's presence came scooting in minutes later to give me a telepathic kiss on the brain and tell me to keep at it.

Each iteration, I sank deeper and deeper into the island, adding small details to the construct until I felt as if I were actually physically there. I'd only ever been to a real beach once, several years ago, but the metaphor felt right, so I did my best. Some scrub trees here, a few sun-baked rocks there. Warm sand between my toes. A gentle, salty breeze on my face.

Nothing but empty blue all around…

"Hal?"

I snapped back to the living room of my Haven quarters with an upright jolt.

Elise was there, hands held up in peace. "You all good?"

"Yeah, fine. I was just pretty deep in there, I guess."

"Well, the good news is that I didn't feel a thing just now." She wrinkled her brow thoughtfully. "Hmm. There's probably a joke in there somewhere."

I laughed. It felt good. I'd been so immersed in my illusion that I'd forgotten what it was I was even trying to do.

"So, nothing?"

She shook her head. "Nothing."

"All right." I looked at the deactivated cloaking pendant on the floor in front of me. "Well that's a start. Now I just have to figure out what these runes mean, and how the scud I'm supposed to make something stick to them long enough to—Holy scud…" I stared in shock at the palmlight display I'd just awoken. "Have we really been at it for four hours?"

Elise smiled. "Was wondering if you'd noticed. Haven't I been a good little student?"

Something about the way she said it…

"The best," I agreed, my eyes tracing along her body.

"Hey, don't go getting any ideas, mister teacher man." She stood with a graceful motion and looked down at me. "I'll have you know I'm spoken for."

"Oh yeah?"

She gave a very studious nod, and I let her haul me to my feet.

"Maybe just a brief repast, then?" I murmured, cradling her close.

She smiled and pecked a kiss on my cheek. "Such a goodfellow, my teacher."

In no mood to brave the crowd at the mess halls, we stayed inside, taking a light meal of fabbed bread and cheese while we chatted over small things and played telekinetically with Elise's orbs.

As encouraging as my early success with conjuring a kind of cloaking field should've been, something told me I'd only just scratched the surface of the task at hand. The Shaping—or the Expression or whatever you wanted to call it—was probably the easy part. Unlocking the secrets of the runes, and perfecting this new technique enough to translate it into a new medium…

If I hadn't been wearing the physical proof that such a thing was possible, I'm not sure I ever would have thought to even try it.

For the moment, though, I tried to push the thoughts aside and simply enjoy some time with Elise. It was the first time in weeks that training—or spending time together, for that matter—was actually fun for both of us. I'd needed it more than I'd realized. And so it came as little surprise when fate saw fit to interrupt us.

We were trying to transfer one of the floating orbs from my control to Elise's when my palmlight started buzzing.

My stomach tightened momentarily at Johnny's name, but I answered the call.

"Hal, you might wanna get over to the shipping yard."

He didn't sound as angry as I'd expected he might, but his voice was tense. This wasn't just a friendly notification.

"Why? What's going on?"

"They're not sure yet, but it looks like we've got a package from Alton Parker."

I dropped the floating orbs, too shocked to focus. One hit the carpet with a light thump.

Elise, apparently so focused on her task that she hadn't properly heard Johnny's words, managed to catch the other one. Then her eyes flicked open in surprise, and her gaze snapped to my palmlight. "Wait, what?"

Her orb thumped to the carpet, punctuating the question.

"We don't have details yet," Johnny said. "They called in the bomb squad, though. I just happened to be with Glenbark when she got the message. She told me I didn't have to bother you until they knew more, but I thought you'd wanna know."

"I—yeah…" I glanced at Elise. "We'll be right over. Thanks, buddy."

"Just look before you leap this time, flyboy," Johnny said.

"Yeah," I grunted through the pain of standing. "Alpha, I really hope it's not another bomb."

"That'd be a pretty crappy plan," Elise said as she went to grab our boots. "Especially for Alton Parker."

She tossed my boots over. I caught them with a wince and pulled them on with another.

"Maybe that's exactly what he wants us to think. So stupid, it's brilliant."

"Seriously?" she said.

At first, I thought she was refuting my joke. Then I looked up and saw her staring incredulously at my boots.

"What?" came Johnny's voice from the palmlight.

"He's lacing his boots with telekinesis."

"I'm in pain," I said, starting for the next eyelet with my mind. "Did I mention the part where I was blown off a ten-floor building yesterday?"

"Yeah, yeah," she said, sinking to a knee in front of me and shooing away my telekinetic grasp. "Drop 'em, flyboy."

"Nice one, Lise," Johnny chimed in. "You tell that flyboy."

I surrendered my telekinetic grip with a sigh. "So that's gonna be a thing, huh? Great."

She smiled and started lacing my boots. "Hey, you need someone to keep you grounded to the planet."

"Who, him?" Johnny added.

I scowled at the palmlight. "We'll be over soon, *buddy*."

"Wait a second," Elise said, just before I flicked the call close. Her fingers had paused on my laces. "Why did Glenbark say not to bother us until you knew more? Why was she even thinking of us at all?"

"Ah, yeah," Johnny said. "Probably shoulda led with that part."

"What part?" I asked.

"Parker's package," he said. "It's got your name on it."

1 1

SWEEPER

Outside, Haven was bristling with the ever-present abundance of precise activity typical of a Legion base. Some legionnaires patrolled the wide traffic ways between the blocky, no-frills buildings that covered the compound. Most hustled about to drills or meetings or shifts at their various stations. Passing a training lot where doceres were barking strings of insults thinly disguised as instructions at their assembled tyros, I felt a strange combination of nostalgia and dread. I thought of Mathis, which in turn dredged up a whole host of memories—a few fond, most painful.

By the time we made it to Haven's main shipping facility, a small crowd had gathered outside, spaced a respectful distance from a high square of the translucent panels I'd seen bomb disposal teams use to cordon off areas as they worked.

A few heads turned our way as we approached, then there were a few murmurs, and several more heads followed.

"Citizen Raish," Glenbark's voice called from the front of the pack.

The crowd parted to give us a clear path to her. She looked as starkly commanding as ever. I strode into the crowd, trying to give friendly—or at least non-demonly—smiles to anyone willing to meet my eyes and wondering if, behind me, Elise was as embarrassed as I was by the sudden influx of attention.

"I told Wingard there was no need to bother you until we knew more," Glenbark said as we drew up to her. She glanced at Johnny, who suddenly appeared to be riveted with something far in the distant sky, before turning back at me. "How are you feeling?"

She spoke in a muted tone, and we were several paces from the nearest soldiers, but I could practically feel them craning their necks to catch any juicy base gossip, so I stuck with, "Fine, sir."

I was too busy studying the scene ahead anyway.

Inside the square of blast panels sat what looked like a plain polymer shipping crate, no larger than the tray Elise had brought me that morning, and less than a foot thick. It looked almost comically small and non-threatening sitting there behind an array of blast panels, but then again, maybe that was the point. Right outside the square, two men in exceptionally bulky suits of armor were fiddling with their instruments, preparing to go in.

"Citizen Fields," Glenbark said, leaning past me to give Elise a polite acknowledgment. "A pleasure to see you again. I hope you've felt welcome with our accommodations."

"Oh yeah," Elise said. "Everyone's been thrilled to see me."

There might have been an undercurrent in her tone, but I was too distracted to decipher it, focused as I was on extending my senses to scan our mystery package.

Polymer strips, full of empty air. Packing supports? And at the center of those, a thin polymer rectangle with a duraglass pane on one side. I narrowed my focus, looking for any dense blips of energy like I'd felt in Alton's rooftop bomb, but all I felt was a small energy cell.

"So what are we dealing with here?" came Elise's voice at the distant edge of my physical senses.

I drew my senses back. "It's not a bomb."

They looked at me, awaiting an explanation.

"It's a tablet, as far as I can tell."

"Told you," Johnny muttered to Glenbark. Then, with much more reverence, "High General, sir."

Someone whispered something behind us, and it seemed to spread through the gathered crowd.

Glenbark was watching me with her usual composure, but I swear she almost looked surprised for the first time.

"That is indeed what the arrival scan showed," she finally said. "But those can be faked with sufficient motivation and resources." She looked toward the blast panels. "Precautions seemed prudent, considering the source."

The two figures in their bulky blast armor were watching Glenbark now. She gestured for them to proceed.

Everyone fell silent as the two brave specialists slid between the blast panels and closed the gap behind them. Elise's hand found mine. She looked apprehensive.

"It's okay," I sent.

"You're sure?"

I hesitated. I was pretty sure I'd felt a tablet—or at least an absence of high-powered explosives—but the silent tension hanging in the air now was contagious.

I gave her hand a squeeze and forced myself to breathe. *"Pretty sure."*

The two men worked with understandably excruciating precision and attention to detail. The anticipation of the crowd grew steadily for the first few minutes, then began to wane as the inspection stretched. Finally, one of the men raised a bulky arm and shot a thumbs-up, and the tension dispersed like a puff of smoke in the wind. A few seconds later, his partner pulled a small rectangle that looked an awful lot like a tablet from the package.

Glenbark touched her earpiece, then turned to look at me with renewed interest. "It's a tablet."

"Looks like you missed your calling as a bomb sweeper, broto," Johnny said.

I watched Glenbark. "So do I get to see what's on the tablet addressed to me?"

"Normally, I'd say that this is a matter of Enochian security and that you'd have to wait until we've assessed the potential risk of whatever information the device contains."

"But?" I said.

"But if Alton Parker actually had the gall to send you a tablet here," Elise said, "you can bet gilders to goja fruit he keyed it so that you'll be the one who can unlock it."

Johnny and I looked at Elise in surprise.

"What?" She shrugged. "It's what I would do if I were a maniacal alien mastermind."

Johnny bobbed his head, turning to Glenbark. "Lady's got a point, si—"

Glenbark silenced him with a twitch of her fingers. "Of course she has a point, Wingard."

Her eyes were crinkled with that composed micro-frown, her gaze fixed ahead, where one of the bomb specialists had slipped out of the blast panels and was lumbering toward us. Back in the square, his partner was still tinkering with the tablet.

It felt like forever, waiting for the encumbered legionnaire to cross the twenty-some yards between us, but finally, he drew up and favored Glenbark with a crisp salute.

She returned it. "Report, specialist."

"Yes, sir. Contents of the package include six standard packing supports and one Rade Tech tablet, sir. The tablet appears to be untampered with, though it is locked, and..."

"Yes, specialist?"

His eyes flicked to me before returning to Glenbark. "The lock display has Raish's name on it, sir."

Glenbark nodded, unsurprised. "Anything else?"

The specialist shook his head.

"Very well," Glenbark said. "Bring the device to me, please. Thank you, specialist."

He gave a crisp salute and hurried off. Behind us, the crowd was aflutter with speculative whispers. Glenbark swiped a few commands on her palm-light before turning to me.

"I think you'd better come to my office, Citizen Raish."

THE AIR FELT ODDLY COOL, rushing through the bandages to my salved face as we sped toward Haven's main operations building in an open ground shuttle. Every soldier we passed stopped to salute Glenbark, who sat at the wheel, steering us through the base and acknowledging her people with a nod here, a slight wave there.

Irked as I still was by her treatment yesterday, I liked that she saw fit to drive herself. Most generals didn't.

I liked less that with each salute to her came a follow up look at me and Elise in the back seat of the shuttle. The looks ranged from pinched-brow suspicion to open-mouthed confusion, but without fail, there was a look. It almost started to be fun after we got over the uncomfortable hump. Almost.

At operations, we disembarked. Johnny launched out of the front passenger seat and attempted to get Glenbark's door, but she waved off his attempt at respectful boot licking before he was halfway around the shuttle.

I liked that too.

Inside, we skirted through the busy sea of specialists, officers, nodes, and displays that was operations, following Glenbark toward a flight of stairs I assumed must lead to her office. The crowd parted readily for us—or for her, at least—and curious stares abounded. Glenbark acknowledged a few updates from officers as she passed, patted a few specialists' shoulders. Her people really seemed to love her—with the possible exception of the ruddy-faced, white-haired man waiting at the base of the stairs. I recognized him.

General Auckus.

I'd never met him before, but, of course, I'd heard a few things in my Sanctuary days. Legionnaires loved to talk about officers, and several of them had had plenty to say about Auckus. Especially the seemingly numerous females he'd treated in a manner most unbecoming of a Legion general.

"General," Glenbark said as we drew close, her tone neutral. "I assume you'd like to join us for the first look?"

Auckus didn't answer immediately. Made a point of taking his time looking over me, Elise, and Johnny.

His dark eyes settled on me. "I knew your father."

There was no fondness in his voice—no reverence for a fallen hero. He said the words simply like they were proof that he was, in every way, my superior. I hadn't needed much of a reason not to like him, but those four words did just fine.

Then he turned to Glenbark, and added, "Updating our procedures yet again, I see? Sharing first look intel with tyros, demons, and concubines." He barked a derisive laugh at his own words, and for a second, I thought he might actually spit at her feet.

I had more than half a mind to telekinetically kick his legs out. Beside me, I could feel Elise thinking about doing worse. Around us, the room had gone quiet. I got the impression this wasn't the first time the two generals had squared off.

"Update the procedures that gifted us with such gracious leadership?" Glenbark said. "Unthinkable. Fortunately, I see neither tyros, demons, nor concubines present"—she glanced to the room at large—"unless we're counting your, shall we say, *rebuffed* conquests, General Auckus."

Several of the specialists and officers snickered at that—particularly some of the females who I had strong feeling must've done some of that rebuffing.

"Charming as always, Freya," Auckus said, turning for the stairs. "Perhaps those assets of yours will yet prove useful. One of these days."

No one snickered at that as Auckus turned the first landing and disappeared up the stairs. Slowly, the room got back to work. Glenbark watched the spot where Auckus had disappeared for a long few seconds, her expression cold, calculating. Then she waved us on, and we all continued up the stairs together.

I was starting to worry now.

First, I thought it was simply the looming mystery of what on Enochia Alton Parker had seen fit to send me. But it was more than that. Much as I despised the way Auckus had put it, I realized I'd been hoping all along that Glenbark would step in and shut Elise out of this thing.

Keep Elise half a planet away from the danger. That had been the plan, right? I should've asked her to wait behind in my quarters. Told her to practice until I got back.

Breathe.

It was fine. This was just an informal meeting. Nothing more than a look at a quite possibly harmless tablet. She wasn't at risk here. But suddenly I couldn't go another step—not knowing that whatever we found here might well put her in harm's way down the line.

I'd caught Glenbark's wrist almost before I knew it. "High General," I said quietly, even though there was no way Elise and Johnny wouldn't hear. "Maybe it's better if we, uh..."

I drifted off at the look on her face. Slowly, very pointedly, Glenbark directed her gaze down to my hand on her wrist. I let go, realizing with a flush of heat to the cheeks how stupid it'd been, grabbing the High General of the Legion like that. Especially when I wasn't even sure what I'd been planning to say.

Luckily, once I'd released her and looked sufficiently guilty about my tactless move, it turned out Glenbark didn't need my advice. "You two had better wait outside," she said to Johnny and Elise, indicating the short line of chairs outside her office.

I tried to keep the relief off my face, but I'm pretty sure Elise didn't miss it. She watched me for a few seconds, probably wondering if I'd step in on her behalf. Once Johnny had finished murmuring his obedient affirmative and it became clear I wouldn't, she turned to Glenbark with a forced smile.

"If it helps alleviate tensions with General Skirt-Chaser in there, I'll sit in the kid's corner." Her eyes went several degrees colder as she turned them back on me and telepathically added, *"For now."*

"LISE, I JUST DON'T WANNA—"

"What? Put me in danger? You're trying to protect me like you did with Johnny, now?"

Her exterior remained deadly cool, but I flinched at the fire in her thoughts. Glenbark looked between us, seeming to gather that something had passed between us, but she turned without another word and strode for her office door, not looking back as she said, "If you please, Citizen Raish, I believe you have a tablet to unlock."

The secure door hissed open at her touch, and she disappeared inside, leaving it open behind her. I looked back to my friends.

Elise extended a hand toward the open door. "Duty calls."

"Well," Johnny said, touching a clarifying hand to her shoulder, "only if you're, like, special though."

"Oh, right," Elise said, nodding emphatically. "How silly of me to forget."

They both turned to me and arched their eyebrows, as if they were surprised to find me interrupting their meeting. It was kind of disconcerting how easily they fell into the act.

"I guess I'll just, uh, be out in a few minutes then, probably," I said, taking a hesitant step toward the door.

"We'll be here," was all Elise said. By the way she said it, I couldn't help but wonder for what kind of duration that statement might remain true.

Not sure I wanted to know the answer, I turned for Glenbark's office without another word.

1 2

POLITICS

Glenbark's office was modest for her station, though still nice by most standards. Darkwood furniture. An elaborate workstation. A spacious conference area, backed by shelves of actual print books. Judging by the lack of any additional decor, I guessed Glenbark might have simply found the office this way upon her recent arrival and either appreciated the aesthetic or cared so little that she hadn't bothered to change anything.

The two generals were already seated, facing one another from across a long, sturdy-looking darkwood table—Glenbark calm and poised with her hands laid to either side of the tablet in front of her, and General Auckus seemingly trying to occupy as much physical space as possible from a seated position.

"Oh, grand," Auckus said, eyeing me, though he was clearly speaking to Glenbark. "You dropped a civie and a pup and decided to stick with the Demon of Divinity."

"The tablet was addressed to Citizen Raish," Glenbark said. "By rights, it's his property."

"Unless we seize it," Auckus grumbled, but he didn't say anything more as Glenbark gestured for me to join them.

I sat with one chair separating me and Glenbark, not feeling particularly close to either of them at the moment, and was a bit surprised when she slid the tablet my way.

"It was addressed to you," was all she said.

The tablet booted quickly and without a single interesting deviation from normal tablet behavior. The lock display, as the bomb specialist had indicated, did indeed have my name on it, in big block letters. *HALDIN*. No missing that. Nor was there any missing the password prompt.

"The sweetest thing?" Auckus said, squinting at the tablet to read upside down from his side of the table. "Riddles. Wonderful. I'm guessing it's not a sweetfizz?"

I couldn't answer for the hollowness in my gut. Because it sure as scud wasn't a sweetfizz. And it wasn't much of a riddle, either. When I noticed Glenbark's piercing eyes watching me, I could see that she'd read as much from my face.

"What does it mean, Haldin?"

I stared through the darkwood table, not wanting to answer, suddenly wishing that I'd fought to have Elise join us—that she were holding my hand under the table right now, whispering in my mind that it was okay.

"My mom," I finally said. "It's what Al'Kundesha—Kublich, whatever you wanna call him… It's what he said about my mom's blood."

So not sweetfizz, I wished Johnny were here to say. But he wasn't, and the silence was palpable. Even General Auckus seemed to feel bad. I slid the tablet closer, refusing to meet their wounded animal stares. My fingers hovered over the letters, trembling.

This was exactly what Alton Parker had wanted, wasn't it? Me, quivering like a broken thing, remembering how many separate ways he could destroy me—already had destroyed me.

Well, grop that.

Except, no matter how fiercely I thought it, my fingers wouldn't seem to move. Beside me, Glenbark extended a hand, palm up—a silent offer to take the burden from my shoulders. I clenched my jaw and swiped in the name.

<Klara Raish>

Through the blur of looming tears, I watched the tablet launch to a tidy home display—nothing but a few standard programs and a single matrix file, again labeled *HALDIN*, as if he'd been worried I might struggle to follow the less-than-subtle trail. I slid the tablet over to Glenbark. Anything to move the attention off me.

The generals pretended not to notice as I hastily dabbed my eyes with a sleeve—Auckus tapping the table with a single finger while Glenbark swiped the tablet feed over to the holodisk on the table and tapped open the matrix file. The file's front layer sprang to life as a pale holo above the darkwood table. I scanned dated rows of numbers, looking for landmarks at the column tops.

Pending. Active. Deployed.

"Troop counts," Auckus said.

"Hybrids?" I asked, morbid curiosity quickly offsetting the painful memories.

Glenbark pointed at the lower rows. "They're dated into the future."

With a few swipes, she displayed the data in graph form, which immediately drew a disturbingly clear picture. Slow, steady growth of all three lines—Pending, Active, and Deployed—dating up until a week earlier, when Pending and Active had spiked and taken off at considerably steeper rates moving into the future.

"Scare tactics," Auckus muttered, though he sounded less than convinced.

I wanted to believe him—because why the scud else would Alton Parker decide to share this kind of intel?—but the significant dip in the lines over the past couple days gave me pause. If the data reflected their losses from the fighting at Oasis and the Vantage facility, was it possible these figures were real? Or had Alton added that touch of realism specifically to bolster the credibility of his lie?

Glenbark wordlessly flipped to the next matrix layer. More column headings and graphs, this time modeling long term population growth and blood supply and demand. My stomach sank at the point where the graphs leveled out about a year from now. The point that had been tagged with bold red text.

Repopulation Complete.

"Baseless models," Auckus said. "Without evidence, this is nothing but empty gesturing."

Glenbark silently swiped to the next layer.

"Scud," I heard myself whisper under Auckus' far more colorful muttering.

Glenbark spared us a stern glance before returning her attention to the array of images floating over the table. There were several rows of them, each clearly showing hybrid chambers, all clearly in different rooms—and not from the lab we'd destroyed yesterday. We watched silently as Glenbark swiped to the last layer.

Nothing but two words. *Good luck.*

"We need to call an assembly," General Auckus said, his sneer having finally died for good beneath the weight of his very real concern. "And I feel the need to reiterate, High General, that a civilian has no business seeing this intel, regardless of his family history."

Maybe it was just the gravity of the findings in front of us, but he sounded slightly less insubordinate now that we weren't in front of a crowd.

Glenbark took a moment to think. "I agree," she said, drawing surprised looks from both of us. "Which is why I'm declaring Citizen Raish an essential operations consultant, top security clearance, effective immediately. I'm also promoting Legionnaire Wingard to the role of personal servitor to the High General, also effective immediately. Witnessed?"

"Consultant," Auckus repeated, eyeing me with open skepticism. "Consultant on what, exactly? Small cell terrorism tactics?" He turned a steely glare her way, daring her to defend herself.

Glenbark was unfazed. "I asked you a question, General."

Auckus sneered and started to say something, then thought better of it and shifted tactics. "You already have a servitor."

"And I'm taking another," Glenbark said. "Witnessed?"

"It doesn't make you a hero, Freya, spitting in the eye of tradition and good sense time and time again." The anger in Auckus' expression cooled, and he shrugged. "But by all means, continue to ignore the lessons of history. I won't argue if you insist on handing me your title and office by season's end."

Glenbark smiled at him then—the first full smile I'd seen from her. It was beautiful, and terrible, and utterly without humor. "The lessons of history?" Her smile froze over. "You saw what happened at Oasis. You've seen what these creatures can do. Explain to me which part of the raknoth threat has any precedent in our illustrious history, General Auckus."

For a second, Auckus looked stumped. Then he snarled and practically spat out, "Fine. Witnessed. And may Alpha see to it that this marks the beginning of your end, High General."

"Call the assembly, Gregor," Glenbark said, looking like she'd already forgotten he was there. "I need a private word with my consultant."

We sat silently until the door had hissed shut behind Auckus' retreating form, at which point, Glenbark closed her eyes and let out a long, deep breath. For a second, she almost looked vulnerable. Which was fair enough, seeing as she'd just all but kicked General Auckus straight in the wrinklies. Even the High General wasn't above punishment if the twelve generals unanimously decided she was failing to operate in the best interests of the Legion and Enochia.

"Was that wise, sir?" I couldn't help but ask.

"Of course not." She frowned at the door. "But less unwise than trying to explain what you're really doing here to a man like Gregor Auckus. They're slowly starting to understand that we're dealing with something out of our depths here. The scudstorm at Oasis saw to that. But if I put it on the record that I'm counting on a kid with seventeen years to his name and a list of crimes longer than his arm, including heresy, to protect our people's *minds* from alien telepaths…" She trailed off, shaking her head at the thought.

"Well," I said after a length of silence, "for what it's worth, I'll at least have eighteen years to my name if we're all still here next Willowsday."

She looked at me like she'd just remembered I was sitting there, and Alpha be damned, she actually smiled a little. "Yes, that'll be much better." The smile faded, and she gestured at the matrix holo still floating above the table. "Let me worry about the politics, Haldin. We have bigger problems to address."

I studied those two words. *Good luck.*

"Why did he send this? If any of it's actually true…"

"It might well be a scare tactic, as General Auckus originally said. Even if the intel is accurate, Parker gets to rattle our cages without handing us anything more actionable than the information that they can produce soldiers far faster than we can."

"That part rattles my cage just fine."

"Oh, it's certainly troubling," Glenbark agreed. "But hardly surprising, given what we've already observed. The true question is what we do in response to this information."

"Which is?"

"Beat him, hopefully," Glenbark said, staring thoughtfully at the holo. "What is it he really shared with us here?"

"That they're expanding?"

"I was thinking more along the line that they're going to win if we don't do anything. Which means at least one of three things, in my mind. Option one, Alton Parker wants us to spend weeks and extensive resources trying to hunt these facilities down, either because he's buying time for something else or because he knows our attempts would be inconsequential. Option two, he's hoping to frighten us into throwing everything we have at Oasis to break their stronghold before they can reinforce it, either because he knows that the effort would end in slaughter for us, or…" She frowned. "Or because he's afraid their advantage won't last indefinitely."

I found myself nodding along, thoroughly impressed by Glenbark's analysis, until the last bit sparked an additional thought. "He did notice I was trying to cover Hound Company with my cloak back at Vantage. Maybe he's worried we're going to, well, you know, do exactly what you want me to do. Cloak the legions and storm Oasis."

Glenbark looked less than thrilled by the news.

"So we either move on Oasis fast," I added quickly, "or we figure out how to locate their breeding facilities and hit them all at once. Therese Brown and the other Vantage researchers might be able to work out some way to track them."

I wasn't sure she heard me at all, lost in thought as she appeared to be. "Sir?"

She blinked away whatever thought she'd been exploring and looked at me like she was suddenly wondering what had compelled her to share her analysis in the first place. Without explanation, she closed the tablet down and stood, turning for the door.

"Wait, what was option three?"

Glenbark paused to study me as if it should've already occurred to me. Then it did.

"You think Alton Parker could actually be trying to help us?"

Glenbark tilted her head in a miniscule shrug. "It's the least likely option in my mind, to be sure, but it is possible. Perhaps the raknoth are not all in harmony. Perhaps Parker has his own motives. Until we understand why he sent this information—and to you specifically—I'm afraid we won't have a real answer."

"Maybe it's all of the above," I said, "with the added bonus that Alton Parker just seems to enjoy screwing with people. Me in particular, apparently."

When it came down to it, I realized, I didn't really know the first thing about Alton Parker. He was an alien, after all. Could any of us really expect to understand what was going on in his head? He *had* seemed rather unhinged when we'd encountered him at Vantage. Scud, maybe he was losing it. But how would we know?

Before I could bring any of this up, there was a low buzz, and Glenbark glanced at her palmlight. "Well, General Auckus certainly wasted no time." She closed her palmlight and started for the door, calling over her shoulder, "Forget Parker for now. I'm going to need you two to start working on these cloaks immediately."

Before I could ask which two she was referring to, she'd already palmed the door open and leaned out into the hallway. "Wingard, Citizen Fields, if you'd be so kind as to join us."

My stomach sank, then sank some more as Johnny and Elise appeared in the doorway, ushering past Glenbark into the office. I didn't like where this was going.

"How's it going in here?" Johnny asked, settling into a seat across the table from me.

"Flowers and sunshine," I muttered, nervously glancing at Elise as she pointedly settled beside Johnny and not me. "All the way."

"Seems like it," Elise said.

"Yeah, General Auckus looked *real* happy when he stormed off," Johnny said. Then, with a frown, he added, "Don't tell me *you* rebuffed his advances?"

"General Auckus was less than pleased with my choices in appointing a new high-level consultant..."

"Ah," Johnny said, eyeing me knowingly.

"... and a new servitor," Glenbark finished, with a meaningful look at Johnny.

"I thought you already had a—Oh." He squinted at her, gauging her expression, then his eyes widened. "Wait, me?"

"Congratulations, Servitor Wingard. I'll expect nothing but your best, each and every day."

I was hard-pressed to recall a time I'd seen Johnny Wingard rendered open-mouthed speechless, but it happened then. Elise actually had to give him a nudge to get him going again.

"Uh, yes sir, High General... sir. Uh, thank you?"

Glenbark considered him warily for another second before turning her gaze to Elise. "Citizen Fields, I would like to informally request your aid in the effort to develop adequate protection against telepathy for our people."

"High General," I started, but she cut me off with a raised hand, her eyes still fixed on Elise.

"You do share some of Citizen Raish's abilities, do you not, Elise?"

I have to give it to her, Elise held her composure far better than I did. Her eyes did flick to me, but she covered the slip without missing a beat, adopting an appraising expression and crossing her arms as she studied me, looking every bit the disgruntled girlfriend. "I guess I can be a stubborn ass at times, if that's what you're asking."

"How?" she added to me telepathically.

I gave a little head shake before I could stop myself. How Glenbark had picked up on it, I couldn't have said. Maybe she was just fishing. But somehow, I was pretty sure she'd pegged Elise as being gifted.

"No matter," Glenbark said, dismissing Elise's deflection with a faint trace of amusement in her eyes. "I won't claim to understand exactly what this project will entail, but I'm assuming two minds will be better than one. That is if you accept, of course, Elise?"

Why are you doing this? I wanted to ask Glenbark—and Elise too as she looked my way, studying my reaction. But what was the point? It wouldn't change anything, aside from maybe irritating Elise more than I already had outside.

So I said nothing as Elise nodded her affirmation.

"Good. Thank you." Glenbark turned to me. "I assume that's not going to be a problem?"

Only if you want me to deliver on cloaking your Alpha-damned legions, I wanted to growl. Instead, I allowed myself a few seconds' indulgence in the fantasy of getting up, telling Glenbark to have fun with her raknoth problem, and walking out of the room. But I couldn't do that either.

You are the best I have to offer this world, Hal, came Carlisle's voice in my mind.

"No, sir," I said. "Of course not."

"Good." Glenbark settled at the head of the table, facing the three of us. "Then I want you two to get to work immediately. I'll continue requesting that the Sanctum pull these so-called Seekers of theirs out of hiding to help as well, but I don't expect it'll do much good. In the meanwhile, whatever resources you need are yours."

She turned to Johnny, her fingers busy over her palmlight. "Wingard, you'll see to it they have what they need and report directly to me."

She offered her hand, palmlight active. Johnny woke his palmlight and carefully set his hand over hers.

"You'll find you now have access to my direct contact ID," she said when she pulled her hand away, "as well as automatic authority on any low-to-mid-level requisitions. Please don't make me regret it."

Johnny looked at his palmlight and back to her. "So I'm *actually* the envoy to The Solemn Nation of Hal and Elise?"

"What?" Glenbark frowned. "You are my servitor, Wingard. You are the extra eyes and hands I am sadly lacking, and right now I need you to do everything in your power to make sure that, when the time comes, our legionnaires' minds are their own. Do you understand?"

Johnny sat a little straighter. "Sir, yes sir."

"And the breeding facilities?" I asked.

"Are a matter for the military minds to handle," Glenbark said. "I'll consider what you said about recruiting Therese Brown and the other Vantage researchers to help locate the facilities. That's a good thought. But I want you to focus on your end. We need a solution to the telepathy threat far more than we need to worry about wiping out a few hundred hybrids at a time."

I wanted to argue—even wanted to drive to have Franco head the team tracking the facilities, both because he was probably the perfect man for the job and because it'd let me more easily keep my finger on the pulse of Alton Parker's operations. But something told me now wasn't the time to push it.

"One more thing, Mister Raish," Glenbark said, and by the slight change in her tone, I was immediately sure I'd been right not to argue. "I'm still investigating how and why, but it appears the Sanctum is already aware of your involvement at Vantage yesterday. The High Cleric finally broke his long silence with me this morning, solely to express his displeasure."

Just what we needed.

"What do you want me to do, sir?"

She studied me, looking conflicted on the matter. "Keep your head down," she finally said. "For now, I don't think it'll be a problem as long as you remain within Haven at all times."

"Sir, I'm not—"

She raised a hand for silence. "I don't like it either, Haldin. And if there were good reason to put you out in the field, I wouldn't let the Sanctum stop me. But you're not a soldier anymore. You reminded us all of that fact by your actions at Vantage yesterday. You are a civilian consultant, and you're here to solve a single problem."

"And if I decide I want to leave Haven?"

"Do you?" she asked, studying me with a look that said she already knew the answer.

I said nothing.

"If it becomes clear you absolutely must leave the base in the line of duty," she said, "I will consider allowing it under armed escort. I'd rather not find out what the Sanctum might do otherwise."

So I was to be a prisoner in everything but title. I guess I'd already seen that coming after being grounded yesterday. But grop that. When the time came, one way or another, I was going to be out there, fighting the raknoth, taking down Alton Parker. But now wasn't the time. Not yet.

Still, I couldn't help but ask, "Why shelter me at all, sir? Why trust us to do a job you're reluctant to even tell your high command about?"

A shadow fell across Glenbark's expression—faint but definitely there. "I gave the order to send those legions to Oasis," she finally said. "I watched legionnaires turn and gun down allies they normally would've died for like it was nothing. Target practice." She looked up, and the intensity in her eyes nearly made me flinch. "My legionnaires. My responsibility. I won't let it happen again."

She calmed a touch. "Unlike General Auckus, though, I'm not deluded enough to think I can push a stone uphill with a rope just by trying harder." She waved a hand at me and Elise. "Hence, unconventional tactics for an unprecedented problem."

"And if we fail?" I asked.

Glenbark's lip twitched. "Then I suppose we'll all find out, won't we? Now, if you'll excuse me, I have an assembly of hungry generals to appease."

1 3

─────────────

ASSEMBLY REQUIRED

"**S**weet Alpha," Elise whispered when I'd finished filling them in on the main points from Alton Parker's mysterious gift of hybrid intel.

"Alpha's wrinklies, is more like it," Johnny said, glancing surreptitiously back at the foot traffic we'd abandoned outside central command to find a quiet spot for the conversation.

Elise spared him a frown. He continued on, unperturbed.

"But these are just, like, wild projections, right? I mean, I can report that in two years I'll have a twelve inch…" He looked at Elise, remembering himself, and blushed a little. "Uh, you get the point. Doesn't mean it's true. There's no way they have that many chambers up and running outside of Vantage."

"It's gotta be a scare tactic," Elise agreed.

"That's what General Auckus said too, before he saw the pictures."

Elise wrinkled her nose, clearly less than enthused at having shared any opinion with the good general—even a reasonable one.

When they'd asked about the meeting, I'd half-considered holding out on them—in part because it was almost certainly classified and Glenbark had definitely not given me permission, but mostly because I was still irritated I'd somehow allowed Elise to get dragged into this thing alongside me. My third day on base, and I'd already been burned, blown off a building, grounded from future missions, and now, it turned out, pathetically inept at keeping my girlfriend out of harm's way.

Not that the cloaking project had any reason to be dangerous. But then again, things sure did seem to have a way of blowing up around me these days.

"Well," Johnny said, standing from the low permacrete abutment we'd been sitting on, "scare tactics or no, I guess it's good we've got the whole gang on the job, huh?" He glanced between us, taking in my dour expression, and Elise's cautious one. "Come on, guys, we're like basically the heroes of Haven now."

"Yeah," I said. "Heroes who aren't even allowed to leave the base."

"Heroes who no one's ever supposed to hear about," Elise added.

"Heroes who haven't actually done a single thing yet," I said.

"Guys. Basically," Johnny said. "I said *basically* heroes. C'mon." He waved a dismissive hand. "We'll figure the rest out as we go."

"Big talk for the non-Shaper," I muttered.

Johnny sagely raised a finger. "I'll kindly refer you back to the point where we've yet to accomplish a single thing. Until we do, hey, anything could happen. No one knows. Could be Johnny's the man with the plan."

Silence stretched.

"Seriously, though," Johnny finally said. "What's the plan, here?"

Elise looked at me. "I guess we'll need some pendants and a phase etcher to start experimenting, right? We might as well just get to work in our quarters."

I shrugged, internally trying to decide if I was pleased or distraught that Elise had decided my temporary housing on a base of war was now *our* quarters. "I guess so. But I was actually thinking I might go visit Therese first. I'd like to speak with Franco, too."

"For Mission Mindsafe?" Johnny asked.

We both looked at him.

"Oh yeah, I decided we're calling it Mission Mindsafe, guys."

Elise shrugged. "I guess I don't hate it."

I kind of did. Or, rather, I resented what this *mission* was quickly turning into: another cage. Everything had changed, and yet nothing had. I was still trapped, the Sanctum might well still be after me, and I still had at least one army—maybe two—standing between me and my vengeance. Worse, I knew that Glenbark was right. In the grand scheme, cracking the secret of the cloaking runes was probably by far the most useful thing I could do to help.

But that didn't mean I had to shut myself in and forget about everything else.

"Hal?" Johnny said. "What gives?"

"Well, Franco might be able to help, or find some helpful resources. Therese, I mostly just wanna check in on. But yeah, pendants and something to make runes with, for sure. And while we're requisitioning goods from our favorite new servitor, I wouldn't mind a good armor skin, either."

Johnny frowned at me. "I'm getting a very non-Mission-Mindsafe vibe here."

"It's just in case," I said. "For all I know, the High Cleric could be ordering to have me killed as we speak. Alpha knows what else might happen on the raknoth front. I'd like some protection, and I'll be damned if I'm gonna start lumbering around everywhere in that scorched, bulky civie armor."

Johnny considered that.

"Or," I said, "I could just ask Franco to find me a good skin. I know he'd come through with the best of the best."

"Ah, low blow, broto. Fine, I'll look into it. Though, full disclosure, I actually have no idea what low-to-mid-level requisitions cover. I was mostly just trying to pretend I had my scud together."

"Trying to impress Glenbark, huh?"

Johnny's brow wrinkled a little too severely. "Why wouldn't I? She's High General, man."

I traded a sideways grin with Elise. *"He's into her."*

"Oh, he's so into her," she sent back.

"You guys aren't..." Johnny looked back and forth between us. "You're not doing it, are you?"

"Hmm?" I said.

"I'm sure she's plenty impressed, Johnny," Elise added, standing and offering me a hand up. "I doubt she'd have taken you as her servitor otherwise."

Johnny eyed us suspiciously for another few seconds, then played at shrugging the comment off as we headed out, Elise and I shooting furtive grins back and forth, and Johnny unquestionably walking with a little extra pop in his step.

WE FOUND Therese lounging peacefully in a quiet corner of the walking gardens beside the medica, warm sunlight soaking her pale skin and sandy brown curls.

"And so my heroes return," she said when she saw us.

"How are you feeling, Therese?" I asked.

"All things considered? Not that bad, I guess." She shrugged. "I got that sleep and juice, at least. How are you boys? And—oh, sorry." She rose with clear effort and offered a hand to Elise. "Sorry, I don't get out of the lab much..." Her face fell, no doubt at the painful reminder of everything she'd been through and lost at that lab. Before we could say anything, though, she blew out a little chuckle, shaking her head. "As I was saying, I'm awful at this. I'm Therese."

Elise took Therese's hand warmly in both of her own. "Elise. Lovely to meet you. And I can't judge." She tilted her head toward me. "I didn't get out of the house much myself until he came along and blew it up."

Therese raised her eyebrows at me.

"That... technically wasn't my fault," I said. "Technically."

A smile pulled at Therese's mouth, but then it faltered, and she swayed. Johnny hurried forward to help her back down to her bench.

"Thank you," she said quietly, looking a bit lightheaded. "Guess that's what happens after two seasons of... well, not bed rest."

Johnny sank down on the other end of the bench.

"I can't believe it was so long," I said, pulling up chairs for Elise and myself.

"Time flies," Therese said. "Sounds like I slept through quite the ordeal. Most of us had been out for a while, so there's been a lot of Q and A in the medica. I've heard some stories." Her light brown eyes shifted to me. "Some more, um, logic-defying than others."

"Yeah..." Johnny said, tucking his arms behind the bench and tilting his face to the warmth of the sun, "I thought the tales of my good looks and heroism were overstated too, but they just keep coming. What's a guy to do?"

Therese smiled, but her eyes remained on me, brimming with curiosity. "Is any of it true?" she asked, looking a bit abashed. "The things they say you can do?"

I looked to Johnny, who turned his hands palms up. "Not my secret society, broto."

Elise didn't offer any words of caution either, so I telepathically bade her to hold on, warned Therese out loud to do the same, and telekinetically lifted Elise a foot into the air, chair and all.

Therese jolted like the bench had shocked her. "Oh my—That's... That's..."

"Oh yeah," Johnny said, watching her closely for any sign she might faint, "he can do that too. See, I thought we were talking about his singing voice."

Elise frowned down at me from her floating throne. "Show-off."

I lowered her back to the patio.

"I don't understand," Therese said, rubbing her temples like she was sure she must be hallucinating. "How do you… How is that possible?"

I spent a few minutes trying to explain the fundamentals of Shaping in the least outlandish way I could. Not that anything I said could really make it easy to swallow.

"Show me again," she said when I'd finished, clearly trying to convince herself the first time had been a fluke.

I floated a leaf from the sun-soaked stone path up to hover over my hand, and channeled the heat to set it to smoking.

She gaped for a handful of seconds then focused back on me, something shifting in her expression. "I would absolutely love to get a look at you under the microscope."

The four of us shared a silent look, Therese's pale cheeks growing redder by the second until she finally sputtered, "I didn't—Oh, that… That came out wrong."

I waved the comment away, smiling.

"It's just that that," Therese said slowly, pointing at the ashes drifting lazily down to the ground, "seems an awful lot like magic."

"I won't argue," I said. "But we call it Shaping."

Therese just stared off like she was trying to piece together how such a thing was possible.

"I probably should've opened with this," I said, feeling the first pang of doubt, "but you can't tell anyone about any of this. For your own safety, I mean."

"Safety?" she asked with an absentminded frown, still clearly lost in thought.

"Yeah, it's just, uh… Well, long story short, the Sanctum keeps a pretty tight lid on this stuff. They've done their best to see to it there aren't many like me left on Enochia."

She focused back on me, understanding dawning in her eyes. "So that's why they really tried to, you know?" She rubbed at her throat, right around noose level. "Sorry, it's just… This is all a lot to take in. A lot, a lot."

"Oh, believe me, we understand," Johnny said. "Especially us boring normal folk."

She looked around at us, remembering herself. "As many million questions as I have, I guess you all probably didn't come here just to tell me about this, did you?"

"We mostly just wanted to check on you," I said.

"Us unsung heroes gotta stick together," Johnny added.

"But we did have a few questions too," I continued. "If you're up for it."

Johnny sat up straighter, frowning at me. "We did?"

"By all means," Therese said, looking between us.

"Hal," Johnny said, "this wasn't what we—"

"Therese and I already talked about it back at Vantage," I said, raising a pacifying hand before turning to Therese. "What I said back there about getting you a lab and a team and everything... How much do you know about those hybrid chambers?"

"Oh." She tilted her head, reviewing something with a faraway look. "Not much. Almost nothing, really. My work, as I guess you kind of already know, mostly dealt with trying to adapt the regenerative abilities of raknoth tissues into something we could use medically in humans. I could certainly hazard some guesses about what those chambers might be doing, and how they might be doing it. If I had a chance to study one, or maybe even a hybrid, I could probably refine those guesses."

"And if I told you we needed a way to track down where they might be building more of them, would you have any ideas?"

Pale as she was after a couple months indoors, the blanching of her face was still noticeable. "Are you... trying to track down more of them?"

"Hal..." Johnny warned.

"We're not sure yet. Alton Parker gave us reason to believe he might be working on other installments."

"Oh, for the love of..." Johnny pointedly waved his awakened palmlight. "It's like you want me to tattle on you. It's okay, Therese," he added, touching her shoulder. "You're safe here either way, but this conversation"—he half-glared at me—"is not Hal's jurisdiction."

"It was my package," I muttered.

Therese looked between us uncertainly. "Well, I'm not so sure I'm the one you want to be talking to for this anyway. There are at least four of my colleagues here who'd know more about the chambers, and... Wait, is this classified?"

"Incredibly classified," Johnny said, shooting me another dark look. "Though I have it on decent authority that this isn't going to be the last you'll hear of it. Hal already told the High General you might be the woman for the job."

Therese looked at me in shock. "Why on Enochia would you do that? Not that I'm not happy to help. Give me hybrid samples and a lab, and I'll do everything I can to try to figure out what's happened to them and how we might try to undo it. But tracking down hybrid chambers? I'm no detective. I wouldn't even know where to start."

"Nor do you need to sweat that right now," Johnny said, rising to his feet, eyes on me. "We need to go have ourselves a refresher course on security clearances and civilians." He looked down at Therese. "I expect the High General will be wanting to speak with you soon, but until you hear more, it's best you pretend this conversation didn't happen. Just like I might have to."

He turned expectantly to us.

I stood, bordering between guilty and annoyed. Elise went to shake Therese's hand and say goodbye. I followed, thinking to do the same.

"You were the only one who had the guts to try to stop what was happening," I said instead as I took her hand. "You had a couple dozen of the best minds on the planet in that lab. You can't tell me a few of them hadn't put things together and realized something was off about Alton Parker's story. But you were the one who decided to stick your neck out and try to do something about it. That's why I know you're the woman for the job. I know we can trust you to do what's right."

I didn't add that I wanted an inside woman on whatever task force Glenbark might construct. That was superfluous—a happy extra.

Therese was watching me like she was trying to decide whether or not I was simply a naive child, spouting nonsense. Her eyes drifted to the bandaged side of my face. A brain-cooked naive child, she was probably thinking.

Behind me, Johnny cleared his throat.

I gave Therese's hand a squeeze and let go. "Get some rest, Therese. And thank you, for everything."

I left the gardens feeling just a bit more confident that this could work— that we'd find Alton's facilities and dismantle them, piece by piece. And that I'd find Alton Parker, and do the same to him.

"So what the scud was that, buddy?" Johnny said when we were back among the busy foot traffic of Haven.

"I didn't want her to be broadsided when Glenbark decides to talk to her people," I said.

He gave me a look that let me know the bullscud was all but leaking out my ears.

"I didn't tell her anything she couldn't surmise from what she already knows," I added.

His look intensified.

"Fine. I'm worried. I'm just trying to make sure we don't lose this thing."

He jabbed a finger at me. "You're just trying to keep your fingers in every little pot there is to finger."

Elise started to say something then thought better of it.

He swiveled his finger to her, his eyes still on me. "Okay. Admittedly, that came out wrong, but you know what I mean. You're acting like you need to be at the center of every part of this fight because you're Haldin gropping Raish and all that, but you know what?"

I arched my brows, waiting for his big punch.

"You don't."

I frowned. "That's it?"

Johnny shrugged. "I figured I'd keep it simple, since you seem to be incapable of noticing the tens of thousands of good men and women on this base who managed to pull their trousers on this morning without your help."

His words might've set me off if it hadn't been for the smile creeping over his face.

"Johnny, I'm not—"

He waved my excuse away. "Just promise you'll give me a heads up next time you're itching to go rogue?"

"I... yeah." I rapped my chest in casual salute. "I hereby swear to keep you informed of my every itch."

"How lovely," Elise said. "At least that'll be some weight off my—Oh."

She opened her palmlight and showed me an incoming call from Franco. Johnny and I pulled over to wait on an out-of-the-way bench beside one of the barracks while she took the call.

"Any luck?" I asked a few minutes later when she was done.

She sank to the bench beside me and shook her head. "Not with the alien ship leads, it sounds like. I told him we could try to talk to Glenbark about him having a look at Legion records when they get in."

"Oh yeah," Johnny said. "I'm sure she'd be thrilled to let more civies into the top secret club. I'll get right on that."

"That would be wonderful, Johnny," Elise said, patting him on the thigh with a smile. "Thank you."

Johnny narrowed his eyes at her. "I have a feeling someone might've noticed by now if there were an alien ship sitting in storage."

Elise just shrugged.

"They're coming to Haven?" I asked.

"Hmm?" She looked at me distractedly. "Yeah, first thing tomorrow."

"Everything else okay?"

She looked at us, concern touching her eyes. "There was just... He said he had one last thing to check on, but he was pretty hushed up about it. Even by his standards."

"No hints?"

She shook her head. "Not really. All he said was that it was something you'd need to be there for if the source panned out."

I frowned. That *was* unusual. I looked at Johnny, wondering what Glenbark would say if I ended up requesting leave from Haven so soon. Johnny, apparently detecting my line of thought, rolled his eyes and stood from the bench.

"Okay, then. Johnny Wingard, servitor report, day one. Hal spilled our secrets to a civie, made some shady requests for covert ops armor, and would like to know if maybe he can go on a super vague field trip soon, for reasons he'll probably only tell us if the mood strikes. Lise heartily abetted, further inviting her civie dad—a world-class information broker, by the way—to have a poke around our secure records. And, oh, our actual progress on Mission Mindsafe, you ask? Ha. Come back tomorrow, maybe." He looked between us. "Does that about sum it up?"

Elise and I traded a guilty look.

"Would it make you feel better if we go get to work right now?" I asked.

"It would, in fact, make me feel better, Hal. Thank you for asking."

"Well, let's get to it then," I said, absentmindedly patting Elise's leg and preparing to stand.

"Best idea I've heard all day," Johnny said. "I'm gonna get these requisitions of ours moving, report, and maybe actually eat something today." He glanced between us. "Unless you guys are up for food right now."

Elise and I traded a smile, not needing telepathy to coordinate what came next.

"We've got important work to be doing here, Johnny," I said.

"Mission Mindsafe, number one," Elise agreed.

Johnny sighed and marched off, mumbling something about damn teenagers.

"You're three seasons older than me," I called after him.

He just threw both hands in the air, middle fingers soaring high.

"And he calls us out on maturity," I muttered.

I turned to Elise and found her watching me with a smile that made me feel like I was seeing her for the first time in weeks. That smile. The sun basking in her raven hair. Her eyes, beckoning to me like cool slices of open sky.

I kissed her. I couldn't have stopped myself if I'd tried. She met the kiss gladly, her lips curling into a delicious smile against mine.

"I love you," I thought, relishing every bit of her closeness. *"But I'm still mad at you."*

"Oh, well that's funny," she murmured, her lips lightly brushing mine, "because I'm still mad at you."

"Well, good then."

"Good," she agreed.

I'll admit to being slightly confused by how outrageously attracted the entire interaction left me feeling toward her, but I wasn't going to argue as we fell into another kiss, deeper than the first. She reached to pull me in closer—

And recoiled with a laugh as her hand found my bandage and came away coated in minty salve. For a second, I thought the moment was gone. Then she wiped her salved hand on my tunic, laughing, and pulled me in for another quick kiss.

"So," she whispered in my head, *"back to work then, partner?"*

I NEARLY FELL off the bench when she capped the question off with a rather captivating mental image. Mostly, I was just glad to be sitting down—especially when I glanced around and saw we were starting to draw attention.

I swallowed. "Work, uh… Work sounds good."

Whatever dangerous—possibly demonic—reputation I might be accruing on base, I'm sure the sight of me chasing a raven-haired beauty through Haven like I was on fire and she was the only water on Enochia didn't earn me many points. Then again, for anyone who got a good look at Elise, maybe it did. I didn't really give a damn either way.

I almost broke the door down getting into our quarters, barely noticing my battered body's protests. Elise pinned me to the wall and kissed me so hard my legs nearly buckled. I reached to pull her in, but she slipped free and vaulted lithely over the entryway divider. There, she paused long enough to make a point of undoing the first few buttons of her shirt. Then she winked and darted into the bedroom.

Sweet Alpha.

I nearly tripped and killed myself in my hurry to rip my tunic off while charging around the divider. Had I been mindful of anything more than the consuming need to feel her skin against mine, I might've noticed her hiding in wait. My focus, however, was a bit narrow in the moment, so it came as a surprise when she caught me on my way through the door and moved as if to hurl me at the bed with an arm throw.

Thankfully, she remembered herself at the last second and instead spun and dropped my battered body gently on the soft mattress. Then she was on top of me, and I was happily lost in a swirling storm of dark hair and delightfully warm lips on my neck, my cheek, my ear. She reached the bandaged side and laughed again. I was too busy ripping off her shirt to care. I spun us around. She hit the bed and wrapped her heels around my hips, pulling me to her. I pressed against her, relishing the smooth skin of her navel and shoulders, burying the side of her neck in kisses, working down, down. She let out a soft, wonderful sigh that made my head spin, and—

Buzz. Buzz.

Elise jolted at the unexpected vibration. I pulled back, Elise searching my face. My palmlight buzzed again. And again. And I slid the stupid thing off my wrist and tossed it onto the bedside table, where it continued to buzz. Elise grinned, and I was powerless to keep my lips from pulling into the widest, most stupid smile my mouth had ever known.

I descended for her, but she stopped me short, cupping my cheek with a gentle hand.

"This is kind of perfect, you know?"

In that moment, I did know. There were a lot of fires to be put out. Too many to count. And a few cargo trams' worth of payback I needed to see served up before I had any hope of sleeping through the night. Things weren't going at all as planned.

But right then, together in that room, her eyes on mine, her heart beating against mine, I couldn't be bothered to care about anything else.

The palmlight stopped buzzing, and we started in again, moving more deliberately this time, removing what clothing remained.

And that's when the alarms started.

Or the *alarm*, rather—a single, nasally wail, blared through amps all across the base. I sighed, pressing my forehead to hers. "You've gotta be kidding me…"

Across the room, the display flickered to life. An emergency alert, I knew. I held Elise's eyes, not wanting to look, not wanting to leave this moment behind. But neither one of us could ignore it.

The news wasn't good. Preliminary reports of half a dozen attacks across Enochia. Small towns. Seemingly at random. Hybrids confirmed at the scenes. I reached for my palmlight. Two missed calls and a string of messages from Johnny.

"Scud." I looked from her eyes, down to the lean, glorious curves of her naked body. Back to her eyes. My hands curling into fists.

She held my eyes, wanting to tell me to let it go. Knowing full well that neither of us could.

"Scud," I all but spat, sitting up and swiping to call Johnny. Frustrated as I was, it took me three tries.

"You can't go out there," Elise said beside me, pulling on clothes like she was preparing to stop me if I tried. "You almost died yesterday. You can't go charging—"

"Son of a gropping…" came Johnny's voice from the palmlight. "Hal! Are you—"

"What the scud's going on out there, Johnny?"

"Oh… Rustled wrinklies, I thought I was upset. You get called away from a perfectly good steak too?"

"Johnny," I growled. "What's the plan? What are we doing?"

"Plan?" He sounded distracted, like he was busy processing something on his end. "No plan, broto. We're grounded, remember? We've already got legions airbound for all six towns."

"We could help, Johnny."

"Not gonna happen. Glenbark's orders."

"What do you mean, not gonna—Why did you even call, then?"

"Can't a guy be worried about his broto?"

"Johnny."

"I wanted to make sure you hadn't caught wind before the alarm and tried to do anything crazy."

"What, like stow away on a transport?"

He hesitated. "It'd hardly be the most drastic move you'd ever pulled."

"Goodbye, Johnny."

"Wait! Wait. I know this sucks, Hal. I know. I'd rather be out there too.

But just because we're grounded doesn't mean we can't save lives. Focus on Mission Mindsafe. You're the only one who c—"

I killed the connection and sat there, silently seething, my mind flashing through a hundred equally futile plans to do something—anything—to help those people.

I wanted to hate Glenbark—wanted to be furious with Johnny—but I couldn't. It wasn't their fault. It was the raknoth. It was my failure to stop them before it had come to this. I needed something to sink my rage into. Preferably something with red eyes and a thick hide.

Elise was holding me, gently stroking me. I realized I was trembling.

"Hey." She tugged on my jawline until I finally met her eyes. "This war belongs to Enochia. Not to Haldin Raish. You know that, right?"

"I know," I said, my voice as mechanical as my movements as I kissed her palm, pulled on my undershorts, and climbed out of bed.

"Where are you going?"

I paused in the doorway. "To do the one useful thing I can right now."

14

MEETINGS

There was no getting around it: it was a long night. My eyes hung half-lidded, full of a dull burning, and my brain had long since been fried, turned to sludge, and fried again. But I kept working. If "working" was what it could be called. In truth, I mostly alternated between trying to hone my mental island technique, staring forlornly at the runes of my own cloaking pendant, begging them to cough up their secrets, and agonizing over the news of the day's attacks.

Abductees. That's what the reels had been calling the several hundred civilians already confirmed missing following the attacks. There were dozens of eyewitness reports floating around—frantic civilians recounting the horror of watching their loved ones dragged off by beasts with pale red eyes, loaded onto transports and carried off to Alpha knew where.

But whether Alpha knew or not, I was pretty sure I did.

Hundreds of civilians, taken by the raknoth? The WAN reels might be hesitant to make the leap, but I couldn't imagine those people were headed anywhere but straight to Alton Parker's facilities to be assimilated into his grotesque war machine—either as new hybrids or as the blood rack victims who'd be feeding them.

The thought had *not* been helping my sleep-starved brain focus on the problem at hand.

Elise and Johnny had fallen asleep on the couch behind me—Johnny softly snoring, Elise curled up in a surprisingly compact ball, her head resting on Johnny's thigh. I'd woken about an hour ago to find them like that, apparently after having drifted off for nearly an hour myself, despite everything. Some corner of my mind insisted that that should irritate me—both my own drifting off and Elise's head in Johnny's lap—but I was too tired to give either thought much credence.

The way I felt, I would've gladly slept on Johnny's thigh.

But I couldn't. Not while I knew those *abductees* were out there, suffering the worst kind of fate because I'd failed to stop the raknoth before this whole situation had exploded. Now more than ever, we needed a way to move on Oasis and disrupt the raknoth forces. Which meant I needed to recreate Carlisle's and Cassius' damn little pendant, sitting there so benignly in my palm—existing, and refusing to tell me how.

We'd copied its runes onto a few dummy models in painstaking detail, despite the fact that the markings were still complete gibberish to us. Hitting them with a fancy piece of Shaping and getting it to stick—that was the hard part. The impossible part.

Maybe it'd make more sense to start simple—trying to imbue a single rune to, say, absorb heat from the air. Something I could do without effort even on the worst of days. That made way more sense… which was exactly why we'd thought of it a couple hours ago, I remembered, shaking my head. Before I'd fallen asleep. Sweet Alpha. But then… There'd been something else. Some reason why I hadn't already tried our brilliant new plan of simplifying the problem…

Because I hadn't been sure if a different application would require a different rune or not. That was why. We'd had an hour-long debate about exactly that, which was right about when Johnny and Elise had drifted off.

And now here I was, thinking in damn circles. Wonderful.

But Past Hal and Present Hal both raised a fair point. The runes on Elise's and Johnny's pendants were quite similar to those on mine—albeit simplified on Johnny's, which lacked the adjustable range of mine and Elise's pendants. But did that mean the runes were some kind of universal, set characters in a language I didn't yet know? Or had Carlisle simply made them up and decided to keep things simple and copy them over and over?

Was it even worth asking these questions when I had no damn way of answering them?

I buried my face in my hands and let out a low groan. Then I made the mistake of reminding myself that untold thousands—and maybe millions—of lives might well depend on my figuring this out. I was on my feet before I knew it, pacing back and forth in a vain attempt to drain the flash flood of panic ripping through me.

I was just a kid. Just a gropping kid, and—

On the couch, Johnny gave a sharp snort, smacked his lips a few times, and resumed his vigilant slumber.

I sighed and reached out with my senses. Carefully, my thoughts all of pillows and clouds, I telekinetically lifted Elise from the couch and slowly, slowly floated her into the bedroom, onto the bed. There, she stirred slightly, her mind brushing against mine in what felt like the equivalent of a sleep murmur. Then she was out again, peaceful as ever.

I longed to go nestle up beside her and sleep for days.

Instead, I telekinetically laid Johnny down to take advantage of the full couch, then I settled cross-legged back to the floor and picked up the light etcher and one of the blank pendants Johnny had brought.

It was time to do some experimenting.

SOMETHING—A sound—jolted me awake. Reflexively, my hand flew for the daggers on the bedside table. I missed the table and hit the carpeted floor with a soft thunk.

"Hal?" came Elise's groggy voice from… not next to me.

I looked up from the floor with a groan and realized I'd missed the bedside table because it wasn't there at all. I was in the living room, where I'd apparently fallen asleep sitting up again. Right in the center of a heaping pile of failure and worthless pendants.

The sound repeated. A knock at the door.

"Wuzzit—Huh?"

I turned to see a bleary-eyed Johnny stirring on the couch.

"Damn delinquents," he muttered, wiping at the dried drool stain at the corner of his lips.

"I swear to Alpha, you're becoming an old man right before my eyes." I pushed myself to all fours and stopped there, allowing my back's indignant cries to subside.

Johnny huffed a victorious laugh. "Who's the old man now, ya wimper-whipper?"

"Probably the guy using the word *wimperwhipper*."

Another knock.

Elise appeared in the bedroom doorway. "Were you boys planning on answering that?"

"Does my answer to that question in any way affect my eligibility for a nice steaming cup of caffa?" Johnny asked.

Elise rolled her eyes and vaulted the divider to the entryway. I pulled myself to my feet to follow by the less acrobatic route.

"Yeah, you guys…" Johnny yawned. "… right behind you."

Elise pulled the door open, and I barely had time to see our visitors before Elise surged forward to wrap her dad in a hug.

Franco Fields was a man whose every inch always seemed to exude sophistication. He had the same raven-dark hair as Elise, but his skin was darker, as were his eyes, deep forest green. Even with several days' worth of unshaven stubble underlying his usual dark, slender mustache, he simply looked roguish instead of unkempt.

Behind him, his two companions, James Bell and Phineas Hammer, were polar opposites of one another—James small and twitchy with light blond hair, and Phineas a stoic mountain with a bald crown at the peak of his dark hair. When Elise finally released Franco from her warm embrace to move on to greeting James and Phineas, Franco strode into the room to clap me on the shoulders.

"I heard about what happened at Vantage." His eyes traced the bandaged side of my head in what was quickly becoming a familiar double-take. I expected him to say something about how I should be more careful, but he didn't.

James shimmied in and pulled me into a jittery embrace, complete with a hefty pat on the back. In the doorway, Phineas didn't so much hug Elise as stand there somberly and allow her to wrap her arms around him—a right I imagined was exclusive to Elise and few others. After a second, he even reached up and patted her back.

It had been less than a cycle since we'd all last seen each other, but we were still close enough to our recent ordeals—most notably, the Legion blasting into Franco's home and driving us apart—that it was hard not to appreciate the times we had together as if they might be our last.

By way of greeting to me, Phineas eyed my bandages then gave a nod and a grunt. There may have even been the hint of a friendly smile buried under that thick beard. I swear, he seemed to like me just a little bit more every time I got my ass kicked and lived to tell about it. Sadistic, maybe, but I chose to take it as a sign of respect from a fellow warrior—Phineas being the only non-Shaper man I'd known to punch a raknoth in the face and live to tell about it. Of course, the fact that that fist was a solid, cutting-edge prosthetic probably hadn't hurt either.

"Ah," Franco said, sliding around the divider and taking in Johnny and the untidy aftermath of our—or my, at least—late night work session. "Charming."

"I might resent that," Johnny groaned, sitting up on the couch and rubbing at his eyes. "Just give me a minute to think about it. Preferably with a nice cup of—Agh!"

He recoiled and awkwardly caught the sack of caffa beans that came sailing through the air and struck his chest. I traced the trajectory to the basic kitchen unit, thinking for a second that Elise had eked out some stronger-than-normal telekinesis from the doorway, but it turned out she'd just moved into attack position quietly.

"Right," Johnny said, standing with his sack of beans. "Cups all around, then?"

James went to help Johnny in the corner kitchen unit while the rest of us pulled the couple extra chairs across from the couch and settled down around the caffa table.

"So no luck on the last lead?" I asked.

Franco shook his head. "Not really. This one might have actually seen something, but if we chart it with the other two probable sightings so far, all we really get is that our red-eyed friends covered a large sweep of Enochia before settling down." Slightly louder, he turned and added, "Any updates on having a look at those records, Johnny?"

"As I told Lise," Johnny said. "I'll get right on that. I'm sure Glenbark would be thrilled to let more civies into the top secret club. Especially ones who think we're too stupid to notice an alien ship sitting around in our records."

"That would be wonderful, Johnny," Franco said, turning back to us. "Thank you."

Johnny narrowed his eyes at the back of Franco's head, then he sobered. "How are things looking out there after yesterday?"

Franco's expression turned grim. "The people are scared," he said finally. "More and more are beginning to wake up to what's happening—hard not to when the stories just keep spreading faster and faster. Red eyes. Humanoid monsters." His eyes flicked to me. "Talk of demons walking the streets. And after yesterday..."

A heavy silence settled over the room.

"What's the count at?" I forced myself to ask.

"Over six hundred," Franco said, his gaze fixed on an uninteresting patch of the dull blue carpet.

Six hundred. Something twisted inside me, kicking in revulsion at the thought of the missing civilians who'd plagued my nightmares, probably already well on their way to becoming helpless blood bags or feral hybrids as we—

"Stop it," Elise sent, taking my hand in hers. *"This isn't your fault."*

I took a careful breath, trying to let it pass.

"In other news, Barbara's still set on nailing down that exclusive with you," Franco said, almost apologetically trying to change the topic. "Could be helpful. For you and for Enochia."

"Hmm," I said, barely even considering. "You can tell her I'll try soon, I guess." It was the same answer I'd been giving for two cycles now, ever since our darling WAN reporter, Barbara Sanders, had saved my life at the gallows and I'd offered to thank her with the true story.

"You know," I added, waving at the room, "after all this is…"

"Yes," Franco said, his eyes flicking surreptitiously to Elise. "Yes, of course. I'll tell her."

"What about the other thing?" Elise asked. "That lead you didn't wanna talk about over the lights?"

Franco's brow furrowed. "Yes. That." He looked around the room. "Not entirely sure these quarters are any safer than speaking over the lights"—he looked at his palmlight, swiped a few commands, and seemed to decide we were safe enough—"but we do need to talk about it."

I waited for him to elaborate, but he seemed to be unsure exactly where to begin.

"How much do you know about the Emmútari?" he finally asked.

That made me sit a little straighter.

"Only what Carlisle told me. Ancient order of Shapers, hunted to extinction by—"

I paused as James came to deposit a tray of five steaming cups in front of us, Johnny trailing him, sipping contentedly at his own caffa. I hadn't told Johnny about the Emmútari—in part because it hadn't precisely come up by itself, but also in part because I wasn't sure he'd appreciate a story that cast the prophet Sarentus and the rise of his Sanctum on a foundation of intolerant slaughter rather than one of peace and unity. He knew that the Sanctum hunted my kind, and for now, that was probably enough. On top of that, I wasn't sure what James or Phineas might know, or if someone really might be spying on us in these quarters.

"Why do you ask?" I said. "You're not saying this lead…?"

"I am," Franco said, also shooting a furtive glance at Johnny, as if debating how much to say. "I was discreetly contacted by a man claiming to have answers to our questions. Both of our questions," he added, pointing back and forth between himself and me.

"Sounds super legitimate," Johnny said, squeezing onto the couch beside Elise.

"I don't suppose this mystery man happened to specify what those questions might be?" Elise added.

Franco looked troubled. "He did, in fact. He knew I'd been… Well, here." He drew something—a piece of paper, I realized—from a pocket and handed it to me. "Read it for yourself. He left this in a deposit lockup for us."

I looked dumbly down at the note.

It felt foreign in my fingers. Too light. Too *old*, I decided, looking closer. Not the off-white of the pages in the few books I'd ever held, but flimsier, stained yellow with age.

"This guy's slinging *paper* notes?" Johnny asked. "He's definitely a murderer."

No one said a thing.

Carefully, I unfolded the paper, taking in the spindly, hand-written script.

BROKER,

YOUR WAYWARD SHIP. The Prospect's shroud. The answers to your questions lie in records long sealed—lost to history, but not lost.

IF YOU SHOULD WISH to find them, bring the Prospect to Humility on third Alphasday, the eleventh of Forge. Go to the Penitent Path. There, you will find further instructions.

DO NOT BRING OTHERS.

THAT WAS IT.

No details. No signature. Just simple instructions for me and Franco to walk straight onto this guy's smashball court three days from now without the faintest clue of what might be waiting.

"Bit of a riddler, isn't he?" Johnny said, leaning in to read with me and Elise. "Records long sealed and all that."

"This doesn't say anything about the… the order," I said.

"No," Franco said. "He used that word when we first spoke by palmlight. It's the only reason I didn't ignore him outright."

Johnny was looking around at us like he'd missed something. "What's the deal with this—what was it? Em-yoo-tary?"

He hadn't missed it, then.

"It's a long story," I said, "from a time before the Sanctum. Old Shapers. Lost secrets. All that."

"Right," Johnny said. "Of course. Classic, really."

I looked back at the note, then to Franco. "And you're assuming I'm this…"

"Prospect," Elise said, wrinkling her nose. "Prospect for what, exactly?"

"I'm more concerned about the next word," I said, handing the paper back to Franco. "How in demon's depths would he know about Mission Mindsafe? The cloaks, I mean," I added at Franco's confused look. "I'm assuming that's what he means by the shroud, right?"

"I believe so, based on our brief communication." Franco stashed the note in his pocket. "As for the how of the matter, I'm afraid I can't say. That he knew I was investigating the trail of the raknoth ship isn't so inexplicable, considering I've had my feelers out, and my anonymity isn't what it once was. But the cloaks, your Project Mindsafe…"

"*Mission* Mindsafe," Johnny corrected. Elise shot him a look, and he shrugged. "Fine. Not important."

"Yes, well," Franco said, "point being, either this man has powerful colleagues and ears in tight places, or—"

"Or he understands enough about Shaping to put two and two together," Elise said. "It's no secret Hal's here in Haven. We've all seen the headlines. If someone out there understands cloaks and telepathy enough to reason out what the raknoth did to the legionnaires at Oasis, it's probably not a huge stretch for them to figure out at least part of what Hal's doing here."

Franco nodded his agreement. My head was too busy spinning with thoughts of this shadowy figure and his purported Emmútari records.

Was it even remotely possible?

I thought back to everything Carlisle had told me about the lost order. I couldn't remember him having ever said anything to remotely suggest he thought they might still be around. And if he hadn't known…

Who the scud was this guy?

"Hal?"

I looked around and realized everyone was watching me expectantly.

"Hmm?"

"We were asking how your work went last night," Franco said, plucking one of my many practice runes off the carpet. "Any progress?"

"Progress?" I had to think about it. Alpha, I needed to sleep. "Yeah, sort of. I… figured a few things out."

Or got one nonsense rune to pull a little heat from the air for a few seconds, at least. I thought. So, progress. Sure. But I was a little too stuck on Franco's odd note to think about it.

"Why not contact me too?" I asked. "Why'd he only go through you?"

Franco gave a helpless shake of his head. "I don't know. There's too much I don't know. If he's reasoned out your current objective here at Haven, I'm sure he's aware your whereabouts are being monitored far more closely than mine. Perhaps it was simply for his own safety."

"Or," Johnny said, "perhaps he's a softsteel-sipping madman who happened upon a fancy old word in one of those creepy paper books and thought he'd take a crack at getting the Demon of Divinity alone for Alpha knows what reason."

"The thought had occurred to me," Franco said slowly. "But, all the same, I'm not sure we can ignore this."

He looked to me, waiting to see what I'd say. I didn't have an answer. It was a risk, and I wasn't even quite sure what the payoff might be. But something in my gut told me this was important.

What would Carlisle do?

"You're right," I said without thinking about it. "We can't ignore it."

If this guy knew something about creating runes—scud, if he knew anything at all about the Emmútari—I couldn't afford to let that knowledge slip through my fingers. Not when it could save lives. Not when my own efforts with the runes were looking about as promising as playing catch without arms.

Johnny polished his caffa off with a noisy slurp before speaking. "Yeah, I don't wanna be that guy, but we also can't ignore that you're sorta on Glenbark's leash right now. You're not leaving Haven without everyone losing their scud."

Much as the thought of asking for permission to leave these walls irked me, he had a point.

"Fine." I said, sitting up. "Then I guess we'd better go ask if I've been a good boy."

"Man," Johnny said, setting his empty cup down with a lamenting sigh. "And I thought today was gonna be a *good* day."

15

CONTACT

"One more time," Ordo Dillard's voice crackled through the skimmer amps.

I traded a knowing look with Franco in the driver's seat beside me.

"We stick to the route," I said.

"We keep our palmlights on at all times," Franco added.

"At the first sign of danger, we walk."

"Should the contact attempt to change the meet location, we do not proceed unless we are able to convey said change to you."

"And, above all else," I said, "we rigorously abstain from any and all urges to be heroes. How'd we do?"

"I feel better already," came Dillard's flat reply. "Just remember, should anything go sideways, you'll have sniper cover, and we'll be nearby."

How could I forget? The thought of steely-eyed Mara watching me through her scope was nearly as unsettling as the worries about what our mysterious contact might have up his sleeves.

"We'll be careful," I said.

"We'll be careful for you," Dillard said. "You just be smart enough to let us."

The connection ended, and so began our comms silence.

Ahead, the mountainside city of Humility was resolving into clear view. It was a fairly small city, compared to Divinity. More of a sprawling town, really. None of the shining skyscrapers of Divinity, and far less air traffic.

What it lacked in bustle, though, it made up for in beauty. Contrary to what one might've expected from a name like Humility, the city gave every appearance of thriving wealth. Lush fields all around. Ancient, elegant architecture—regal stone towers and scenic walkways, all in seemingly good repair.

The name, Franco informed me, was more in reference to the city's position in the shadow of the mighty Byahnan Mountains, and to the fact that Humility was, for the most part, a Sanctum city—light in Legion presence and home to many simple but thriving shops, bustling marketplaces, and, above all, worship halls. A dozen in total, according to Franco. I didn't have to look hard to spot the largest one, right at the base of the mountains, though all of them would be equally packed right now for Alphasday ceremonies.

"Nervous?" Franco asked as the city drew near.

A vague meeting with an unknown entity who already knew more than he should and claimed to know a whole scudload more about an ancient order that'd been so far buried that even the High General of the Legion hadn't heard about it? Mostly, I was just surprised we were here at all.

Glenbark hadn't been happy.

"Maybe," I said, shifting in my newly requisitioned armor skin. "But more about what we left behind than anything else."

Because Glenbark hadn't been the only unhappy one.

Franco gave me a sympathetic smile, clearly understanding. If it hadn't been for him, I wasn't sure we would've escaped the meeting back at Haven without bloodshed. Not that Glenbark had given one shiny damn about his dashing charm and silver tongue. It was more just that Franco had a knack for speaking the truth in a way that made it hard to ignore. And the truth was that, if there was even half a shot this contact of ours could help us with the conundrum of the cloaks, this little outing was well worth the risk. The past two days of my ineffectual rune blundering had proved that clearly enough.

That said, even Phineas had come close to cracking his unshakably stoic veneer when Glenbark had demanded he, James, and Elise remain on base for the operation to minimize potential complications. Watching those two stare one another down, I'd been reminded of the old saying about an irresistible force meeting an indestructible object. I hadn't really been sure which was which, but it turned out to be a crappy metaphor anyway, seeing as Phineas had bowed in the end. Elise, on the other hand...

"I don't know how much more of this she's going to put up with," I said quietly.

Franco studied me for a long moment. My relationship with his daughter was about the last thing I wanted to discuss with Franco, but, at the same time, I also longed for his reassurance that it was going to be okay.

"I'd say it depends," he finally said.

"On whether I stop running off without her?"

He tilted his head back and forth as if to say *Maybe, maybe not.* "More on whether you can bring yourself to be honest with her about *why* you do, I think."

I opened my mouth. Closed it. I wanted to argue. Wanted to point out that Glenbark had left us no choice in today's arrangement. That is wasn't my fault. More than anything, I wanted to pretend that I wasn't secretly relieved Elise had been made to stay at Haven. But I was. So I said nothing instead, and we sat in silence as the skimmer banked gently down toward the mountain side of the city. We passed over the regal stone perimeter wall of Humility, the autopilot navigating us toward the nearest landing pads.

"Take it from a man who's made a pretty bit of coin selling secrets," Franco said, reaching for the controls. "Honesty is everything in anything that really matters."

If I hadn't seen him take the controls then, I might've sworn it was the weight of his words alone that guided the skimmer down to a gentle landing in one of the structure's hundreds of parking alcoves.

"For now," he added, reaching for the door and pausing, "let's just see to it the two of us don't earn her eternal wrath by falling prey to any hapless tricks out there, yes?"

I nodded, pulling on my hood and shaders and trying to focus on the task at hand. "Fair enough."

We climbed out of the skimmer and headed for the mag lift that would take us to ground level. Under my street clothes, the new armor skin felt as nice as I knew it was. Meant for stealth and undercover work, it was snug, but not restrictive, and rated for light to medium gunfire. I wasn't sure how it would hold up to raknoth fists and hybrid claws, but it sure beat the scud out of the civie armor.

Outside, the streets were plenty busy, probably mostly with traffic headed either from the morning worship sessions or to the more popular noon sessions, which would be starting shortly. Plenty more, though, were stopping here and there, haggling at merchant carts or simply enjoying a nice, sunny Alphasday with their families. After the wild, permacrete jungle of Divinity, it was actually kind of nice walking the stone streets among the quaint old taverns and homes of Humility. At least until I felt the tingle creeping up my neck.

I glanced around, wondering if it was simple nerves or if maybe my senses had caught some flicker of Mara's scope settling on me from a distant tower. If everything was going according to plan, which it seemed to be, she'd already been waiting for hours, with Davis for her spotter and a second pair similarly posted elsewhere, watching her blind spots. I wondered if her trigger finger had been aching all this time, itching for something to do—some demon to end.

But *that* was just the nerves talking. Probably.

Whether she liked me or not, Mara was a professional, just like Davis, sniper team B, and the other sixteen legionnaires of First Squad who'd trickled in over the past few hours, dressed in civilian clothing, to post up in the vicinity of the Penitent Path.

As we'd all taken turns noting, Franco's mysterious contact hadn't elected to actually designate a meeting time, which we'd taken as a sign that it'd be safest to assume the area was being watched at all times. Hence the slow trickle, and the impetus for keeping Ordo Carter's Second Squad with their transport on the other side of the city, out of the way but ready to deploy in full armor if needed.

Franco and I were both fairly certain the precautions were either ridiculously overdone or woefully inadequate. I tried to convince myself it was the former, but as we worked our way down the bumpy cobblestone street to the smoother, more contemporary trafficways, I started to feel some of that nervousness Franco had asked about in the skimmer.

We walked on, not really talking but to keep on course and kindly refuse the many offers of goods from the merchants we passed. A paunchy fellow with sun-baked skin and kind eyes waved a box of delectably ripe goja fruit as I passed, and I felt a flicker of annoyance and guilt as the smell conjured the memory of Melanie leaning in to tend my face in the medica, her lip balm fragrant with the sweet red fruit.

Walking out here in the sights of multiple high powered rifles, hooded and shaded to avoid being recognized by the public, risking our lives for what could well turn out to be a trap or nothing at all, and *that's* where my mind went. Amazing.

At least my face wasn't covered in bandages anymore.

After a few more streets and several more vendors, musicians, and public gatherings, we reached the open square at the city end of the Penitent Path. A fountain burbled merrily at the square's center, boasting one of the mighty sculptures of the Prophet Sarentus that were so common across Enochia.

On the far side of the bustling square, the Path rose up and bridged its stony way across the Byahnan River that ran down from the mountain and through Humility. Any who wished to cross the river and reach the great worship hall from this side of Humility did so via the Penitent Path, many of them stopping along the way to beg Alpha's forgiveness for their transgressions. Two such faithful worshipers stood at the side of the bridge now —a lone woman, who leaned sobbing on the stone lip, tossing coins one by one into the river below, and a middle-aged man who stood stark nude for all to see, his head hung low, a devastated-looking woman standing not far behind, watching him.

A gambler and an adulterer, I guessed.

I didn't want to cross the Path. I wasn't really sure these days how Alpha might feel about me, but something in me balked at the thought of being laid bare for his judgement. Not that I needed to cross a bridge for that. And besides, it didn't matter what I wanted anymore. I was here for a reason.

We were crossing the square to the stairs of the Path when something whispered in my mind, oddly atonal, as if spoken by a machine.

"Demon."

I froze.

Pulling my defenses tighter, I glanced around the square then closed my eyes to sweep for a telepathic mind.

There was none. None that I could feel, at least.

"What is it?" Franco asked quietly beside me, tense but composed.

"I'm not sure. Someone just—"

"The riverway underneath the Path," that perfectly flat voice sent. *"Come."*

Franco was still watching me expectantly.

"He wants us to meet him below the Path, I think."

"He's a telepath?" Franco asked.

That was a damn good question. If he was, why couldn't I feel him?

"Maybe. I don't know, exactly."

"I don't like this," Franco said.

I didn't either. Not even a little. But I wasn't turning away now.

"Come on."

I started across the square, Franco reluctantly falling in beside me.

"At the first sign of danger..." he said softly, repeating our promise to Dillard.

I kept my senses open, sweeping around us, telling myself that, really, there hadn't been anything to suggest danger yet. Just extreme creepiness.

"Why can't I feel you out there?" I sent out wide.

No response.

Maybe he was simply cloaked, but I didn't really believe that. I hadn't felt a presence at all, even when he'd sent his thoughts.

Yep. Extremely creepy.

At the far side of the square, we stopped on the right side of the Path at the top of a stone stairway leading down to the footpath alongside the Byahnan River. There were a few pedestrians below, out for a leisurely walk, and a few barges tied off along the river. Other than that, all was relatively quiet.

I looked up and around at the buildings and distant towers of Humility, trusting that at least one of our friendly snipers would see me. Pointedly I looked down the steps. Back to the surroundings. Back down the steps. *Going down.*

If our mysterious contact was watching, he didn't deign to break telepathic silence and tell me to stop. No buzzing palmlight telling me to abort, either. Franco looked far from happy, but he wasn't about to turn away either.

We reached the riverway path at the bottom of the steps without molestation. No dastardly assassins hiding in the brush. The path was fairly quiet thanks to the permacrete embankment separating it from the crowd in the public square, and its length was empty aside from the few pedestrians to the right… and the hawk-nosed man who was sitting on a bench beneath the first arch of the Penitent Path.

Staring straight at us.

He looked away as soon as I noticed him, his eased posture forced, like he was trying too hard to look uninterested. His face was gaunt behind that hawkish nose, his dark hair greasy and his clothes threadbare. I started toward him, intuiting it would be unwise to give this man time to think his next move through.

"Easy," Franco murmured from slightly behind me, apparently uncomfortable with the pace I'd set.

"That's far enough," Hawk Nose called before I could say anything. We paused ten feet away from him, trading an uncertain look, as he continued staring pointedly straight ahead.

"What comes next?" Franco asked him. "You were careful getting us here. I assume there's a next step before we talk?"

Hawk Nose let out a deep breath. "I suppose there is."

Something about his tone…

I was already throwing my senses out when he leapt to his feet and pointed something—a wand?—in Franco's direction. I fixed my mind on the strange device, preparing to rip it from his hand.

Something streamed into my head before I could, a liquid dose of pure dizziness, topped with a side of nausea. My knees hit hard permacrete, the world blurring around me. Somewhere, Franco cried my name.

I tried to answer. Couldn't move. Couldn't even focus to reach out and smack the gaunt man into the river.

We gropped up, was all I had time to think.

Then the world went dark.

16

TOMES

I fell out of darkness with no memory of where I'd been and landed in the rigid embrace of a wooden chair with no idea where the scud I was. Then I lurched against the constricting tug of bindings on my chest and wrists, and pieces started falling back into place.

Hawk Nose. The bastard had hit me with some kind of... I don't know what.

"Hal," someone whispered beside me. Franco.

He was seated beside me at a rough wooden round table, watching me with clear concern. And he wasn't tied up, I realized. But he wasn't moving to help me, either. Why?

Franco's eyes flicked elsewhere. I followed his gaze across the room and froze.

Someone was watching us. But not Hawk Nose. This man was bald and slightly plump beneath his voluminous brown robes—robes similar to those many Sanctum acolytes wore. His face was deathly pale, like he hadn't seen the sun in decades. And he was holding a wand like the one Hawk Nose had pulled right before I hit the floor. He held it loosely now, pointed at the floor, and he didn't look particularly threatening. More just curious.

"He won't talk," Franco croaked. At first, I thought he was speaking to our apparent captor, telling the man I wouldn't crack, but then he added, "He's just been watching us with that wand."

I opened my mouth to speak. Realized my throat was as dry as Franco's sounded. "How long have I been out?"

"Don't know," Franco croaked as I looked around the room. "I haven't been awake long. Can you…?"

I forgot about the room for a second as I caught his drift and turned my attention to assessing my bindings with my senses. Except I couldn't. Couldn't feel anything but my own stiff body.

"Scud," I whispered.

Franco nodded, unsurprised. "I was afraid of that."

Maybe Dillard and Hound Company are coming, I wanted to say. *They'll probably come blasting in any minute.*

But as I processed our surroundings, my hope dwindled.

We appeared to be in some kind of underground dungeon. Ancient-looking stone walls and floor. Wooden furniture that looked hand-carved. The room was meticulously clean and full of an odd juxtaposition of old and new. A heavy-looking wash basin and washboard. Cauldrons. Stoves. And then, amongst all that, a fab, and a full node workstation. And around it all, books. Shelves and shelves of them.

"Where the scud are we?" I muttered. And how the scud had we gotten there?

Louder, I called, "What do you want from us?"

The pasty-faced acolyte recoiled a little at the jump in volume, then recovered and pointed at the table with his wand. It was only then I noticed the books that lay open in front of me and Franco. There were three of them, all as ancient-looking as the stone walls. More so. Old enough that it looked like their dry pages might simply disintegrate were a strong breeze to sweep the room. Far more interesting than the antiquity, though, was what was on the pages of the first book.

Runes. Runes unlike any I'd seen in Carlisle's work.

I leaned hungrily forward—or tried to, only to tug against my bindings. I scanned the pages as best I could from where I was. There was little text on the page, and I was unsurprised to find that it was written in such archaic language that I only recognized pieces, and still stumbled over those.

I glanced at the next book over. A faded ink drawing of a long, bulbous ship stretched the two open pages, disgorging hundreds and hundreds of tiny figures at the base of some mountains. The Byahnan Mountains? It was impossible to say, but judging by the ratio between the ship, the mountains, and the people—if that was indeed what they were supposed to be—the ship would've been gargantuan in size. There was no text. No explanation.

My gaze was already shifting to the next book, which was open to one full page of text and one full page illustration of an epic battle between three people, clearly Shapers, and one dark figure with—

"You've gotta be gropping kidding me," I muttered.

"I had similar thoughts," Franco said.

I was too busy scanning the text for some explanation. There. Something about some kind of council, I thought it said, and a man named Valen… defeating the prophet… the *false* prophet…

"Sarentus," I whispered.

"Praise Alpha," Franco replied.

I stared at the illustration, dumbstruck. Stared at Sarentus, wreathed in shadow.

His eyes were red.

Even faded as the ink was with age, it was unmistakable. But that didn't mean anything, did it? It was just a drawing. Just a drawing in a book that looked to be hundreds of years old. A book, I saw now, that mentioned the Emmútari more than a few times. As did the rune book, I saw now at a closer look.

Unless some forger had gone through a lot of trouble, I was pretty sure I was looking at honest-to-Alpha records of the Emmútari.

"Can you turn the pages?" I asked.

Franco shook his head, not moving his unbound hands. "I tried." He tilted his head. "Our friend didn't seem to like that."

I looked up at Pasty, still watching us from his corner of the room.

"Who are you?" I asked. "How do you have these?"

He blinked at me. Looked around at the shelves of books. Sweet Alpha, was he a simpleton? Was that wash basin of his lined with softsteel?

"What the scud do you want from us?"

I hadn't meant to yell, but between Pasty's seemingly perpetual state of dumb surprise and my own frustrations at being powerlessly bound, it just happened. Pasty flinched, wide-eyed as if he'd never heard such barbarism. He hung his head, trembling slightly.

"I… I'm sorry," I was surprised to hear myself say. "I didn't mean to yell."

What in demon's depths was going on? Where were we? Where had Hawk Nose gone? And why the scud was I apologizing to the guy who was at least complicit in holding us prisoners?

He just looked so damn pathetic.

"What do you think he wants?" I asked Franco. "Why's he doing this?"

"Because you've clearly hurt his feelings, Demon," came a voice from somewhere behind.

I craned around and caught a glimpse of a slender build and dark, unkempt hair. Hawk Nose, returned from whatever the scud he'd been doing—unless he'd just been sitting there listening all along. When I looked back, Pasty had perked up at his partner's arrival. He wasn't exactly smiling, but it still made me think of a hound greeting its master after a day home alone.

"I believe he was referring more to the abduction and silent prison master act," Franco said, "to which I'd like to pose the same questions. Why did you attack us, and what do you want?"

"Only way to bring the Prospect in safely," Hawk Nose said, scooting around our table to stand in front of us.

"What does that mean?" I asked. "Am I the Prospect? Prospect for what?" I eyed the wand in his hand. "And what the scud is that thing?"

He glanced down at the device himself, frowning a little. "Thought you might've known."

What was it with these people? Even when they talked, they managed not to answer a single question. I was about to try again when Hawk Nose held out his wand for us to see more closely.

The device was less than a foot long and maybe an inch in diameter. It was made of a dull metal, and now that he held it out, I could see that its surface was covered in etchings inlaid with what might've been silver. Runes. They were intricate, and very well-ordered. More like the ones in the book than those on my cloaking pendant.

I looked between Hawk Nose and Pasty, trying to understand, to fit the pieces together. "Are you Emmútari?"

The question seemed to amuse Hawk Nose. Unsurprisingly, he didn't answer—just turned to his pale companion. "It's safe now. Let's get this over with."

Pasty gave an excited little clap and padded across the room toward us. He was barefoot, I realized, pasty white feet smacking the stone floor. He went to a nearby trunk, rustled around, and withdrew a battered old helmet straight from the ancient history lessons. Except not quite, I realized as I got a closer look. Because the helmets in the lessons hadn't been covered by intricate silver runes.

I got a funny feeling as Pasty padded forward, holding the helmet as if he intended to slip it onto my head.

"What are you doing?" I asked. "What is that?"

"Just relax a minute," Hawk Nose said, wand held at the ready but not quite pointing at us.

"If you'd simply talk to us, goodfellows," Franco said, "I'm sure we could come to understand what it is you—"

Hawk Nose held up a hand to silence him. "You'll get your answers if and when it's time." He waved at Pasty, who'd paused nervously, to continue. "We need to be sure first."

"Sure of what?" I growled, jerking my head away as Pasty held the helmet out. I couldn't move enough to fight. Couldn't feel a damn thing with my senses. Beside me, Franco was tensed, ready to spring at Pasty.

Across the table, Hawk Nose raised his wand at Franco. "Don't."

Franco was about to try anyway. I could see it in his eyes. I was just about to warn him off when Pasty surprised us both by darting forward and jamming the helmet over my head. I froze, scared to even breathe.

Nothing happened.

"Congratulations," I said, looking between our captors. "You got me. Now can one of you please tell us what the scud is going on?"

Pasty made a series of impatient gestures, tapping his head with both hands, then turning them out, palms up, as if to say *What are you thinking?*

I wanted to scream. What was wrong with these people?

Pasty tried again, this time placing both hands over his heart and spreading them to the open room before bringing them back to cup his head.

"You want me to… open up? To a helmet?"

Pasty nodded excitedly.

"No." I looked between Hawk Nose, who watched impassively, and Pasty, who looked suddenly crestfallen. "No. Why in demon's depths would I let you crazy bastards in my head?"

"Very well," Hawk Nose said. "We'll find another."

He raised his wand at Franco.

"Wait," I snapped. "Sweet Alpha, what's the matter with you two?"

Hawk Nose said nothing—only waited to see if I had more to add.

"What's this thing gonna do to me?"

"You will be measured," was all he said.

Helpful as always.

"Hal," Franco said, "you don't have to—"

"It's fine."

In truth, I hadn't the faintest clue what the scud it was. Certainly not fine. But hey, if I could fight my way out of a raknoth's telepathic prison, I should be able to handle an inanimate object, right? Hopefully. Besides, Alpha only knew what they'd do to us if I refused.

We'd come here for answers, hadn't we?

"Put that damn wand down," I said.

Then I lowered my mental defenses.

It happened quickly—a kind of slow, sweeping warmth scanning across my mind from one side to the other, like a sliver of sun sliding across the floor in accelerated time. There were bursts of emotion and pain. Flashes of memories of my parents and my days as a tyro in Sanctuary. Of Elise and Carlisle. Of the raknoth. Most came and went too quickly to process. Some lingered too long—the night Al'Kundesha had murdered my parents, the slaughter at the White Tower. I didn't like it. Didn't trust it. But at least there seemed to be no sign of impending torture or struggle.

Distantly, I was aware of Pasty hovering beside me, leaning in to inspect something on the helmet. Light of multiple colors flickered at the edge of my vision. Could he see what was happening? There was no inkling of another presence sharing in this experience, but he seemed awfully intrigued by the side of the helmet. I tried not to think about it, hoping it would be over soon. And it was.

Sooner than I'd expected, the device's odd warmth retreated from my mind, leaving me alone in my head once more. I drew my defenses back around me and shifted my focus back to the room, feeling vaguely ill.

Franco was watching me with a tense expression. Hawk Nose had ignored my command to lower his wand and was watching his partner expectantly. I turned to Pasty.

He recoiled a few steps, lower lip trembling, eyes wide, watching me like one would watch a snarling wolf.

"What?" I said. "What happened?"

Franco looked as confused as I felt.

"Is it him?" Hawk Nose asked.

Pasty shook his head frantically, refusing to meet my eyes.

Hawk Nose closed his eyes. Let out a deep breath. "Scud," he whispered.

Apparently I'd failed their test. But I'd also had enough. Far more than enough. They weren't going to answer our questions—I was pretty sure of that. Whether they were planning on letting us live was less clear. But I'd be damned if I was going to wait around to find out.

I caught Franco's eye. Tried to give him a signal.

He crumpled in his chair like his strings had been cut. It took me a second to realize what had happened. By the time I whirled on Hawk Nose, he was already shifting his wand in my direction.

"You bastard!" I cried.

Then the world went dark.

THIS TIME, I sprang up from the darkness with a gasp. Franco was hovering over me, occupied with his palmlight. Some of the tension bled out of his face when I stirred.

"Good. I was starting to worry. Come on."

I sat up too quickly with Franco's assistance and tried to look around past the spinning in my head. "Where is that Hawk Nosed bastard?"

"Gone, I think. Thought I caught a glimpse of him running off when I came to. We need to move."

"Why?"

The world steadied around me. We were tucked away in a stone alcove on the edge of a quiet garden square. There was no one in sight, which seemed kind of strange, but—

In the distance, an alarm keened a long, mournful note.

"That's why," Franco said. "I'm calling Dillard."

I checked my palmlight. Dozens of messages and missed calls. And no wonder. It had been a couple hours since we'd first confronted Hawk Nose by the Byahnan River. Hound Company was probably tearing this city apart looking for us.

But that alarm…

I was reaching to return Johnny's last call when Ordo Dillard's voice crackled from Franco's palmlight.

"Fields! Where the scud are you two?"

"We're safe, relatively speaking," Franco said. "The contact surprised us. Took us somewhere. We're back on our own, now."

"Good, then you two need to—"

A transport roared by overhead, flying far too fast and low to be Legion. I craned my neck out of our alcove and saw others descending on the city. A shrill scream carried to us from across the garden, followed by an inhuman roar.

"Do you confirm?" Dillard's voice crackled.

I scrambled woozily to my feet and watched in horror as, a few blocks down, the speeding transport slowed to a hover and began disgorging ravenous hybrids into the streets.

"Repeat," came Dillard's voice, "Humility is under attack."

17

INCURSION

Maybe it was the civilian clothes I wore over my armor skin, making me feel the part. Maybe it was a residual effect of how powerless I'd felt being handled by Pasty and Hawk Nose in that Alpha-cursed dungeon. Whatever it was, in those first moments seeing the hybrids descend on Humility, I felt just as terrified as every other screaming civilian.

"Call your skimmer and get your asses the scud out of here!" Dillard was snapping through Franco's palmlight. "That's an order."

Franco was busy doing just that, tensely swiping commands into his palmlight. I could only stare in dumb shock as, three streets down and about a hundred yards away, feral hybrids crashed into their first kills of the day. Only they didn't kill them. They grabbed them up and dragged them off, kicking and screaming.

It was happening again.

"Hal," Franco was calling. "Get back here. The skimmer's on the way. Hal!"

But I was stuck—frozen by the dull wringing in my head, unwilling to watch the horrors unfolding, but unable to look away. More hybrid transports coming down now. More civilians running, screaming, carried away. More dying. The crack of gunfire as Humility's meager local forces stepped into action.

Dillard barking at me through Franco's palmlight, pinging me on my own.

"Stay where you are, Raish," he called. "I repeat, do *not* engage. You are to return directly to Haven and—"

In the chaos ahead, I saw a hybrid turn from the screaming woman it was carrying to tear out the throat of the man who was pounding on its back, trying to stop it. Everything condensed to that point, my heart hammering in my ears like detonating thumpers. I was only distantly aware of Franco and Dillard's voices in the background. Somewhere, multiple hybrids roared.

Then a man and woman stumbled into the garden square at a disoriented run, and I was moving before I knew it, tearing across the garden as their sickly green pursuit came howling after them. I tore through a line of shrubs and vaulted the parapet, not stopping to think.

The hybrid caught my presence just in time to catch my fist—and a considerable hunk of panic-fueled telekinesis right along with it. The creature hit the adjacent building with a wet cracking sound and dropped limply to the ground along with a few falling bits of stone debris.

My abilities were working again, then. That was good to know.

The two civilians turned wide eyes to me, and I realized the man was cradling a baby.

"Go," I said. "Straight out of town. Go!"

They backed away, looking as shocked as I'd felt a moment ago, and finally turned to run.

"Hal," Franco called, jogging up behind me, "they're ordering us out of here. I know what you're thinking, but—"

"These people need help, Franco." I spotted a loose building stone next to the fallen hybrid and called it to my hand with telekinesis. Holding an image in my mind, willing it to be so, I started channeling. My head buzzed, the air cooled, and the stone shifted to form a simple spike in my hand.

I looked back to Franco. "You should go."

He searched my face, came to some decision, and went to grab himself a stone.

Crude weapons in hand, we charged down the uneven stone street toward the sounds of fighting. It didn't take us long to find it. The first hybrids I'd seen were still there in the square a few streets over, some just beginning to spread out to the north and south, several others rounding up —or feeding on—the few civilians who hadn't yet made it out.

The hybrid at the eastern entrance of the square whipped around just in time to take my telekinetic spike to the eye. It dropped with a keening growl. I was already yanking my spike free, darting into the square. Almost as one, five hybrids turned from their mayhem and bellowed a horrible challenge. I was about to hurl my spike at the leftmost when another choir of roars sounded to the south. Another to north. And again, further out, spreading through the city like the cries of some demonic wolf pack.

That couldn't be good. But I didn't have time to worry about it as the hybrids charged. I dropped two with my telekinetically propelled spike before they closed. The other three, I blasted backward to buy time to reset. Or tried to. The rightmost hybrid, either sensing an attack or looking to surprise me, launched itself into the air just before my blast hit.

Which left me with a healthy hit of channeling fatigue and a bloodthirsty hybrid plummeting for my head.

Stupid. I'd been stupid. That was all I had time to think before the beast crashed into me. Reflexes kicked in, and I at least managed to hit the ground with an intact throat. The impact drove the air from my lungs. I struggled with the hybrid, my hands clamped to its wrists, trying to focus enough to hurl the thing off me.

Franco stepped in and buried his stone spike in the hybrid's head before I could.

It jerked and crumpled on top of me. I was opening my mouth to thank Franco when my senses buzzed a warning. I telekinetically ripped Franco's spike from the fallen hybrid. Franco gave a yelp of surprise as he caught sight of the other hybrid charging toward us. I couldn't see where I was aiming, but I didn't need to. My senses guided me, and the fourth hybrid died. I rolled the other dead hybrid off me in time to see the fifth and final beast tilting its head back to roar.

Half its head disappeared in a cloud of red mist before the first breath left its mouth.

"What?" Franco said.

I waved westward as I climbed to my feet. "I think we have a guardian sniper."

I glanced at my buzzing palmlight, expecting a private message or call from Dillard—likely of the furious variety—but it wasn't. He was pushing me to Hound Company's channel. I slipped in my earpiece and accepted.

"What the scud are you doing down there, Raish?" came Mara's frosty voice.

"Was just singing your praises," I grumbled, retrieving our spikes. "Thanks for the cover."

"Cut the chatter," Dillard snapped. Then, in a private channel, he added in a hard voice, "I *told* you to get to the damn skimmer, Raish."

"I'm sorry, sir, but I can't leave these people behind," I said, already moving toward the cluster of people the hybrids had been moving in on when we'd reached the square. They were dressed in worship attire, and staring around the carnage of the square with wild eyes.

"I don't like it either, Raish," Dillard said in my earpiece as Franco stepped in to tell the good people to run for their lives. "But I have my orders. And you do too."

"You have orders to protect us," I said, watching the worship-goers turn and heed Franco's advice. "Not to turn tail from a hybrid attack."

"We're coming to collect you," he said. I almost wondered if he'd even heard me until I noticed he'd added Franco to the channel. Just ignoring my protests outright, then.

"Hybrid forces are estimated at four hundred," he added, "and look to be driving half the city toward the great worship hall."

"Probably because they're planning to abduct them like before," I growled.

"We'll rally here," Dillard continued as if I hadn't spoken, dropping a nav pin several blocks to the west of our position.

"We can help them, Ordo," I said. "We can—"

"Get to the rally point, Raish. Both of you. We'll reevaluate from there."

With that, Dillard cut our private connection.

At least he hadn't told me to stay put this time. And he hadn't said an outright no to helping once we'd met up, either. Of course, he might've just been trying to get my stubborn ass to play along, but I wasn't so sure. Dillard seemed like a good man.

And these people needed them right now.

Either way, thinking about it wasn't doing anyone any favors, so once Franco and I had seen the square safely cleared, we set off for the western exit.

Tendrils of dark smoke were rising in the distance off to the left as we hurried on. I tried not to dwell on the bloody bodies we passed—those brave spirits who'd fought and lost—but I ended up looking at every single one anyway, each another cold punch in the gut. No one in their right mind would have considered Humility a military target. No tactical value in the position. No significant resources. Just innocent, Alpha-fearing citizens. But that was the point, wasn't it?

They were the resources.

How many more had already been dragged off in transports, or driven toward the great worship hall to be collected there? I didn't want to think about it, and I had no idea how we could even hope to stop the hybrids. Between Humility's entire Legion garrison, their enforcers, and Hound Company, our forces probably only barely matched their numbers in total —and Alpha only knew how many of Humility's precious few gun hands were still fumbling to gear up and hit the front lines. Add in that we were fighting in the middle of a populated city against inhumanly strong predators, and that put us at a strong disadvantage. No question. They'd wreak their havoc, grab a few hundred new screaming recruits, and be gone by the time major reinforcements could arrive.

These thoughts circled through my head with increasing desperation as Franco and I pushed on, passing a few small packs of civilians, killing three hybrids that were hounding after a family of four. We were approaching an intersection with one of the major streets when I felt something quite large thundering our way. I held up a hand to slow Franco, gripped my spike tight, rounded the corner—

And nearly ran headlong into Johnny, who's cloaked mind I'd missed completely.

Behind his helmet's transparent faceplate, Johnny's face went from startled to relieved to confused all in the space of a second. Then he threw me into a quick, back-thumping hug. "Dammit, broto. What did we learn?"

Between our near-collision, the chaos screaming around us, and the remaining disorientation from the mess of our run-in with Pasty and Hawk Nose, I was speechless.

Johnny disengaged and fixed me with a serious look. "Never trust a man who uses paper. That's what we learned today."

"That," Edwards called, plodding up behind him, "and never visit Humility on Alphasday."

That explained the giant *something* I'd felt approaching. Edwards and Johnny had traded in their civilian disguises for their proper gear—probably around the same time Franco and I had gone missing and spoiled all the clandestine undercover fun—and were both armed to the teeth.

A scream in the distance shattered our moment of relief.

"Come on," Edwards said, handing Franco his sidearm. "Let's get to the rally point."

Johnny slipped me his sidearm, and we set off into the chaos. Mostly, we encountered fleeing civilians over the next couple blocks. We shot a pair of hybrids that were corralling a mother and her two boys, and waved the rest on, urging them to the outskirts. A Hound fireteam fell in with us at the next intersection. Then another at the next. Judging by the sounds of fighting, most of the action was centering in on the great worship hall a few blocks ahead. A quick update from Dillard confirmed as much.

When we reached the square that was our rally point, I clicked my cloak off and cast my senses out to sweep ahead—too far to pick up many fine details, but the picture was clear enough. People—too many to count—gathered in a dense cluster ahead, their minds burning with crazed fear. Several more minds with the unmistakably alien feel of hybrids neatly corralling them in tighter, tighter. Too tight. Too neat.

Either the hybrids could operate more autonomously beyond their feral instincts than I'd imagined, or someone was controlling them. One of the missing Seekers, maybe? Or had one of the raknoth come to Humility?

Chatter from the group drew my attention back to the small square. I dialed my cloak back in to combat range. Dillard was coming, along with the rest of First Squad.

I was opening my mouth to call out what I'd felt when a nearby gunshot jolted me to silence. In the blink of an eye, half a dozen rifles were aimed in the direction of the sound. But I was still staring at Dillard's party, where the legionnaire next to him had fallen to the pavement, clutching at his throat.

He'd been shot.

Another gunshot barked somewhere else. Another soldier fell.

"Cover!" Dillard yelled.

My mind was whirling—my heart hammering, eyes scanning for the shooters. The hybrids weren't tacticians. They didn't ambush. Didn't even use guns.

Another shot from above.

Johnny drove into me, pushing us toward the cover of a stone fountain. First Squad was firing back now, their slugs ripping through the parapets above at the hunkered down forms of our deadly shooters.

I started to reach out, thinking to end them quickly.

Then the hybrids came.

1 8

LIMITS

Glass shattered. Hybrids roared. Legion rifles replied in kind.

In the space of a breath, the quaint town square morphed from quiet rally point to full on war zone, dozens of hybrids pouring out through doors, windows, and—in a few cases—the walls of surrounding buildings, charging with bloodthirsty howls.

Johnny's rifle barked to my right, Edwards' heavy rifle thumping to my left. Behind, Ordo Dillard was barking orders I only barely registered in my earpiece. The thought of Dillard tingled some internal alarm, and I whipped around right as a hybrid launched from a rooftop straight for him. I hurled my mind out to catch it and only partially succeeded in time. The hybrid wobbled into an ungainly spin, slowing just enough for Dillard to backpedal clear. He put a healthy number of slugs into the beast before it had even hit the stone, then went straight back to shouting orders.

"Hal!" Johnny was grabbing me by the arm, yanking me back toward the fountain.

I turned and glimpsed something that made me freeze.

It was a hybrid—I was almost certain—but its hide was a far darker green than those of its kin, its mouth more elongated in a fanged snout. It perched on a nearby rooftop, watching me with eyes that glowed soft crimson, almost like those of a true raknoth. And it was pointing a rifle straight at me.

I threw my hands out, focusing my will. In the chaos of the battle, I didn't hear the hybrid's rifle specifically, but I saw the muzzle flash. Felt something slam into me. Not slugs, I realized, but Johnny, throwing himself in front of me.

My focus teetered dangerously with the impact, as did my balance, but I held on. Johnny jerked in front of me. My insides wrenched with dread. Then I saw the three slugs floating a few inches from his throat and faceplate.

For a moment, it felt as if everything had frozen around us. Then I let the slugs fall to the stone, and Johnny exploded into a stream of inventive curses, raising his rifle. Above, the hybrid shooter's chest erupted red mist before Johnny could draw a line. Mara's long-range work, I had a feeling. The creature hit the rooftop, and I didn't resist as Johnny pulled me back to cover.

The hybrids looked to be retreating from the square now—a few leaping from rooftop to rooftop, one carrying a rifle like our late shooter's, and another dozen or so darting off down alleyways or crashing through windows into the surrounding buildings. Just like that, silence descended on the square, thick with the scent of gun smoke, all the heavier for the thunderous chaos that had preceded it. It stretched for a few breaths, unmarred, then sound resumed.

The clicks and clacks of empty slug feeders ejecting and fresh ones slapping home. The groans of the wounded. The low chatter of legionnaires checking on their squadmates, asking one another what the scud was that, and since when did those things learn to use proper weapons.

I was more than a little curious myself. Curious, and horrified.

"Double tap the fallen," Dillard's voice crackled over the squad channel, admirably level, if a bit short of breath. "Every hybrid gets a slug in the brain, people."

"And speaking of slugs and brains," Johnny murmured beside me as First Squad swept out to see it done, "you can catch gropping gunfire?" His eyes were still a bit wide.

"All two times I've tried, at least," I said quietly, trying to brush it off before the legionnaires who weren't busy pumping slugs into fallen hybrids could stare any harder.

A couple seemed to be questioning if they'd truly seen what they thought they had. The rest looked at me like they were wondering why the scud the Demon of Divinity hadn't seen fit to save the first two men who'd fallen to the shooters. And why hadn't I, dammit? I should've been ready—should've felt the shooters coming.

"That's… good to know," Johnny was murmuring, shaking his head. "Guess I owe you one."

It was my turn to stare. "Johnny, after what you just did, you don't owe me—"

"You would've done the same," he said, waving the comment away as he looked across the square. "At least someone cored that bastard before… Huh."

I followed his gaze up to our shooter's perch.

The hybrid was gone. Only a spatter of dark blood and a heavy collection of debris and slug holes remained. We traded a look, both wondering if it was possible that hybrid had walked away from a high powered slug to the chest. Dillard's call for attention broke our silent reverie.

Seven of our squad were down in total, three of them fatally. It wasn't much comfort that we'd made them pay with twice as many hybrids. Especially not when one of the fallen creatures who'd apparently avoided the double tap sweep snapped up to grab another Hound. I reached out too late to stop the beast from tearing into the legionnaire's thigh. We all scrambled to help, but Franco was closest. He shoved his borrowed handgun to the hybrid's head and pulled the trigger.

Crack.

A fleck of dark blood spattered Franco's cheek. He didn't seem to notice, reaching absentmindedly down to help the fallen legionnaire. He looked to be in shock—which, given the carnage he'd just witnessed, was completely understandable. He hadn't been there at the White Tower. Not inside, at least. He'd been busy helping coordinate the civilian evacuation, which meant he hadn't had to see the rivers of blood on dark stone, and the silent screams frozen on the faces of the hundreds we'd failed.

The hundreds I'd failed…

"Lock it down, First Squad," Dillard barked beside me, nearly making me jump. "Wounded evac in sixty seconds, then we've got a date with Second Squad. Ordo Carter's betting a round of ale they cut through this scudstorm to the great worship hall before we do."

That raised a round of shouts and chest thumps. Edwards stomped a dead hybrid's head in with the heel of a massive boot. The legionnaires all played in, psyching each other up, trying to pretend like a third of the squad wasn't already down for the fight.

"Any idea what the scud that was?" Dillard said beside me, too quiet for anyone else to hear.

I didn't have to ask what he meant. The ambush. The coordination. The red-eyed hybrid with its rifle, and the way its appearance was shifted from its brethren, more like a full raknoth.

I thought back to the hybrid that had reacted to my telepathic touch at the labs. "Maybe… maybe the older ones are developing new skills as they mature. Maybe. I don't know. I think the ones with the rifles might've even organized that ambush." When Dillard didn't react, I added, "With telepathy. None of the hybrids I've seen could do that."

He frowned. "And what does that mean, exactly?"

I was still thinking about the strange hybrid at Vantage. Was it my imagination now, or had its mind actually felt like more of a *he* than an *it?*

The thought chilled me. "I'm not sure yet. I didn't think what happened at Oasis could happen without the raknoth present, but now I've got a bad feeling these older hybrids might be growing into their parents' abilities."

That finally got a flicker of horror from Dillard. As quickly as it came, he buried it, looking around at his assembled legionnaires. The transport was arriving now, descending to collect our wounded. Dillard took a moment to call out a few commands before turning back to me. "Get Fields and make sure our people get to safety."

I tried to keep the tension from my face. "You need me out here, sir."

It was a mistake. I could see it in the immediate flash of derision in his eyes. I pushed on.

"Someone's controlling these hybrids, Ordo. A strong telepath. Maybe even a raknoth. Let me help you stop them."

His eyes flicked to my pendant. To me. To the transport.

"Let me keep their minds safe," I said quietly. "Please."

That did it. I could see it in his eyes. He grimaced, muttering a curse to himself, then skewered me with a firm glare. "You'll stick with the squad."

"Yes, sir."

"You'll do as you're told." His glare somehow intensified. "To the letter, Citizen."

I nodded.

"Even if you're told to retreat."

"Of course, sir," I said a bit too quickly, trying to keep the reservation from my face.

He chewed on that, staring me down all the while.

"Somebody get Raish a gropping helmet," he finally called over his shoulder. Then, to me, he added. "Get Fields on that transport before he collapses. You're with Edwards and Wingard."

I resisted the urge to salute, figuring it might only agitate him further. "Thank you, sir."

"Just don't die on my watch, Raish," he growled. He stomped off, clearly still plenty agitated as he cried, "Lock it down, Hounds! We've got hybrids to kill."

THE GREAT WORSHIP hall lay only a few more blocks ahead. The sounds of fighting throughout the city, I couldn't help but notice, seemed to have diminished during the stint of our ambush in the square. Had the rest of Humility's defenders fallen prey to similar traps? Was it possible the hybrids had coordinated that well across multiple engagements?

I wanted to think the unsettling quiet was just a product of my confounded helmet muting my sense of hearing with its clunky bulk. But it wasn't. I knew damn well the helmets actually amplified hearing to an extent. Which in turn reminded me that I should be able to ping any friendly Legion forces in the vicinity on my display.

Apparently I'd been an apostate terrorist a little too long. I was getting rusty.

A few gestures and spoken commands later, the news wasn't good. Only eighty-four enforcers and legionnaires in total converging on the great worship hall—some skirting toward the western side where the bridges were more plentiful and less exposed than the Penitent Path, some sweeping around our way to where the hall's courtyard was accessible by land.

Eighty-four.

Where were the rest? Had so many fallen?

I dropped the display overlay. There were no signals to ping, but I didn't need them to know there were still at least a couple hundred hybrids ahead. We could hear them now—a low, steady choir of growls and guttural grunts, punctuated here and there by a scream or a roar. First Squad prowled forward, telling the few civilians we spotted to clear out and wait for the reinforcements that were on the way.

At the last intersection, a lone, slender civilian rounded the corner at a dead sprint, wild panic in his eyes, and crashed straight into Edwards' hulking form.

"They're taking them!" he cried. "They're taking them all!"

"You're okay," Edwards said. "Try to take a breath."

"We thought the worship hall would be safe," the guy continued as if he hadn't noticed Edwards at all. "But those things… They kicked down the doors, started grabbing people. I ran." His frantic eyes widened in realization. "I left them. Alpha help me, I left them all to die."

"Well, don't stop now," Edwards said, pushing the shocked man on his way. "Keep running. We'll take care of it."

The guy's gaze flicked confusedly from Edwards to the rest of the squad, then he took off without another word.

We set off again, trading uneasy looks at the growing sounds of hybrids and wailing captives ahead. Behind me, Dillard was speaking to someone in a steady stream—coordinating by the sound of it. As we drew up to the mouth where the street emptied into the wide open courtyard of the great worship hall, he sent one fireteam inside to take up supporting positions and bade the rest of us take cover and wait for our allies around the courtyard to get in position.

Angling myself to peer through the windows of two perpendicular walls of the adjacent building, I caught a small sliver view of the courtyard beyond. I saw hybrids. So many of them. And even more civilians, cowering in tight huddles. Parents clutching children to their breasts. Others on their knees, pleading in futility with their reptilian captors. Several of the hybrid's transports were waiting near the crowd, and—

"Oh, son of a beardsplitter," Johnny muttered beside me, confirming he heard what I'd just picked up on.

The low thrum vibrated oddly in my gut, drawing closer, growing like a deep hum in the chest of a giant.

"Bastards are bringing in a carrier," someone growled.

Curses all around, including my own. I'd been hoping my gut had been mistaken. One carrier could easily fit an entire legion—over five-hundred men and women. Between that and the twenty or so transports the hybrids had ridden in, they were going to have the space to abduct that entire courtyard.

"We can't let them load that thing," I muttered, edging closer to the corner of the building with Johnny.

Edwards, apparently feeling the same urgency, was leaning to poke out and take a look.

"Hold," Dillard said, somehow having appeared right beside us without a sound. "Mara says we've got shooters on the worship hall, tucked outside her line of fire."

As if in reply, gunshots cracked in the courtyard, and a spray of dirt kicked onto Edwards' boots.

"We've got companies arriving on our north and south in a minute," Dillard said. "As soon as they're in position, we move."

"I can cover us," I told Dillard quietly. "If we push out now, I can block their fire and we might be able to—"

He cut me off with a sharp look that lasted until the sound of gunshots across the courtyard drew all our attention. It was coming from the directions of the Path and the other side of worship hall, where Second Squad had been approaching from—sporadic at first, then picking up, more insistent. Our allies moving in.

"On the ready, Hounds," Dillard said, turning away from me to walk the line. "When we move, stick to the perimeter, make them come to..."

I stopped listening.

He wasn't going to trust my abilities. Not when it might mean his people's lives. But that carrier was a game-changer. We didn't have time to slink around out here, trying to pry the hybrids from their neatly corralled prizes before it landed and carted away Alpha knew how many new recruits for the raknoth horde.

So I gathered my focus, pulled a barrier into place, and stepped into the courtyard before anyone could stop me.

I caught sight of them just as they opened fire—four tiny pairs of crimson dots already sighted along their rifles, waiting. Slugs slammed into my barrier—a few at first, then several more when I didn't fall dead. They weren't particularly skilled shots, but I felt the cost of stopping each one all the same, each slug a jolt of electricity through my chest.

Catching on that something was amiss, one of the shooters lowered his rifle and bellowed a throaty battle roar. It was quickly taken up through the courtyard, too many pale red eyes turning to fix on me. I wanted to turn and run.

But the sight of the enormous carrier descending from the west reminded me I couldn't.

I turned back to my allies, who were gaping at me in open shock.

"Let's go!" I called.

Johnny took a step forward. Traded a glance with Edwards. Everyone else looked to Dillard. I met the ordo's gaze, acutely aware of each slug pinging off my invisible barrier. For a second, I thought he might shoot me himself. But then he shifted his weapon to one hand and waved the other forward.

"Move in, Hounds! Spearhead on Raish. Go!"

First Squad stowed the incredulous looks and launched into action with grim resolve. Hybrids were charging now. Dozens of them. I prayed to Alpha those other companies were close and pushed forward, trying to keep myself between First Squad and the shooters, shifting the coverage of my barrier as best I could to maximize our protection and minimize the chances I might accidentally block friendly slugs on the way out.

It half worked, at least.

First Squad opened fire on my flank, several of them cutting down charging hybrids. And a few, unfortunately, smacking me right in the mind with slugs that caught the edges of my barrier.

Confused curses from behind. My barrier faltered as I tried to adapt. I'm not sure it mattered much anyway.

Focused as I'd been, I hadn't noticed the hybrids on the worship hall had stopped shooting until a rough hand caught my shoulder and Dillard shouted in my ear. "We've got friendly fire across the way. Tell me how to shut it down."

I looked around, focus fully broken now.

Hybrids charging. Dying. Closing on us. Humility's legionnaires were arriving to the courtyard now, those at our backs hurrying to our aid. Those to the right, closer to the hybrids, were engaged in a disorderly tangle, half their people wrestling one another for control of weapons that had gone indiscriminately lethal. Judging by the screams and the spike in gunfire from the direction of the Penitent Path, the situation must've been similar there.

And ahead, our hybrid shooters had disappeared behind the parapets of the worship hall. Taking cover while they orchestrated a telepathic attack?

The carrier was groaning down behind the worship hall now, its drives whipping the air into a wild frenzy even at this distance.

We had to stop them. Had to—

"Raish!" Dillard snapped. "How do we—"

I yanked my pendant off and shoved it to his chest.

"Hey, whatever you're—"

But I was already running. "Keep them off my back!" I cried, half-expecting him to try to tackle me down. Maybe he did. I wouldn't have known. I ran for the worship hall faster than I'd ever run before, Dillard and Johnny crying after me from behind. Hybrids roaring for my blood. Slugs whistling through the air around me. And through it all, the desperate screams of the civilians, wailing for aid, several making a break for it only to be smacked back down by the hybrids still guarding them.

I kept running, pulling energy from the cells in my pockets, preparing myself. Something slammed into my shoulder. It must've been a slug from above. I kept running.

Then I focused my energy and jumped.

I'd once watched Carlisle nimbly scale a thirty foot wall in a single leap. That memory was the only reason I even believed such a feat possible—and almost certainly the only reason my half-cocked plan worked.

It just wasn't nimble.

I slammed into the stone wall of the worship hall's first tier hard enough that bones might've broken if not for my armor skin. I wasn't really sure they hadn't. Especially not as I crashed down to the slate of the steeple I'd been aiming for. But I managed to catch onto a handhold anyway before I slid off to the twenty foot fall below.

Above, one of my hybrid prey roared from the second parapet, and it was only then that two thoughts occurred to me. First, that I could've effectively cut these four apparent telepathic threats off from the rest of the battle if I'd brought my cloaking pendant instead of giving it to Dillard.

And secondly, that I'd just thrown myself straight at four telepaths without a cloak.

I had all of a second to relish in my own brash stupidity before four minds crashed into mine. I slumped to the slate, physical senses falling to distant background as I poured everything I had into my mental defenses. The four minds pressed in, crushing down on me until I was sure I'd suffocate.

"It fights," hissed a cold, awful voice.

What the holy scud?

"Not long," said another.

I was speechless. I wanted to scream. All I could do was hold on, and that only barely. They weren't tremendously strong, but there were four of them, prying at all sides, clawing and ripping. I couldn't hold on. They were going to pull my walls down and—

Somewhere far away, the world shook with an explosion.

"Leave now," growled a third voice. *"Bring manstock. Eat the Raishman next ti—"*

All at once, their minds vanished. I went from crushed to floating free in the space of a blink. I drew back to my physical senses, tightening my defenses behind me, and found Johnny below, shouting up at me. He had my pendant in his hand, and First Squad wasn't far behind. My pendant. Reaching out, I confirmed it: he'd cut me off from the hybrids, whether he'd meant to or not.

He'd saved me.

"You good up there, flyboy?" his voice crackled in my earpiece.

I tried to wipe sweat from my forehead but only smacked my translucent faceplate. I looked around, panting. "I think so."

"Whatever you did worked," he added. "Second Squad recovered and fragged the carrier's engines. Half the one-oh-seventh legion is about to drop in."

Worked? All I'd done was jumped up there and nearly gotten broken by four hybrids. But now transports were lifting off from the rear of the worship hall, packed to the seams with retreating hybrids. Our forces were focusing fire on the craft. Several wavered. A few went down. Below, the civilians were scattering in a maddened frenzy, running for their lives as their would-be captors fled the scene. And there, in the distance—a whole fleet of transports approaching from the south. Half the companies of the 107th legion, apparently, coming to squash this incursion and restore order.

"Get your ass down here," Johnny was saying in my earpiece, "and help us... ah, scud."

Looking back to where my telepathic opponents' perch, I saw the problem. Or at least one of them. The four dark hybrids were vaulting the parapet straight into the transport hovering on the other side. The transport that was clearly packed with hybrids *and* civilians.

The last hybrid leapt from the worship hall into the ship and reappeared at the open side hatch a moment later, hauling a man and a woman by the backs of their tunics as if they were children's playthings. He dangled them over the edge for all to see as the ship began rotating around to the east. Human shields to protect their escape. The crafty bastard.

I hauled myself to my feet on the pinnacle of my little steeple, my gut plotting a course that my brain balked at. But if I could get close enough...

"Hey," Johnny's voice crackled in my ear. "What are you—"

I gathered the energy and jumped for the next steeple, twenty feet over. Adjusted my course with telekinesis, thudded to the slate, and jumped again. Johnny was yelling something in my ear, but I was too engrossed in not falling. Not missing. Another jump. Almost there. One more jump. The ship was beginning to pull away.

Close enough.

I thudded to the next steeple and threw my senses out, reaching for the transport's engines. But my approach hadn't gone unnoticed.

Ahead, the dark hybrid was watching me with cruel fiery eyes.

"Human catch," it called in a raspy, guttural voice.

Then it hurled one of its human shields from the transport like an over-sized smashball.

I threw my mind out for the screaming man plummeting to the ground. As far as he was, my efficiency was shot, and I felt it—brain buzzing, dark spots in my vision. But the guy touched down safely. Catching the woman that followed left my head spinning. And that's when I realized that was exactly what the hybrid wanted.

The transport was pulling away from the worship hall, the dark hybrid reaching back to pluck out his second set of human shields.

Below, the Legion forces were too busy sweeping up what hybrids remained in the courtyard to do anything, and the few who spotted the transport held their fire at the sight of the dangling civilians.

I couldn't let them escape. Couldn't leave those poor people for hybrid food, or worse.

So I gathered my energy and leapt from the steeple before I had time to think about it.

The bolstered jump took me farther than expected. I had several seconds to take in the wide-eyed legionnaires and civilians gaping up at me before the ground came rushing to meet me. I slowed myself just enough to fall into a roll and come up running. Not fast enough.

Ahead, the transport was easily pulling away.

A jolt of panic shot through me, burning off the haze of exhaustion.

"Hal!" Johnny barked in my earpiece.

I pushed harder, ignoring his voice, sprinting as fast as I could. Faster. Refusing to acknowledge that a man could not outrun a transport. Opening my body to the energy around me. Bending it to my stubborn will. Forcing my body to go faster, to be more.

Cool electricity crackled through me like I'd never felt before. I ran faster. Faster than I'd ever imagined, the soft ground flying beneath my feet at an alarming rate. I was moving too fast—sure each step would my last— but I clenched my teeth and pushed on.

It wasn't enough.

The transport continued to pull steadily—almost lazily—ahead, cutting low over the buildings at the eastern edge of the courtyard.

I was losing. Failing. Again. I saw the civilians kicking for life. Saw my mom's bloody corpse. Carlisle. The White Tower. I screamed, tearing after the retreating transport, and threw everything I had into one last jump.

Even enraged as I was, it was terrifying.

The ground fell away far too fast, my vision swirling with darkness in the wake of the channeling fatigue. Swirling right up until some rational corner of my brain astutely raised the question of how the scud I planned to land on the rapidly approaching rooftop.

Roughly. That was how.

I don't know exactly how fast I was moving when I slammed down to the rooftop, but it was too fast for my exhausted body and mind to control. My legs buckled. I did my best to roll, not that I had much choice in the matter.

When I found my feet again—body oddly burning, stomach threatening to void its contents—the transport was waiting for me fifty or so yards ahead, swiveled around so that its open side faced me. Several sets of red eyes watched me. The one with the darkest hide, their apparent leader, had handed one of his human shields off to another hybrid. He raised his free fist to his chest in mock salute.

He wanted me to watch. The sick bastard wanted me to see my failure.

He barked a command, and together, the hybrids pitched their last four hostages out of the transport.

My hands shot out reflexively, as if they could somehow quicken the projection of my will.

Too far. No time.

I tried anyway, casting my will like an enormous net, freely channeling the energy to make it so. I closed my eyes, focusing. I couldn't watch. My vision was swimming too much anyway.

The first two hit like a pair of hefty boulders dropping on my back. The next were like speeding slugs punching through soft tissue.

Something jammed into my knees. The ground. I tried to hold on.

Were they slowing?

I couldn't think—couldn't even feel them now.

The world crashed violently down all around me.

I'd fallen.

I'd failed.

1 9

———————

BREAK

The night was dark and moonless, and windy this high up.

This high up?

Alton Parker faced me from the high ground of the slanted duraglass rooftop, his dark hybrid pet at his side, its eyes burning with the same cruel red intelligence as Parker's.

We were atop the White Tower, I realized.

I looked down, and my world lurched. They were all there. My parents. Carlisle. Johnny. Elise. Hundreds more—the Great Hall piled nearly to the brim. A mountain of the dead. Of my dead. My failures.

Movement ahead. Alton and his new pet lunging for me. My legs were too sluggish, my arms too clumsy. I moved as if I were underwater. They fell on me without mercy, batting me back and forth like a smashball, speaking in casual tones of the rebirth of their people and the hilarity of human weakness. They beat me methodically, until I was senseless—until, finally, Alton Parker grew bored.

He gave a disinterested wave in my direction, and his hybrid yanked me off the ground, studied me with scornful red eyes, and hurled me from the tower.

The fall was too long, every wind-whipping foot of it tinged with some horrible familiarity, like the embrace of a long-dead loved one in the night. I plummeted for the streets, reaching for my power. But I couldn't.

Again I reached, and again it failed me, slipping through my fingers like falling water. Something was missing. A part of me, real as any limb or organ.

Again I tried. Again. The hard ground rushed closer. I screamed in despair. The sound caught in my throat at the sight of two faces below, looking up, calmly watching me plummet toward them. Johnny and Elise. They weren't dead. Weren't...

"Help," I said. Then, louder, "Help! Please!"

The fall stretched on, impossibly long. For too long, they studied me, their expressions cold, detached. Then they turned to one other, disregarding me. The ground rushed up to meet me.

"No!" I yelled. "No! Please!"

Impact.

Blinding, thunderous impact, tearing through every fiber of my body—so hard it seemed a small miracle I didn't simply explode into a pool of blood and mashed biomass. The pain was oddly disembodied, not so much the crushing sensation I expected but more a deep, inescapable certainty that it was there, overwhelming and terrible, and that I was actually, in fact, dead.

Except I could still hear them talking.

"It's nothing he can't sleep off," Johnny said. He sounded doubtful. Which made sense, seeing as I was clearly dead.

"Look at this," someone else hissed. Elise. She was staring down at me. "Tell me this is okay, Johnny. Go on."

They watched my smashed body in silence, their faces oddly blank.

"I've never seen him move like that, Lise. It was like something out of a storyvid."

Was he talking about me? That didn't seem right. I'd just been beaten senseless—disintegrated into the pavement like a powerless idiot.

"Most of the squad was too scared to go pull him off that rooftop," Johnny continued.

That didn't make any sense. Except...

"I don't give a crap if the squad is scared of a rodent's shadow," Elise snapped. "I just..." There was a long, heavy sigh. "I can't..."

"Why don't you get some fresh air? I'll stay here, message you when he wakes up."

"I'm not leaving," she said. Then, almost to herself, "Not until he wakes up, at least."

Wakes up. Why would they expect that? Didn't they see me here, broken and dying? They had to. Unless...

Unless—

I GASPED AWAKE, eyes snapping open to a world of bright light and even brighter pain.

"Talk about timing," Johnny muttered to my left.

We were in the medica. Something warm planted itself against my right cheek. A hand. Elise's. I recognized it by feel and scent even before her face appeared over mine.

She looked terrible.

The tired worry, I'd expected. It was nothing I hadn't seen before, and completely understandable. But this was something more—a kind of deadness in her eyes that chilled my insides.

"I'm losing count of the times we've done this," she muttered, more to herself than me.

She withdrew her hand and straightened, glancing at something in the corner. The door, I realized with a sickened feeling.

What had I done?

I tried to reach for her, to say her name. Between the pain, the disorientation, and the driest mouth I'd ever had, it mostly came out as a weak fumble and a pitiful groan.

"I think that's hybrid for *I'm sorry,*" Johnny said, scooting past the foot of my bed and over to the spot opposite Elise.

"Not... funny," I groaned.

The reminder of those fluent hybrids sent a fresh wave of nausea-tinged horror through me.

"Not even a little bit," Elise added, though the comment seemed directed more at me than at Johnny.

"What..." I tried. My throat was raw, like I'd been screaming. Because I *had* been screaming, I remembered—chasing after that transport, doing things I hadn't known I was capable of. "Those civilians..." I looked expectantly at Johnny and winced at the protests of my sore, beaten muscles. I didn't like the look on his face.

"They're... They'll live. Some broken bones and such, but they're definitely a lot more alive than they would've been if you hadn't... done your thing. What was that, by the way?"

"I'm not really sure. Some kind of Expression, I guess. Didn't really have time to think about it. Just kinda opened the taps."

Elise's exasperation was palpable.

"Didn't have time to think about it?" she repeated. "You charged into enemy territory against orders, nearly got yourself killed once, and *then* decided it was time to start channeling Alpha knows how much energy for you don't even know what… and you didn't have time to think about it?"

I glanced at Johnny. "I see you filled her in."

"Don't look at him," Elise said. "It's not Johnny's fault you decided to run off."

Anger bristled in my chest.

She hadn't been there. She didn't know what it had been like. How it had felt to watch those civilians pulling away in that transport. The terror in their eyes.

"I did what I had to," I said, trying to keep my voice steady. "But we have bigger problems right now." I turned to Johnny. "Those hybrids… We need to talk to Glenbark."

I moved to sit up. The pain was exquisite. Especially when Elise pressed me back to the bed with a firm hand to my chest.

"No. You need to listen to the medics for once in your life."

I opened my mouth to point out that I hadn't even been awake long enough to speak to one of those medics, then hesitated at the look on her face. She wasn't just exasperated, or worried, or tired. It was more than that. She was angry. More than angry.

"Lise," I said softly, "what's going on? I'm okay. I'm—"

She bent down to pluck something from under my bed and held it out for my inspection. A translucent polymer bag, full of some unpleasant, rust-colored liquid. Across from her, Johnny gave a little groan and looked pointedly away from the stuff.

"Do you know what this is?" Elise asked.

"Uh… kinda looks like bloody urine."

"*Your* bloody urine," she growled. "You tore yourself up inside. They showed us the scans. Your muscles, your joints… Medics said you tripled the record for the most micromends they'd ever had to pull on someone who hadn't been hit by a bomb or a moving vehicle. They gave you so many nanites they wanted my dad to sign off on the dosage before they—"

"Okay!" I grimaced at the bag of bloody urine. "Scud, okay, I get the point."

"I don't think you do," Elise said, bending to reattach the bag below.

The anger flared in my chest again, stronger this time, begging for release. I'd nearly killed myself trying to help people, and—

"I think I'd better let you two talk," Johnny said, inching away from the bed as if he were afraid we might spontaneously explode.

Elise and I spoke at the same time, her telling him that would be much appreciated right as I told him it wasn't necessary. We traded a look that made me feel cold inside.

"Yeah, I'll be outside," Johnny said, hurrying for the door. He disappeared, then poked his head back in a second late. "You crazy kids just remember you love each other, okay? And that—Right, leaving."

The door slid shut behind him with an electronic hum, and I turned to meet the glare Elise had chased him from the room with. Her gaze didn't soften when she turned it to me.

"So what? You want me to apologize for saving lives now?"

The words were pure venom leaving my mouth. I practically spat them.

Her fists were clenched. For a split second, I thought she might even hit me.

She visibly forced herself to relax, keeping her gaze fixed on the bump of my feet beneath the blankets, safely away from my eyes. "You can't keep throwing yourself at every problem in the world," she said, her voice flat. "Giving it everything, every time. Giving more of yourself than you have." She hesitated, jaw tight. "We've both seen what happens when you tap too much power."

It was like she'd punched me straight in the gut.

For a second, I was back at the White Tower again, watching in horror as Carlisle wielded wild power beyond anything I could have imagined. Watching as he smote our enemies down with that barely-contained fury, the bleed-off whipping the entire Great Hall into a violet maelstrom.

Watching as that arcane storm turned on him, consuming him until he lost control. Watching as he vaporized the entire Great Hall with him and our enemies still inside.

Something between a gasp and a whimper escaped my throat, hot tears pressing at my eyes.

How could she do this? She didn't understand what I'd been facing back in that Humility courtyard. Didn't know what I owed Carlisle.

You are the best I have to offer this world, Hal.

She didn't know. I hadn't been able to bring myself to tell anyone about Carlisle's message. Hadn't even been able to listen to it again myself. And for her to use his death like this… for her to wield my grief against me like a weapon for trying to save innocent people…

It was unforgivable.

When she finally looked up to meet my eyes, I could see that she wanted to take it back. I looked away before she could try, refusing to let her, a dull ache settling in the back of my throat.

"I know you feel like you have to save everyone you can," she said quietly after a while. I felt her start to reach for my hand, and hesitate. "I would've wanted to do the same, Hal. I know that. But you won't be able to save anyone if you wind up in an urn."

Like Carlisle, I could practically hear her saying. Except there'd been nothing left of Carlisle to put in the urn, had there?

I rested my head back on the pillow, staring pointedly at the pristine white ceiling, avoiding her eyes. I didn't want to think about it. Whatever I'd done back in Humility hadn't been anything like what Carlisle had...

No. I couldn't think about it right now. About any of it. About Carlisle's final moments, or the fact that Elise would stoop so low as to use it against me like this. The woman I loved, stabbing me right in the deepest of wounds.

"Hal..." She took my hand, her expression torn. "I didn't mean to... I just—"

"I'd like to be alone."

They didn't feel like my words. Not really. Those words belonged to the ugly, wounded thing inside me. The same broken thing that pulled my hand away from hers—refused to meet her eyes.

No. They weren't my words. But they left my mouth all the same. And I didn't take them back.

I felt Elise teetering there. Heard her swallow, open her mouth, close it. Then the door slid open with a low hum. I closed my eyes, unable to cope with the thought of adding anyone else to this mess.

"—all due respect, sir," Johnny's flustered voice drifted in, "I'm not sure right now is the best—"

"Raish."

My eyes slid open at the sound of Glenbark's voice in the doorway.

"I need to speak with you," she said. She didn't add the *alone* or the *right now*, but they came across clear enough in her tone.

I wasn't sure whether to dread what was coming or to be relieved for the excuse to escape my skimmer wreck of a conversation with Elise. Glenbark strode into the room without waiting, not quite fuming—she was too controlled for that—but clearly not happy. Elise hovered uncertainly beside me.

"Elise was just leaving," I said.

The look she gave me told me the words cut deeper than I'd meant. Or maybe exactly as deep as I'd meant. I couldn't tell anymore.

She hurried for the door, barely even acknowledging Glenbark, averting her face as if to hide tears, and vanished into the hallway. Outside, Johnny called her name, hurrying after her.

Glenbark paid the display little more attention than to close the door when Elise and Johnny had gone.

Silence.

Then, in a quietly menacing voice, "What were you thinking?"

I caught myself before the excuses started. Willow whipping wouldn't do me any good here.

"There were enemy telepaths on the field. I stayed to stop them."

Anger flashed in her eyes like I'd never seen.

"You stayed to—"

She closed her eyes, jaw tight. I waited, speechless. It was oddly terrifying, seeing her like this.

Finally, she regained her composure and opened her eyes to fix me with a stare that was slightly calmer if no less frightening. "Can you make me these cloaks, Haldin?"

I swallowed, surprised by the question. "I… Yes. I'm doing my best, sir."

"Your best," she repeated, as if testing the idea out. She shook her head. "No, I don't think I believe that."

"Sir, with respect, I'm—"

"Do you remember what I told you after Vantage, Citizen Raish?"

I took a breath, trying to collect my thoughts. Trying not to explode. I couldn't handle another person telling me I'd gropped up. Not even the High General.

"You told me that I should get used to following orders or get off your base, sir."

"No one gets a free pass," she agreed. "No matter what they can do. And today, you defied orders for the second time."

"I saved lives, General. Maybe hundreds. If I hadn't been there—"

"You defied orders, Raish. It's as simple as that. And before you go tallying how many lives you think you saved, tell me this: did you even stop to think how many lives you were endangering, putting your neck on the line like that?"

I froze, mouth half-open, realizing I had nothing to say to that.

"Just as I thought," she said when I'd been silent too long.

I scowled down at my hands. "You don't understand what it's like, being told to stand back and play it safe when you can do the things I can do. When you're the only one out there who can."

She was silent for a few moments. I kept my eyes pointedly averted, studying my fingers without hardly seeing them at all.

"Look at me," she finally said, when it became clear I wasn't planning on rejoining the conversation.

I didn't want to look at her. Didn't want to talk to her. Didn't want a single Alpha-damned thing to do with any of this anymore.

"Look at me, Haldin," she repeated, calm but firm.

I met her gaze with a scowl, and was surprised to find empathy in her stern blue eyes.

"Every day, I make decisions that I know will mean the deaths of good men and women. Every day I wrestle with my choices, wishing it could be different, that I could save everyone. That I could do the impossible." She shook her head. "Don't be so quick to assume what I do and don't understand. More importantly, never forget that every action, no matter how small, has a cost."

I opened my mouth—to say it wasn't the same thing, or maybe even to apologize, I barely knew—but she silence me with a look before I could start.

"It was a mistake sending you out there," she continued. "I see that now. Which is why it won't happen again. I'm placing you under house arrest, pending the completion of your assignment."

"*That's* your small cost?" I cried. "Sir, you can't—"

"You don't understand, Raish. This isn't a discussion."

I bristled, preparing to argue, but she stared me down with pure adamantus in her eyes.

"This is larger than either of us now, Haldin. You have no idea the scudstorm you kicked up with your display back in Humility."

That gave me pause, a familiar dread creeping in my gut. One more thing I hadn't had time to think about…

"The reels," I murmured.

"Are filled to bursting," she said, "and far too many are talking about you, calling for the Sanctum to step in and give you the noose again." She tilted her head. "Of course, some are calling for heroic busts of you in the town squares as well. Enochia doesn't quite know what to think."

"But you do."

She adopted an expression reserved for pouting toddlers. "Believe it or not, I have more pressing issues to think about at the moment."

I frowned. "What else is happening?"

The faintest sneer pulled at her lips. "What? Outside the world of Haldin Raish?"

Despite how much this was all making me want to hit something, I found myself staring back at my hands, heat rushing to my cheeks at her words.

"Humility wasn't the only target," she said, all traces of derision gone.

My stomach sank, my own freedom forgotten for the moment. "Where else?"

"Service. New Amestown. A few smaller towns you've probably never heard of. All the same. Hybrid forces, in and out. Thousands taken across Enochia."

I stared at her, unbelieving. I was going to be sick. All that effort. The trouble I'd apparently stirred. The legionnaires we'd lost. I'd nearly killed myself trying to save those four last civilians. And it didn't matter. Because, meanwhile, the hybrids had been snatching up thousands more.

"Do you understand now why I need your uninterrupted focus?" she asked. "We have to strike back. Now. And we need those cloaks to do it."

"Keeping me prisoner isn't exactly gonna help me focus."

"And letting you run wild isn't going to help you survive. You leave me with little choice."

"Sir… Please. Don't do this. I'll be more careful next time. I'll…"

"It's for your own safety as much as anything else, Haldin. General Auckus is already calling for both our heads on pikes, and after today, something tells me the Sanctum might be all too willing to answer that call.

"You're the High General of the Legion."

"And I know the limits of that power," she shot back with a pointed stare. I recoiled at the rebuke in her words, half-expecting her to dig in again, but she only let out a heavy breath and sank into the chair at my bedside.

"I need you and Elise to give me something to work with, Haldin. Ordo Dillard already explained what you think is happening to the older hybrids, and what it seems to mean for engagements moving forward."

"If we could get a sample to Therese Brown and her people, maybe—"

She cut me off with a wave. "It's being handled. I need you to set that aside and focus on what the rest of my people can't. We're looking at a complete paradigm shift, here. One we're completely unequipped to handle."

"One we wouldn't have recognized if I hadn't been out there," I added quietly.

"And one which you are, by far, our best hope of fixing," she continued, surprising me with her lack of argument. "We can sit here and bandy words about the fault and the blame and the fairness of it all until we're both blue in the face, but I'd prefer it if we could move past that and you could simply tell me if your meeting was worthwhile."

My meeting?

"Did you learn anything that could help during your abduction?" she added at the apparent confusion on my face.

The memories of Hawk Nose and Pasty hit me like an electric jolt. Since waking up in the middle of a hybrid attack, I'd barely had time to think about the mysterious duo, with their rune wands and their dungeon of impossibly old books.

"I'm not sure," I admitted, trying to remember what little I'd seen in their open tomes. "I think they had answers, but they wouldn't give them to us. Not before…" I thought about the rune-powered scanner helmet Pasty had crammed on my unwilling head. "They gave me some kind of test, but I don't think I passed."

What the scud had that been about, anyway? And the fear on Pasty's face when he'd recoiled from me at the end…

Alpha, that had been one bizarre encounter. I couldn't make sense of any of it. But after glimpsing those tomes, and the rune-powered devices they'd been packing, I was pretty sure of one thing.

"We need to find them again."

Glenbark nodded. "I have teams looking. I believe Citizen Fields may be conducting his own investigation as well." She fixed me with a heavy look, almost apologetic. "Even so, I need you and Elise to proceed on the assumption that you won't be receiving any help from the outside. We're well past having the luxury to rely on good fortune and happenstance."

Furious as I wanted to be at Glenbark's punishment—and much as the thought of facing Elise again made me want to flinch—I couldn't seem to find anything but cold, dreadful exhaustion in my heart as I stared at her staring off into space.

"I'll do my best, sir," I said quietly, too tired to decide whether I resented the words, wanting little more than to close my eyes and leave all this scud behind.

Glenbark hardly seemed to notice I'd spoken, lost in her own thoughts, her brow pinched with more concern than I was used to seeing out of her.

"Sir?"

She straightened, returning from some distant thought with a surprised look in her eyes. She looked almost as tired as I felt.

"How bad is it out there?" I asked. "Really."

She shook her head at the question, and for a second, I thought she was going to stand and leave without answering. "They're spreading us too thin," she finally said. "Chipping down our numbers while they replenish their own."

The defeated look on her face only deepened the discomfort in my gut. I wanted to say something useful—to point out that maybe this was all part of Alton Parker's plan to get us to move on Oasis again before we were ready, or that maybe there was some deeper vulnerability they were trying to hide. But what vulnerability?

The hybrids were growing stronger, not weaker. What if the raknoth were simply stepping things up because they were that assured of their own victory? And why wouldn't they be? As far as I could tell, they might soon have hundreds—if not thousands—of mature hybrids that were nearly as strong and dangerous as true raknoth. What force could possibly hope to stop that?

Maybe this fear and doubt was exactly what Parker had wanted us to feel all along. Or maybe the truth really was that—

"We're losing, Haldin," Glenbark said. "Not decisively. Not yet. But losing all the same, piece by piece."

Cold fear gripped me to hear her say it. She stood, and for a brief moment I wanted to tell her to stay—to please not leave me all alone. It irritated me as soon as the thought landed, the idea of prostrating myself to the woman who'd just placed me on house arrest for trying to save people's lives. But then she surprised me by reaching down and planting her hand on my chest, over my heart. Her fingers looked more delicate there than I would've expected.

"I need you to set this aside," she said, pressing her hand to my beating heart, her voice intense though it was barely above a whisper. "There are going to be a lot of people calling you demon in the coming days. Some calling you hero, as well. I need you to stay above it. I need you to see that *this*"—her fingers found the bump of the pendant beneath my gown and gave it a tap—"is the way you get your revenge. The only way you find the justice I know you're seeking."

She hesitated, her other hand going to her own chest, where I assumed her pendant was concealed beneath her dress tunic. She held my gaze, and I saw the hard barrier of discipline and professional distance fading from her eyes. Saw the deep sorrow that lay beneath.

"Let this be your redemption, Haldin."

I can't adequately explain the way those words made me feel. For one fleeting moment, it was like she truly saw me—saw me in a way that no one else seemed capable of doing anymore. Like she understood the weight on my heart. I searched her face, lips trembling, waiting for more. But she only withdrew her hand and stepped back, leaving me alone with the weight of the darkness, her wall of professional distance once again returning.

She watched me for a moment, just long enough that I thought she might say something more. Then she turned to leave. Again, I had the impulse to ask her to please stay. But that was ridiculous. Freya Glenbark was not my friend. She was the High General of the Legion, and I was nothing to her but a means to an end.

The door whirred open. She paused there, looking back with something in her eyes that made me wonder if I was wrong. "The four you tried to catch at the end," she said slowly. "One of them will never walk again. I thought you should know."

Then she left, and I was alone—more alone than I'd been since Carlisle. Since my parents. I couldn't stand it. I wanted to call for Johnny and Elise, but I couldn't stand the thought of what Elise might say. Couldn't stand that maybe this might be the time I would call and they wouldn't answer.

So I sat quietly alone as the tears came, unable to quantify what it was I was crying for, too exhausted and broken to try. For a long while, I just cried, trying my best to stay in that room, away from the lives we'd lost. The people I'd let down—was *still* letting down every single day the raknoth went on walking this planet, killing and maiming and taking everything we had to give. More.

I'm not sure how long I'd been crying when the door whirred open— only that I was in no mood to be seen in that state.

"I heard you were awake," a female voice said. "I have to tell you, as your personal medic, I think you—Oh."

Melanie drew up short as she stepped in and caught sight of what I could only assume was the red-eyed, tear-streaked face of a crying child. I turned my face away, not bothering to wipe my face, but not wanting to meet her eyes either.

The door closed. I closed my eyes, drawing into myself. I didn't want to know what she thought about what she'd stumbled into—whether she'd left or stayed. I suppose I felt it anyway.

Footsteps.

A hand settled over mine. It wasn't warm or particularly soft. But it was gentle.

"Do you want me to leave?" she asked softly.

I swallowed and opened my wet eyes to look at her. There was concern in the wrinkle of her brow, and caring in the depths of those golden brown eyes. So much caring that I couldn't understand it.

I tried to answer. Tried to nod. Or maybe to shake my head. I didn't know. My lips were quivering. And then, before I knew it, I was crying again—not the silent, mournful tears from earlier, but great ugly sobs that wracked through me, sparking fresh waves of pain and pathetic noises from my throat. I was too tired to fight it. I gave in completely. And Melanie held on all the while, saying nothing.

Part of me wanted to be appalled at the display of wretched vulnerability, but something about Melanie's calm aura gently dispelled any such notions. She didn't ask questions. There was no stroking of the thumbs. No soft touches on the cheek. She wasn't even looking straight at me.

She just held my hand tight, simply being there, allowing me to purge my emotions without judgment.

At some point—I'm not sure how long had passed—the sobs faded, leaving behind only a light shaking and the occasional shudder. I wanted to talk to her, then. To explain something of what I was feeling. To at least thank her, for the love of Alpha. But I couldn't seem to find the traction to open my mouth and start.

My eyelids hung heavy, half-lidded—my thoughts sluggish and slowing. The soft bed felt suddenly all too welcoming.

Melanie seemed to understand.

"Sleep," she whispered, moving closer to meet my eyes for the first time with a sad smile. She gave my shoulder a gentle squeeze. "You're okay, Haldin. Just sleep now."

I didn't argue.

2 0

—————

SHADOWS

Something was wrong.

That was all I knew as I jolted upright in the dark room. Or tried to.

In the dark dead of night, it took me a moment to remember where I was. Another moment to understand what was happening.

I was fixed to my bed in the medica. Tied down by restraints I could hardly make out in the darkness.

Instinctively, I opened my mouth to cry for help. Something soft and dry jammed its way into my mouth. I recoiled, trying to spit it out. Something smacked an adhesive strip over my mouth before I could. A gag.

Whose?

There was no one. Heart thundering, I reached out with my senses—only to realize I was trapped to the confines of my body, trapped inside a dialed-in cloaking pendant.

That's when the blind panic took me.

I'm not sure I can explain. There's the terror of facing down bloodthirsty monsters—of knowing the odds are hopeless, the outcomes bleak. And then there's that of being totally, utterly helpless. Cut off from all control. Powerless.

It wasn't hard to decide which I preferred.

I bucked against the restraints like a wild animal.

"Oh shush," said a soft voice.

I froze.

"It'll be over soon," the disembodied voice added from somewhere to the left. Feminine. Sultry. I didn't like the sound of it one bit. But at least it jarred me back to my senses enough to start using my head.

I might be trapped inside a cloak, but at least part of the bindings were in physical contact. A chill spread through me as I channeled the heat from my body. I couldn't reach far enough with my senses to sever any of the bindings all the way through, but if I just got them started…

I felt as much as heard the binding tear against my right forearm.

"What was…" my shadowy captor muttered. "Oh really, now," she sighed with the exasperated tone of a mother who'd just caught her child making a mess of the pantry.

I was halfway through the second binding and yanking the first arm free when something bit into my left side—a sharp clamp of pure, sizzling electricity. It coursed through me, irresistibly convulsing every battered muscle on my left side and half of those on my right until I couldn't breathe for the pain—couldn't see, couldn't think anything at all aside from a hopeless prayer for it to end.

It did, eventually. I couldn't say how long it was. Couldn't think or say much of anything, really. A stun rod, my muddled brain finally pieced together. That's what that had been.

"There," the voice said, sounding satisfied about something. There was a clunk of something being tossed into the waste receptacle. "That's better."

Slender fingers snaked under my chin and pulled my face to the left with wiry strength. And there she was. A lithe silhouette in the dark. One that I was certain hadn't been there just a moment ago. My attacker.

"The Demon of Divinity," she said softly, stroking my cheek with a thumb. "My, oh my."

I tried to say something. Sluggish as my stunned brain was, it took me entirely too long to remember the reason I couldn't seem to speak was that I was gagged. Just like it took me too long to register the importance of her glib gesture.

She was touching me.

I coiled my mind, preparing to strike at her through the physical connection. But something was wrong. My thoughts. My body. All disjointed. Effects of the stun rod?

Warmth creeping through my limbs.

Why was it getting worse?

I pushed the thought aside and attacked as best I could anyway.

There was resistance. Then she yanked her hand back like she'd been burned, breaking the connection before I could make any real progress. "Hmm," she said. "You *are* a wild one, aren't you?"

I gaped at her, the room beginning to tilt oddly, warm honey flooding my brain. Resistance? That meant something. Meant…

She was a telepath.

"It's a shame, really," she said, coming closer, planting a hand on my chest.

I tried to use the connection to attack again, but the warm honey was spreading, melting my mind from inside out, covering me like a softsteel blanket weighing me to the bed. She caught my mental attack without discernible effort. Leaned in until her lips tickled my ear.

"The reels just don't do you justice, Demon," she whispered.

Then she took my earlobe in her mouth, her tongue hot against my flesh, and gave it a gentle bite. I tensed, barely able to process what was happening, sure this was just the sadistic foreplay to something terrible—another round of the stun rod, or a dagger in the gut. Demons to the wind, I half-expected her to bite my ear off. But then she gave a contented sigh and drew back with a breathy laugh.

"You should see your face right now."

She straightened and took a few lilting steps toward the door, still facing me.

Who the scud was this woman?

"Sadly, I must be going. I imagine I'll see you in the nether, Demon."

My head was humming, sinking—the room spinning around me now, a drunken ocean of undulating shadows. Her silhouette was still there, head cocked, like she'd heard something. My head fell to the pillow like a thousand-pound stone.

There was a mechanical whirring somewhere to the left. A sliver of light split the ceiling, spreading.

The door. Someone was at the—

"Step away from the Raishman, lady."

Johnny. Thank Alpha.

"I'm serious. Don't make me—Dammit!"

Gunfire. Multiple shots. Shouting from the hallway.

With effort, I lifted my head. The world lurched around me, the scene coming to me in hazy flashes.

Two legionnaires down in the hallway. Johnny in the doorway, sidearm in hand—raising the weapon, hand shaking, all the way to his own temple. Horror plastered across his face.

I screamed into my gag, adrenaline cutting through the fog. I tore my right hand free from the ripped binding. Reached desperately for the cloaking pendant with numb, clumsy fingers. Too late.

Something plowed Johnny over from behind—a streak of dark hair flying into the room before he'd even hit the floor. There was a hissed curse and a thud of impact, and I turned my head in time to see a shadowy figure crash into the wall beside the window with a heavy *thunk* and the sound of cracking plastwall.

My savior stood at the foot of my bed, fury radiating from her silhouette.

"I don't know who you are," came Elise's voice, "but you picked the wrong gropping day, lady."

Lise, I tried to say. It came out a mournful gagged groan, and my head thudded back to the pillow, the shadows spinning my world, reaching for me like living things.

"What'd you do to him?" Elise growled.

Darkness folding around me.

"Ah, the Demon's concubine," groaned my attacker somewhere far away. She sounded like she was in pain. Probably because Elise had just put her halfway through the wall.

A light buzzing at the edge of my senses suggested she might've said something else, but I could hardly be bothered at this point. I was sinking into the bed, spinning. I didn't need to worry. Elise had it under control. Though, there was something… Something I should tell her? The thought buzzed at the edge of my mind like an irritating insect. The room spinning faster, faster.

Then my world exploded—a concussive boom that ripped through me, shaking my bones. Somewhere in the distance, glass shattered.

I was still alive?

Bright light pierced reddish-orange through my eyelids. Someone had turned the room's lights on. Voices shouting back and forth. Someone's hands on my neck, peeling off the cloaking pendant.

"—take this back," someone was muttering. "Alpha-damned crazy blondes with their thumpers and their—Hey, Lise? He's not looking so hot!"

My eyelids fluttered open.

Johnny looked down at me with a decidedly unhappy slant to his features. Was it me who had him so upset? Something to do with the way my limbs were floating in a sea of warm honey? But that wasn't upsetting, was it? It was actually kind of nice. Perfect, even. If I could just breathe a little easier…

"Hang in there, buddy," he said with a weak smile. He glanced back at the door to yell something about *gropping* and *help* before turning back to me and unceremoniously ripping the adhesive strip from my mouth.

It should have hurt, some corner of my mind decided, but I barely felt it. Little more than an odd, numb tugging sensation. Elise was at my other side now. I couldn't move my head to see what had become of my attacker. I tried to ask, but I'm not sure much came out.

"She's running," Elise said, her face tight, her hand on my cheek, though I couldn't seem to feel it.

A ruckus in the hallway outside. Sounds like a full company charging into battle. With effort, I flicked my eyes toward the door. Legionnaires were pouring into the room, sweeping with their rifles, a squad of medics right on their tails.

Elise yelled something I couldn't quite understand. Added something to Johnny in a tense tone. And then they were gone, replaced by half a dozen medics, all buzzing about my bed like a frenzied colony of grasscutter bugs —all serious faces and methodical movements. Something turned my world, and then there was Melanie, standing where Johnny had just been, eyes wide with concern. Her lips were moving. She was talking to me, touching my face, shining a light in my eye. I couldn't seem to hear a thing. Couldn't feel her hands on my face.

Something was wrong, I knew. It was impossible not to know with this army of grim-faced grasscutters busy at work around me. My world was closing in. Melanie abandoned her light. Put her face right in mine, mouthing something with big, deliberate movements of those goja fruit lips. She did it again. And again.

Hold on.

Hold on.

But I couldn't.

RUMORS

I woke to dimmed lights, a world of pain, and an unstoppable need to vomit.

"Medic," someone rumbled in a deep voice to the right.

There was a gasp to my left. Then I lost it, lurched forward, and retched into... into a bucket?

Where the scud had that come from?

"It's okay," said a gentle voice, an equally gentle hand rubbing my back. "Get it all out."

I didn't have time to question or argue. I retched again. And again. On and on for what felt like an hour, until I was left simply shaking, clinging to the bucket like a life raft. Cold sweat on my forehead. Hot, tangy bile coating the back of my throat, the taste seeping unpleasantly along the sides of my tongue.

"He's good?" the deep voice asked—Edwards, I realized as my sleep-muddled brain finished rebooting.

"He's good," said the second voice. Melanie.

I pulled my face from the bucket opening with a groan. "I think..." I tried. Alpha, my mouth was dry. "... think good's a pretty scuddy choice of words."

Edwards chuckled in the corner. "Damn, kid. Keep it up and I might actually start believing the rumors about you."

"Rumors?" I tried to sit up. Winced. Glanced weakly around to where giant Edwards was crammed into an armchair, his feet propped up on a smaller stool, uncannily large sidearm in hand and heavy rifle propped nearby. Beside him, the windows had been covered over with some dark opaque polymer, shutting us off from the outside world. "But you've seen me."

"Oh yeah," Edwards said, following my gaze to our newly installed privacy panels. "Catching slugs and jumping buildings, sure. But I'm talking about the rumors that're saying you can't be killed."

I snorted, then profusely apologized when the act spewed a few lingering flecks of my sick onto Melanie's hand, still holding the bucket at the ready. She barely seemed to notice, finishing her professional inspection of me before handing over the bucket, shooting each of us a stern look, and going to the sink.

"Just to be clear," she said, washing her hands with a kind of absent-minded precision, "we won't be testing that rumor anytime soon." She smiled at me, patting her hands dry. "Medic's orders."

"Alpha be kind," Edwards affirmed quietly.

I touched fist to chest in a casual salute, my lips returning her smile of their own volition—at least until everything else started coming back to me. The reason for the dark panels stifling us in place of windows, and Edwards' presence, and the fireteam I felt outside my door.

"Where are Johnny and Elise? What happened to that… person?"

That *telepathic* person, I wanted to say, but I wasn't sure it was wise to broadcast what had truly happened here. Because if that woman had been what I thought she was, I wasn't sure what was safe to say, or whom it was safe to say it to.

Who did you turn to when a Seeker of the Sanctum tried to assassinate you in the middle of a Legion stronghold?

Maybe I was being paranoid. Maybe I'd hallucinated the entire bit about her being a telepath. How would I know? It wasn't like I'd been clear of mind. But at least the fact that I had armed guards and that Johnny and Elise had deemed it safe to leave me here suggested they'd talked to Glenbark and had the situation under control. Hopefully.

I came back from my thoughts to find Edwards and Melanie watching me expectantly.

"Sorry, what?"

"I said they stormed off to catch your, you know," Edwards said, with a wave of his fingers, "your person."

"What?"

"Wingard and your lady. They left after the medics told them they had control of your situation. Went to go try to find—"

"No, I got that part. I meant *what* as in what, you just let a pair of teenagers go chasing after the woman who infiltrated Haven and nearly killed me?"

"They're both okay," Melanie said, taking the bucket from my hands and sitting down to begin a series of light exams.

"It was fine," Edwards said, waving a dismissive hand. "Half the base was already sweeping for intruders by then. You couldn't throw a stick without hitting a legionnaire out there."

"And yet they came up empty-handed?" I guessed.

"Yeah." Edwards frowned. "Kinda spooky, right?"

"Spooky," I muttered. "That's one word for her."

"Go on," Edwards said, leaning forward expectantly.

It was my turn to frown. "About what?"

"No. Nothing." Edwards glanced hesitantly at Melanie, then back to me. "Rumor just has it she was, shall we say, on the pretty side. Confirmed?"

"I don't know, man," I mumbled, my hand drifting to the earlobe she'd quite unexpectedly molested. "I was kinda busy dying in the dark. What is it with you and rumors anyway?"

Edwards gave an innocent shrug and leaned back into his chair, looking disappointed.

Honestly, aside from the clear conclusion that *someone* wanted me dead, I wasn't sure what to make of any part of the dangerously close encounter. Mostly, I just wanted a damn shower. Which wasn't surprising considering my last one had been *before* I'd crammed into an armor skin, gotten kidnapped, fought through an incursion, and then spent a day mostly unconscious in the medica.

It was turning out to be a rough couple of days.

"Did Elise say…?"

Again, I faltered over the thought of revealing that my attacker had been gifted.

"She didn't say much," Melanie provided when I failed to continue. "They came back to check on you a couple hours ago. She, uh… well, she wasn't very happy."

Something about the way she said it, the way she pointedly avoided my eyes.

"Wasn't happy about…?"

"About any of it, I'd think." She turned away to consult the machines at my bedside. "I'm sure they'll be back soon. Guess you can ask her yourself."

Behind her back, Edwards gave me a pointed look then hooked his fingers like claws and bared his teeth like a hissing feline.

What in the love of Alpha was happening? Pervy assassins in the night, and now what? Had Elise and Melanie butted heads when I'd been out?

My heart beat faster at the thought. Had I been caught? Caught at what? I hadn't done anything wrong, had I?

I suppressed a sigh and tried to ignore Edwards as I swiped out messages to both Johnny and Elise that I was awake and wanted to talk. Then, chiding myself for not thinking of it first, I added a message to Franco.

<Any word yet on what the scud that was back in creepy dungeon land?>

Franco, for his part, responded in the time it took Melanie to finish her inspection of my vitals. She settled into the armchair at my bedside with a contended sigh as I pulled up his message.

<Tracking leads. I'll find them. You rest today. I'll keep you posted if I find anything before I see you. We should talk soon, either way.>

That was for damn sure. Between the hybrid attack at Humility and the one on my life right here in the medica, the run-in with Pasty and Hawk Nose almost felt like it was just a dream that had never really happened at all. But I couldn't forget those ancient texts, and that strange telepathic helmet Pasty had forced on me.

Could those two really be some kind of remnant of the Emmútari? Descendants of the original members, maybe? Sworn guardians of what knowledge remained?

Each explanation that occurred to me felt more ridiculous than the last. Maybe I'd get lucky and the raknoth would manage to finish me off before I had to worry about any of this mess.

But then I remembered what Glenbark had said last night, and Carlisle's words weren't far behind. True guilt poured through me. Because there was an entire planets' worth of people to help before I could earn the right to even joke about giving up.

I had to find Pasty and his tomes again. Or I had to figure it out myself. Either way, I had to do *something* other than lie here in this damn bed, *resting*. I glanced at Melanie, wanting to ask for something I knew was impossible. I was too fried to be useful to anyone, no matter how badly I wanted to be.

Somehow, Edwards chose that moment to stand up, stretch, and declare he was going to check in with the fireteam out in the hall. I swear to Alpha it was like he was mocking my bedridden corpse—swore it firmly enough that I forgot to say anything. Melanie just gave him a tired nod.

Once he was gone, silence stretched between us, tinged with an uncomfortable edge.

"Do you need to go see your other patients?" I asked.

Her lip twitched. "Trying to get rid of me?"

"No." I shook my head. "No, I just don't wanna be a burden or get you in trouble or anything."

"Well, that's sweet of you, but…" She yawned. "But I'm technically not on medica duty right now."

Not on duty? Had she stayed here all night for me?

"Orders came down," she said, reading my unspoken question. "I volunteered."

Somehow, the admission made her look three times more exhausted.

"Melanie… You should get some rest." My eyes flicked to Edwards' hulking form out in the hallway. "Rumor has it they already work you medics to the bone as it is."

She bobbed her head in tired agreement, but didn't move—warring with some unspoken thought.

"What is it?" I finally asked.

"I just… I'm worried. About you."

I patted my chest as if to say *Look, all good here.* It hurt. "I feel fine," I said anyway. "Whatever she gave me, whatever you did, I think I'm okay."

She frowned a little, like she wanted to launch into an extensive list of the reasons I was not okay, but the look passed. "That's not what I meant. I'm not worried about your immediate physical health." She cocked her head. "Although we might have to talk if you're looking to make a habit of jumping off worship halls and everything."

When I said nothing, she pushed on.

"It's just that… there's been a lot of talk about you."

"In the medica?" I asked, knowing full well that wasn't what she meant.

"In Haven. On Enochia." She swiped a few commands on her tablet and handed it to me. "Pretty much every headline on the WAN and anywhere else is either about the attacks or you."

Glenbark hadn't been kidding last night. Mostly, the reels were filled with news of yesterday's planet-wide attacks—reports, reactions, and wild speculations about what it all meant. But there, peppered with unsettling frequency between the real news, were the pieces that made my pulse race and my stomach squirm.

Haldin Raish - The Demon Who Lived.

Haldin Raish - The Savior of Humility.

Demon of Divinity Strikes Again.

There were dozens of them. Hundreds. Praising my name. Cursing it. Saying pretty much everything else in between.

"Apparently there was an amateur videographer in the crowd," Melanie said as I opened one and was greeted by a vid straight from Humility. "She caught it all. Threw the vid on the net within the hour, declaring you the savior of Humility."

I watched with morbid fascination as a disheveled figure with the torn tatters of civilian clothing over his armor-skin leapt from the worship hall steeples, impossibly far. I flinched as he hit the ground and rolled. Hopped to his feet and took off like… Sweet Alpha, like a demon. Seeing it from the outside perspective, I couldn't believe that had been me. It barely looked real. It certainly didn't look human. Especially not when Screen Hal let out a blood-chilling scream and launched himself a good thirty feet into the air.

No wonder I was pissing blood.

The vid cut from the scene at Humility to a headshot of a commentator I didn't recognize. Melanie reached over and froze the vid before the guy could get two words out.

"You're a hero," she said firmly. "Never mind what they might say."

"I might have to mind it if the Sanctum decides they made a mistake playing along with the Legion's pardon and allowing a demon to live."

Assuming they hadn't *already* decided that and sent a certain slippery Seeker to end me in my sleep—which, given the evidence, was kind of looking like exactly what they'd done.

"This is why I was…" She sighed and took the tablet carefully back from me, avoiding my eyes. "You're not a demon, Haldin."

A dozen responses shot through my head, from *No scud*, all the way to *You can't prove that, and so what if I am?*

"Do you believe in Alpha?" I finally asked.

She looked taken aback. "Of course I do."

"So why wouldn't you believe the Sanctum about me?"

She faltered and dropped her gaze like she already knew her answer wasn't really an answer at all. "The High Cleric has yet to comment on any of this."

"And what if he said I was pure evil? That I was a demon of the nether, and that I needed to be purged from Enochia?"

She was silent for a long while, conflict heavy in the furrow of her brow. I was about to tell her to forget about it when she spoke, quietly.

"I believed them the first time they said those things about you. And I was wrong. And I'm sorry for that." She looked up to meet my eyes. "I don't know what His plan is or how it's going to work out for us in the end, but meeting you"—she gestured to her tablet—"seeing you fight for those people… I believe Alpha gave you these gifts to help us. And if using them means you face persecution, then I have to believe that's part of His plan as well. I… believe in you, Haldin. And I'm not the only one. I want you to remember that when you're out there, dealing with all the looks and the headlines, and the whispers behind your back. That, no matter what they might say, there are a lot of people out there who are alive because of you."

Hot tears were pressing at my eyes by the time she finished. Part of me wanted to disagree with everything she'd said—to tell her that she was wrong, that she simply hadn't been there to see the people I'd failed along the way. Part of me just wanted to fall at her feet, bawling like I had the day before.

I was opening my mouth to at least attempt a *thank you*—and to point out that Glenbark's house arrest probably meant I wouldn't be heading into the chaos anytime too soon anyway—when Edwards strolled back into the room with all the subtlety of a dancing bull.

"So Raish, what's the deal with—Oh." Edwards froze, looking between us. "You guys look real serious."

Melanie and I traded an embarrassed look.

"Should I go?" he added, making no move to do so and instead studying us like we were a particularly captivating storyvid.

I glanced at my palmlight, which was still uncomfortably devoid of responses from either Johnny or Elise.

"Actually," I said, looking up, "I was hoping one of you might be willing to stand guard in case I fall over in the shower. My coin's on you, big guy."

Edwards looked at Melanie like he was hoping for her to shoot the idea down.

She considered me, then shrugged. "If he feels up to it, I won't argue."

"Me or him?" Edwards and I both said at the same time.

Melanie stood, smiling a little as she reached over to disconnect my equipment and fluid lines. "I'll let you two figure that out. My orders were to see Haldin through to sunrise. If you don't mind, I'm going to go give my report and get a couple hours of sleep before my shift starts. My replacement will be back in a few minutes to put you back together."

"I should've listened to Evie," Edwards grumbled as Melanie touched my shoulder in farewell and headed for the door.

"Melanie," I said.

She paused by the door, turning back.

"Thank you. For everything."

A small smile pulled at her lips. "Just don't fall over in the shower, please. It'd be a pretty embarrassing way for the Savior of Humility to go."

2 2

THE NEW NORMAL

"This is humiliating," I declared as water began cascading down my body in delightfully hot streams, carrying away entirely too much grime.

"For you or for me?" Edwards asked, taking a cautious step back from the open shower. "Actually, don't answer that. It's me."

I didn't argue. Getting over to the shower had not been enjoyable. Disrobing and climbing into the shower under the watch of the heavy gunner even less so. But now that I was here under the pour of blessedly hot water, sweet Alpha, did it feel good. So much so that an appreciative grunt escaped me before I could stop it.

"Yup," Edwards said, "it's definitely me. I'm moving around the corner, kid. Don't die."

I didn't argue with that, either. Just tried to enjoy the feeling of knotted, battered muscles relaxing in the warmth without falling over.

"Hey, Edwards?" I called as I began rubbing soap on with one hand, clinging to the rail with the other. "Can I ask you something?"

"Wondering what to do when you want 'em both?"

I almost slipped off the hand rail. "What?"

A low, rumbling chuckle. "Nothing. Yeah, kid, as long as it doesn't involve the words *can you* and *scrub my*, ask away."

"I was just wondering... Davis and Mara and..."

"You're wondering why I'm here when my fireteam isn't?"

"Sorta."

"I heard Dillard tell Carter to send over a couple fireteams from Second Squad to watch you. They were a bit more grateful than most for your spooky scud after said scud got those things out of their heads back at the worship hall. I just offered to tag along."

"Why?"

"Alpha, kid, you trying to throw *all* your friends away?"

"No, I just…"

"I'm gropping with you. I just came to help. Couldn't pass up the chance to chafe Evie's hide, either. She was *not* a fan of me coming here. Says you're cursed, demon or not."

It took me a second to recall that Evie was the name he called Mara by, but when I did, I wasn't overly surprised by the news. Those steely eyes of hers had never tried to hide the fact that it was an abomination she saw when she looked at me.

"And you're not worried she's right?"

"Eh, not so much. They're a superstitious folk, those specters."

I frowned. "Mara was a specter?"

She certainly wasn't one now, unless she was hiding the shroud and parading with Hound Company for fun.

I nearly slipped again as Edwards jerked his head around the corner to shoot me an incredulous look. "Of course she was a specter, kid. Alpha, have you seen her shoot?"

"I, uh, yeah—But…"

Edwards seemed to remember himself then, and retreated back around the corner. "Look, I'm not gonna pretend like the stuff you do out there doesn't put a little frost on my wrinklies. But I also can't help notice you haven't done a thing but try to save lives with your, uh, magic stuff. Hard to condemn that, as far as I'm concerned."

I finished rinsing off lathered soap and waved the shower off. "I uh… Thanks, Edwards."

I was surprisingly comforted by his words. And it only made me feel worse to realize that, in all my burning need to stop the raknoth and my indignation at being a tool for the very people who'd so recently been trying to kill me, I hadn't even bothered taking the time to get to know the people who were more or less becoming my squad mates.

An apology was halfway to my tongue when Edwards' massive hand reached around to offer me a fluffy blue robe. "Don't mention it, kid. Just don't ask me to pat you dry."

I took the robe with a smile, deciding that I liked Edwards. "So why do you like pissing her off so much?" I asked as I cautiously stepped out of the shower, robed and feeling immeasurably better for the soft fabric and damp freshness pleasantly hugging my body.

"Who, Evie?" Edwards turned and looked at me like I'd asked why he bothered working out so much. "Because it makes the sex a thousand times better."

"Oh. I didn't know you two were… Oh."

He grinned broadly at the look on my face. "Take my word for it, kid, there's nothing hotter than an angry specter on top of you, going so hard you're not quite sure if she's trying to grop you or kill you." His eyes went distant with some fond memory. "Or both."

"Well, that's uh… I don't know. But speaking from recent experience, I think I could do without ever having a woman try to kill me in bed again."

He came back from his daydream with a chuckle. "Nonsense, broto. You just haven't pissed off the right lady yet."

Stomach sinking, I glanced at my palmlight. Still nothing.

"Oh, I think I pissed her off just fine."

"Ah, you kids…" He clapped a fatherly hand on my shoulder, then recoiled at my wince. "Oops. Sorry. But seriously, if it's really right, you kids'll make it work. Just don't be a scudhead. Oh, and uh, while you're at it, maybe don't tell Evie I said any of this stuff about her either, huh? Unless…" He looked thoughtful for a second, then shook his head. "Nah. Not worth it."

When we left the privy, there were two people waiting for us in the room—a dark-haired medic I didn't recognize, and…

Son of a goat-gropper.

"Docere Mathis," I grunted as Edwards looked between us in confusion, probably wondering why I'd stopped cold in the middle of the room. The medic, too, looked less than pleased by my reaction, frowning at the docere as if wondering if he should ask him to leave.

None of our reactions fazed Mathis' stony-eyed stare, of course.

"Please," he said, waving to the medic without averting his eyes from me, inviting the man to do what he would while also nixing any thoughts of his being asked to leave.

The medic turned to me, still frowning, and gestured for me to get back in bed. I almost argued, loathing the thought of taking a submissive position for whatever lecture my old docere might've come here to give, but my shaking legs were hardly pillars of dominant masculinity, so I let Edwards help me back into bed.

"Did the High General send you?" I asked Mathis as the medic went to work reconnecting my lines and checking the bedside machines.

Mathis was a rigid column of darkwood disapproval. "Something like that."

Great.

"Here to berate me some more?" I asked, trying to spread my hands in indignant scorn and instead only earning myself an apprehensive tut-tut from the medic, who'd moved on to a light physical examination.

"She didn't think the house arrest was enough?" I added, not to be silenced.

Edwards slunk back to his chair in the corner—at first, I thought, to retreat from the impending unpleasantness. But then he kicked his feet up like he was ready to enjoy the prime storyvid drama unfolding before him.

It might've made me smile if not for the look Mathis was giving me.

"I'm here to ask you some questions about last night," he said flatly. "Though I'll happily admit I think you deserve a lot more than house arrest, if you're asking."

"I'm not."

His dark eyes burned, and I could practically hear him yearning for the days when he would've been able to take me to the sparring mats and beat that kind of attitude straight out of me. A cold smile pulled at my lips just thinking about how it would go for him if he were to try such a thing these days.

If I didn't know better, I would've thought something about my expression actually made him uncomfortable. "Perhaps you could just answer my questions, then," he said, uncrossing his arms and—I think—trying to adopt a more neutral pose.

"Isn't this a job for the enforcers and Haven patrol?"

"It is," he said, taking a few steps closer to the foot of my bed as the medic finished his work and retreated from the room. "But I offered to help."

I frowned. I vaguely recalled Mathis had spent time as an enforcer in a past life—and granted, I was a bit rusty on these things—but that didn't really check out with my working knowledge of protocol in this situation.

Was he here as a favor to someone, or just to stick his nose back in my business and maybe fit in a shot or two at my integrity of character while he was at it?

"Fine," I said. "I didn't see much last night, but ask away."

"Why don't you just start from the beginning?" he said, priming his palmlight to record the conversation.

With only a small sigh, I launch into as thorough a recounting of last night's attack as I could, leaving out nothing but the ear nibbling and the fact that she'd been a telepath. I even considered telling Mathis the last part. Far as we were from being one another's biggest fans, Mathis was an honorable man. I was pretty sure I could trust him as much as I could trust anyone else in the Legion.

Still, the words hesitated on my tongue. "She was… I think she was sent by the Sanctum."

It was enough of the truth to set their investigation on the right path for now—assuming there *was* a right path in this scudstorm. But I could see in the slight furrow of his ebony brow that he knew I was holding something back.

"Why do you say that?"

"Just a feeling."

"A feeling," he repeated.

I tried not to wilt under his stare. "A strong feeling."

He held my gaze for a silent stretch, and I thought for sure he was about to call bullscud when he instead rounded on Edwards, who was so engrossed now he was about ready to fall out of his chair.

"Give us the room, specialist."

Edwards snapped to, remembering himself, and hopped to his feet. "Sir, yes sir."

I wasn't glad to see Edwards go—or, more precisely, to be left alone with Mathis—but there wasn't much to be done about it. Mathis turned back to me, and I waited for the drill instructor face to make its appearance, but he surprised me.

"I'll recommend they take this hunch of yours under advisement." He closed his palmlight, ending the recording but still clearly wanting to say something. "You know we're not your enemy, don't you?" he finally asked. "You've been given every grace since—"

"Since you all tried to kill me?" I asked before I could stop myself.

He crossed his arms. "Did you see me pointing a gun at you, Raish?"

"You would have."

"You were an outlaw."

"A *framed* outlaw."

He looked unimpressed by the distinction. "You broke into a private research facility—"

"Where they were killing people."

"—and infiltrated a Legion stronghold—"

"To wake your asses up to—"

"To a crisis that should've been reported to the proper channels."

"They *owned* the proper channels!" I growled, half a second from telekinetically removing his maddeningly calm ass from the room.

But to my surprise, he nodded. "They did. And what's your excuse now?"

That caught me off guard.

"I won't deny that what happened to you before was… wrong," he pushed on before I could catch my balance, and I could see that the admission cost him something. "I don't have to tell you that we're dealing with a completely unprecedented situation. What I will point out is that we're all still here, doing our best to adapt and overcome as a team, just like we were taught. Just like *you* were taught."

So that's what this was about…

I scowled at him. "I thought you weren't here to berate me."

"Old habits die hard, I suppose." He gave me a pointed look. "But no harder than should the discipline of a legend's son."

"Yeah, there we are. Back to basics, right silver spoon?" I shook my head. "I'll never be the man my father was. You think I don't know that?"

"I think you convinced yourself that that's what I thought about you all those years."

"Oh yeah? And what did you think, Docere? What was it you were trying to teach me with all the silver spoon this and daddy's boy that?"

His brow was knitting like he was wondering how I could've missed it— or maybe even questioning himself as to how he'd failed so completely. "I was trying to teach you the one thing you needed to learn."

"And what the scud was that?"

The doubt on his brow disappeared. "That it's not enough to be the best on the mat—the strongest, the fastest, the smartest. It's not enough to be the best *everything* if you don't know how to respect your fellow soldiers, if you can't value them for their strengths and trust them to have your back when it matters."

I opened my mouth to argue, but I had nothing to say. I had nothing but the emptiness his words left at my core. Because I'd had a partner I'd truly trusted to watch my back. And he'd died doing it.

"I was trying to teach you," Mathis continued, more calmly now, "that you could be more than a record on the tyro performance indices. More than any of that." He gave an honest shrug—the first I think I'd ever seen from him. "I was trying to teach you that you could be more than your father, if you'd just step out of your own way."

I couldn't help but stare. *That* was what he'd tormented me for? Some vague aspiration that I was *more* than a boot-licking silver spoon?

He'd sure had a scuddy way of showing it.

"Well thanks for pointing all this out now that I'm a civie with the world's brightest target painted on my head," I muttered. "I'll try to keep that in mind next time I decide to get in my own way."

"I hope you will," he said, ignoring my sarcasm. "Because it's not too late. You're in this thing, civilian or no, and people are counting on you. So next time you find yourself thinking it's your place to try to outdo every man and woman who's given their life to this planet—"

"I'll be sure to think of you, Mathis."

There it was—the old flash of docere anger I remembered in his eyes. But as quickly as it came, it was gone. "You do that. But for now, get your rest, Haldin. We need you."

Unable to find a suitable reply, I watched him go, wondering how much of all that he'd actually meant and how much Glenbark might've told him to say—how much any of them cared about anything beyond the fact that I was their best bet at fixing their telepathy problem.

I didn't have long to dwell on it before Edwards leaned into the room bearing two generous platefuls of eggs and toast. "Chow, broto?"

I was hardly hungry, but Edwards took my noncommittal grunt as an affirmative. I was still absentmindedly poking at a mound of egg a few minutes later when my palmlight finally gave the merciful buzz I'd been waiting for. My excitement was immediate, and nearly as profound as Edwards' enthusiasm for the food he was scarfing down in his corner chair. When I saw the message was from Johnny, my spirits only grew.

And died back down almost immediately.

<Wrapped up all day with stuff for Glenbark. Helping Therese get things set up, too. No news on your attacker yet, but we're working on that. Someone will be by to ask you for a report. Get your rest after that. I'll catch you up tomorrow.>

My fingers hovered over the palmlight display, a hundred different replies flying into my head and back out again. I felt angry, betrayed. And oddly deserving of Johnny playing the hand of the busy servitor, keeping *me* at arm's length.

And meanwhile, not a word from Elise…

"You'd better eat that," Edwards rumbled through a mouthful of eggs, shoveling more in and eyeing my full plate with borderline frightening intensity. "I make no promises for my behavior after this plate is empty."

I sighed, picking up a piece of toast with a solemn prayer that—much as I appreciated Edwards' time and company—this was not the new normal for my life.

23

GALLOWS

"There he is," Johnny said from my bedside when I awoke the next morning. "The talk of Haven."

I groaned, groggily fumbling for the memory of where I was and what was happening.

"Is he the Demon of Divinity?" Johnny continued. "Or could he be the Savior of Humility?"

"Don't rule out the murderer of wise-ass gingers, either," I said, rubbing the sleep from my eyes and laboring to sit up with aching muscles, which, while still plenty stiff, already felt considerably better than they had yesterday. Thank Alpha for nanites.

We were alone in the medica room, Edwards and my resident medic either waiting outside or having finally been cleared to leave me alone like a normal patient—or like one under normal room arrest by the fireteam outside, at least.

"And since when are you in a good mood?" I added, turning back to Johnny.

He shrugged, his cheery demeanor flickering for a second. It was a small glitch, but plain enough to one well-versed in Johnny-isms. "I dunno, man. Maybe I feel bad for you, what with all the headlines and the things people are saying."

"What things?"

Johnny scrunched his face up, as if wondering where to begin.

"Where's Elise, Johnny?"

His face fell, taking my stomach along with it.

"Why didn't she…? Why didn't either of you…"

"There was a lot to be done yesterday," he said, looking everywhere in the room but my eyes. "Still is. Glenbark's got me on three separate projects, and Therese and the other Vantage rescues are getting up and running to start tracking those facilities and everything."

"Johnny."

"Glenbark even agreed to bring Franco and his people onto the team since they're… yeah," he continued, as if he hadn't heard me. "And then there's the case of Codename Siren, and everything else, and by the time we had a chance to breathe yesterday it was… Well, we figured you needed to sleep, and—"

"Johnny. What's going on?"

For a long moment, he teetered on the edge. Then he let out a heavy sigh and finally met my eyes. "She's not happy, Hal. Neither of us are."

"What did she—"

He held up a hand to stop me. "Broto, you know I'll always be here for you." He cocked his head. "You know, provided you stop trying to go die without me and everything. But you two need to talk. Like, really talk. To each other. You don't want the wise-ass ginger playing messenger between you."

He made a fair point. Enough so that I agreed and asked him to go find a medic to discharge me. They weren't in any hurry to abide, but agreed to at least talk about it after I ate a solid breakfast. So, I settled for shoveling down fabbed something or another while Johnny briefed me on some of what I'd missed yesterday. The latest damage report from the hybrids' last round of attacks didn't exactly stimulate my appetite, but I forced the food down anyway, needing to get out of the medica.

"So what's up with Codename Siren?" I asked when Johnny reached the news—or lack thereof—about my mysterious telepathic attacker. "Who came up with that one?"

A rare look of embarrassment crept over him. "That was Lise. I was, uh, with the boys outside your room when our new blonde friend rolled up and, well… I mean, they didn't have cloaks on, which gives them a fair excuse, but I…" He was full-on blushing now. "Look, let's just say she's got charm, and she knows how to use it. So, you know… Siren."

I couldn't help but smile a little, despite everything. "I can't imagine why Mathis didn't think to tell me about that bit yesterday."

He grimaced. "Yeah, sorry about that, by the way. Not that I had any say or anything, but…" He shrugged. "Was he a beardsplitter about it?"

"What do you think?"

He shook his head. "Gropping doceres, man…"

"Yeah," I said, eager to change the topic. "So, this Siren person. I take it Elise noticed she was, you know…" I tapped the side of my head.

Johnny nodded. "We told Glenbark and Franco. No one else."

"Good. I only told Mathis I suspected the Sanctum, but… Yeah, that was good thinking."

It was only at Johnny's curious look that I realized I was still bobbing my head. He arched an eyebrow in question.

"She, uh… She licked my ear," I explained, unsure how else to put it but suddenly needing to tell him. "It was weird."

Johnny frowned, then crossed a leg and adopted a decidedly scholarly pose in his chair. "Do go on, my goodfellow."

I dropped my gaze to my plate. "I don't know why I brought it up. It was just… Yeah. Right after she pumped me full of drugs, and right before she left me to die, she just leaned in, whispered that it was a shame to kill me, then she, you know, sorta sucked on my ear, like…"

I gave up and abandoned the thought to silence.

"Broto," Johnny finally said, "that confuses me in strange places."

Gropped up as it was, I kind of knew exactly what he meant.

"I think she was a Seeker," I said, eager again to change the subject. "Which probably means one of two things."

"The raknoth or the Sanctum," Johnny agreed. "We're trying to uncover what we can, but Ol' Siren Earsucker didn't leave much of a trail." He frowned. "I'm not gonna say you *shouldn't* tell Elise that you were kinda sorta molested by the sexy assassin lady, but you might not lead with it, by the way."

I grunted as I scooped the last bite from my plate. "What would I do without you, buddy?"

He shook his head, stared pointedly at my ear all the while. "Alpha only knows where those lobes would end up."

AFTER TOO MUCH waiting and several emphatic promises to the medics that I would refrain from anything more physically intensive than walking for the next few days, I was released to my two fireteams' worth of house arrest troops to be escorted to my domestic prison. I limped out of the medica beside Johnny wearing my armor skin—the civilian clothes I'd worn over it in Humility being a few degrees too battle-tattered for decency. At least the medica servitors had washed the armor, though it still smelled vaguely of sweat and battle.

Still, as we walked across Haven, I decided I was kind of glad for the extra protection.

I'd thought I'd been getting used to the strange looks around base, but this was unquestionably different. Before, it had been furtive glances, curious looks, and a few whispers behind my back about how I hadn't fallen when the Sanctum hangman had thrown the gallows lever—about how I'd survived a bomb and a ten floor fall back at Vantage, and how they suspected the nickname, Demon of Divinity, might well not be a nickname at all.

But now they knew. They'd all seen the vids of me leaping around like something inhuman. All the world had seen. Gone were the furtive glances and the whispered rumors. Now they stared openly, some in horror, some in awe.

I kept my eyes forward and marched on as best I could. Johnny stayed close to my side the whole time, Carter's Second Squad fireteams in neat formation around us. As pissed as I was about the house arrest thing, I had to admit I was glad for the guard detail when the shouting began.

It started with one zealous legionnaire loudly condemning my spirit to burn. Then another pitched in. And another. The first few were hushed by the more conscientious spectators, but slowly, surely, it built—a rising tide of their collective loathing for the unholy demon who'd infiltrated their ranks, tricked their High General. Murdered their friends.

I was sure it was about to reach a boiling point and spill over into violence when a hush began to spread through the crowd that'd somehow grown to the point of blocking multiple trafficways by then. Legionnaires shuffled, making room for a procession of passing ground shuttles.

I half-wanted to take advantage of the distraction and try to make a run for it with my escort, but curiosity got the better of us all. Like Johnny beside me, I craned my neck to see who had calmed the storm… and met eyes with General Auckus passing by.

He sat in the back of his ground shuttle, letting his servitor drive him around like high royalty, and the look in his eyes as he met mine… I wasn't sure what to make of it. Only that it made my skin crawl.

Quickly as it came, the moment passed, right along with Auckus' procession.

"That was weird," Johnny said beside me, confirming that I hadn't been imagining the strange edge in Auckus' stare.

"Probably wishing Siren hadn't botched the job," I muttered back.

He didn't argue.

Thankfully, with the momentary lull in their angry shouting, the crowd seemed to have lost crucial momentum. It slowly began to disband—some walking away with disappointed looks and others, while still clearly displeased with my continued propensity for drawing breath, resigning themselves to glaring daggers at my back as we continued on.

For the time being, their ill-will didn't escalate beyond that. The closer we got to the civilian barracks, though, the more I almost wished it would. Because as much as I didn't want to deal with General Auckus' malicious looks and the malcontent of Alpha-fearing legionnaires, I was even more worried about what was waiting for me ahead.

Marching to our quarters, I couldn't help but think of the way I'd felt back in the White Tower, shuffling barefoot and chained across the Great Hall to the waiting gallows. It felt like a lifetime ago. And yes, logically, it seemed kind of ridiculous to compare to the two situations—literally walking to my death versus going to face the girl I loved. But as far as my dread-steeped gut was concerned, there was very little difference. If anything, this march actually felt more dire than the last.

At least at the gallows, I'd known what to expect.

Johnny's grim expression when we reached the civilian barracks didn't help matters. "Fare thee well, dear goodfellow," he said, laying a hand on my shoulder.

"This isn't an execution," I said, maybe more to myself than to him.

He tilted his head as if to say *Maybe, maybe not*, thought about adding something else, then said, simply, "She loves you, broto," before turning to leave.

I watched him go. Turned slowly to the door to our quarters.

"I can feel you standing there," came Elise's voice.

"This isn't an execution," I mumbled to myself, reaching for the access panel.

In the tiny entryway, the click of the door shutting behind me felt a little too reminiscent of a gun being cocked. I braced myself and rounded the divider to find Elise sitting on the living room floor, meditating in the dull gray light that filtered in through the long window.

She opened her eyes, looked me over, then tilted her head toward base. "Tough crowd out there, huh?"

For a second, I wanted nothing more than to leap on the thread she'd just cast me—to play it up, hammer it home that I was the real victim here. "That's not important, Lise," I forced myself to say. "Not right now."

No more putting it off.

I can't adequately describe what it felt like as we moved to the couch by some unspoken agreement and settled awkwardly in—not quite separate, but not quite touching, either. We moved with an air of deep discomfort, like two strangers sitting down for an interview. It put an ache in my chest.

How could the bond between us suddenly feel so tenuous? It didn't feel real. My head was spinning.

I reached out to grab hold of her hand. The touch was jarring—not a romantic spark but a collision alert, forcing us to meet one another's eyes. I was surprised to see my own turmoil reflected in her. She was just as lost as me right now.

And I *was* lost, I realized—suddenly certain that something had gone critically wrong between us but blind as to how or why, or even when.

I wanted to grab her and pull her to me, refuse to let go. I wanted to kiss her. But she dropped my gaze before I could, stroking my hand absent-mindedly with her thumb.

"I don't know if I can do this anymore, Hal," she said finally.

Something shattered in me.

It was breathtaking—almost fascinating, in a morbid way—to hear her say the words. The words I'd somehow convinced myself she wouldn't say even when I'd known deep down that they'd been coming.

"Lise…"

"I'm not mad at you." She thought about it. "Okay, I am. I'm pissed. Furious. But that's not the problem. The problem"—her voice wavered—"is that I can't keep sitting by and watching this happen. Watching you kill yourself. Watching you…"

"Lise, I know it's—"

She silenced me with a look. "Do you? You really think you know what it feels like to sit by and watch the person you love run off into battle? A person, I might add, who has an almost perfect record of nearly getting himself killed. You know what that does to me?"

I opened my mouth and closed it, fumbling for words. It wasn't my fault, I wanted to say. I didn't want this. Didn't ask for it. I hadn't even been the one to bar her from joining the excursion to Humility. That had been Glenbark.

But I'd been glad for it, hadn't I? Glad for the knowledge that Elise was stuck safely back in Haven. Glad for the chance to throw myself at the hybrids —to live up to Carlisle's legacy—without the fear of losing the person I cared about most. And was that really so wrong?

"I didn't know what else to do, Elise. I'm sorry. I was just trying to help."

"Trying to help?" She shot me an incredulous look. "Working on the cloaks—that's helping. Advising Glenbark on the raknoth. Scud, maybe even riding along with a squad for a mission. That's helping. But tackling Alton Parker solo? Disobeying orders to charge into a field of hybrids? Pushing yourself so hard that you almost die from exertion? That's not helping, Hal. That's suicide."

"That's not—Look, I'm fine."

"You're not. You've been to the medica twice in seven days, Hal. Tell me how you think this turns out if you keep on—"

"WHAT DO YOU WANT ME TO DO?" I roared.

I rocked back from the violence in my own voice. I hadn't felt it coming. Hadn't meant to slam my fists to the table. But there were Glenbark and Mathis in the back of my head, telling me to step it up. There was Alton Parker and his intelligent hybrids, sweeping across Enochia, consuming it whole. And there were the deep, pulsing aches in my forearms, confirming that I'd just snapped and lost control yet again.

"What do you want me to do?" I croaked, rising to my feet, heart pounding in my ears. I couldn't meet her eyes. Couldn't stand what I might see there.

I pointed out the window instead. "They're killing people out there. Right now. People are dying, and I have the power to stop it."

"You don't," she said, shaking her head at the edge of my vision. "No one has that power. No one can handle that responsibility alone."

"I..." I blew out a long breath. "I know that. Guess it doesn't matter anyway now that I'm on house arrest."

Gently, I settled back onto the couch and reached for her hand. "Look, I know how hard this must be for you to—"

She hissed a bitter chuckle, pulling her hand away. "Really? So you *have* stopped to think about it? I mean *really* think about it? How it would feel if we switched places? If the Legion had come to me for help? How you'd feel if I told you to stay put like a good little boy while I ran off to tempt fate one more time? How you'd feel sitting here, wondering if maybe that's actually what I wanted—if maybe I was just going to keep pushing myself until I winded up dead and didn't have to feel the weight of the world on my shoulders anymore?"

I opened my mouth to tell her she was wrong and realized that I'd be lying. I *didn't* know what she was going through. How could I?

"How would you feel," Elise whispered, "if I came back from all that just to shut you out, tell you to leave. How would you feel if you found me crying on someone else's shoulder within the hour?"

Melanie.

I felt sick.

She'd seen me crying to Melanie the night Siren had come for me—or heard me, or felt me from the hallway. It didn't really matter.

"Elise, that wasn't… After Glenbark left, I was upset. I was crying when she found me. It didn't mean—"

"I don't care about that," Elise said, wiping her eyes. "I don't love it, but I'm not some jealous little girl thinking I should be the only one allowed to comfort you. That's not what this is ab—" She took a sharp breath, shaking her head. "You don't even see it, do you? You let her in, Hal. You showed her exactly what you've been hiding from me ever since the Tower."

Her words hit me like a mag tram, ringing with an intensity of truth that left me wondering how the scud I'd been so blind. Had I really been so closed off?

"I've been here for you," she said, the grief draining from her tone, leaving it flat and weary. "I've done everything I know how to do. And I'm sorry I pushed you about Carlisle the other night. I'm sorry. But I can't just grin and nod while this thing you're carrying around eats you from the inside out."

"Lise, I didn't… I've been so absorbed in everything else, I never stopped to think…"

I'd thought I'd been handling it. I'd thought, being with Elise in those crumby little Legion quarters, we'd been healing together. But no.

Once. That was how many times I'd allowed Elise to see me grieving for Carlisle and my parents and everyone else. One time, right after the White Tower, I'd cried into her arms—allowed her to help me. And since then… I'd avoided it all like a disease-ridden dumpster around her, hadn't I?

I'd spent plenty of time thinking about Carlisle and my parents and everything else, certainly. But always when I was alone. Always when times were already dark. Never when Elise might see.

I'd kept her at arm's length. Shut her out from everything she needed to understand and given her nothing but brooding silence and erratic bursts of anger. And somehow, getting back to work and feeling useful again in these past days, I'd actually fooled myself into thinking it was getting better.

Alpha, how had I not seen it before now? Before she stood from the couch with a look that made me feel broken inside?

I grabbed her hand, desperate. "I can't lose you, Elise. Please. I can't. I can't live through it."

She cupped my cheek with her other hand. "And I won't sit here and cheer you on while you ride yourself to the pyre. I won't be the princess you convince yourself you're doing this for, watching you cry out for help over and over again only to refuse everything I have to offer..." She shook her head, jaw tight, trying to pull her hand from mine. "I can't, Hal. I won't help you kill yourself."

"Lise, please." I clung to her hand like it was my last lifeline. "I can't—I won't... I love you."

Her lips quivered. A tear rolled down her cheek. "I love you too, Hal. I always will."

The look in her eyes hit me like a raknoth fist to the diaphragm. My hand loosened around hers. She slid her hand free and stepped past me. I stared blankly at the space she'd vacated.

This couldn't be happening. I was on house arrest, for Alpha's sake, I couldn't... I... I couldn't breathe. The world tilted drunkenly around me. I tried to turn as she stooped down to pull on her boots but couldn't even seem to do that.

Do something.

The words rolled through my head like a chant, over and over, until they lost meaning. I had to say something. Had to explain it to her, whatever *it* was. The thing that had been trapped inside of me, festering there as surely as if it had died with Carlisle and all the others.

At the edge of my vision, she stood, boots on. Hesitated. She was going to say something. But then she moved out of view, toward the door.

I tried to follow her. Why couldn't I move? I had to tell her. Had to say something. A weight wrapped around me, pressing in on my chest until I was sure my heart and spinning head would both burst. I was going to vomit. Words came out instead.

"It should've been me."

I turned, finally unfrozen by the words I hadn't expected or intended to say.

Elise had paused by the door, waiting for more. "What should've been you?"

The words clung in my throat, desperate to stay.

"At the White Tower," I finally managed. "It should've been me."

She looked up to meet my gaze, her eyes full of empathy and desperate longing. My jaw trembled. Tears began to fall, loosening the words in my throat.

"I shouldn't be here." My voice was thick and wet. "It should be Carlisle. He could have handled this, could have protected the legionnaires as easy as —" I fought down a sob, burying my face behind clenched fists, tears dripping from my chin into my lap. "He should've left me in the tower. He should have gotten you out himself. Shouldn't have come in the first place. All those civilians. All the soldiers who died because of—"

A sob wracked my body. I tried to hold it together—needed to get it out, for both of us. But then she was there, her hands cradling my head, warm and kind and loving, stroking my hair, wiping the tears from my cheeks, and for a few minutes, all I could do was cry. She pulled my head to rest against her stomach, and I fell to my knees at her feet, burying my face into her. She held me tight, silently stroking my hair until I had no tears left to cry.

"I can't do it, Lise," I said when the sobs had faded, my voice hoarse and wavering. "I can't be what he was. What my dad was. I'm not good enough." I looked up at her. "Why did he leave me here? I... I don't feel like I deserve to be alive."

She sank to her knees, so that our faces were level, and planted a gentle hand on my cheek. "He did it because he loved you, Haldin. Because he couldn't bear the thought of losing you. He sacrificed himself for *you*. Not Divinity, or Enochia. You. If all he'd cared about was stopping the raknoth, maybe he would've traded places. But he wanted you to live, Hal."

I was shaking. She held me, nothing but love and conviction in her eyes. She truly believed what she was saying. I sniffed hard in a futile attempt to keep my runny nose from overflowing, then tried to wipe the sopping mess from my face. Elise balled her sleeve and did it for me.

"There's something I haven't told you," I said.

She finished wiping my nose and planted a light kiss on my forehead, the ghost of a smile touching her lips. "I think now seems an appropriate time, don't you?"

I wasn't sure how to answer that. Wasn't sure there was an appropriate time at all, or that she'd ever be able to understand the scope of what it meant to me. But now was the time to try. So I wordlessly slid the holodisk I'd been carrying all this time from my pocket and handed it to her. She studied it uncertainly, then activated it. Her eyes widened at the sound of Carlisle's voice, but she settled, listening attentively, stroking my hair all the while.

It was the first time I'd heard Carlisle's farewell since finding it.

"Do you understand?" I asked when the ghost of my mentor had finished.

She studied my face. "I think so."

"He wanted me to stop them, Lise. To save Enochia. It's the only reason I'm alive."

She rejected the idea. I could see it in her eyes. But she considered her words carefully before speaking.

"Astute as you can be from time to time, I fear you will struggle to see what I see when I look at you."

I frowned. Those were Carlisle's words. "Lise, I know—"

"I have faith in you," she recited, pulling me close. "More, I fear, than you have in yourself."

I tensed in her arms. She didn't understand. "You are the best I have to offer this world," I recited in kind. "He had faith that I could stop them, Elise. Faith that I could take care of this world when he was gone. And he was wrong. And—What?"

She was shaking her head against mine, like I was spouting nonsense. "Just… Both of you. You say you can't be like Carlisle, and yet you're doing exactly what he did, looking at the whole picture and only seeing the darkness you think you deserve."

She held up the holodisk to belay my protest, scanning back until she found what she was looking for.

"If you are hearing this, Hal," came Carlisle's voice. "If I've indeed perished, know that I will have done so gladly if it meant life for you and peace for Cassius. Know that it is not your fault. Mourn if you will, but do not for a second give in to despair."

"That's not… He only said that because…"

She hugged me then. Squeezed me harder than I understood—hard enough that my aching muscles cried out in protest. "It wasn't your fault, love," she whispered. "Carlisle. The Tower. I know you blame yourself. But you didn't do those things. You're not letting yourself see how much worse it all would've been if we hadn't done what we did. And I've just been here, watching it kill you. Watching this wall grow up around you. Looking for some crack, some way in to find you and—and—"

Her voice broke, and then she was crying, and I was squeezing her tight, wondering how in demon's depths I'd ever been so blind—how I'd convinced myself for a single moment to shut this woman out.

"I'm so sorry Elise," I whispered, my eyes brimming with fresh tears. "I didn't mean to hurt you. I never wanted to…" I squeezed harder. "I love you so much. Please. Please don't—"

Her lips pushed into mine, wet and salty with tears, her hands clinging to the back of my head, pulling my face to hers.

"I thought I'd…" she started to whisper against my lips, then shook her head, fingers twining through my hair. She rested her forehead to mine. "Just please don't do that again. I know we can't always be side by side. But please just don't go somewhere that I can't follow you again."

I cupped her cheeks. Wiped her tears away with my thumbs. "I guess it's a good thing I'm on house arrest."

We shared a tear-filled laugh, and Alpha did it feel good, kneeling there together, trading breaths, holding one another and just relishing the closeness while I tried to work up the momentum to say what I knew needed to be said. It scared the scud out of me, but I got there eventually.

"Where I go, you go?"

She opened her brilliant blue eyes, so close to my own, and cupped her hands over mine. "You sure you mean that, flyboy?"

I swallowed, holding her gaze. "I do."

"Alright, then." She inclined her head. "Where you go, I go."

The smile she showed me then was one of the good ones, tear-streaked cheeks and all. The kind of smile that would've beam pure warmth and happiness straight into the spirit of whomever it struck.

And right then, it was just for me.

2 4

ARRESTED

We didn't get back to work that morning.

We laid in bed and held each other close. We talked and laughed and reveled in one another. We made love like it was the first night all over again, clinging desperately to one another as if gravity had inverted and we were the only thing keeping one another from falling away to empty sky.

For a few wonderful hours, we let ourselves be teenagers again—together and in love and just… happy. Plain and simple. No cares in the world.

I'm pretty sure it was the best day of my life.

Which almost softened the blow of coming back down from the clouds to remember that I was still on house arrest. Almost.

But that was okay too. Because I had work to do.

Yes, there was still a wild horde of hybrids pillaging Enochia's population. And yes, Glenbark and the Legion were depending on me for a solution to the telepath problem. But for the first time since the White Tower, I felt like I truly had Elise back—like I truly had *myself* back.

Lying in bed that morning with the exquisite comfort of her naked body pressed to mine, there wasn't a single obstacle on Enochia that felt insurmountable.

My confidence threatened to waver somewhat when we finally called an end to our tryst to get back to work and I remembered that I didn't have the faintest clue what came next in the grand plan—or lack thereof—of Project

Mindsafe. For starters, I practiced my mental island technique to reacclimate to the cloaking technique I planned to eventually use on these runes. Once Elise confirmed it was working, I had her start practicing the technique while I turned to the runes and back to the starter task of trying to imbue one with the simple function of pulling thermal energy from the air.

I won't claim it was fun work, but it was kind of impressive how quickly the time passed when I was toying with runes and new techniques. Maybe it was a product of the countless hours I'd spent sitting on Carlisle's practice mat, determined to hone my abilities into fighting shape as quickly as humanly possible. Maybe it was just the pressure of Enochia riding on the line. Whatever it was, the work possessed me.

After finally achieving limited success with a few heat sinks, I turned to the more abstract task of trying to imbue a rune with my mental island effect, but that only ended in a long string of failures with a frustrating lack of understanding as to what aspect was off. Was I simply failing to effectively cast the cloaking effect onto the rune? Or was it the rune itself that was incorrect—incapable of holding the desired effect? Or was it something else completely?

There was no way to know.

Elise, having found little success with her own practice at the mental island technique, broke from her meditation to posit that—even if I was successfully expressing the cloaking field effect onto the rune—there was no reason the rune *should* work in isolation. In fact, she said, it made more sense to expect that a rune meant to accomplish something that required energy—something like generating a cloaking field—would probably itself require a secondary rune which could supply the primary rune with power.

It made perfect sense, and it felt like a major breakthrough, but my excitement only lasted as long as it took me to realize I had no idea how the scud one would go about powering one rune with another.

This entire endeavor was quickly proving itself to be one endless stream of flopping awkwardly from one unknown to another, without even the most basic reassurance that we were even flopping in the right direction. And meanwhile, thousands of people were dying.

I needed help.

I needed those Emmútari texts. Why the scud had those two even yanked us into that dungeon if they were only going to chuck us back on the streets? Didn't they realize what was happening on Enochia—how many lives might've been saved if they would've just told me what they knew? What had Pasty seen on that helmet that had so terrified him at the end?

The more I failed to spark any new progress, the more these questions pushed into my mental space, swirling on a dark cloud of frustration.

Finally, when I couldn't look at a rune without hearing Pasty's bare feet slapping across the stone floor of his dungeon, I broke from the work to have a bite with Elise and call Franco for any updates.

"Hal," he said, sounding a little surprised. "Good timing. I found something this afternoon. Was planning to visit once I'd confirmed."

"What is it?" I asked, trading an eager look with Elise.

"I'm not in the best place to talk right now. Here…"

My palmlight threw up a buffering icon then populated with a vid feed of Franco. He was sitting at a desk in a busy room I could only assume must be Therese Brown's lab. Or soon-to-be lab, at least. The room was bigger than I'd expected—though it was sort of hard to tell from our fixed viewpoint in the corner—and currently awash in chattering scientists and poorly arranged equipment, or so I gathered by the copious debating and emphatic hand-waving. There were maybe twenty people in view, a roughly equal mix of Legion specialists and civilians. The gaunt pallor of cycles spent on the blood racks marked most of the latter as ex Vantage employees.

"Welcome to the United Hybrid Trackers of Enochia," Franco said, waving a hand at the mess behind him.

"Is that seriously what you settled on?" Elise asked beside me.

Franco gave her one of the cryptic smiles that only she seemed capable of deciphering and turned his attention back to something in front of him. "I'll send you what I have for now." He turned from his work at a voice I couldn't quite make out, and nodded. "Of course. Come say hi."

Therese Brown drew up behind Franco with a wave and a warm smile. "Hello, there."

"Hi Therese," Elise said.

"How are you feeling?" I asked, though I could guess well enough from her appearance. Her eyes were tired, and her brunet curls frizzy and a little wild, as if she'd been working too much and sleeping too little, but she still looked better than she had in the days after being rescued from Vantage— her face less sunken, and her cheeks full of a healthy flush.

"Better than you, from what I hear," she said with a concerned look. "Are you holding up okay?"

"I'm doing fine."

That earned me a skeptical look from all three of them at once.

"More fine than some would prefer," I clarified.

"Well not this frazzled old survivor," Therese said. "I hope you're eating, and getting enough rest."

I couldn't help but smile a little at that. Therese might not have been particularly calm or collected, but there was something about her that always seemed to put me at ease anyway—a kind of soft-spoken goodness that seeped peacefully into my spirit even though we weren't physically in the same room.

My palmlight buzzed with an incoming message from Franco, and I saw that Elise's did as well.

"Elise knows how to access that," Franco said, I assumed more for my benefit than hers. She was already busily swiping and tapping away at her device.

"Sorry," Therese said, glancing between Franco and us and taking a step back. "I didn't mean to interrupt. I'll let you three—"

"Hey, you got those freezers!" came a familiar voice from off-screen a second before Johnny drew up to join them. "What's going—Oh, hey guys. Long time, no riots."

"Speaking of interruptions," Franco murmured.

"You're telling me," Johnny said, clapping a hand to Franco's shoulder. "Seriously, though, guys. Check this out." He must've plucked the camera from Franco's node then, because our view lurched wildly around until I found myself looking at two long surfaces that almost looked like bulky tables on wheels until Johnny raised the camera and I got a look at what lay beneath the translucent panels on top.

Each bulky chamber contained a frozen hybrid.

I suppressed a shudder, staring at the things. Beside me, Elise's fingers had paused over her palmlight as she took in the garish sight. One was newly turned from the look of it, pale and still smooth-skinned in a few places. The other was fully covered in dark green hide, which I took to mean it was one of the older specimens from Humility or maybe one of the other attacks.

Therese was saying something off camera that I couldn't make out.

"Nice," came Johnny's voice from much closer, holding the camera on the frozen hybrids for a few more seconds before taking us on another lurching ride back to Franco's desk. "Nice and creepy."

Therese shrugged as Johnny stepped back to let us see them all again. "Better than keeping them in the food freezer. People were starting to complain."

"That's a joke," Franco added at Johnny's quizzical look.

Therese winced. "A bad one too, I take it. Sorry, it's been a while."

"I think you have the mother of all valid excuses there," Elise said.

Therese just looked around the room, cheeks reddening, until she found an adequate diversion. "Oh, there's James with the ion exchange filter. And…"

"Hey guys!" called an energetic voice. Then, as James bounced into view and caught sight of us, "Oh! Hey guys!"

Phineas wasn't far behind him, pushing a cart laden with a heaping, bulky machine whose function I could only guess at.

James shook his head, patting the thing. "You won't believe the hoops we had to jump through to—" He paused, looking back and forth between Phineas and Therese, who were furtively eyeing one another. "Oh yeah. I guess you two haven't actually met yet, have you?"

"No," Therese said, "we, um…" She smoothed her blouse. Wiped a rogue brown curl out of her face. "Funny we've both been in and out and haven't crossed paths yet." She extended a hand as they drew up. "Pleased to finally meet you, Phineas."

Phineas abandoned the cart and gripped her hand. "It's… an honor. After what you did for Enochia… We owe you."

I was almost positive it was the most words I'd ever heard him say at once. And demons to the wind, was that an artifact on my palmlight display, or was he *blushing* beneath that bushy beard?

"Oh, um, thank you," Therese said. "But it was nothing, really. I just…"

They only seemed to realize then that they were still shaking hands.

Phineas straightened, releasing her hand.

Johnny and James were watching the interaction unfold like they'd just stumbled upon a rare animal and were worried any movement might spook it. Beside me, Elise was equally mystified.

"So… they're like, in love, right?" I sent to her.

"Like, at first sight. I almost feel weird watching."

"Ah, to be young again…"

She failed to stifle a smile. *"If you'd tried to make that joke yesterday, I might've killed you."*

I just took her hand, lacing our fingers together and deciding I was glad it wasn't yesterday. On my palmlight, Phineas was retreating with some mumbled explanation about needing to go grab something from the skimmer, and Therese was positively red-faced. After an uncertain glance back and forth, James decided to follow Phineas.

"So, uh, did you learn anything new from those hybrid samples?" I asked, in part to fill the silence that followed, but also because I was intently curious to know.

"We're still working on it," Therese said, composing herself and glancing toward the freezers. "I haven't had the samples or the equipment long enough to say much, but there are a few interesting preliminary observations."

"What'd you find?"

"Well, the samples from the, um, *articulate* hybrid have noticeably higher concentrations of foreign nitrogenous materials than the samples we harvested from one of the, uh, newborns before Vantage was destroyed."

I frowned. "Foreign nitrogenous…"

"If you're willing to overlook a few minor technicalities, I suppose we could say the articulate hybrid's samples are expressing more foreign proteins and have lower human cell counts than their newborn counterparts."

"Foreign meaning raknoth?"

She hesitated. "Well, technically, we haven't confirmed that. But it seems quite likely, yes."

"So they *are* basically turning into full raknoth as they age?"

"In a way, perhaps. But not in the way you may be thinking." She tapped at her lips with a forefinger, as if wondering how to explain. "The true raknoth are discrete beings that invade a host and take control, yes?"

I nodded.

"Right. Well, while the relationship between raknoth and host clearly isn't symbiotic," she said, "it seems the raknoth at least strike some balance with their hosts' bodies, modifying and altering without completely smothering what was there to begin with. Based on what we're seeing from these hybrid samples, I'm starting to suspect they lack that crucial aspect of balance. Their raknoth side might be more like a cancer than a sentient being. If my work at Vantage was any indication, it might just keep growing until it smothers every human cell in the body."

"What does that mean?"

"I can't say for sure. But, if that's indeed what's happening, given what I've seen studying their tissues in the past, I'm going to guess that a fully developed hybrid will require a tremendous amount of human blood to survive."

"And meanwhile, they'll just keep getting stronger."

She turned her palms up. "Possibly. It's also possible there could be an inflection point where they start to weaken if the blood demands grow too high. We're doing our best to develop a workable model from what little data we have. There are a lot of complications. For instance, it's possible the daily average volume of blood consumption might alter the rate of development. A hybrid who feeds more frequently or in higher volumes may transition more slowly. We have no idea, really. We just need more data."

"Well," I said, "guess it's a good thing we've got the best in the world working on it, then."

Therese blushed, waving away any intended compliment. Franco just smiled.

"Plus," Elise said, "who knows, maybe the hybrids outgrow their feeding capacity and their entire army ends up just croaking overnight."

"That," I said, "or we find ourselves facing five raknoth and an army that requires a few small cities' worth of blood a day."

"Or that," Therese agreed quietly, ushering in a silence far more somber than the last one.

"This is why we can't take you places, broto," Johnny said.

I shrugged. "Just saying."

"We'll all keep doing our jobs," Franco said. "It's all we can do." He gestured toward us. "Check what I sent you. I'll be over soon to discuss it."

With all the commotion and the talk of hybrids, I'd nearly forgotten about Franco's mysterious finding. We all said our goodbyes, and I ended the call and eagerly turned to Elise, who was already back at work, sifting through folders and tapping commands into the custom application I'd seen her and her father use a couple times for sensitive data transfers over the lights.

Finally, the file in question popped open. Some kind of personnel file. A full blown official citizen registry file, I realized. The kind that wasn't supposed to be accessible to the general public. And while the picture ID was probably at least a decade out of date, the longer I stared, the more certain I was.

It was Hawk Nose.

Franco had found him. But that realization wasn't as shocking as the name listed on the citizen registry file.

Burton Kovaks.

"You were kidnapped by Andre Kovaks' *brother*?" Elise finally asked.

I waved helplessly at the file, unsure what to say, too busy remembering the night I'd watched Andre Kovaks hanged in the Great Hall for his blasphemy and his multiple crimes against the Vantage Corporation. It had been my last full night with my parents—the last night I'd slept in my own bed in Sanctuary, certain that, uneasy doubts or not, I was bound for a long life of Legion service.

"Was he one of them?" Elise asked. "One of these Emmútari record keepers? Is this some sacred familial tradition or something?"

"I don't know," I said, shaking my head, which was threatening to overflow with those questions and a thousand more like them.

Franco couldn't get here soon enough, I decided—though, at the same time, I knew he wouldn't have concrete answers to these questions. All I really knew was that I still had a telepathic cloaking problem to solve, and even more questions now than I'd had fifteen minutes earlier.

I turned my own cloaking pendant over in my fingers, looking between it and the somber-faced image of a younger Burton Kovaks, mind whirling around, and around, and around.

And so the endless stream flowed on.

SPURRED by cheerful thoughts of Kovaks family trees and hybrid armies growing city-sized appetites, the next few days passed like a sandcloth over chaffed skin. Another round of civilian abductions came and went with a feeling of frightening routineness around Haven. Not that I was allowed to leave the apartment to see, or anything. I just gathered as much from my friends and from the reels.

I also gathered from the reels that, despite the fresh round of attacks and the increasingly clear picture of a war slipping out of control, reel coverage of my demonly episode in Humility somehow only seemed to be gaining traction instead of fading away as it should have. That was a problem, but there wasn't really anything I could do about it, sequestered as I was. Instead, I did my best to follow Glenbark's wishes, keep my head down, and crack the cloaking rune problem.

It was just that my best wasn't good enough.

Worse, despite Franco's discovery, the odds of our getting help from the Emmútari texts still seemed about as thin as optical shroud film. Franco agreed that Andre Kovaks had likely been involved with the remnants of the Emmútari. In fact, that assumption, made de novo from the odd circumstances of Andre's arrest at Vantage and the unique level of knowledge that'd been contained in his publicly released logs, had been what had led Franco to check the Kovaks family connections and find Burton in the first place.

But finding his name hadn't landed them any closer to finding the man himself. Franco was doing his best, of course, and Glenbark had agreed to put out a planetwide alert for Burton Kovaks' capture, but that was going to take time—if it even paid off at all. Meanwhile, they were busy in Therese's lab, hatching a system for identifying likely locations of undercover hybrid breeding facilities.

Maddening as it was to not be able to simply walk out the door and go visit—or even to just take a stroll and clear my head—my aching legs didn't much lament the chance to remain on the floor or the couch, unburdened by the nuisance of locomotion. My antics in Humility had taken a heavy toll.

That said, I gladly would've paid that toll again three times over for some kind of break with the confounded runes. I'd spent so much time staring at them that they were still there when I closed my eyes—still there when I slept, taunting me throughout the fitful nights.

The only bright side through all of it was Elise.

We trained. We talked. We worked on solving the mystery of the runes. And when it was all too much and our eyes met just so, we took the kind of breaks that only two teenagers locked in an apartment together could take.

It was during one of these breaks that Elise took me by the hand and led me into the bedroom, telling me she had a special surprise for me. I'd like to say I played it cool, but mostly, I followed like a hungry hound. There may have even been slobber.

"What did I do to deserve a surprise?" I asked, as she guided me to the corner of the bed and pushed me down onto it.

She gave me a smile that would've left me weak at the knees if I hadn't already been sitting. "You don't know what day it is," she said softly, sliding down to her knees in front of me, "do you?"

My body was already responding to her. "Uh…"

What day was it?

I couldn't think of anything but her hand sliding up my thigh, and her head dipping closer to my lap. She shot me a wink, dipping lower… and pulled a small dark box out from under the bed before leaning back to offer it to me with a brilliant smile.

"Happy birthday, flyboy."

"Holy scud," I muttered, absentmindedly laying a hand over my thundering heart. Had I honestly forgotten my own eighteenth birthday? "I… thanks, Lise. Can't believe it's already…"

Her smile only widened, and she forced the box into my hand. "Open it."

I studied her face for a moment, drinking in her infectious smile, then I did as she said, flipping open the dark lid with growing anticipation. My breath caught—a thousand different memories and emotions flashing through me all at once.

It was my dad's pendant. The very same darkened silver sigil of Alpha he'd worn at his breast every single day of his life. I would've recognized it anywhere.

I looked dumbly at Elise, who was watching me with an expression teetering between concerned and hopeful.

"Johnny managed to pull it from records. Apparently it was one of the few things that survived the fire. We thought you should have it."

I stared at the silver pendant in my hands. Turned it over to the back side, which had clearly been polished, but not enough to completely hide the charred evidence of the fire it had seen.

Elise's face fell. "Is it… too much?"

"I… No," I croaked, finally finding my voice. "No, Lise, it's… It's perfect."

She leaned in close, cupping her hands to the back of my head. "Are you sure? Because it kinda looks like you're gonna cry."

"I'm not gonna cry," I said as the moisture brimmed dangerously in my eyes.

She pulled me in for a deep, lingering kiss that ended with a few quick pecks on the cheeks and nose. "I love you, Haldin Raish."

"Dammit," I whispered as a single tear spilled over. "I guess that means I love you too, Elise Fields."

"Well that's good to know," she said, rising from her knees and leaning in with a satisfied smile. "Because the rest of the surprise comes later," she whispered in my ear before standing back up and pulling me to my feet. "After cake."

I sniffed and cleared my throat, an odd mixture of sadness, tender emotion, and animalistic arousal all warring in my body. "Cake?"

But she just backed to the closed bedroom door, beckoning with a single finger and a mischievous smile.

"You didn't," I said, wiping my eyes and pulling my dad's pendant on as I went to join her.

She just shrugged and gestured to the door. I pulled it open, and there were Johnny, Franco, James, and Phineas, all standing there waiting.

"Surprise!" called James.

"I thought we *weren't* doing the surprise thing," Johnny said.

"I got excited," James said, looking embarrassed.

Franco brandished a small cake, smiling. "I know it's hard to think of celebrating anything in times like these, but we just wanted to remind you that we're here for you and that we're all going to come through this thing together. Happy birthday, Haldin."

"And may Alpha grant a thousand blessings on your cursed ass," Johnny added, clapping an arm around Phineas' shoulders and then immediately rethinking the move.

I just looked from Elise's shining smile to the rest of them, all watching me, all of them radiating caring warmth—or at least mild fondness, in Phineas' case. It was the love of a family, and it pulsed through me as I stepped into the room, pretty sure I'd been overly optimistic with my promise that I wouldn't cry.

Then my palmlight buzzed.

I thought little of it—didn't even consciously intend to check it. But my damned fingers reflexively uncurled, and once my eyes flicked over the message info, I couldn't look away.

It was a full message, with a title line and everything: *A Peaceful Request.* And below that, in the ID line: *The Sanctum of Alpha.*

Just like that, the magical warmth of that moment evaporated. Someone might've said something back in the room, but I wasn't there anymore. My world had condensed in on that single line.

Since when did the entire establishment of the Sanctum send private messages to Haldin Raish?

The message wasn't extremely long, but I skipped it anyway, scrolling straight to the signature with a sinking suspicion. And there it was, signed in some fancy tailored digiscript, right next to the sigil of Alpha.

Servant of the Almighty Alpha, and High Cleric of the Sanctum.

"The High Cleric," I muttered to myself.

I looked up and was almost surprised to find my friends all staring at me.

"The High Cleric sent me a message." My tone sounded flat and dumb to my ears.

They all looked as dumbfounded as I felt. All of them but Franco, who pressed the cake into James' hands and stepped forward. "What does it say?"

I scrolled to the top of the message and started reading, only barely comprehending through the mental haze. I reached the bottom and held the palmlight out to Franco, needing him to tell me that I was actually seeing what I thought I was.

"What does it say?" Elise asked beside me, watching her dad's face with frightened eyes.

I felt dizzy, my head whirling with all of it—the scudstorm of the past cycle, the implications of receiving this message now, mere days after an unidentified telepath had tried to murder me in my sleep.

"The High Cleric peacefully requests Haldin's presence at the White Tower," Franco said slowly, holding my wrist as he scanned through the message once more, just to be sure. "He wants him there tomorrow at noon."

Turned out, I had read it right, spinning head and all.

Happy birthday to me.

2 5

OLD WOUNDS

"Remind me again why this isn't the worst idea ever," I muttered to Johnny, keeping my eyes ahead on the gleaming tower that utterly dwarfed the descending transport's front viewport. The White Tower.

"High General says so?" Johnny replied in an equally hushed tone.

"She also said I was on house arrest," I grumbled. "What happened to that?"

The transport touched down with an easy jostle, and Ordo Dillard leapt straight to it, issuing orders to First Squad with precision. I'd always thought he was a good ordo, but today he was perfect—his stance crisp, the authority in his voice absolute. First Squad snapped to his commands with a discipline that would've made Mathis proud, disembarking to form a perimeter in pristine order.

That's what happened when the High General of the Legion came for a ride-along with your squad.

Glenbark stood from the seat ahead of us, paying little outward attention to the disciplined display around us and instead turning to fix me with a look that let me know our comments hadn't gone unheard. She was especially decorated and composed today—the High General of the Legion, in all her calm fury and decorum. She even had her ceremonial sword belted on.

Her stare made me want to squirm.

"It isn't the worst idea ever," she said, leaning in close enough that only we would hear, "because the only alternative you've left me with, Citizen Raish, is to deny the invitation of the High Cleric himself and invite war with the Sanctum and open rebellion from half my generals. Our coming here today—your playing nice in there today—might be the only thing that changes that." She favored Johnny with an approving look and the faintest ghost of a smile. "Plus, I say so."

Demons below, was he starting to rub off on her?

Given that we were about to meet the man whose predecessor had tried to execute me a few short cycles ago, I sure hoped not. Especially since the last High Cleric had only wanted to kill me because he'd been a raknoth and I'd been screwing with their plans. He probably hadn't given a damn that Carlisle and I were Shapers or demons or whatever else they wanted to call us. The new High Cleric clearly did.

And looking out at the crowd of spectators amassing around our perimeter and the front courtyard of the White Tower, I wasn't even sure I could blame him.

My existence was becoming a public disturbance.

"I should've listen to Lise and given Barbara that interview when I had the chance," I said, mostly to myself.

Johnny patted my shoulder. "Hey, at least you two got one last good swive in, right? Plus, cake."

Glenbark and I both turned frowns on him.

He shrugged. "What? Tell me that's not worth something."

Glenbark turned back to me. "You're not dying today, Raish. Certainly not before I have my cloaks, and preferably not until long after." She started to turn away, then paused as if remembering something. "And for the record," she added, "you're still on house arrest."

I wanted to say something smart and sarcastic about just how evident and touching her concern was, but I held it in, thinking diplomatic thoughts. Play nice. That was the theme of the day. Play nice with the High Cleric who may or may not have already signed my execution order.

This was a mistake.

But Glenbark was already waving us toward the transport's exits, busy checking in over the battle channel with the other ordos in our escort detail. Johnny was taking his feet, offering me a hand up.

I was already here.

It was already done.

All I could do was stick to the plan.

What plan? whispered a voice in the back of my mind.

Stepping back into the streets of Divinity—or the grand courtyard of the White Tower, as it were—felt wrong, somehow. Foreign. Not that it had actually been that long since I'd been in the city. It hadn't even been a full cycle since Johnny and Mathis had come to our cramped little Legion hideaway. It was just that I felt out of place in the sprawling city, under the gleaming majesty of its towers.

Under the watchful eye of its people.

There were hundreds of them along the edges of the expansive courtyard. Thousands, maybe. More pouring in by the second, staring and pointing and animatedly chatting back and forth. Too many people watching our meager detail of three Legion companies marching for the might of the White Tower.

Too many eyes on me.

I looked northeast and forced a smile at the distant towers, imagining that Elise could see me—which she probably could. That had been the entire point of having them tag along in a civilian skimmer, right? A means of escape that wouldn't risk starting a civil war between the Legion and the Sanctum.

Just in case.

The White Tower loomed above us, still the tallest structure in Divinity even after the Great Hall and several floors below it had all been obliterated by Carlisle's final act. I'd wanted to ignore the sight of it on the flight in. But then I'd thought of everything Elise had said yesterday, and how I'd been failing to handle things since the incident. I'd decided it was time to look. I'd even tried to think thoughts of gratitude instead of guilt, staring down at Carlisle's wreckage.

"Deep breaths, buddy," Johnny said beside me.

I nodded and did as he said, noticing how tense I was.

So maybe it was going to take more than some deep-cutting words and a day of reflection to get me centered. But it was a start, at least.

"Hey look," Johnny added, pointing off to the right of the tower, "they fixed the windows."

He didn't have to explain what windows he was talking about. I'd been unconscious by the end of our big fall from the tower, but Johnny and Elise had later told me about the way the glass had shattered in my wake as I'd acted like a human brake, venting our plunging velocity off in a raw outpouring of telekinetic force.

It had been a terrible night. The worst of my life, next to the night Al'Kundesha had taken my parents from me. And not just because of the fall. The fall, arduous as it had been, had been little more than a hard punctuation on the end of a night of horrors I knew would be with me as long as I lived.

And here we were again.

Maybe that's why everything felt so wrong, marching across the courtyard, with its lovely flowers and its happily burbling fountains all continuing their cheery existence, refusing to acknowledge the darkness that had touched this place not even three cycles past. Or maybe it was the larger-than-life-sized sculpture of the prophet, Sarentus, at the base of the great Tower steps, his head bowed and his hands spread wide, palms upward, ready to receive the word of Alpha.

My mind flashed to the illustration Franco and I had seen back in Humility, in Pasty and Hawk Nose's dungeon—Sarentus the prophet facing down the last of the Emmútari elders, his eyes so clearly rendered in faded blood red. Yet another reason we needed to find those two. Even thinking about the implications of that drawing this close to the White Tower filled me with concern that I might simply burst into blasphemous flames where I stood.

But no such luck.

Above, Glenbark was cresting the wide stone stairs at the head of our party beside the ordo prime of Bear Company. Dillard and First Squad kept closer to me and Johnny. I was glad Glenbark had chosen to keep the Hounds with me after Humility. Mara's frosty looks aside, my shaking nerves were comforted by the familiarity of the legionnaires around me— especially Edwards, who lumbered along beside me opposite Johnny. I still wished I'd had the chance to speak privately with Dillard to apologize for once again complicating his life, but that would have to wait.

We passed under the great arch at the top of the sprawling steps and proceeded past the large sculpture of Alpha's sigil. The shouts of the crowd seemed to grow more insistent the closer we drew to the Tower.

Demon. Savior. Scudbucket.

None of them knew the first thing about me, but every single one seemed to have an opinion about who and what I was. Some shouted thanks and words of encouragement. Others tried to rush in and throw rotten fruit, only to be quickly repelled by our Wolf Company escorts.

I did my best to shut it all out, staring up at the Tower instead—the jewel of Divinity. Of Enochia, really. Unlike most of Divinity's architecture, there wasn't a square inch of permacrete to be glimpsed on the Tower's exterior. It was still there, of course, reinforcing the Tower's formidable hardsteel skeleton. But no one saw that side of the Sanctum's holy palace. To the outside observer, the White Tower was all sleek duraglass and glossy white alloys—so pristinely glimmering that it could be mistaken for a beam of pure, condensed light when the sun hit it just so.

We reached the tall duraglass doors. A small army of servitors and Sanctum acolytes were awaiting us with uneasy stares in the atrium, but I was mostly focused on the dozens of cream-and-gold armored Sanctum Guard lining the space. Most of them had been raised by the Sanctum, trained from the ages of twelve to eighteen as Legion tyros like Johnny and me, and then returned to take their stations here. I might have even known a few of the Guard in this room, but you never could tell through the opaque golden faceplates of their helmets.

As far as most civilians were concerned, Sanctum Guard weren't so different than legionnaires, enforcers, or any other vessel of authority. The Legion, after all, almost exclusively followed the will of the Sanctum in times of peace. But this wasn't a time of peace, and right then, I could tell I wasn't the only one in our group thinking about just how much the Sanctum Guard were *not* the Legion's soldiers. They belonged to the High Cleric—his own private army, nearly twenty-thousand strong. And right then, I couldn't help but feel they were not our allies.

A tall wisp of a cleric swept across the polished atrium floor to meet us. He walked with a chronic hunch in his back, his arms crossed and his hands hidden within folds of his robe sleeves.

"High General Glenbark," he said in a thin, airy voice. "Alpha's blessing to you and your regiment." His rheumy eyes found me and lingered as if to make it clear that said blessing did not apply where demons were concerned. "I am Cleric Housfeld. The High Cleric is expecting you if you'd allow me to show you the way."

"Please, your holiness," Glenbark replied.

It made me slightly uneasy, the subtle air of deference that came over her in this place. Or was that just my imagination?

I followed along, trying to ignore the frightened gazes riding me through the atrium. Together, the Tower's massive mag lifts were plenty large enough to accompany our three companies of legionnaires, but Glenbark left Bear and Wolf Companies to wait below, keeping only Hound with us. I did my best to trust her reasoning and distract myself with the spectacular window view of Divinity as we climbed.

"The High Cleric has had to relocate to smaller quarters ever since the...

incident in the Great Hall," Cleric Housfeld said as we ascended, his tone carrying a hint of apology or embarrassment.

Incident? He knew who I was—knew that the *incident* he referred to had in fact been my botched execution, which had led to the death of hundreds, including Carlisle—and he was going to act like the unsettling part of all of this was that we had to meet the High Cleric in less regal quarters?

Johnny's hand on my arm was a silent warning my control was visibly slipping. I closed my eyes. Relaxed clenched muscles. The lift slowed, and I opened my eyes to catch Glenbark glancing at me with what might've been a look of sympathy or warning. Maybe both.

Cleric Housfeld was pointedly avoiding looking at me. "This way, please," he said, stepping smoothly between the opening doors as if he were eager to avoid spending a moment longer than necessary in the lift with us —or with me.

The wide hallway we stepped into was elegant to say the least. Rich, cream-toned marble floors. Vaulted ceilings, twice as high as you'd find in any other skyscraper in Divinity. Two dozen Sanctum Guard adorned the walls, their lines centered on an ornate wooden door I assumed must lead to the High Cleric's current quarters. They stood at rigid attention as we approached, rifles in hand. I couldn't imagine they normally kept a full squad posted outside the High cleric's door, but it wasn't any mystery why they were here now.

I fought the urge to squirm as a few detached from the wall to pat me down. They didn't find anything. Bringing a few meager weapons would have served little purpose. Of course, if anyone thought that meant I was unarmed, they hadn't been paying very close attention. Still, the two Sanctum Guard appeared satisfied—though it was hard to tell through the golden faceplates—as they backed away and nodded to Cleric Housfeld, who promptly rapped his spindly knuckles on the door.

To my surprise, the High Cleric answered the door himself. He was a short, unassuming man, with thinning brown hair and kind eyes. "Alpha's blessing to you all," he said in a gentle voice, his eyes settling on me. "Please, come in, Haldin."

His casual air threw me off balance. Here was the closest thing Enochia had to a supreme world ruler, and he was inviting me in as if for a friendly cup of caffa. I couldn't help notice Glenbark looked a touch off balance as well. She was opening her mouth to say something when the High Cleric turned to her.

"If you wouldn't mind, Freya, I would like to speak with Haldin in private for a moment."

Glenbark didn't look thrilled about it, but after a second, she relaxed and bowed her head. "Of course, your holiness."

It didn't exactly put me at ease, but when everyone's attention settled back on me, I didn't seem to have much choice in the matter.

I traded one last look with Johnny and strode into the High Cleric's quarters.

<hr>

OPULENT AND SPACIOUS were the first two words that came to mind as I entered the High Cleric's quarters. Rich dark wood trimmings. Lush rugs. A reading loft that was itself far larger than my entire Haven quarters and well-stocked with real, hardbound books. If this was what qualified as inferior quarters in the White Tower, then—

My idle inspection drew to a sharp halt as I sensed them.

Six of them, so still in their dark armor that my brain hadn't registered them as living things at first glance. The High Cleric's elite Onyx Guard— the unit whose legendary reputation made even the specters sound unimpressive. They watched me from behind their black faceplates, motionless as their namesake.

I remembered to breathe, chiding myself for having thought for even a second that *in private* would have possibly meant *alone.* I was the Demon of Divinity, and he was the High Cleric. Of course we weren't alone.

Behind me, the High Cleric closed the door, leaving the two of us *in private* with his six elite killers. He turned to me with something of a sad smile.

"Well then... Tea? Caffa? Anything else?"

Cup-full of poison, did he mean?

"I'm fine, thank you."

He bobbed his head and went to one of the cushy leather armchairs facing the wide, curved duraglass panel that looked down on Divinity. "Please," he said, waving at the armchair beside his.

I strode slowly around to the chair, wishing I'd thought ahead to dial my cloak out far enough to sweep the entire room for threats, but hesitant to adjust it now for fear the Onyx Guard might try to put me down if I did anything other than sit. So, I sat and did my best not to fidget. The High

Cleric barely seemed to notice, staring thoughtfully out at the lines of skimmer traffic glimmering in the sun.

Now that I had a moment to think, I noticed the High Cleric's mind felt different than that of any man I'd ever met—not telepathic, but not exactly defenseless, either. The minds of his Onyx Guard felt much the same. It was disconcerting, but I took some comfort from the fact that they didn't seem to notice my probing.

"You know," the High Cleric finally said, still staring out at the city, "the High General has messaged me no less than four times about you and those like you. Her most recent correspondence could even be reasonably construed as a warning about harming you. She seems to be under the impression that you are a vital resource to the war effort, regardless of your standing in the eyes of the Almighty." Slowly, he turned to study me. "What do you think about that?"

"I'd rather not be harmed, if that's what you're asking."

He smiled, and it looked genuine. "Oh, and I'd rather not cause harm, if that's what *you're* asking. But the fact remains that your existence is a challenge to the order of things, and a slight to the will of Alpha."

The words teetered on my tongue, caught between caution and anger. "Is that why you tried to have me killed?"

He continued studying me, his face betraying nothing, until he finally looked back to the city and its air traffic.

"Do you remember your lessons on the black pin beetle scourge in the eight-hundredth and fifty-seventh year of Enlightenment?"

"Not… particularly. Why?"

He shook his head, unperturbed. "Perhaps something a little closer to your area of expertise, then," he said. "Do you recall your learnings on Project Sentinel?"

That one was kind of hard to forget. As tyros, we'd heard all about the Legion's pioneering effort to create a new, more potent form of combat stims. And it had even worked—at first. Radically increased alertness, analytical reasoning, reflexes, and a dozen other metrics that made the users perfect little super soldiers. It was only after years of using Sentinel that the underlying degradation started to show itself between doses. Deranged psychoses. Violent mood swings. All kinds of other unpleasantness we'd heard about in class.

"You were barely a child when the worst of it was breaking," the High Cleric said, seeming to detect that his point had landed, "but I'm sure you saw some of the horrors your classmates with affected parents had to go through."

He wasn't wrong about that.

"I take it this is your way of saying we shouldn't mess with nature?"

He tilted his head. "I'm merely pointing out two of the several thousand potent examples that've showed us, time and time again: when men think to bend nature to their will, it is the good, innocent people who are made to suffer. Mind-enhancing drugs. Well-meaning ecologists. Interventions so seemingly beneficial at the time, leading to such unintended consequences." He raised a palm as if offering up something tangible. "The decline of natural order. The degradation of what is good and just."

I clenched my jaw, quelling the flood of arguments I wanted to hurl at his bullscud point. "If you're suggesting what I am is unnatural," I said slowly, calmly, "then with all due respect, holiness, I believe there are gaps in your own understanding of this planet's history."

His lips quirked—not quite smug, but not far off. "You speak of the Emmútari. The great deceivers of old."

The use of the order's proper name caught me more off guard than maybe it should have. "Well, you know what they say about history and victors."

His expression darkened, and for a flicker of a moment, I glimpsed something in him that gave me pause—a glint of righteous rage, brilliant as it was brief. It shook me.

I couldn't imagine many had seen that look before. They say the office of High Cleric can only be held by one so devout as to have transcended such flawed things as hatred. And while I couldn't have said for sure if the man hated me, in that moment, I saw something else, clear as day.

This man despised what I was. Despised it in a way that defied every inch of his kind eyes and holy grace.

"At any rate," he said slowly, settling with unnerving speed back to a place of control, "the history is irrelevant. The simple existence of something in nature does not imply that it is something to be embraced or tolerated. Diseases. Cancers. Natural predators. We must defend ourselves by the means becoming of servants of Alpha."

And there it was. *The means becoming of servants of Alpha.* Implying he had it on holy authority that my abilities didn't make that list.

Never mind the glaring hypocrisy of the entire existence of the Seeker core. That was surely fine, right? Because he was the one ordained to decide where we as Alpha-fearing humans were supposed to draw the line, and he said so.

Scud, maybe it wasn't even shoddy logic on his part. Maybe it was just that, to him, I wasn't human at all. To him, I was a walking abomination—a threat to the natural order of things.

"Fine," I said. "Never mind the history, and never mind the sanctity of what I am. You have a raknoth problem on this planet, and I'm guessing the fact you're talking to me at all means you realize you don't have a solution."

He studied me. "Alpha will provide for us, as he always has."

I stared at him, trying to gauge whether or not he was serious. "We have a host of tremendously powerful alien beings taking over our planet, using our own people to build and feed their army, and you're telling me... Fine. You're expecting a solution to fall from the sky?" I touched a hand to my chest. "Here I am. How are you so sure *that's* not the will of Alpha?"

That shadow flashed across his face again, but was quickly swept clear by righteous tranquility. "All is the Will of Alpha, child." He gestured out the window. "The routine tribulations." Gestured to me. "The dark temptations. But it *is* curious, isn't it? That these... aliens, as you say, would come here of all places in the universe and threaten us with abilities which only you and your kind possess any power to resist?"

"What I find curious, your holiness, is that you seem more concerned with casting blame and condemnation on my shoulders than with addressing the fact that there's an enemy out there you don't know how to beat. An enemy who can turn our legions against one another and grow their own armies as fast as ours can fall. The raknoth will consume this planet whole—millions dead, hundreds of millions—and you're more concerned about the morality of my existence?"

The High Cleric raised a hand for pause. Focused as I'd been on what I was saying, I hadn't even noticed the Onyx Guard ghosting closer around us, ready, waiting. I held very still, readying my own energy, trying not to look tense.

"And should I not be?" the High Cleric asked, calmly lowering his hand. "You are the one who seems to think you alone possess the ability to stop them."

"I'm *going* to stop them." I glanced pointedly around at the Onyx Guard. "The only question is whether you're going to have more of your people try to kill me while I'm at it."

He narrowed his eyes infinitesimally. Once again, he made no denial, but there was something else—some flicker of recognition, or something like it.

"Why did you invite me here, your holiness?"

He snapped his fingers. I tensed as the Onyx Guard in my left peripheral moved, but the Guard only moved to the door, gliding across the stone with eerily silent grace.

"I invited you here to judge what manner of man you are when the air is not thick with slugs," the High Cleric said. "And to discuss your position moving forward."

The door opened behind us. I turned as Glenbark and Johnny marched in, both tense, followed by a striking blonde girl who—

I sucked in a breath.

It was Siren.

I'm not sure if I cursed or made a sudden movement or what. Something set the Onyx bastards off. My extended senses trilled, my reflexes kicked, and the next I knew, I'd made a flipping leap right over my chair and landed beside Johnny and Glenbark, six stunner bolts all crackling to a halt a hair's breadth shy of my raised hands, every Onyx Guard in the room prowling my way with weapons raised.

"Enough," called the High Cleric.

The Onyx Guard responded robotically, weapons lowering, still ready but not quite aimed at me. I let the caught stunner bolts fall, drawing my defenses tighter.

"Someone's jumpy," Siren muttered, swinging the door shut behind her. "Can't imagine w—"

"Silence, Seeker," the High Cleric said.

Siren flinched as if he'd struck her, bowing her head and saying nothing, her fingers tracing the slender dark strip of the collar she wore at her throat.

"What is the meaning of this, your holiness?" Glenbark asked, her tone stern but seeming to lack its usual authority in this place of Sanctum power. "I was given to understand we had an agreement."

An agreement? What agreement?

I risked dropping my gaze from the Onyx Guard to take in Glenbark's expression. She didn't look happy. Neither did Johnny.

"Careful, my child," the High Cleric said. "These are dark forces you tamper with. I would merely see to it they are properly controlled."

Glenbark's face was stony as she glanced at Siren, then back to the High Cleric. "Forgive me, holiness, if I'd rather not have assassins loitering on my base, babysitting my assets."

Understanding dawned like a den of wriggling ice worms in my stomach. I glanced at Siren, expecting to see glib victory in her eyes, but she kept her gaze fixed to the floor, real fear in her eyes.

"—cept prudent cautions," the High Cleric was saying, "then I'll have to insist you leave your asset here to be properly handled."

My mind was whirling. This was unfolding too fast, Glenbark talking like she'd already made a deal for my spirit. I looked back to the High Cleric, fixing the positions of the six Onyx Guard in my mind. I didn't know where this was going, but I was sure I didn't like it. If I could move fast enough, I might be able to—

Don't do it, came a soft voice—Siren's, I realized. The raw, vulnerable plea in her tone caught me off guard. I hesitated.

Then something jabbed into the back of my neck, and before I could move, electric jolts arced through me, locking my limbs rigid until I toppled. I hit the ground, convulsing, uncomprehending. Something slipped around my neck. Johnny's pendant, I realized. He was crouched over me, an odd look in his eye, and a stun rod in his hand.

It didn't make sense. He couldn't. Wouldn't. And yet here I was, twitching uncontrollably on the floor, liquid warmth crawling up my spine.

"Johnny?" I tried to croak past a dry mouth and a sluggish tongue.

He avoided my eyes, rolling me over. Restraints tightened around my wrists. The warmth was spreading, weighing my eyelids like softsteel anchors.

I tried to look up. Saw only Johnny's furrowed brow, and Glenbark hovering over his shoulder.

"Don't fight it, Raish," she said. "Your fate's already sealed."

2 6

HEAVY LIFTING

I blinked out of darkness on a rippling wave of disorientation and found myself staring at a set of green-blue eyes hovering startlingly close to mine.

"Buddy, you're gonna need to take a deep breath and—"

I lashed out before I could fully recall why. Those green-blue eyes widened as they flew away and thunked into a wall—no, a bulkhead—just as my brain caught up.

Johnny.

I rolled off the bench and stumbled to my feet.

Johnny had taken me down with a stun rod. Why? And why—

A pair of preposterously large arms closed around me from behind.

"Easy, kid," someone said. "No one's gonna hurt y—agh!"

I lashed out again, and something heavy hit the bulkhead behind me. Adrenaline screamed through my veins, telling me to fight, to run. To not trust a single one of these bastards. But why?

"Listen to me, Raish," a voice called, hard and resolute. *Glenbark.*

Because Freya Glenbark had betrayed me. That was why.

"We need to talk abou—"

I whirled, casting my will out, and yanked her a foot off the deck, tightening my telekinetic grip hard enough that she'd have no illusions about what was happening. It was only then that I really registered we were back on the Legion transport.

And that all of First Squad was aiming weapons at me.

"Lower your weapons," Glenbark snapped. "Everyone. Now."

First Squad complied with unerring discipline, though the wary stares remained.

Behind me, someone was laughing softly. I glanced back and saw Siren sitting in the last seat, one leg crossed, elbow propped to the knee, resting her chin on the palm of her hand and looking generally amused. She smiled at me. "This is so much more exciting than Sanctum life."

"Mara," Glenbark said, surprisingly calm and poised for someone floating in a tight telekinetic cage, "if she talks again on this flight, hurt her."

"I don't think the High Cleric would appreciate that very much," Siren said.

"You're here as his eyes," Glenbark said, "not his mouth." She looked back to Mara. "Not another word from her."

"Your will, my hands, sir," Mara said, cracking her knuckles and starting toward Siren, careful to give me a wide berth.

"Citizen Raish," Glenbark said.

I was too distracted watching Johnny pull himself back to his feet, rubbing his head. On the opposite side of the cabin, Edwards was doing much the same.

"Scud, broto," Johnny groaned, "I know that was rough back there, but —" He touched the back of his head and winced. "Ouchie!"

Glenbark's voice cut through my swell of guilt. "Haldin."

I turned to meet her eyes and was almost surprised to find I still had her suspended over the deck.

"If you would kindly put me down, I'll explain what's happening."

I did, the beginnings of embarrassment burning at my cheeks as I looked around at the twenty-some legionnaires all watching me, waiting to see if I'd explode or not. But why should I be embarrassed? Wasn't I the one who'd been back-stabbed back there?

Glenbark found her feet, gathered herself with grace, and tilted her head toward the transport's front cabin. "In private."

I looked around, mumbled a few apologies to Edwards, Johnny, and the squad at large, and followed her up the steps.

Siren's sultry voice called after us. "Don't go sharing all your secrets without m—"

There was a sharp smacking sound, followed by Siren's, "Oww! Bitch!"

Another smack followed. Then silence.

That, at least, gave me a tiny bit of feral satisfaction. I'm sure Mara enjoyed it more than I did.

Up by the pilot's nook, out of sight of the main cabin, Glenbark pointedly gestured to the back of the transport then to her own ear, one eyebrow arched in question. I adjusted my cloaking pendant until it was just the two of us inside, and spoke quietly. "If you're asking if she can hear us, I highly doubt it. If you're asking if I'd like to know what the scud is going on, then—"

"It had to look convincing, Haldin," she said quietly.

"Convincing as my best friend stabbing me in the back?" I hissed.

"I did what I thought was necessary," she fired back. A hint of hesitation touched her brow. "For what it's worth, I am sorry. I didn't enjoy keeping you in the dark. But we won't win this war without Sanctum support, and that meant proving I have you contained. It had to look genuine. I'm doing my best to keep both our heads off the chopping block, here."

I clenched my fists, wanting to be angry but only finding that she was making too much sense. It was no secret General Auckus and his supporters were in arms over Glenbark involving me with the Legion at all. Keeping Glenbark from having to spit in the Sanctum's face by denying the High Cleric's invitation was exactly why I'd agreed to play along in the first place.

Not that I'd had much of a choice.

It had either been that or escaping Haven by force and going back on the run for real. Still, deterring civil war within the Legion had seemed a worthy enough reason to play along. But she was right—none of the Legion politicking would even matter unless the High Cleric believed that Glenbark had me under control—that I was nothing more than a tool in her fingers. And that was exactly what she'd just shown him.

Plus, on top of all that, I was pretty sure she actually meant it when she said she was sorry, and I doubted those were words she said often.

"Fine," I finally forced myself to say. "Fine, I understand. But I'm not working with that woman watching over me."

She opened her mouth to say something, but I pressed ahead, refusing to budge on this.

"No. I don't care what the deal is, sir. He tried to have me killed, and now his assassin is sitting on our transport. I don't want her anywhere near me or my people. Get rid of her, or I'm gone."

"You can't leave, Haldin."

I clenched my jaw. "You think you can stop me?"

She didn't bristle at my challenge—just shook her head, barely even seeming to hear it. "There's more I need to tell you. The High Cleric made it clear his agent's presence was an unnegotiable condition of my taking you back into Legion custody, but—"

"Unnegotiable? You really don't think having her try to kill me under your nose sort of breaches any agreement you two could ever make?"

"He's the High Cleric of the Sanctum, Haldin. I can't ignore his demands any more than I can afford to fight two wars at once." Her face darkened. "But there's more you need to know. He also made it clear that your life will only be withheld from the Sanctum's kill list as long as you remain in my custody. And he's officially re-declaring you an enemy of Enochia."

My fists clenched, the news burning through me like a wave of pure rage. *That* was why she was so sorry. Not for lying to me. She was sorry because I'd listened to her—tried to help her, for the love of Alpha—and now I was headed right back where I'd been before the White Tower. Hunted. Hated.

An enemy of Enochia.

"Officially, you are to be my prisoner," she said quietly. "As long as you remain within Haven, you—"

"I what?" I snarled. "I won't be killed on gropping sight?"

She grabbed me by the shoulders, then, her grip like adamantus, and the conviction in her eyes so intense I nearly forgot I was angry for a moment. "I won't let it come to that, Haldin," she hissed. "You need to trust me on this."

Trust her? Trust the woman who'd just led me into a trap—just had me stripped of what little freedom I'd had?

For a moment, something inside me screamed for me to lash out—to smash her into the bulkhead. Reach out and blow the transport engines. They wanted a demon? I could show them one.

I could take this entire damned escort down, starting with her.

I looked into her eyes, trembling, her adamantus grip unwavering on my shoulders, and all I could see was her own righteous outrage, burning right against mine. I couldn't take it. Any of it.

"Why can't you gropping people just leave me alone?" I growled, jerking her hands from my shoulders with a sharp twist. I dropped to the nearest seat, burying my face in my tense hands until the emotion surged forth again. Before I knew it, I was spinning around, facing down into the rear cabin, and shouting at the top of my lungs. "What the scud is wrong with you people?"

No one answered. The few pairs of eyes I could see down there flicked away, pretending they hadn't been staring. Only Johnny's eyes stayed on me

—apprehensive and guilty—but as unwavering as Glenbark's grip. He held my gaze until I turned back around to find Glenbark watching me with pity in her eyes.

"What gives you the right?" I asked quietly. "Any one of them could've been born like me. Why should any of you get to have your gropping hooks in my life? You might as well execute me for the color of my eyes."

Her face was tight, her eyes angry. But not at me, I thought—and not even at herself—but at the injustice of it all. The injustice she'd led me to. I couldn't not see it in her eyes.

Freya Glenbark might not be my friend. I wasn't even sure she particularly cared about me on a personal level. But she wasn't the villain here, either. She was pissed. About all of this.

She settled stiffly in the seat beside me, not speaking for a while.

"The Sanctum is ready to join the fight in earnest," she said finally. "The High Cleric agreed to grant me secondary control over the assignment details of the Sanctum Guard across Enochia. They'll retain ultimate control, of course, but this will considerably free our resources to go hunting for Parker's hybrid facilities."

I looked at her. "Are you saying my freedom really made that much of a difference?"

She shook her head. "I'd like to think the two are as unrelated as they should be, but I can't claim to know the workings of the High Cleric's mind."

"Don't you mean Alpha's will?"

She studied me with those piercing blue eyes, her expression unreadable. "We're all bound by something, Haldin," she finally said, "be it honor and duty, service to Alpha, love and friendship…"

"Or a holy decree that you're a monstrous threat to humanity?"

"Your shackles are unique in shape and size," she admitted, "as are your abilities to affect change in this world. But you'd do well to remember that, fair or not, just or not, we all have our shackles to bear."

I studied her tired face, wanting to call bullscud and to tell her that was easy for someone in power to say, but the weight of her words settled over me, giving me pause. She touched my forearm—lightly, this time—and rose to leave me to my thoughts.

Demon's depths, maybe she did care after all.

I was even starting to flirt with the idea that maybe this development with the Sanctum had been inevitable anyway when the sounds of a scuffle in the main cabin caught my attention.

"—et me go, you crazy—Raish! We've got a problem!"

Siren's voice.

I frowned, leaning over to check it out. She couldn't possibly think I'd be on her side just mere days after she'd tried to kill me, could she?

"Sir?" one of the pilots called.

On the stairs, Glenbark caught my eye for a split second before we both turned to the pilot's nook.

"Sir, I'm picking something up down in that—"

That canyon, I assumed he meant to say, eyeing the rocky canyon a little ways ahead.

Instead, his face went slack without warning.

Vigilant one second, then just blank the next.

"Pilot?" Glenbark called. "Pilot, sitrep."

Commotion from the main cabin below.

"Hal?" Johnny called. "Siren's not looking so hot back here."

My insides went cold as the pieces all fell into place. I reached desperately for my cloaking pendant—just as the pilot turned his blank face back to the controls and jammed down on the stick.

The transport plummeted for the dusty grasslands that led up to the canyon below, dropping sharply enough that I left my seat and hit the ceiling. A thud and a sharp curse to my right told me Glenbark had done the same. I was too busy fumbling with my pendant, dialing out the cloak so that—

Ahead, both pilots came back to their senses with surprised yelps. One of them recovered and yanked back on the stick.

I reached out to help Glenbark back to the deck as the transport leveled out, but she landed fine on her own and whirled to the main cabin. "Lock it down, Hound Company!"

Affirmative cries from behind.

The pilots scrambling to regain control ahead.

Glenbark threw herself into the chair beside me, working the restraints. My fingers lingered on the pendant, my mind whirling with possibilities and half-formed plans. I didn't know what to do, which way to move. Then the transport engines gave a series of sharp cracking pops, and the decision was made for me.

Down.

Straight down. Like a powerless lightsteel death trap.

Screams and curses from the cabin. The acrid stench of fried electronics. The pilots trading their own curses, slapping at the controls.

I started to reach out reflexively. Realized there wasn't a chance in demons' depths I could catch a falling transport full of geared soldiers.

The backup engines sputtered to life.

Too late. Not enough.

I threw my power into slowing what I could anyway, tugging my own seat restraints across my chest with shaking hands.

We hit.

It was like Alpha himself had dropped an ocean on me. The impact was ferocious, smashing and jerking and crushing me in so many directions at once that I simply collapsed into myself, barely clinging to consciousness. Then it receded. The world expanded into five senses once more, and we were sliding—the entire transport cruising on with too much forward velocity, sliding across dirt and stone with a horrible wrenching screech.

Sliding straight for the canyon. Too fast.

I stared at the gaping maw of the approaching canyon and the unreasonably calm blue sky beyond, clinging to the hope our considerable weight and drag would bleed off our equally considerable momentum in time.

Maybe.

The pilots were in a frenzy, flaring the brakes, dropping the landers.

Maybe.

We were slowing, the lip of the canyon crawling closer, closer to the prow.

Maybe.

The prow crested the lip of the canyon with a mournful crack, barely at a crawl now. But still too fast. I felt the edge of the canyon slide by beneath the pilot's nook, beneath me and Glenbark. Too far. We were tipping.

I threw myself into the transport's lightsteel skeleton and heaved with everything I had.

Our slide was slowing, slowing, but at the same time surrendering inch by agonizing inch of leverage. The prow of the transport began to dip into the canyon, the rear tilting up to follow.

I pulled more energy, my body screaming in protest.

Still tipping.

More energy. *More.*

Too much energy, ripping through every inch of me. I was going to explode with it. I opened my mouth and let the scream tear out of my throat.

The transport yanked to a halt, half-pitched into the canyon.

Shocked silence. Groaning metal. A crackling inferno of energy burning me alive, and—

Why the scud weren't they moving?

"GO!" I roared.

Glenbark dropped her wide-eyed surprise in an instant. "You heard him, Hounds!" she shouted. "Out the back! Go!"

A flurry of activity from the cabin. Ahead, the pilots disengaged themselves from their restraints with shaking hands and crawled carefully from their dangling nook. I closed my eyes, holding on, each second like a crushing infinity, trying to distract myself with the tiny weight shift of each legionnaires piling out of the rear hatch.

A tugging sensation at my chest nearly broke my focus. The ship teetered, groaning. Men were shouting somewhere behind.

"Don't give up now, soldier," came Glenbark's voice, right in front of me and yet oddly distant as immersed as I was in my personal wrestling match with a ten-thousand pound transport.

Easy for you to say, I tried to get out. Mostly, I think I just growled as she hefted me over her shoulder and set off down the steps.

The world was closing around me, receding to nothing but the tilt of the ship and the blinding light of the energy ripping through my body. I was burning and freezing from the inside, all at once. I thought I might've heard Johnny's voice nearby, running beside us. I couldn't tell. Couldn't seem to notice anything but the electric torrent roaring through me and the thudding of astonishingly shiny boots on the deck above my head.

Above my head? That didn't seem—

Focus.

But it was too late. With slow, inevitable certainty, the transport began pitching further into the canyon. I tried to hold on, tried to restore the balance, but I'd lost it.

That was okay, whispered some dark corner of my mind. I'd tried my best. At least now the pain would end.

But then the world flooded back into my senses, taking shape in the form of Freya Glenbark's athletic backside by my face, the groaning wreck of our transport lurching away from us… and the gaping canyon depths the three of us were all currently falling into.

This, I decided, was most certainly *not* okay.

I opened my mouth in a silent scream, trying to reach out—to do anything.

Then my legs smashed into something on Glenbark's front side, and a pair of arms shot around her backside, nearly cuffing me on the head from both sides at once. Grunts and curses. We were moving, falling. We crashed to the ground, my legs crushed between Glenbark's weight and the body of our rescuer. Momentum carried my top half off Glenbark's back, and I caught myself on the dusty rocks, earning myself a scraped hand and a jarred elbow.

Head spinning from channeling fatigue, I glanced down to find Glenbark's head rising from our pile, looking around in surprise at the pale hands clamped firmly to her buttocks. As if they felt her gaze, the hands shot into the air, fingers splayed, trying to play it cool. Glenbark opened her mouth to say something.

Then the thunderous crash of our transport meeting the canyon floor below jarred us all back to the present.

Glenbark was back on her feet in an instant, waving off the concerned legionnaires pressing in around her. "On your feet, soldiers!" she cried.

"It's a fine ass, broto," a voice rumbled underneath me, "but I could do without it on my face, all the same."

I rolled off Johnny, thinking to get to my feet and help him up, but the channeling fatigue wasn't done with me. The world spun, my vision wavered, and I hit the dirt and retched.

"Thanks for the catch, ass-face," I groaned when I was done.

"Lock it down, kids." Edwards' startlingly strong arms grabbed me beneath the arms and hauled me to my feet. "Grab-ass time's over."

"Tell me about it," Johnny mumbled, dusting himself off and accepting a hand from Mara.

My legs were shaky, my body trembling with fatigue, but we had bigger problems. More transports were down in the dusty stretch behind us—three more clearly having crashed short of the canyon, the other two in the process of landing to come see what the scud had just happened. And at the sight of a wide-eyed Siren rushing toward me, I remembered what it was that had brought us down in the first place.

I was opening my mouth to call out to Glenbark when the first enemy transports rose out of the canyon, side doors thrown wide to reveal the small army of hybrids waiting inside. And there, in the center transport—

My breath caught, my mind flashing back to the battle at the White Tower.

There, in the center transport, stood Frosty, the dark-haired, icy-eyed Seeker who'd nearly burned Elise alive before fleeing the Tower with the old High Cleric.

And her eyes were alight with crimson raknoth fire.

27

FROSTY

For a moment that probably felt longer than it actually was, the world stood still—hybrids standing at eerily silent attention, legionnaires watching with tensed trigger fingers, or looking up from tending wounded squad mates, waiting to see what the beasts would do. As if there was any real question.

Raknoth eyes pulsing bright crimson, Frosty tilted her head back and gave a chest-shaking roar.

The hybrids charged, taking up her call and leaping from their hovering transports like bloodthirsty demons. The air filled with the cracks and hums of legionnaires opening fire all around us. Edwards and Mara were hauling me and Johnny back, away from the canyon ridge and toward the rest of our downed transports and the heart of our forces. I was too busy gaping at the hundreds of spent softsteel slugs slamming into a wall of thin air just shy of the hybrids' charging line.

Frosty.

She stood at the lip of her transport, eyes burning and hands thrust out in a manner that confirmed my fears.

She'd been taken by a raknoth, abilities and all.

We had another Zar'Faenor on our hands.

A hasty twist of my cloaking pendant cut the charging edge of her army off from her protection. The hybrids faltered from the interruption in tele-pathic command and the sudden onslaught of slugs tearing into their ranks.

Then their beastly instincts took hold, and chaos broke loose. They swept into the legionnaire ranks like a wild storm of claws and fangs, killing whatever they could reach, dying in swaths only to be replaced by more.

Johnny pressed a sidearm into my hand as we drew up against one of the downed transports and Edwards and Mara turned to open fire. At the back of the transport, Glenbark rose from a pale-faced legionnaire she looked to have just finished dragging to relative safety, rattling a steady stream of commands over the battle channels as she stalked toward us, sidearm in hand.

"What in demon's depths is that thing?" she cried over the sounds of fighting when she reached us.

It wasn't hard to imagine what *thing* she was talking about.

"She used to be a Seeker," I called back. "Disappeared at the White Tower. Now she's—"

"RAISH!"

The cry was inhumanly loud, and so distorted I wasn't really sure I'd heard it right. At least not until I saw Frosty tense and leap from her hovering transport straight for us. She arced impossibly high, sailing through the air, her transport bucking and nearly crashing into the canyon behind her from the force of her launch.

"Holy scud," Johnny said, gaping up at our coming doom.

Glenbark ripped her sword free from its scabbard, grim determination in her eyes. Much as I appreciated her spirit, I dialed my cloak out, preparing to catch Frosty and throw her straight back down the canyon.

Not that that would stop her.

Before I could, though, a dark skimmer came soaring through the air, aimed to plow straight into Frosty's side. The instant before it struck, though, Frosty threw out a hand, snarling, and the skimmer crunched to a violent halt, the hood crumpling against thin air a few feet from her outstretched hand.

Frosty hovered there in midair, holding herself and the crashed skimmer aloft with telekinesis, favoring her would-be attackers with a deadly, fanged smile.

Franco, I realized.

That was Franco's skimmer.

I was already running.

"Get out of there, Lise," I sent desperately, pumping my legs faster. *"All of you. Jump. Now."*

They didn't hesitate. Frosty was yanking the skimmer closer, looking like she intended to rip it open with her bare hands, when the skimmer's doors kicked open and four lightly armored forms dropped out. I started reaching out to catch them, then cursed when Frosty beat me to it.

Elise, Franco, Phineas, and James all yanked to a halt barely five feet into their fall, caught again in the raknoth's telekinetic grasp.

"Mara!" I cried.

She didn't require any more explanation than that.

Frosty jerked as the slugs pelted into her, her skin rippling light green as her battle hide emerged. But it worked. Elise and the others resumed their fall as the raknoth threw up an arm to cover her face and directed a blind roar in Mara's general direction. I drew to a halt beneath Elise—or as close as I had time to get—and threw my mind out to catch her and the others.

They thudded to the ground on wobbly legs, and I had to fight to keep my own knees from buckling, drained as I already was from earlier. At a horrendous crash from behind, I turned to find the front half of Franco's skimmer buried through the roof of the transport Mara had been shooting from. Mara was scrambling back to her feet behind the wreckage. Edwards, Johnny, and the rest of First Squad were still firing, mostly on the encroaching hybrids, but some at Frosty, who was falling their way, crimson eyes fixed on Mara.

"Come on!" I shouted to Elise and the others.

All around us, the fighting raged. The hybrids must've been young, scattered as they were in a wild killing frenzy, utterly without organization. The legionnaires, reduced largely to small unit tactics, weren't faring much better, but they seemed to be pulling it together, regrouping. I couldn't worry about that now. Not with Frosty rampaging up ahead.

On fresh legs, Elise handily outpaced me, drawing and extending her collapsible spear in a fluid motion as the first hybrid caught sight of her. It died a moment later. She rolled clear of a second creature's charge, drew a dagger, and tossed it out in front of me along with a telepathic, *"Catch."*

I did as she said, catching the weapon with telekinesis and burying it straight into her attacker's eyeball while she pivoted and paid a third hybrid in kind with her spear.

We pushed on, Franco and the others keeping our flanks clear. Several hybrids were converging on the transport ahead with bloodthirsty howls, now, spurred on by Frosty's approach. The raknoth herself finally hit the ground and sprang straight for Mara, who was perched atop the transport, dropping target after target with short, controlled bursts.

I lashed out reflexively and caught Frosty with a telekinetic blast that sent her skewing off course—and straight into First Squad.

Mara, having already hit the deck, took a split second to shoot me an exasperated look then sprang to her feet and resumed fire. On the other side of the transport, the screaming started.

"Dammit," I growled, pushing my legs harder.

We darted past the transport's prow, around the corner, and—

Voom!

An enormous wall of air and telekinetic force crashed into me like an explosive shockwave. I left my feet. Felt Elise do the same beside me. I clipped something—James or Phineas, maybe—and came out spinning. Reached out and managed to slow our combined flight. Hit the ground too hard next to Elise and James with nothing but empty space in my lungs and a sharp burning in my diaphragm.

"Ah, High General," came a cold, feminine voice from the transport. "I didn't see you there. What a pleasant surprise."

I sat up, wincing, gasping for air, and saw that we hadn't been the only victims. Everyone on that side of the transport was down, legionnaires and hybrids alike. That had been a monster of a blast. And Frosty didn't even look bothered by the channeling fatigue as she stalked toward Glenbark, her skin almost fully transitioned to scaly green raknoth hide now.

Alpha, she was powerful.

But it didn't matter. If Zar'Faenor had been killed, she could be too. I started pulling myself to my feet.

Ahead, Glenbark was already up, facing the supercharged raknoth with her sword in hand and grim resolve in her eyes. Frosty darted in with an almost playful air, like it was a rowdy pup she was trying to catch, and not the High General of the Legion. Glenbark moved with precision, avoiding Frosty and landing a rapid succession of cuts across her arms and throat. Or strikes, at least.

She might as well have been trying to cut permacrete.

Recognizing as much, Glenbark changed tactics and went for Frosty's underjaw with a hard stab. It might have even worked, if Frosty hadn't caught the blade in one bare, scaly hand. She raised the other, sprouting long claws to strike... then whirled as Johnny and Edwards charged in, lunging for her in tandem.

Johnny, she batted away with an invisible wave of force. Edwards, she caught by the throat, yanking the massive man aloft without discernible effort.

I threw my mind out, panic gripping me, the final moments of my dad's life playing before my eyes—when Al'Kundesha had snapped his neck just like this. I reached, desperate to tear Frosty's hand away before I had to watch someone else die.

A falling blur of dark armor and auburn hair struck Frosty before I could, and there was Mara, kicking Frosty's knees out, riding her to the ground with her wicked combat knife held ready for the kill.

For a second, I had a glimmer of hope it would work—even shifted my focus, preparing to help Mara drive the knife home. But then Frosty flung Edwards bodily against the transport hull, caught Mara's knife arm, and flipped her to the ground hard enough to break bones. Mara barely flinched. Just rolled over and jammed her knife into Frosty's knee.

Frosty let out a piercing shriek, slapping Mara's knife hand away, raising her foot to stomp her into the ground. I drew energy for a telekinetic blast to knock Frosty away. Something ripped into my left shoulder first—a line of fiery pain blossoming to the tune of a guttural growl and Elise crying my name.

Focus broken, I tried to rock away only to feel it dig deeper. A hybrid's claws, I realized, right before I felt the hand give a jerk and fall away, dead by Elise's spear.

A pair of sharp snaps and Mara's raw scream ripped me back to the fight ahead. It was a horrible scream—all her hardsteel discipline evaporating in that moment, burned away by all-consuming pain. I whirled in time to see Mara hit the transport hull and thump limply to the ground. Frosty was turning to Glenbark, a glimmering blade in her hand—the end of Glenbark's sword, I realized. Frosty had snapped it in two. The raknoth raised the broken blade, poised to strike.

I wrapped my mind around her and yanked. Hard.

The raknoth sailed toward us, covering half the gap in the air before slamming down to the stony dirt and bouncing a few rolls further. I was already charging forward, Elise at my side, with no better plan than to sink my dagger into one of those crimson eyes. Then I felt the tide of energy pouring into Frosty. She sat up, raising a hand our way.

"Split!" I all but screamed at Elise's mind.

We dove apart just as the air shook with a low boom. By the whipping wind, it felt like we'd just dodged a damn mag train. I rolled to my feet and launched my dagger at Frosty's face as she rose. She took it carelessly on the forearm and lunged straight for me. I twisted away from her first grab. Let my extended senses take control, ducking and weaving me through a flurry of attacks.

"Don't think I've forgotten you, Raish," Frosty hissed between brutal swipes. I could feel the aura of energy swirling around her, the air growing frigid as she drew more and more energy, her raknoth body seemingly unperturbed by the effort of containing it. "Too stubborn to die…"

That dam of energy broke open, and a wave of telekinetic force fell on me, crushing me to the ground. Frosty crouched down in front of me, shaking her head.

"… Too weak to matter."

Barely able to lift a finger, and firmly out of options, I threw my mind at hers like a cornered animal.

She was strong—every bit as strong as I expected a raknoth to be. But our footing in the telepathic arena wasn't nearly so laughable as our physical discrepancies. The pressure on my body weakened, her scaly lips pulling into a snarl as she repelled my attack.

"*This is what Al'Braka warns us against?*" she sent, and I thought I could hear just a hint of strain in her voice. "*Pathetic.*"

"Maybe so," I growled back, laboring to split my attention. "*But it makes you think, doesn't it?*"

And that's when Elise's spear came sailing through the air to strike Frosty square in the throat. The raknoth staggered back with a disturbing wet coughing sound. I tried to telekinetically drive the spear in deeper, but she was already ripping it free with a growl, snapping the composite haft in two like a twig. I rolled out of the way as she flung one piece at my head. When I came back up, she was already leaping past me, straight for Elise.

I caught the raknoth in my mind and slammed her to the rocky ground as hard as I could, stumbling to my feet.

"Shoot her!" I yelled, keeping the pressure on.

Half a dozen legionnaires gladly opened up, having been waiting for their shot. Around us, the rest of the fighting seemed to be dying down, Frosty's hybrids largely wiped out. Not that that meant we were at an advantage.

The first outpouring of slugs slammed into Frosty's invisible barrier, a line of spent softsteel quickly forming on the rocks between her and the legionnaires. She tried to rise, but I slammed her back down with telekinesis, holding her firm. Her crimson gaze snapped to me, and then she really put her back into it.

I was on my knees before I knew it, head spinning with the effort of keeping her immobilized. It was too much. I'd channeled too much. Was exhausted to my bones. I felt my body lilt forward, ready to topple to the rock.

And would that be so bad, if I just laid down and went with it?

Maybe not. I could all but feel the blessed emptiness of unconsciousness embracing me, like gentle hands lacing around my chest and shoulders from behind. A soft body pressing against my back. A daydream of Elise, inviting me to give in and—

"Hold on, Demon. Help is almost here."

I jerked a few inches from the darkness at the sound of Siren's voice in my mind. The hands were still there, wrapped around me.

Her hands.

What in demons' depths was she—

But I felt it then, like plunging into a cool, clear lake on a stifling Midsummer day—a gleaming reservoir of support and relief radiating from where she touched me, right there for the taking. And I didn't have time to ask questions.

What happened next was hard to understand by sensation alone. It wasn't so much that my fatigue went away as that I shared some of it, diluting its effects between myself and... Siren? I didn't know. Didn't understand what was happening. All I knew was that when I dug deeper to keep Frosty pinned down through another frantic surge, the effort was noticeably easier.

"Alpha be sweet," Siren groaned in my mind. *"Take it easy on a girl."*

Not easier, then, I guessed. Just distributed.

I wasn't sure whether to apologize or push harder.

More legionnaires were joining in from mopping up the hybrids now, a small mountain of slugs piling around Frosty. A few were even starting to punch through. I saw Edwards limping up with his heavy rifle. If we could just keep Frosty immobilized a little longer...

But then I felt them—two telepathic minds, howling through the sky straight for us—and my stomach fell.

More raknoth, coming to rescue their pinned ally?

I reached out, trying to investigate, and—

"No!" Siren sent. *"They're with us. Don't let it break your—"*

A low boom ended her thought as Frosty pounced on the distraction and let loose with a blast of force that sent most of the spent slugs rocketing back at the legionnaires like bomb-propelled shrapnel.

And I was too late to even try to stop it.

Slugs ripped into the ranks as legionnaires tried and failed to take cover in time. Some fell dead on the spot. Others hunkered down and returned fire, their armor taking the worst of the attack. I rose to wobbly feet, Siren slumping down behind me, apparently too exhausted to follow.

Frosty was already up, in full, monstrous raknoth form now, surveying her wreckage with a snarl from her elongating muzzle. Past her, near Elise, a gray skimmer was landing, carrying the two telepaths who'd pulled my attention a moment ago.

"*—here to help,*" Siren sent weakly.

Did that mean more Seekers?

Judging by Frosty's reaction, I was guessing so.

The raknoth called my dagger to hand from the dirt and turned my way, crimson eyes flaring bright. She touched fist to chest in mocking salute and flashed a fanged smile. For a second, I thought she'd charge—try to end me before any of us could recover.

Instead, she turned and hurled the dagger over the Legion line. Straight for Glenbark. The High General was bent over a wounded soldier, unaware. I let out a wordless yell. Reached out. All too late.

The blade rocketed forward, guided by Frosty's telekinetic desire.

"FREYA!" someone bellowed.

Glenbark snapped around, eyes wide, the blade mere feet away.

Then Johnny slammed into her side in a rough tackle, driving them both to the ground.

I nearly fell over in relief, then forced myself to turn back to Frosty instead. But she was already sailing through the air, back for the canyon from which they'd sprung their ambush. Her transport was waiting there, rising from the canyon depths to catch her in midair on the second inhuman leap.

She turned back, crimson eyes glaring down on us. "*Until next time, Haldin Raish.*"

Then the transport turned and sped off into open sky, leaving behind a desolate battlefield, overflowing with dead hybrids and wounded legionnaires. Dread weighing on my chest, I looked over to check if Johnny was okay.

Bleeding a bit maybe, judging from the way Glenbark was inspecting his shoulder, but decidedly not dead. *Thank Alpha.* I turned to see Elise jogging my way. She was unharmed, the worry on her face solely for me and the wounded. I thanked Alpha a second time, then allowed myself to buckle to a seated heap on the ground.

"She was always a bitch," Siren groaned beside me, "even before she went all red-eyes."

"Frosty?" I mumbled, my thoughts not quite all there.

She raised her head to look at me, looking amused despite her light pallor. "She is, isn't she?"

"Hal?" Elise called nearby. She took the last stretch at a run and dropped to her knees to wrap me in a tight hug. "Sweet Alpha, I can't let you out of my sight for a minute." She pulled back to look at me. "When your transport went down…"

"The Demon gave us quite the ride back there," Siren agreed, sitting up.

Elise shot a dark look at her but said nothing. Had Johnny already filled her in on why my assassin was sitting within spitting distance, then?

Elise focused back on me. *"Is Haven still safe with these people around?"*

"Probably not, but…" I lost the thought as Elise's words clicked. These people. Plural.

I'd nearly forgotten about our two telepathic arrivals.

They were watching us from beside the gray skimmer they'd landed in—a tall, slender man with long dark hair and the dark clothing to match, and a giantess of a woman, dressed all in dull grays and stern-faced beneath her short blond hair. Both, I noticed, wore slender collars just like Siren's. They had their hands raised in casual surrender, but neither one seemed all that troubled by the several legionnaires aiming weapons at them. I felt a flicker of something passing between them and Siren as Dillard parted from the crowd to go inquire as to what the scud they were doing here.

"Don't shoot them," Siren called, rising to her feet with a wince and a languorous sigh. "Pretty please."

At a look, Elise stood and hauled me to my weary feet to follow after her.

"—what you're doing here," Dillard was saying when we drew close enough to hear.

"It's none of your concern," said the slender dark-clad man in a voice that was deeper than I would've guessed. He wasn't quite stand-offish so much as dismissive, slightly tense, like he had somewhere to be, and this wasn't it.

"If you won't tell my ordo who you are," Glenbark called, pushing to the front of the ranks beside Dillard, "I'm going to have to grow insistent."

"He's a Seeker," I called, drawing confused looks from the legionnaires and dark scowls from the two telepaths.

"They both are."

28

BATTLE PLANS

"I can't believe Glenbark agreed to this," Elise muttered.

We were huddled together in the back of the fresh transport the closest outpost had sent to collect us from the canyon and see us back to Haven. I followed her gaze to where the three Seekers were surveying us from the opposite corner of the cabin—Siren with her sultry blond charms, and Dark Eyes and The Giantess with their brooding silence.

I wasn't entirely sure myself why Glenbark had so forcefully suggested they come along to explain themselves back in the safety of Haven. The safety of Haven seemed a whole lot less safe with them around. That the Seekers hadn't argued with Glenbark only increased my uneasiness. I was almost certain it would've been better to send them on their way.

Even without my extended senses, I got the impression they were conversing telepathically at that moment. Dark Eyes scrutinized me, then shook his head as if to say *No way*. Siren shrugged at him as if to say *Believe what you will* then shot me a wink that made no pretenses. Elise's scowl darkened. I squeezed her hand, trying to bring her attention back to our quiet corner.

"I can't believe I grabbed her ass," Johnny said quietly, having missed the entire interaction as he stared at his own hands in awe. It took me a few seconds to place that he too was talking about Glenbark, and the brush he'd had when he'd caught us leaping from the tumbling transport.

I looked between them. "I can't believe either of you are thinking about anything but the fact that there's another Zar'Faenor running around out there." I gave Johnny a pointed look. "While we're at it, though, I also can't believe you stunned me in the back."

Johnny shook himself from his reverie and scrunched his face up in half-apology. "Yeeeah. Look, you know I love you, broto…"

"Do I sense a *but* coming?"

"Eh, not really a but…" He cocked his head. "*But*, do you see how it feels now, when your broto decides to go and do things his own way without telling you?"

"Landing your friend back in the Sanctum's sights seems kinda steep for a lesson," Elise said.

"Yeah," I added, "next time I have an issue with your teamwork skills, I'll be sure to help Glenbark throw your ass on the world's most dangerous hit list, *broto*."

"Ooo…" Johnny made a face like he needed a minute. "Don't talk to me about Glenbark and asses right now."

Elise sighed, but I saw the trace of a smile on her lips.

"Maybe keep your voice down just a sliver, Captain Grabby Hands," I said quietly while Johnny glanced longingly toward the head of the transport.

"Was that—" Johnny glanced furtively around the cabin, seemed to assure himself that no one had heard, then turned back to me. "Fine. I heed your point, goodfellow. I'm sorry I stunned you."

"And lied to us?" Elise asked.

Johnny glanced between us with a look that said, *That's rich, coming from you*, but finally relented. "And lied to you. But for what it's worth, I honestly believed Glenbark's plan was the best bet we had for your long term safety, buddy." He glanced down at his hands, real remorse creeping over his face. "I'm sorry it went the way it did back there."

I said nothing. Elise stroked my hand with her thumb, all of us silently contemplating the High Cleric's new ruling. Enemy of Enochia. Part of me wanted to be angry with Johnny. It hurt, knowing my best friend had willingly conspired behind my back. But thinking of how the situation might have erupted if he hadn't…

I wasn't entirely sure if I would've done what Johnny had done. But what I was sure of, beyond the shadow of a doubt, was that Johnny was my friend.

"Hey," I finally said, "at least Glenbark stuck around to pull me out of the transport back there. That's something."

"Yeah, man," Johnny said, shaking his head. "It really was. I mean, I knew she was in good shape, but damn." He looked between us, gauging my expression. "Oh, you meant, like, because of the betrayal and the redemption and all that. Yeah, that too."

Elise gave me a look of conspiratorial amusement before turning to Johnny. "You seem just a touch smitten, my goodfellow."

"What? No, I just—Lady's strong, okay? She hauled your man there out of that transport like a little Hal doll. And besides, it's *smoten*, isn't it?"

Elise's smile widened. "It's not."

"And not to sound insecure or anything," I added, "but I *was* a little busy holding up the entire damn transport at the time."

It was my turn to receive Elise's patronizing stare. "I still can't believe you tried that." She shook her head in wonder. "Or that it worked."

Johnny waved a hand. "Well he didn't actually lift the entire thing." He glanced at me. "Right? I mean, granted, I'm not really sure how you... you know, do your thing. But there were, like, leverages involved and whatnot, right?"

I just watched, waiting for him to arrive at his own conclusion.

He sighed. "Okay, you're basically the son of Alpha. Are you happy?"

I shrugged, smiling a little, and decided that—in that moment, with Johnny and Elise by my side—I was, in fact, reasonably happy. The moment only lasted until I accidentally glanced over and saw Dark Eyes still staring at me intently, but it was still nice to be reminded, if only for a moment, that there was something to be fighting for.

Having finished whatever damage control she was coordinating, a grim-faced Glenbark descended from the front cabin, eliciting rapt attention from all the legionnaires present—particularly Johnny. She spotted me, indicated she wanted to talk above, and turned to ascend without a word. Once she was gone, the curious eyes turned our way.

"Shall we?" I asked quietly.

Elise and Johnny rose to lead the way. Across the isle, Franco rose from his place with James and Phineas to follow us. After the near riotous stares I'd experienced back in Haven, I was sticking to my new practice of keeping my eyes front and center when, only a few steps in, something extended into my periphery. A legionnaire's fist, I realized, held out to me in a gesture of friendly camaraderie.

For a second, I could only stare, not quite understanding. I stared long enough that the woman started to abashedly lower her fist. I hurriedly raised mine and leaned in to touch my knuckles to her with a muttered, "I, uh—Thanks."

Thanks?

I wasn't really sure why I said it, but she smiled and nodded. I turned to find another fist waiting. And another. I moved all the way down the line, every single legionnaire touching their fist to mine—some reserved and respectful, a few openly smiling.

I went with it, not really understanding what had suddenly changed but grateful for the building sense of acceptance with each fist I touched. As we reached the front of the cabin, Siren extended her closed fist on the left with a mischievous grin. I ignored it, too caught up in the legionnaires' sincere gesture to heed her silly little game.

Elise, on the other hand, looked like she would've been all too happy to lend Siren the use of her clenched fist.

"I don't get it," I said quietly to Johnny when we'd reached the more isolated upper cabin. "What did I do?"

"You fought yourself half unconscious twice over to save the legionnaires who'd just helped deliver you to your unsuspecting trial," Glenbark said, turning in her seat to face us. "It shouldn't surprise you that we care about that kind of thing, Haldin."

It didn't surprise me when she put it that way. It just hadn't occurred to me to even see things from that angle.

Glenbark's eyes flicked from Franco to Elise to Johnny, not so much protesting their presence as merely documenting it, then she waved for us to join her. Elise and I took the two empty seats opposite her, Franco settling in the next row over. Johnny, having no other convenient option, chose the seat directly beside Glenbark. That seemed to amuse Elise, which in turn seemed to turn Johnny's cheeks roughly the same color as his hair.

If Glenbark noticed, she didn't say anything. Which was understandable, given the stellar levels of *gropped up* our day had already reached and handily surpassed.

"That... thing," she started.

"We call her Frosty," Johnny provided.

Glenbark pursed her lips, considering, and seemed to decide now wasn't the time to start rejecting odd ideas. "Fine. Frosty. You said she was a Seeker."

I nodded. "She was at the White Tower the night of... the massacre." Elise squeezed my hand, and I pushed on. "She escaped with the raknoth posing as the last High Cleric, along with another of her colleagues."

"Smirks," Johnny added.

A pang of guilt moved through me at the memory of Smirks. Bastard that he'd been, he'd tried to do the right thing in the end. He'd helped me break free of Al'Kundesha's telepathic hold. And I'd failed to repay the favor when Frosty and her raknoth master had snatched him up and fled into the night.

"Well," Glenbark said, "at least we have no shortage of cute nicknames for our enemies. So I'm to understand that this Frosty has been… taken by one of the remaining raknoth? And that this raknoth now possesses abilities like yours?"

I nodded.

"How powerful does that make her?"

I looked around the quiet space, pretty sure they all already instinctively knew the gist of the answer. "I'm not sure. I think she's playing by the same rules I am, at least. As in, she's limited by how much energy she can channel before she passes out or hurts herself.

"But?"

"But raknoth bodies can handle a lot of abuse."

Glenbark glanced at her empty scabbard, all too aware of just how much punishment a raknoth could give and take. "And what of the fallen raknoth, Zar'Faenor? Your reports indicated he was similarly capable. Had he also claimed a Seeker for a host?"

"Zar'Faenor used the body of Carlisle's old teacher. I didn't think the detail was necessary back when I…" I dropped my eyes to the deck. "It just didn't seem important at the time of my report."

Glenbark said nothing.

Elise broke the silence. "If we're sure there were twelve to start, there could still be at least seven Seekers out there, unaccounted for. We already know the raknoth probably have Smirks, if he's still alive."

"And that Al'Kundesha promised power and freedom to those who joined him," I added.

"Right," Elise said. "So, worst case scenario, it's feasible we could eventually be looking at five of those things if the rest of the raknoth decide to copy Frosty."

"That might explain why we haven't seen much of the raknoth themselves lately," Franco said, stroking his mustache. "Therese and I were talking yesterday about how the raknoth might alter their hosts once they've taken them. She thinks it might take months or even years for them to make their vessels as strong as what we've seen. Perhaps they prefer to stay hidden while they're… transitioning."

"How many of the raknoth were actually confirmed at the attack on Oasis?" I asked.

"Three by our count," Glenbark said. "Not that we can really be sure. But it still leaves the possibility that this raknoth has been adopting its new host, Frosty, ever since the White Tower. Perhaps it was the raknoth she absconded with. That would help explain why we haven't seen a trace of his former holiness."

"Are you positive she was still human at the White Tower?" Franco asked.

"Pretty sure," I said.

Her mind certainly hadn't *felt* alien. Of course, I wasn't sure my telepathic impression was infallible there, but the fact that Frosty's abilities had grown multiple times stronger since then seemed to support the idea that something had radically changed.

"So what we saw today was probably what a raknoth can make of a Seeker in about three cycles," Elise said.

"Which paints a scary picture of what we could be looking at if others make the transition," Franco added.

"And also kinda makes it sound like Frosty might keep getting stronger," I said.

Glenbark looked around at us. "Much as I appreciate the analysis, I was quite hoping it might conclude with a handy proposition as to how we counter such a threat moving forward."

"Well, Frosty ran today when those two Seekers flew in, right?" Johnny asked.

"I'm not sure she really needed to," I said, trading a look with Elise.

"You don't think she was afraid?" Glenbark asked.

I shrugged, unsure how to answer. I hadn't exactly been on fresh legs by the end of the fight, nor had Siren. If Frosty had decided to fight on, I wasn't sure we would have stopped her. Alpha only knew how much she'd had left before she reached her limits.

"I think she was testing her abilities against mine," I finally said, looking down at my hands. "And I think she passed."

Silence.

"Hey, come on, big guy," Johnny finally said. "Remember when you caught an entire transport with your mind?"

"With leverages, you mean?"

Johnny grimaced at his own words.

"Imagine what she'll be able to do if Therese is right," I continued. "If she grows stronger…"

"If she does," Glenbark said, "then we'll find a way to deal with it. You saved lives today, Haldin. Don't let hypothetical developments undermine that."

It was kind of hard to take her words to heart when I could see the loss in the hollowness of her eyes and the set of her shoulders. Because no matter how many we kept alive today, we both knew there'd been plenty more we'd failed. If the Legion actually survived this war, I knew they might one day teach this engagement as a victory in the classrooms—a stirring example of a successfully routed ambush.

But it was hard to see victory when the blood of the fallen was still fresh on your hands. Or on your dress tunic, in Glenbark's case.

I thought about Mara, and the stomach-turning scream that'd ripped from her throat when Frosty had stomped her down after taking Mara's knife to the knee. Thinking of the way she'd looked, her left leg and hip pulverized, her face so bloodless, and the way Edwards and Dillard had hovered over her…

Franco's voice snapped me from the grim recollection. "Do we have any confirmation that the three raknoth who attacked Oasis are still there?"

"No," Glenbark said. "They've kept most of their forces underground since we attempted bombing runs. We've done our best to contain Oasis from a distance, but I'm not putting it past question that a raknoth could have escaped. They could be hiding back among civilization, for all we know."

"Raknoth are pretty damn good at blending in," I agreed.

Franco grimaced. "So we have no idea where they're at or if they might currently be undergoing similar upgrades."

No one needed to point out that it was probably safest to assume the worst. I was pretty sure we were all thinking it. I cringed inwardly at the thought of a supercharged Alton Parker, or whatever name the raknoth might take if he switched to a gifted host. All that insidious cunning, armed with the kind of power Frosty wielded…

"We need those cloaks," Glenbark said, looking between me and Elise. "Now more than ever."

"We're getting closer," I said, hoping I sounded more convinced than I felt. To Elise's credit, she managed to nod her agreement without looking like she was wondering what the scud I was talking about. Maybe she actually believed it.

"But I have to point out," I added, "even cloaked legionnaires won't be safe from all her abilities. Something like what she did with those slugs today would still—"

"It doesn't matter." Glenbark looked around at all of us in turn. "We stick to what we can actually control. We find the breeding facilities and cut off their army. We cloak our legions and retake Oasis. I don't care how strong they are, even five of those things couldn't survive against our cloaked legions once their hybrid reinforcements are cut off. We stay the course. Agreed?"

"Agreed, sir," Johnny said with one of his rare serious looks.

"Agreed," Franco echoed, followed by Elise.

They all turned to me, but my head was too busy whirling with doubts to answer immediately. What if Therese and Franco couldn't track down the facilities, and—much more realistically—what if *I* couldn't come through with the cloaks? It wasn't like I had any bright new ideas, short of going back to Humility and ripping the city apart for Burton Kovaks and Pasty's Emmútari archives. Which, I realized, would be considerably more problematic now that I had the official *enemy of Enochia* sign hanging around my neck in addition to my existing house arrest.

And scud, what if none of that even mattered? What if five supercharged raknoth blasted into Haven tonight with an army of mature hybrids at their backs? What would we do then?

The thought chilled my insides.

But they were waiting for my answer. Counting on me.

"Agreed," I said quietly.

"Good. Then I have an assignment for the two of you," Glenbark said, looking between me and Elise again. "The Seekers. They might know something that could help you, yes?"

"I doubt it," I said before I even had time to think.

I didn't need to look at Elise to know she didn't like where this was going either.

"But there is a chance," Glenbark said. "And furthermore, I doubt they're going to be forward with me about what they were doing following us, and whether it's by the will of the High Cleric or otherwise."

I frowned. "You think they're acting on their own?"

"I think I'd like to know what they're doing here and if they're capable of helping our situation. I also think they're considerably more likely to open up to a fellow practitioner than to the High General of the Legion."

I traded an uncertain look with Elise. "You do realize their entire function is to kill people like us, right?"

Glenbark looked pointedly between me and Elise. "All the more reason to find out what they're doing here, then, don't you think?"

EVENS & ODDS

By the way Dark Eyes and The Giantess scowled at the back of her head from the transport, I was guessing it hadn't been a group decision when Siren came straight up to me on the Haven landing pad and asked if we could all go somewhere to talk. At least that saved me the awkwardness of trying to organically get the Seekers alone. Not that it wasn't obvious enough that we weren't alone at all when half of Hound Company fell in behind us, following at a respectful distance. Less obvious were the dozen or so snipers Glenbark probably already had watching us.

But Dark Eyes and The Giantess said nothing of it, simply looking displeased with Siren but also keen on not letting her out of their sight for some reason. No one protested when Johnny and Elise stuck by my side either. Three and three just seemed fair.

In a strange way, it almost felt like we were the cool kids, sneaking off to do as we pleased. Dark Eyes and The Giantess might've been in their mid-twenties, and Siren couldn't have been more than a couple years older than me.

For a second, it was almost like they weren't professional Shaper killers. But they were. And I kept that fact firmly in mind as Johnny guided us toward a nearby rec zone as Glenbark had instructed.

I got the impression they were equally cautious of us. Aside from a few glib remarks from Siren about finally seeing Haven in the daylight and one tiny reminder of how Johnny had succumbed to her wily charms the last time she'd visited, barely a word was spoken in the five minutes it took us to reach the rec zone and find a quiet corner in the garden. It wasn't exactly a beautiful space, but it was clean, and the modest collection of sun-kissed flowers and shrubberies at least attempted to alleviate the tension as we sat about, waiting for someone to start.

"Chatty bunch today, aren't we?" Siren said, looking around at all of us.

Elise joined the other Seekers in scowling at her. I was a little surprised Johnny didn't fire something back, but he seemed a little hesitant to engage Siren, whether because of his slip up last time or because he assumed I had a plan.

I didn't.

"You're the one who asked to talk," I said. "What did you wanna talk about?"

Siren rolled her eyes. "Oh please. We're sitting here with the High General's servitor and a full squad hiding in the bushes, for the love of Alpha. Don't act like she didn't ask you to crack the scary Seeker shell and harvest our juicy little secrets."

"Maybe she didn't have to ask," Elise said. "Maybe some shells, I crack for free."

It was slight, but I swear Dark Eyes grinned a little at that.

"Nice cover-up, by the way," Elise added to Siren.

It was only when she said it that I noticed the faint discoloration in skin tone where Siren had applied pigment to her right temple to cover up the bruise Elise had given her back in the medica.

Siren just raised her delicate eyebrows, feigning innocent surprise. "It seems to me I've done something to upset you, sweetling."

"Easy," I telepathically crooned Elise's way, thinking calming thoughts as I felt her tense beside me. *"She's testing you."*

"Yeah," Johnny said, his gaze near Siren but not quite on her, "I hear that's what those non-lizard folk do when you try to murder their loved ones. Getting all upset and such. How quaint, right?"

Siren all but ignored him, watching Elise like a predatory feline. When Elise failed to explode, Siren let out a sigh and lounged languorously back in the sun, as if having lost interest.

"Look at you, knowing women," Elise sent.

I stifled a smile. *"Women, no. But I might know a thing or two about serpents."*

Siren opened an eye to peer at us. "So are we going to be honest with one another here, or are you two just going to keep talking behind your guests' backs?"

That surprised both of us, seeing as we'd set our cloaks close enough to cut us off from the Seekers.

"You pick up on a lot of things, being around our type half your life," Siren said. "We don't need to feel the mind whispers to recognize the look."

"Fine," I said. "We can do honest. Let's start with what you want and why your friends here were following our convoy."

"Our convoy that just so happened to get ambushed," Johnny added.

"Careful, servitor," Siren said, "or you might upset Eight's pristine moral sensibilities."

The Giantess, who'd frowned at Johnny's words, shot a dark look at Siren.

"We didn't lie to your officers," Dark Eyes spoke up in his deep voice. "We came to confirm Six made it safely to Haven. If we'd known there was going to be trouble, we would've been closer behind."

"Hmm," Elise said. "So you weren't planning to, say, sweep in and carry away your friend Six here when we were all too tied up or dead to notice?"

Anger flickered across Dark Eyes' face, so convincing that I almost missed the way the blond titan of a woman beside him—the one Siren seemed to refer to as Eight—visibly swallowed, shifting uncomfortably. Maybe Siren hadn't been kidding about those moral sensibilities.

"You really think I would've stuck around to fight if that'd been the plan?" Siren asked.

"Funny," Elise said, fixing Siren with her most piercing stare, "I didn't seem to see you doing much fighting. Not until the very end."

Siren's lazy smile returned. "You mean when I juiced up your man, sweetling?"

"You think Glenbark would be mad if I killed her?"

I just rested my hand on Elise's thigh and squeezed, noting Dark Eyes' exasperation as he massaged his temples.

"Enough with the kid games, Six," he said. "You wanted to talk, talk. Eight and I don't need this crap."

Beside him, Eight nodded her dignified agreement. Something passed between the three of them, and I was tempted to dial my cloak out and try to listen in.

"Now who's being rude?" Johnny muttered.

We all looked at him in surprise.

"What?" He spread his hands. "I have eyes, people."

"My friends and I," Siren said, "are merely having a bit of a disagreement as to how significantly the red-eyed reemergence of our old colleague, Lady

Bitch Face"—she smiled at me—"or Frosty for short, is going to grop up our plans."

"Those plans being?" Elise asked.

It was Siren's turn to shoot a dark look at her friends. "Oh, I'd tell you, but then Four here might try to set me on fire."

"Four, Six, and Eight, huh?" Johnny said. "What, do you guys eat all the odd numbers or something?"

Siren showed him a serpentine smile. "Would that it were us doing the eating." She looked at me. "That's kind of why we wanted to talk."

"You're afraid the raknoth are on the hunt for more Seeker hosts?" I ventured, looking between Siren and Four.

"They're afraid the raknoth will hunt them down after they've fled the Sanctum's protection," Elise corrected.

As soon as she said it, everything clicked into place, from the circumstances of their arrival to every little look and twitch I hadn't even realized I'd noticed. Elise had seen it all and pieced it together with an intuition that would've made Franco proud.

What little doubt remained was quickly swept away by the look in Eight's eyes. She looked caught. And so did Four.

Elise was right.

The Sanctum hadn't sent the Seekers here. They were on the run—or getting ready to be, at least. But if they were worried about the raknoth finding them…

"We're done being their killers," Four practically snarled, yanking me back to the moment. "Done with all of it." He traded a look with Eight and regained some composure before turning back to us. "We just need to make sure our people will be safe."

Siren patted his leg and smiled at us. "He's such a good Seeker Core Dad, isn't he?"

Four ignored her. "We need to know what you know about what that thing did to One so we can make sure it never happens again." He glanced wearily between me and Elise. "We'd also like to learn how to replicate the devices that hide your minds from detection."

We sat silently, waiting to see if he'd go on.

"Is there an *in return* clause you're forgetting about somewhere in there?" Johnny finally said, "Or would you prefer they each throw in two kidneys while they're at it?"

Four eyed him before turning his wary gaze on me. "Is there something you'd wish in return?"

There sure as scud was. Namely, the answers to the cloaking rune problem. But the way Four had just referred to their pendants—like he didn't even quite know what it was he was asking—pretty much settled it in my mind.

These Seekers had no idea about the cloaking runes, much less how to help make them. So I decided to try another route.

"Do you know anything about the Emmútari?"

The three Seekers exchanged confused looks. A clear *no* on that one, then.

"How about Expression?"

"Like, of an opinion?" Siren asked.

Alpha be damned, what did they teach these people?

In their defense, they might well know the art of Expression by a different name, but I wasn't sure how to probe at the topic in a useful way without revealing what I was indirectly searching for. For multiple reasons, it seemed like a bad move to let it slip that I didn't even know how to make the cloaking pendants they were after. Thankfully, Elise was ready with her own questions.

"How about something easier?" she said. "Can you at least tell us how many Seekers you can account for, and how many might have gone missing or joined the raknoth? For some reason, the Sanctum seems a bit tightfisted with those details."

"We know roughly where at least six of us are at right now," Siren said, "One—the bitch you call Frosty, I mean—being included in that number." Four was giving her a sharp look, as if intending to cut her off, but Siren didn't back down. "What? You want them to give us everything for nothing?"

By the look on Four's face, I guessed she wasn't usually the voice of reason in their group. With a dark frown, he relented and resigned himself to staring broodingly off toward the landing pads while Siren continued.

"Five, Seven, and Nine are missing, but none of us would be surprised to learn they'd joined Team Red Eyes. I *know* Twelve flipped sides." She gave me a pointed look. "And rumor has it Three took a bullet in the head trying to bring down the mysterious Carlisle and the Demon of Divinity."

The memory put an aching itch in my right shoulder, where I'd taken a slug from the same Sanctum Guard who'd accidentally shot his own Seeker in the middle of the rain-soaked streets of Divinity.

"And Two..." Siren started and faltered, her air of lazy smiles and sultry winks giving way to one of consternation.

Four stirred. "Six, if One sided with those things... Two's gone. You know that."

"Two is Garrett?" I asked quietly.

I already knew the answer. I'd seen it when I'd been inside the man's head with Carlisle. But even if I hadn't known, Siren's reaction would've confirmed it—the slight hiss of breath, the attentive straightening of her posture. I got the feeling she didn't often care so much about anything.

"That's Smirks?" Johnny asked.

"Alpha be damed," Siren half-growled under her breath, "what is it with you people and nicknames?"

"Well, we didn't know about your nifty number system, did we?" Johnny said. "I mean this with all due diplomacy and everything, but listening to you guys talk about each other is kinda giving me flashbacks to all the jokes our instructor used to tell in basic arithmetic."

Siren ignored him in favor of skewering me on the end of her resolute stare. "Where is Garrett?"

Probably playing host to a transitioning raknoth as we speak, I didn't say.

"Frosty and your old High Cleric took him when they fled the White Tower," Elise said.

Four frowned. "Took him?"

"He had a change of heart when he saw those monsters in the Great Hall," I said. "He was injured helping me break free from one of the raknoth. I tried to get him out, but they grabbed him first."

Four looked mildly surprised by the news. Siren just looked frustrated. It was Eight, though, who caught my attention as she stirred and leaned forward to speak for the first time.

"Two had a good heart. We all know this deep down. Deep, even, as he chose to hide his own goodness beneath bitter words."

Her voice was like the smooth stone foundation at the base of a powerful river, and her words lingered in the air, hovering until she gave a minuscule head bob of approval and settled back into her stony silence.

No one argued with her, but her words stirred something in me in a way that I didn't quite understand until Four spoke again.

"Will you help us avoid Two's fate? Help see to it more of our talents don't fall into their hands?"

And there it was, rankling deeper this time. Because sure, we could all agree that the rise of more Seeker-powered raknoth was the last thing this planet needed. But for these people to come here asking for our help... These people whose precious High Cleric had tried to kill me multiple times. These people who'd spent their lives mercilessly murdering their own kind only to now pretended like they actually knew the first thing about what made a heart good…

I consciously relaxed my hand from Elise's thigh and moved it back to my own lap, where it couldn't do any damage, trying to get a grip on the rising storm inside me.

Because, for a second, I'd almost forgotten who and what I was dealing with.

"I understand why you hesitate," Four was saying. "Were I in your place, I'm sure—"

"How many Shapers have you killed in your life, Four?"

His face darkened, but I was already turning to Siren. "What about you?" She dropped my gaze. I turned to Eight. "And you?"

Eight was the only one of them who didn't react. She merely held my gaze, steady as a rock. No challenge in her eyes. No apology. Just calm reflection. "Twenty-three," she finally said.

Shock rippled through me, followed on the heels by a deep, churning nausea. Four shot Eight a dark *Why the scud would you tell him that?* look. She paid it no mind.

"Twenty-three," I repeated, looking between the three of them. "So it's probably safe to say I'm looking at a total of more than fifty dead Shapers between the three of you."

"Raish," Four said slowly, "trust me when I say you don't—"

"Don't what?" I snapped. "Don't know what I'm talking about? Don't know what it's like to have no choice? To have your back to the wall? To be all alone, hunted by the entire gropping world?" I was on my feet, now, on the verge of shouting. "After everything I went through, do you really think there's a damn thing you can say to me to justify what you've done to your own kind?"

"This was a mistake," Four said with a dark look at Siren. He stood, moving slowly, as if he were frightened he might startle me. "We'll leave as soon as your General allows us to do so peacefully. We'll manage on our own."

"Manage," I repeated, looking incredulously at Johnny and Elise. "They'll manage." The concern in my friends' eyes only fanned the flames inside me.

I rounded back on Four. "That feeling deep in your gut right now? The one that's got your heart beating around the clock? That voice whispering that any minute now, they'll come blasting through that door or stalking around that corner? That's what every one of your victims lived with from the day they learned what they were and what they had to fear from people like you. Why should you be the ones who get to walk away from that?"

Four paused from hurrying his fellow Seekers to their feet to shoot an incredulous glare at me. "Walk away? You really think any one of us could…" He shook his head, at a loss for words. "You think *they* were scared? You have no idea what we've lived through. You don't know the first thing about us."

"I know you're asking for my help when at least four of your order have already tried to kill me." I glared at Siren. "Some more recently than others."

She held my gaze, unflinching. "Do you really think you'd still be here if I'd actually wanted you dead?"

That caught me off guard, right along with the look in her eyes.

"Forget it, Six," Four said, gesturing for her to come along. "He doesn't even know how that thing on his neck works. This was a waste of our time."

I gaped dumbly, trying too late to hide the way his words all but knocked the breath out of me. Whether he was confident about the claim or just fishing for a reaction, I was pretty sure I'd just confirmed I had no idea how to give them what they wanted.

And I was too pissed at that moment to much care.

"Because this is all about you, right?" I practically spat. "We're just busy trying to save Enochia, but please, don't let us waste your time. Never mind that you three could've been helping if you'd stepped out of your White Tower before now, or that there won't even be a White Tower anymore if we don't stop the raknoth. No Sanctum. No anything but hybrids and human blood bags. We're talking about stopping the end of our world, and you're telling me I should help you run away and hide. So yeah, I might not know much about you, but I know enough to say you're either ignorant or cowards."

Eight's knuckles audibly cracked as she balled her massive hands into fists. Four held up a hand to warn her off.

"It's not worth it, Eight," he glared at me. "He already has us all figured out."

And with that, he turned on his heel and stalked off.

Eight considered us for a tight-jawed moment then turned to follow. Siren remained a stretch longer, looking between us and her departing allies a few times in clear frustration before finally rolling her eyes, heaving a sigh, and storming off muttering something about grown men and grop- ping children.

I clenched and unclenched my fists, watching them go, watching Ordo

Carter step forward to meet them and confer about something—probably where he'd been ordered to take them. I found myself hoping Four would do something stupid, lash out, give me a reason to go pound him into the permacrete. But Carter's squad formed up around the Seekers and escorted them off without incident.

I watched them go with trembling fists, feeling like I was going to explode. I wanted to scream. I wasn't even sure why I was so angry. And worse, for some infuriating reason, some part of me actually felt bad—dirty on the inside, like I'd stooped somewhere I'd once despised.

Had I been too harsh?

Too harsh to the Seekers who'd spent their lives murdering innocent Shapers?

It was ridiculous to think. And yet, as I watched the Seekers and their escorts vanish behind a distant building, I couldn't ignore the nagging feeling that maybe I was missing something—and that maybe I was treating them exactly the same way the world had decided to treat me.

3 0

BREACH OF CONTRACT

"Well," Johnny finally broke the silence when we were quite alone in the garden. "I'd like to think that went well."

"Yeah," Elise said. "I especially liked the part where we now have three angry Shaper killers walking around Haven with no illusions that we can give them what they want."

"We're on it," Johnny said, busy on his palmlight. "We've already got multiple squads keeping their collective eye on 'em." He frowned. "Not that they can't just, you know…" He waved a finger at the side of his head. "But at least we know what they want now. Probably. Maybe."

We both stared at him.

He shrugged. "I'm telling Freya it went well."

Elise arched a dark eyebrow at me and mouthed, *Freya?*

I tried to force a smile, but I couldn't.

"What are we gonna do about them?" I asked finally.

"I dunno," Elise said. "Something tells me Glenbark's not gonna be inclined to let them just fly off once Johnny fills her in. The Sanctum would be furious with her for one thing. And evil or not, they might still be able to help."

"Civil war or invasion by raknoth…" Johnny shook his head. "Never a dull moment in Haven."

Elise nodded along until her brow folded at some other thought. "Sweet

Alpha, I do not like that Lady Swive Eyes, or the way she looks at either of you."

"Yeah," Johnny said, absentmindedly bobbing his head. He froze. "Wait, me?"

Maybe it was just my guilty conscience talking—not that I had *reason* to be guilty—but the tone of his question told me his mind had gone right to where mine had landed. A dark medica room, a near-lethal case of honey-brain, and Siren's hot mouth nibbling on my ear.

Thankfully, Elise took his tone to suggest a different motivation.

"Johnathan Wingard," she said, raising a stern finger at him, "do *not* let that woman get you alone in a room. The aura she gives off..." She shuddered a little. "She reminds me of one of those snakes that starts eating its mate while the poor bastard is still"—she made an inarticulate gesture—"doing his thing."

Johnny gulped audibly, some combination of horror and infatuation warring on his features. "That's... terrible to think about," he said slowly. "Definitely... definitely terrible. Definitely."

Elise patted his leg. "Just remember Freya."

"Yeah," Johnny said, still stuck in whatever delightful horrors were playing out in his head. "Yeah, I'll just—Wait, what? I told you, I'm not—She's not..." He stood, drawing himself up with a most dignified air, and shook a finger at Elise. "That would be highly unprofessional, my goodlady. Now..." He looked between us, finger pivoting with him. "Who wants to go see if Therese will let us poke a dead hybrid with a stick?"

His playful expression faltered as his finger landed on me and he seemed to remember that I wouldn't be going anywhere but straight back to house arrest with an armed guard detail.

"We mustn't let the Sanctum think the demon's slipped the leash," I said in a bad Glenbark impersonation.

"We don't have to go," Elise said.

"Yeah," Johnny added. "I was just gonna swing by for an update, really. See what the fuss is about this big delivery."

Franco had been rather excited when he'd received word from Therese on the flight back to Haven—something about the rather colossal collection of data drives he'd requisitioned from the Central Enochian Repository being delivered. Whether or not his excitement was born of a sincere belief that they'd find the hybrid breeding facilities by cross-referencing the data on those drives with the list of conditions they'd drafted in Therese's lab, or just a general enthusiasm for data diving, I wasn't entirely sure.

Either way, I waved Johnny and Elise on. "You two go. Those data drives aren't gonna sleuth themselves."

"All right, then," Johnny said, clapping a hand on my shoulder before leaving me to say goodbye to Elise. "First one there gets the stick, Lise," he called over his shoulder, "and I'm not sharing."

Elise only smiled and came to wrap her arms around me. She planted a soft kiss on my cheek, and I nuzzled into her, closing my eyes and wishing with everything I had that we could simply stay there in that garden and forget about everything else.

"I don't have to go," she said quietly. "My dad hardly needs my help combing through a mountain of corporate records."

"Go. You're the best he has."

She smiled. "Oh, I know that. I'm just saying he'll probably be sad I'm stealing some of his fun."

I smiled back and kissed her forehead. "Sounds like there's enough to go around, even for Franco. I think I could use a couple quiet hours to myself anyway."

She pulled back and looked up at me with those beautiful blue eyes. "Just make sure you eat something before you get back to it?"

Some part of me thought to answer, but I was too caught up just admiring her. The look stretched and gave way to one of those moments where the entire world just simply fell away without warning, leaving me with nothing but the feel of her in my arms and the overwhelming epiphany of just how much I loved this woman.

She searched my face, idly stroking my cheek, seeming to garner at least some part of what passed through me. Maybe she felt it in my mind.

"Go," I whispered. "Before you make me change my mind."

She cupped my cheek. *"No dark thoughts until I'm back to hold the light?"*

I smiled. *"Deal."*

And as I walked back to our quarters under armed guard to resume my house arrest, I even managed to keep my promise. Yes, there might've been three Seekers, a full Sanctum, five raknoth, and a whole damn hybrid army trying to kill me, but life still could've been a whole mountain of scud worse.

I had my friends. I had Elise. And I might not know exactly how we were going to solve this cloaking problem, but we *were* going to solve it.

And demons to the wind, maybe I'd even throw in a hot shower and fresh clothes while I was at it.

NECK deep as I expected he would be in ripe data drives, I was surprised when my palmlight buzzed a couple hours later with a call from Franco.

"Have you seen the reels?" he asked before the vid feed had even finished establishing.

Having been well-conditioned over the past seasons to automatically dread those words, my stomach was already sinking by the time his concerned expression resolved on my palmlight, flanked by Johnny, Elise, and Therese. They all appeared to be watching something on Franco's display, eyes wide and mouths agape.

"That's… impossible," Therese said.

"It's just…" Johnny muttered.

"What happened?" I asked.

"… Leverages and… scud," Johnny concluded, as if he hadn't heard me.

Leverages?

I didn't like where this was going.

"Check the headlines, Hal," Franco said. "The story just broke."

I was already swiping their vid feed over to the wall display and pulling up the reels on my palmlight. I looked at the top story—and froze.

Haldin Raish declared Enemy of Enochia, saves High General, entire transport of legionnaires, from enemy ambush.

"Freya is not gonna be happy about this," I distantly heard Johnny groan. I was too busy tapping the headline, my stomach sinking further at the vid file waiting at the head of the story.

It started with an aerial shot of a transport—our transport, I knew, by the sight of the approaching canyon and the growing dread in my gut. The vid must've been from one of the transports behind us. It was surreal, watching the engines die, watching from the outside as the transport plunged to the rocky ground below, knowing I'd been inside of that falling death trap. Then the vid cut to one of our transport's interior cams, and I got to watch myself and Glenbark slam into our seats so hard we might've momentarily shrank by a foot.

Whoever had put the vid together made it perfectly clear what had happened next, cutting back and forth between the two perspectives to show us sliding for the canyon, clearly doomed. Me inside, eyes closed, brow furrowed. The transport, cresting the lip of the canyon, going over. Me, fists clenched, mouth tearing open in a silent scream. The transport yanking to an inexplicable halt over the gaping mouth of the canyon.

I watched in a numb stupor as the rest played out. Siren and the legionnaires pilling from the rear. Johnny and Glenbark dramatically jumping from the transport as it pitched into the canyon. The hybrid-packed transports springing their ambush.

The vid ended with the appearance of Frosty and her blazing red eyes.

"Not happy at all," Johnny was murmuring on the wall display, still shaking his head. "And they missed the best part." He slid a hand through the air as if revealing a dazzling headline. "Ruggedly daring legionnaire saves High General from raknoth-propelled dagger." He craned his neck to shoot a mournful look at the opening said dagger had rent in the armor on the back of his shoulder. "Sacrifices were made."

I might have smiled if I wasn't busy drowning under the sea of how gropped I felt. Glenbark was going to be furious. And probably for good reason. Everything we'd just gone through to placate the High Cleric about my position at Haven, and now this happened.

I almost could have laughed. Almost.

I swear, I could practically see whatever edgy coordinator had chosen that headline leaning back in their chair with a proud smile, telling themselves that they'd done a brave thing, taken a stand, made a difference.

I wasn't sure if it would even occur to them that they may well have just signed my execution orders.

Because, as furious as Glenbark would be at whoever had salvaged that footage and put it out there, I couldn't imagine the High Cleric wasn't going just as red at that pristine cream collar of his right then. The vid alone was bad enough. The headline, though, couldn't have been more inflammatory if they'd come straight out and said *High Cleric of the Sanctum, big stupid villain who condemns Enochian hero moments before he saves the day?*

I could only imagine His Holiness was currently bumping my status back onto his *To be killed, IMMEDIATELY* list, regardless of whatever deal he'd struck with Glenbark. And with three Seekers on base, potentially looking to renew favor with their holy master…

"I'm coming back," Elise said, as if reading my mind. "Right now."

"Lise, it's—"

"We need to tell Glenbark to send more guards to the apartment," she said to Johnny, ignoring me.

"I'm fine, Lise," I said, more insistently this time. "I've already got an entire squad posted around this place. Any more men and they're just gonna be running into one another."

We all fell into a short staring contest.

"Are you having any luck with the drives?" I asked, desperate to get them to stop looking at me like I might spontaneously sprout a slug hole in my forehead.

Elise frowned at the deflection but said nothing.

"No significant breakthrough yet," Franco said, "but we're circling the fringes of a pattern," Franco added. "It's just a matter of time before we have our first location." He cocked his head. "Assuming our criteria are actually any good."

"Right," Johnny said, busy on his palmlight. "Well, thrilling as that sounds, I think that's my cue." He winced at something on his device. "Nope, that's the one. Time to run damage control." He glanced back my way. "And I'm requisitioning reinforcements for your apartment, per Glenbark's approval. No buts."

I rolled my eyes. "Great. I feel safer already."

He thudded his chest in salute. "Just get back to work, flyboy."

Try as I might to do as Johnny said, getting back to work proved challenging even after I'd managed to say my goodbyes and talk Elise and the others into carrying on over at Therese's lab. For a while, I sat on the couch, scrolling through the reels as the duplicates of my story began to proliferate, some focusing more on the High Cleric's announcement, others on the canyon ambush.

None of them were good news for me. But it certainly put things in perspective when I saw that there'd also been two more hybrid attacks earlier that day. Both against smaller settlements. Both ending with several hundred more civilian abductions.

It was getting to be almost every day with the attacks now.

If not for that thought, I might have gone on lamenting my cursed existence for the remainder of the afternoon. But cursed or not, there was still one thing I could do to actually help Enochia.

I got back to it.

Deep focus took a while to find, amped as I was by the slim-but-existent possibility that the High Cleric could've seen that vid, thrown demons to the wind, and told his three Seekers to screw the treaty and bring him my head, immediately. Eventually, though, I settled back into the task of trying to link one rune to another.

It was actually going pretty well. I couldn't say for certain how I knew, but I swore I could feel the breakthrough lingering there at the edge of my awareness, closer and closer with each try. Maybe it was just wishful thinking, but I wasn't going to complain. I kept my head buried in the work, where I couldn't spare the attention to worry that each and every moment could be the one when someone would knock down my door and come get me, or the one when my palmlight would buzz with a message from Glenbark or the High Cleric himself, ushering in some fresh addition to my growing collection of shackles. Nothing would come of the worrying. So I did as I'd promised Glenbark, and I focused on what I could control.

At least until I heard the sound from my bedroom.

31

ROUGH

Someone was there.

My hand flashed to my pendant and dialed the cloak in close before I even had time to register anything else. *The guard detail,* my adrenaline-buzzed brain insisted. It had to be one of the legionnaires.

Inside the apartment?

It made no sense—even before my racing brain honed in on the sound that'd startled me and realized that my mysterious *someone* was running the shower.

I was already on my feet, frozen between storming the bedroom and running for the hallway door, crying for the guards and not stopping until I was comfortably surrounded by a dozen friendly gun hands. I teetered, mind screaming with a hundred questions of who and how, and raknoth and Seekers, and the fact that whatever was in my bathroom had already surpassed my guards, and that I had to stop it before it could finish whatever it was up to and slip back out.

I found myself prowling forward almost before I knew it, dialing the cloak out a little as I went. Defenses raised. Boots silent on the carpet—more silent than my thundering heart, at least. I forced myself to breathe, trying to separate the useless jitters of fear from the healthy respect of the potential danger waiting ahead.

I drew my sidearm. Respectfully. I was glad I'd been paranoid enough to climb back into my armor skin after my shower earlier.

The trickling patter of the shower doubled in volume as I pushed the bedroom door open. Empty. To the left, one wide window stood clear open. I didn't bother gesturing to close it, or looking around for any more evidence than the steam wafting gently from the privy entryway on the right.

I didn't tease out with my senses to feel for the enemy presence. I cast my mind out like a battering ram, fully expecting it to be there. And it was.

It tensed at my sudden attack, recoiling in on itself. I was already charging around the corner into the privy before the intruder had time to recover, gun raised, telekinetic fury crackling at my fingertips.

But there was nothing. Nothing but my own clouded reflection staring me back in the steam-fogged mirror.

Then something moved in the thick steam ahead. An incorporeal spirit, ghosting for cover. I grabbed the wispy wraith with telekinesis, preparing to slam it into the poly-tiled wall, and—

And at once nearly lost control of my telekinesis, my weapon, and my voice as Siren materialized out of the steamy air, wearing a blue shower robe. *My* shower robe. And nothing else.

"Alpha be sweet, will you relax?" she snapped.

The exasperation on her face only made me gape that much harder.

"Siren? How... What..." On a sudden impulse, I swept the bedroom behind me. No knives plunging for my kidneys. Just Siren watching me flounder with a decidedly amused expression.

"What the scud are you doing here?" I growled.

"Using your shower," she said, like it was the most obvious thing on the planet. She looked down at her state of ruffled near-undress, rectified it only marginally, and met my eyes again. "I hope you don't mind. Alpha, did you think assassins were waiting in your bathroom?"

"I..." I fumbled for coherent words, half-raising and half-lowering my gun until I gave up and shoved it back in the holster with a mental curse. "The thought crossed my mind, yeah. Now what the scud are you doing here?"

She adopted a confused expression, looking to the shower and back to me. "Did I not just...?" Delicately, she touched the back of her head, the movement causing her robe to shift dangerously. "Maybe I hit my head harder than I thought."

"Yeah, hilarious. Now, if you'll kindly get dressed..." I reached out and telekinetically turned the shower off.

"Hey!" Siren looked from the shower to me with an indignant pout. "Some host you are."

"I didn't invite you."

She arched an eyebrow, her robe—*my* robe—somehow shifting open to reveal more cleavage even though I could've sworn she hadn't moved. "You can join, if you'd like."

I pointedly turned and walked out of the steamy room, keeping my extended senses alert just in case. "What I'd like is for you to tell me what you want and to get the scud out of here. And not necessarily in that order."

There was a loud, exasperated sigh, then she padded after me into the bedroom, still wearing my damned shower robe.

"Okay, okay," she said. "I wanted to talk to you, you big stubborn"—she shook her hands, searching for the right word—"*demon...* Alpha, what tingler crawled up your tunic?"

"I don't know. Maybe it's the mountain of people trying to kill me on a daily basis. Maybe it's that I'm not used to finding strange women hiding in my shower robe with a..."

The words died in my throat as my thinking brain finally caught up and realized she wasn't wearing an optical shroud at all. Which meant...

She was watching me with a sultry smile, clearly enjoying watching me fumble through the logic. "Well, I'm not sure I can do much about the first bit, but..." She reached down and began undoing the robe's cinch with slow, confident movements, her eyes locked on mine the entire time. "... if you want your robe back..."

"Stop," I said.

Or meant to say, at least. But something was stirring in me—a slow, tingling wave, tickling my pounding heart with electric trills of excitement, pulsing down through my anatomy with a delicious warmth. It tied my tongue, telling me to let her keep going. Insisting that I help her. That I throw her down on the bed and *have* her. She would let me. She wanted it. Was silently begging for it.

The cinch came undone.

She took one sinuous step forward. Her hands tracing slowly up her navel, to her chest, teasing the robe apart to reveal another inch of soft, voluptuous cleavage. Another. Her eyes burning into mine.

Forget about the Sanctum. Forget about...

Elise.

The thought was like a small prayer—an emergency signal to my aching fingers. They found my pendant before my curve-drunk brain could tell them.

As soon as I was alone in my cloak, it was like a spell had been broken. My head took a sharp shake by its own accord, and the bedroom settled back around me, once again in control.

Siren's face was scant inches from me—when had she gotten so close?—her body pressed to mine, her eyes studying me now like she thought I might've just suffered some critical system failure. My hands were on her arms, I realized, having darted there to stop her from finishing her grand unveiling.

"Did you…" I started before realizing there was no tactful way to end the question. "What did you just do to me?"

The confusion on her face was genuine this time. She searched my eyes like she thought I was gropping with her, then dropped her gaze pointedly down at my groin. "I think the real question is what you're planning on doing to me."

She shifted her hips then, and I became painfully aware of how extensively my anatomy had already responded, and just how close her body was pressed to mine. I stumbled back a step, but she moved with me, sliding a hand up my chest, around the back of my neck. Her lips nearly found mine before I jerked my head to the side. She didn't miss a beat—just ran her fingers possessively through my hair, nuzzling her way to my ear instead.

I tried to back up, but my body wouldn't listen. *The skin contact,* some dim corner of my mind noted. Skin on skin. That was a problem, but I couldn't seem to remember why past the maddening sensation of her hot mouth on my ear, and the thoughts and images pouring into my mind. The two of us wrapped together on the floor, right on the very spot where we stood. Every inch of her warm flesh pressed to me. Every inch of me inside of her. The sure, passionate rhythm of her body, her hips grinding against mine. Her back arching. Her head tilting back to cry my name.

All I had to do was let it happen.

My hands were on her hips, trembling, squeezing hungrily, refusing to let go. Her free hand was sliding down the front of my armor skin. Not stopping. She grabbed me like I belonged to her, her other hand pulling my lips toward hers, demanding I give in.

I was falling. Falling straight toward her, watching everything else in my life fly past. And there was Elise, watching me fall by, the hurt and betrayal in her eyes like a churning sickness in my gut.

I latched onto that sickness—used it like a weapon to pry myself from the electric tingles of anticipation rippling from her flesh to mine. Hurled it at the dull stupor clogging my brain. I pushed myself back with every tenuous fiber of willpower I had.

Something rushed through my body. The air split with a low thunderclap, and next I knew, I was standing in the middle of a half-wrecked bedroom, trembling, and Siren was sprawled across the bed, disheveled and gaping at me like I'd gone insane. Her robe had fallen open in the blast. I started to look away—suddenly feeling no desire to see the flesh my blood itself had been screaming for not five seconds ago—but she tugged the robe closed before I had to. She looked almost embarrassed by the concession, like somehow she felt more vulnerable with her clothes fully on. And for a second, that's exactly how she looked. Vulnerable. Hurt.

I half-wanted to apologize. Half-wanted to yell at her to get the scud out. Couldn't seem to say anything at all. Then the second passed, and the surprise died on her face, replaced with a startlingly sudden snarl.

"So you like it rough?"

She spun to her knees in a fluid movement, putting her back to me, shot me a feral grin over her shoulder, and dropped the robe to her waist. My breath caught.

Scars.

Dozens of them. Hundreds. Her entire back a dense web of pale lines.

"Do you like what you see, Demon?" She dropped the robe the rest of the way and bent over on the bed, turning back to me with a wicked grin, hatred burning in her eyes. "Is this how you want me? You wanna add your own mark?"

I averted my eyes, choking on a dry swallow. "Who did that to you?"

There was an irritated sigh and the sound of shifting on the bed. "Like you give a scud," she muttered. Then there was a flicker of motion, and something soft struck my chest. I jerked back, but it was only my robe.

When I looked back up, Siren was gone.

No, not gone. Just not visible. I saw the telltale shimmer in the air as she slid off the bed and padded back into the bathroom. I said nothing. Didn't know what to say. I dialed my cloak out a little, just enough to give me fair warning if she tried anything, then glanced around the corner in time to see clothes I hadn't noticed on the drying rack earlier tugged off and disappear into thin air, consumed by her shroud effect.

I stood there listening to her hop back into her clothes, her feet smacking lightly on the polymer floor tiles, three million questions rolling through my head and zero desire to break the silence with any one of them.

I couldn't even wrap my head around what I was feeling, aside from that it involved a vague sense of nausea.

"What the scud just happened?" I finally managed to ask.

A bitter laugh trickled out on the lingering tendrils of steam. "I'm just trying to decide in here if Ponytail is the luckiest girl on Enochia, or just the most sexually frustrated."

I wasn't really sure what to make of that, so I stuck to the basics.

"Were you ordered to kill me?"

Silence.

It stretched long enough that I was pretty sure she didn't plan on answering. When I felt her start to leave the privy, I moved to block the way.

To my surprise, she didn't look angry when she materialized in front of me, fully dressed. Just uncharacteristically somber.

"You know I was."

"I meant again. A second time. Today."

She studied me with those alluring brown eyes. "Alpha, what is it with you? You're just…" She waved a helpless hand, shaking her head. "I don't know what you are."

She glanced at the open window behind me.

"Does the High Cleric want me dead right now or not?"

The first touch of her humor returned. "Oh, I'm sure he does." I opened my mouth, but she rolled her eyes and pushed on before I could speak. "But he didn't order any of us to do it, as far as I know. Not yet, at least." Her lips quirked. "He's probably a bit busy wondering where Four and Eight wandered off to right just now."

"Right…" I frowned. "So why did you… What were you actually looking for here?"

It was brief, but I swore I saw her gaze flick toward my pendant before she smirked and dropped her stare pointedly to my groin, arching her brow in a most suggestive way.

"You wanted to steal a cloak," I said, thankful my voice came out steady.

"I wanted to know your secrets," she said, frowning and eyeing the window impatiently now.

"So you tried to… to…" Alpha be damned, I couldn't quite bring myself to say the words, *seduce me,* any more than I could keep the heat from spreading through my cheeks.

Siren ate it up.

"Oh, poor, poor Ponytail," she said, shaking her head. "I hope that girl knows how to take care of herself while you're busy blushing in the corner."

That only made me blush harder—though from embarrassment or anger, it was hard to say.

"How did you even get in here?"

She gave me another one of those *Have you been licking softsteel?* looks and turned her head between me and the window.

"I'd better not find out you hurt anyone getting over here."

"Or else?" she asked, taking a step closer. Her satisfied smirk only grew when I took an involuntary step back.

"What about the other night?" I asked, giving her a light telekinetic nudge to let her know I was ready to stop her. "I need to know how you got on base. Did someone let you into my room?"

She stepped forward and found herself pressed firmly into my telekinetic barrier. She didn't seem to mind. "You mean aside from your ginger guard pup?"

She leaned into my barrier, tracing her fingers lightly over its surface. I'd never seen anyone do that. It freaking tickled. I almost shuddered—with what, I couldn't have said. All I knew was that even holding her telekinetically felt too intimate right then. I released her, stepping aside.

"My sincerest thanks, goodfellow," she said, reaching to stroke my cheek as she passed and only grinning wider when I leaned away from her touch.

"I'm not going to hurt you, Haldin. Are you really so scared to be touched by a woman?"

"You didn't answer my question."

She shot me a sickeningly sweet smile. "Well that must be just so frustrating for you."

"I could make you answer."

She held my gaze, unflinching. "I bet you could."

She began to fade from sight, starting with the legs, her arcane shroud rising slowly this time, as if to highlight the fact that, whatever else had happened between us today, she was the one who was in fact going to be leaving me hanging at the end.

"How do you do that?" I asked, not really expecting an answer, nor willing to force anything else out of her at the moment. "I've never seen anything like it."

With nothing but her shoulders and head remaining visible, she gave a huff of bitter amusement. "Sweetling, I can't even begin to imagine the scope of the things you haven't seen." She started to turn for the window, paused, then faced me with a sneer. "You wanna know my secret, Demon? Here it is. I've been invisible my entire gropping life. Sometimes I just put energy into it."

And with that, she blew me a scornful kiss and vanished.

But she didn't leave. Not immediately. I felt her lingering there, one hand on the window sill, hesitating.

"I didn't even need to work my charm on him," her voice came from the seemingly empty room. "One look at me and he would've been slobbering to let me in even if the High Cleric hadn't already ordered him to."

"Who?"

Silence. But still she lingered.

"Six, please."

"Six? What happened to my nickname?"

"Siren, then. Please, Siren."

I could hear the smile in her voice. "I like that you call me that. Fitting, I guess. You be careful, Demon."

I felt her start to climb through the open window and teetered there, wanting to stop her and force the answer but feeling somehow that it would be the wrong move.

Outside the window, she paused. "And while you're at it, you might wanna ask your General Auckus what he was up to the night we first met."

Then she was gone.

I stared at the open window for what must've been five minutes before finally dialing my cloak out to make sure she was actually gone. Then stared some more, wondering what in demon's depths had just happened.

3 2

GRAY

"Raish?" The legionnaire's eyes came more focused and alert as he took me in and realized I was standing outside of the apartment I was supposed to be confined to. "Raish? You're... and that woman, she..." He looked around, noting the open window I'd climbed out through, and I could see him struggling to remember what had happened.

"She's gone," I said. "I just wanted to make sure she hadn't hurt anyone out here."

"Scud," he finally muttered. "I didn't even see her coming. She just..." He frowned, clearly coming to the memory of something that seemed not quite right—like a voluptuous blond assassin swirling into existence out of thin air, maybe.

"It's not your fault," I said, offering him a hand and nodding over to where the guard by my living room window was likewise laid out. If it was anyone's fault aside from Siren's and maybe the High Cleric's, it was probably mine. Yet another reminder that I'd failed to protect the Legion against telepaths—not that my cloaks would've saved them from Siren's charms once she'd ghosted in close enough, as I'd found out all too intimately.

"Just hit me outta nowhere," the guard muttered to himself once I'd helped him to his feet. He looked around again before remembering himself and fixing me with a closer inspection. "Are *you* okay?"

"She wasn't here to hurt me," I said, thinking back to how she'd hesitated at the end, and how she'd ended up deciding to tell me what I wanted to know.

General Auckus.

Had he really been the one who'd helped her on base for her near-lethal medica visit? Or had Siren merely been stirring the Haven pot with a clever lie because that's what she liked to do—or, worse, had been *ordered* to do by the High Cleric? Maybe I should've just broken into her mind and found out for certain.

When I noticed the odd look the guard was giving me, I quickly added, "Doesn't mean she won't be back to finish the job."

The last thing I needed were Haven rumors about the Demon of Divinity sneaking around with the mysterious Sanctum girl.

I gestured to the other passed-out legionnaire. "You got him?"

The legionnaire nodded, blinking the last of his disorientation off and shifting back into proper soldier mode.

"Good. Then I think you'd better put me back under arrest before you make your report, soldier."

He showed me the trace of an abashed grin. "Sir, yes sir."

I climbed through the window back into my bedroom, went straight to the front door, and invited the squad leader inside to calmly—and privately —fill her in on what had just happened. She wasn't happy. Understandably. But at least she was on the same page that we should keep the incident quiet and report straight to Glenbark.

I didn't argue when she left to make her report and to tighten the defenses on my windows and any other potential points of ingress. I opened my palmlight and swiped out my own message to the High General.

<Need to talk. There's been a breakthrough.>

Perhaps it would've been fairer to add that the breakthrough had nothing to do with cloaking runes, but I needed to get her attention on the Auckus lead as quickly as possible. I added Johnny to the message and sent it out, trusting he could help expedite things and would also be wise enough not to immediately cue Elise in. Not that I intended to keep her in the dark. I just needed a minute to clear my head and figure out how to explain to her what Siren had been doing in our bedroom.

As soon as I sat down to take that minute, though, I was nearly overwhelmed with the urge to slip my guards, run straight to Therese's lab, fall down at Elise's feet, and tell her then and there. Tell her that I was sorry and that I loved her and that the memory of her had been the only thing that had let me break free from Siren's telepathic head games in the end.

I'd like to say it was the house arrest and the threat of potential execution for bad behavior that kept me rooted in place. But, if I'm being honest, I think I was just scared. Scared that I'd fumble the words and grop everything up. Scared that I'd tell the truth too completely, and do the same.

Because what if Siren actually *hadn't* been working some strange telepathic mischief at all? What if I was simply that weak for a warm touch and some soft curves?

No. That was bullscud. I knew the difference between desire and mind control. My first time with Elise, I'd been so consumed that it hadn't even occurred to me to stop, but thinking back on it, I was sure I *could* have stopped if there'd been good reason. If I'd wanted to. But earlier today... wanting to stop only to find my body unresponsive... that had been something different. Something externally imposed on me.

Right?

I crossed my legs, plucking a practice pendant from the floor, and tried to settle into some manner of focus. I felt dirty—to the extent that I almost wanted to take another shower. Which in turn only reminded me of Siren in my shower robe.

I let out a heavy sigh and woke my palmlight, pulling up my running messages with Elise.

<There was a little incident over here, but I'm fine. Didn't want you to worry if you heard anything. You should finish your work and>

I stared at the incomplete message for a few seconds then cleared it, positive that any mention of an incident, large or small, would have her storming the apartment with the cavalry. And much as I would've loved to feel her arms around me right just then, I wanted a couple hours to cleanse my pallet and maybe even get something done so I could stop feeling so damned guilty.

<Looking forward to holding you tonight.> I sent her instead.

Her reply wasn't long in coming.

<Did something happen?>

I shouldn't have been surprised that even that would pique her curiosity. She was truly her father's daughter.

<I found something out, but it'll keep until tonight. Crack the facilities and we can celebrate together.>

That was enough truth to see us through for a couple hours. Tonight, though...

Her reply buzzed through the gathering clouds of my thoughts.

<Guess I DO still owe you that birthday surprise...>

A ripple of delicious anticipation shot through me, followed almost immediately by an even bigger wave of dirty guilt.

Alpha be damned, I was really starting to hate how complicated my life had become.

Hours later, after my guard detail had been doubled and the windows had all been reinforced to the extent that I could no longer see day passing to dark night outside, I was still sitting on the floor, alone in our quarters, toying with my runes and trying not to think about all the wild scud that had happened that day. Looking around at the mess of etched and drawn runes scattered about the room—and at the melted decorations and copious scorch marks on the couch table—I decided I'd been less than successful on both fronts.

Empowering runes, at least, was becoming quite doable. I'd made at least a dozen successful heat sinks that night, hence the scorch marks in the table. I'd firmly established that a given rune did not necessarily have a set purpose and could in fact be made to hold whatever effect I empowered it with. I'd even managed to link two runes together—one that drew thermal energy from the air, and another that expelled it like a big, cozy heater. Or, it turned out, like a small, focused death beam. Hence the melted decorative orbs.

At one point, I was even pretty sure I'd technically succeeded in empowering a linked rune combo to draw thermal energy and produce my island-method cloaking effect. It just hadn't lasted long enough for me to confirm. Which was exactly the problem.

No matter what I did, I couldn't get a single damn rune to function for more than a minute or so before the effect just bled out and died.

Re-empowering the same rune again worked. I could do it for hours. Had done it for hours. But it was like filling a leaky basin. Over and over again, no matter how hard I tried, how carefully I focused, the effects simply wouldn't stick. And I didn't know what to do about it.

I glanced at my palmlight for what must've been the hundredth time in the past ten minutes, starting to worry. Probably, Elise had simply gotten caught up in the thrilling contents of yet another data drive, but from her last message nearly an hour ago, I'd expected her to be back by now.

With a sigh, I rose to go get a much-needed glass of water. The thought of her walking through the door any minute pretty much nullified any chance of my finding the deep focus required for more rune work. Mostly, it made my insides crawl with apprehension.

I was just going to tell her what Siren had done. Straight up. There was no other option. No option but to tell the girl I loved that a madwoman who'd recently tried to kill me had somehow turned around and damn near seduced me.

This was going to be a tram wreck.

I was surprised I'd managed to get anything done at all today, as aggressively as the whole situation had been eating at me. I'd tried and failed to discreetly ask Johnny via message about his own experience being incapacitated by Siren. He'd assured me her touch had been positively unnatural —*like a triple IV dose of NitroSteel,* in his words—which had made me feel a bit better. But then, of course, he'd wanted to know why I was asking.

I was still going to have to explain that one at some point.

For the time being, I occupied myself staring at my half-full water glass, studying the way the light passed through and thinking about Siren's phenomenal little invisibility trick.

Had she actually meant to let me live back in the medica? I was honestly starting to wonder, but after today, I was also hesitant to trust anything my gut had to say about the woman.

After a few worthless minutes of speculation, I decided it didn't particularly matter right then and plucked the cloaking pendant from my chest to return to the all-too-familiar ritual of studying it. Johnny and Elise had both informed me that the amount of time I spent staring at the runes had officially reached full-on-creepy status, but how could I not stare?

There it was, the answer to our most pressing problem, sitting in the palm of my hand, just waiting to be understood.

The flowing, nested design of the interconnected runes had made it somewhat hard to determine where one ended and another began, but after my creepy amounts of studying and sketching, I was fairly certain there was a grand total of five runes on the cloaking pendant. One to generate the cloak, and another to pull the requisite power from the air—those two seemed to be a given. And given that Johnny's non-adjustable cloak only had four runes, one of the five on mine must be controlling the range of the cloak.

That still left two runes unexplained.

I obsessed over those two runes. The more I thought about them, the more I was sure at least one of them must be the key to keeping their fellow runes powered up for good—or for at least eleven years, seeing as Elise's had apparently been working that long. But if I was right, and one or both of those runes was preserving the others, then what the scud was keeping *them* going?

It was like the old riddle some casual worshippers loved to pull out when they'd been too long at their drink. *If Alpha created Enochia and everything that we know, then who made him?*

Lucky for them, they got to just keep drinking until they forgot their questions. No one was depending on them to figure out where the infinite loop began.

I wasn't so lucky. All I could do was resign myself to thumping the back of my head against the cabinet, waiting for inspiration to jiggle loose. At the apprehensive jolt that shot through me, I actually thought for a second that it might have. Then I realized my palmlight had buzzed.

My stomach fluttered at the sight of Elise's name.

<Sorry, love, we got caught up. Might actually have something here. You still at it? I'll be back soon. Get your celebration pants ready.>

I smiled at that, then grimaced at my own audacity in smiling. My fingers hovered over the palmlight.

<Something's better than nothing, right? I'll be>

I paused. Started to delete my words. Paused again.

Gropping scudbuckets, I wished I could just go over there now. A night-time stroll through Haven sounded indecently tempting. For a few seconds, I even considered asking the ordo outside my room if she might run it up the chain, just this once.

Please, sir, I know it's a matter of Enochian security and everything, but I'm REALLY scared my girlfriend's gonna be mad at me...

As if.

"Whatever," I muttered to myself, swiping at my palmlight.

<Still at it, pants and all. See you soon, love.>

Alpha, with wit like that, how would she ever bear to be without me?

I glanced at the door, wondering if the ordo might at least be amenable to sending someone for flowers. Because nothing said romance like flowers someone else had to fetch for your house-arrested public enemy boyfriend, right?

I'd just crawled back over to my pile of practice pendants—literally crawled, because that's where I was at that point—when someone knocked at the door. Had someone been in the room with me, they probably would've gotten a kick out of my jerky reaction and the position I ended up in, sprawled across the floor with my sidearm trained on the door.

Alpha, I was losing it. I let out a deep breath and confirmed with a quick mental sweep that it was only one of the guards. They knocked again right before I reached the door. I pulled it open and was greeted by an unfamiliar face. Her insignia marked her as belonging to the 122nd Wolf Company.

"We've got a potential Code Gray on base, sir."

Code Gray. I rifled through dusty memories. "Intruders?"

"It's probably nothing, and we've got this place locked down tight out here, but Ordo said to let you know to keep an ear open, just in case."

I nodded uncertainly, my mind filling with thoughts of Siren and her friends sneaking around on base—or other Seekers, even, dispatched by the High Cleric to come find them. But it was probably actually nothing. Just a confused courier or a jumpy watchman on the wall. It happened.

"Okay," I said. "Yeah, thanks. Will do."

I started to retreat into the apartment, then paused.

"Uh… This is gonna sound weird, but um… if I were to ask you to get me some flowers…"

I trailed off at the expression on her face and was about to stammer a never mind and close the door when I realized she hadn't even heard me. It was something she must've been hearing on her earpiece that had her eyes widening. I looked down the hallway and saw similar expressions on half a dozen legionnaire faces, then I glanced at my own palmlight.

Nothing.

I looked back to my hall monitor. "What's going on out—"

A distant alarm split the night.

I waited, tense, holding my hesitant guard's gaze and praying—as I'm sure she was too—that it had been a mistake. Five long seconds of silence. Then the alarm blared again. And again.

"I'm getting my gear," I said, turning back into the room.

She didn't argue, but probably only because I didn't add the part where I was going to Therese's lab to secure Elise and the others whether my guard detail liked it or not. The fourth blare of the alarm left me little choice in the matter.

Because Haven was under attack.

33

CODE BLACK

"Hear the call, Haven," the speaker in the corner of the bedroom boomed as I frantically pulled on dark clothes over my armor skin and retrieved my helmet from the closet. "Code Black. Repeat, Code Black."

"Tell me something I don't know," I growled at the wall.

"Raknoth forces have breached the perimeter," the voice boomed, making me regret my words. "Repeat, raknoth forces have entered the base. Arm yourselves and proceed to your designated defense zones immediately. This is not a drill. Repeat, this is not a drill."

The voice went on like that as I reached for my daggers and the wall display came to life with a live stream of relevant details and updates. I scanned the lines and paused to make sure I'd seen what I thought I'd seen.

Only a hundred estimated hostiles?

My breathing eased a little. A hundred hybrids rampaging through Haven in the middle of the night was no laughing matter. Far from it. People were groggy, mistakes could well be made, and the hybrids could do some serious damage. If they'd made it past the perimeter guards, they probably already had.

But still, a hundred hybrids weren't going to take Haven on their own. There were over five thousand legionnaires on base, and they weren't going to be scudding themselves with surprise and fear as many had understandably done when the hybrids had made their debut in razing Sanctuary.

So why send such a small force at all?

I had a dark mental image of Alton Parker watching this all from a high-flying skimmer, waiting to unleash some devastating surprise in the midst of this seemingly ill-conceived attack, and what little ease I'd felt quickly dissipated.

I needed to find Elise and the others. From there, we'd see.

My guards were pounding on the door when I made it back to the entryway.

"My fireteam has been ordered to remain in the room with you, sir," the one I'd spoken to earlier said. Or at least started to say. The words sort of died off at the end as she took in my battle garb.

"You can post up wherever you'd like, Talia," I said, reading her name on my helmet display, "but if you're interested in watching my back, it's headed to engineering."

I wasn't overly surprised when she didn't step aside and tell me to carry on. Or when one of the legionnaires behind her started speaking quietly with one hand to his ear—probably telling the ordo I was getting ready to bolt.

For a second, I considered doing just that. But I couldn't deny how much nicer it would be to have a squad's-worth of friendly eyes and weapons checking corners with me out there rather than hunting me down and trying to drag me back.

So when Talia started to tell me, "We can't allow that, sir," I picked her and the two legionnaires at her flanks all up with telekinesis and scooted them neatly aside, at once clearing my path and, hopefully, making my point clear.

The legionnaires who still had their feet on the ground jerked back at the display, and tensed when I turned my hard gaze on them. I started walking before their shock could wear off.

"Tell your ordo I'm going to engineering," I called, not looking back. "And that I wouldn't say no to some cover."

I heard their urgent whispers behind me. Felt one of the closer ones tug the stun rod from his vest. Just to make my point as clear as possible, I grabbed the weapon with telekinesis, still not looking, and ripped it from his hand. I probably shouldn't have smiled at the resultant *thunk* of rod striking carpet, or the collection of hissed curses that followed, but at least none of them tried to shoot me in the back.

They followed, and I could faintly hear one of them muttering quick updates to their ordo. Talia drew up beside me, showed me a stern frown, and patched me into their battle channel.

Nothing like a good crisis to stir up some reluctant camaraderie, I guess. That, or the fear of demonic powers.

"Dillard told me you were a royal pain in the ass," came a wry female voice in my earpiece—Ordo Grotski of the 122nd Wolf Company, according to my palmlight.

"My apologies, Ordo," was all I could think to say, busy as I was swiping messages to Elise to stay put and to Johnny to let him know where I was headed. He'd either be with Glenbark or reporting to a defense area. Either way, he was probably safe enough. Scud, if it was truly only a hundred hybrids, neither one of us should probably even see any fighting.

"What's in engineering?" Ordo Grotski was asking.

"A whole bunch of important resources, sir."

Beside me, Talia shot me a look that almost made me wonder if it wasn't actually her voice in my head when Grotski said, "One of those resources happen to be your mate, Citizen?"

"I promise you," I said, approaching the barracks doors, "we don't wanna lose what's in that lab."

"All right, then," Grotski said as Talia palmed the access panel to the right.

The night air wrapped me in a muggy embrace as I stepped through the barracks doors... and my extended senses screamed in alarm.

I yanked a barrier into existence around me, not having time to resolve what was incoming or from where. No sooner had my foot touched down outside than I felt a rapid string of concussions on my barrier and found myself looking at a small flock of stunner bolts hovering in front of me. *Friendly* stunner bolts, I realized.

To complete the betrayal, another Wolf made a lunge with his stun rod from behind, and yet another one actually dropped down on me from some handhold above the barracks doors. I shoved the one behind me back into Talia's fireteam, redirected—if not quite tossed—the falling Wolf, and rounded on Talia just as she was yanking her own stun rod free.

We froze like that—me tensed to run, solidifying my telekinetic shield, and Talia and Alpha knew how many other Wolves out there trying to decide whether or not to rush me with even more stunners.

In the corner of my mind, I noted that something about the sporadic gunfire reporting from a dozen directions around Haven sounded wrong— far too staccato and scattered for well-organized squads gunning down wild hybrids.

"At ease, Wolves," someone called, stepping forward from the shadows.

Ordo Grotski, I took it from the voice and the command. She tugged the Wolf who'd tried to take me from above back to his feet before turning to me with an unabashed shrug. "We had to at least try to get you back to safety."

"Does that mean you're done?"

"Well, I'd still prefer you'd turn around, but…" Reluctantly, she nodded.

I swallowed, preparing to run. "Is that why you still have half a dozen Wolves waiting to take their shots?"

Her genteel expression flickered with surprise, but that was only part of what had my heart racing. The gunfire was definitely wrong out there, waxing and waning with the give-and-take rhythm of armed combatants trading bursts of softsteel.

I needed to move.

"I can feel them out there," I said, taking a few steps forward with my barriers held tight. "You can't lie to me. Now, I'm going to engineering. It's up to you whether you—"

"Get down!" someone shouted from the shadows—just as the barracks courtyard lit up with gunfire.

Blood sprayed from Ordo Grotski's throat. She fell dead before I could so much as twitch, an expression of shock frozen across her weathered face. Someone crashed into my right flank—Talia, I realized, shoving at my barrier with fierce conviction.

"Take cover!" she growled, pushing us toward the permacrete abutment at the edge of the walkway to our left.

I regained my senses and stopped fighting. Around us, the courtyard was coming alive with return fire as we dropped into cover. Slugs thwacked into the permacrete just behind us, spewing specks of debris against my faceplate and cutting down one of the Wolves who'd been tight on our backs.

I shifted my barrier, trying to cover the other two rushing to join us, and peered out from cover, drawing my sidearm. I traced the muzzle flashes to the rooftop across the courtyard, and there they were, silhouetted in the flood of Haven's lights—four hybrids, fully armored, but recognizable by the soft crimson glow of their eyes through their helmet faceplates.

As one, the hybrids roared, and as quick as they'd drawn a line on the hybrids, four of the Wolves turned and opened fire on their own squad. I dialed my cloak out as far as I could, cutting them off from the hybrids, but not before two more legionnaires had fallen.

Above, the hybrids had already vanished into the night, leaving the remaining Wolves gaping at each other in pale, wide-eyed shock.

"What the scud was that?" one of them cried, his shaky voice echoing the dread in my own gut. Because it wasn't just a hundred hybrids Haven was facing. It was a hundred gun-toting telepathic super soldiers. Maybe more. And they'd apparently seen fit to properly armor themselves this time.

"You have to get back inside," Talia said, looking warily from me to the legionnaires tending to Grotski and their other fallen brethren.

"I can't," I said, realizing just how true it was as I said it. Talia started to argue, but I cut her off. "We can't. Those things could be coming back with reinforcements. We need to get the wounded to a defense zone and keep moving."

I didn't add that I had a sinking feeling it might be me they'd been looking for—and that they seemed to have known where to start—but Talia seemed to come to a similar conclusion on her own. I half-expected her to curse me or at least point out that this was a scud assignment, but she just stood and started calling orders to lock it down and get the wounded ready to move. But Ordo Grotski and four of the fallen were already dead, and the fifth legionnaire who'd taken a hit was already stimmed and back on his feet, refusing to be carried or even helped.

"Keep them close to me if you're coming," I told Talia quietly. "I can keep the hybrids from gropping with their heads."

She relayed the orders, not bothering to ask what the scud I meant by any of it, and fell in beside me as I oriented myself and headed for the courtyard exit, morosely thinking that my first visit to Therese's lab was really shaping up to be one miserable bitch of a scudstorm.

WANTED

As we pushed on, I saw that Haven was rousing to life and pulling its defenses together every bit as quickly as I'd hoped. Knowing what was loose on base, though, I was still worried it wouldn't be enough.

Dark shapes seemed to move in every shadow. Some leapt from rooftop to rooftop, gunning down a legionnaire here, or forcing a few bursts of friendly fire there. Other beasts darted across the permacrete, their red eyes burning behind their faceplates as they cut down whatever stragglers they came across with fang and claw.

Were there really only a hundred?

There was no way to tell, and nothing to be done about it but to press on. I kept my cloak extended as we went, periodically clicking it off completely to scout for enemies farther ahead, and otherwise lending what telepathic protection I could to the Wolves and to what legionnaires we passed. But it wasn't even close to enough.

Soon, the battle channels were filling with reports of friendly fire and heavy losses. We saw a full squad open fire on two hybrids only for the hybrids to gun down a few, rip apart a few more, and vanish to the rooftops with inhuman speed. I was torn—desperately wanting to go join the fight and help, even more desperately needing to get to Therese's lab and make sure everyone was safe there.

We pressed on, Talia, who knew Haven far better than me, moving to shortcut us through a mess hall. We were approaching the exit on the far side when the doors burst open and three legionnaires flew in like a pack of feral haga beasts was at their heels. One whirled, raising his rifle, just as the first of two hybrids came lunging through the door.

I caught it in the air with telekinesis. "Shoot it!" I roared, telekinetically ripping its helmet off as it began bucking against my hold with exceptional strength.

The soldier who'd turned quickly complied, the Wolves and his allies joining him. The hybrid's skull took more of a beating than seemed possible, but when I released my telekinetic hold, it crumpled to the floor, dead. I cast my senses out, preparing for the next hybrid, but it had backed away from the door.

"Raishman," came a harsh, throaty voice from outside. Then again, at a half-roar. "Raishman!"

The legionnaires turned wide eyes my way. I reached out, intending to immobilize it so they could step out and take it down, but it had already bounded out of my cloaking field.

"It's gone," I told them.

We pushed on with three new allies and a collective feeling of unnerving dread at where and why that hybrid might've fled. Outside, the sounds of fighting seemed to be slowing marginally. There were still bursts of distant gunfire every half minute or so, too-often accompanied by hair-raising screams and inhuman shrieks, but the sounds seemed to be spreading, hunter and hunted both becoming more cautious—though I wasn't entirely sure which was which at this point.

We were only a few minutes from Therese's lab when we came across the bloody aftermath of a fight between twenty-some legionnaires and two hybrids. All dead.

I stared down at the two monsters who'd claimed the lives of an entire squad, trying to hold onto my stomach's scant contents. Under Haven's bright floodlights, I noticed inky lines spanning the hybrids' exposed hides like dark spiderwebs. My mind flashed back to the raknoth sickness I'd briefly glimpsed in Al'Kundesha's memories when we'd tangled back in Sanctuary. Was that what I was seeing now?

A groan from the lake of bodies reminded me that now wasn't the time to worry about anything but surviving. Two of our party hurried toward the sound and pulled a wounded soldier out from under one of the dead. Somewhere off in the darkness above, I thought I heard a low growl.

"We should keep moving," said Talia, apparently having heard it too.

Once they got him on his feet, the wounded legionnaire seemed capable of moving with only light support, so we pushed on. For the last couple minutes of our trek, the sounds of fighting continued to grow more distant and sporadic, mostly focused toward Haven's center. We also didn't pass anyone, which wasn't overly odd since we were moving into a less-populated corner of Haven.

But I couldn't shake the feeling we were being followed.

At first, I attributed it to battle nerves. As the building that housed Therese's lab came into view, though, I finally caught it at the edge of my senses on one of my quick, uncloaked sweeps—a hybrid, prowling after us from the shadows a couple rooftops back. It seemed to feel me noticing, because when I looked back, there was nothing. I watched the shadows uneasily. Finally, two dots of crimson fire appeared in the darkness, watching right back. Waiting.

Suddenly, I had the horrible feeling our presence might be more a danger than a boon to Elise and the others. But it was too late to turn back. Almost as soon as the one hybrid made itself known, another appeared behind us in my extended senses, and another off to the far right.

They were boxing us in. Like intelligent predators.

"We need to get inside," I said quietly to Talia and the others, dialing my cloak in and hoping the hybrids' senses weren't sharp enough to catch my words. "We have company closing in around us."

They perked up and acknowledged my words silently.

I gripped my sidearm and led the way across the mostly open lot in front of the lab building, feeling horribly exposed. For the first several steps, I allowed myself to hope. Then I toggled my cloak for another quick sweep and brushed against three more hybrid minds lurking on top of the lab building, and I had to swallow the truth.

We weren't going anywhere without a fight.

I motioned us to a halt next to a few bulky cargo transports that were the best thing for cover anywhere nearby, drew one of Carlisle's daggers, and readied myself. The legionnaires fell in around me, doing the same. The closest enemy was still over fifty yards away, but for hybrids leaping from rooftops, that might not mean more than a few seconds' warning. I made one last mental sweep, then dialed my cloak in to keep us protected from telepathic attack.

There were at least ten hybrids around us now, their minds abuzz with nearly as much telepathic power as I'd felt from any of the Seekers. Together, I had no doubt they could break my mind. It might only take a few of them.

"Raishman."

Skin crawling, I leaned around the large skimmer and followed the guttural voice up to the several pairs of red eyes looking down from the shadows of Therese's rooftop.

"Master sends for you," came another voice from the building behind, more airy than the first.

"Weapons down and we spare men," called a third voice from somewhere off to the right.

Their timing was that of one mind speaking through three mouths. It was creepy. I glanced around at the Wolves. Talia gave a curt shake of her head. They were with me.

"I think you can tell your master to shove it," I called. "And meanwhile, I'd suggest you clear out of here before all of Haven finishes with your friends and comes raining vengeance on your asses."

"*Fool.*" The word came from all around us, as if hissed by the darkness itself.

It had been worth a shot, at least.

In the silence that followed, a small voice pleaded with me to move—to make a mad dash for the lab building while we could. But we were pinned, I knew that. At least out in the middle of the lot, we'd have time for a few shots when they inevitably grew impatient and came for us.

The legionnaires must've agreed with my conclusion, because they all held their ground. We were tense as suspension wires, sure. No amount of training in the world could have changed that as we waited there for clawed death to descend upon us. But we were ready. For what felt like an hour but might have been a minute, we were ready.

Was it my imagination, or were the sounds of fighting growing louder now? Heading our way?

Depending on how the next few minutes went, that probably wouldn't matter too much, but it at least made me hope we might have reinforcement soon. Whether the hybrids noticed the same thing or simply grew bored, I'm not exactly sure. But I swore I felt the change in the air when something set them off.

They came with shrieks and growls. More than ten of them.

I caught sight of four dropping from the closest rooftop, raised my sidearm, then ducked back behind the skimmer with a curse as the ones on Therese's building opened fire. The legionnaires responded in kind, and within seconds the lot went from dead silent to thunderous cacophony.

Two hybrids slammed down to the skimmer behind me with bone-shattering force and a pair of thick roars. Reflexively, I reached to blast them away with telekinesis, only registering after they sailed away that I'd only cleared the line of sight for the shooters on the roof. I cursed again, and turned to fire on another charging hybrid, hunkering down as best I could.

Things fell apart quickly after that.

The hybrids were fast, relentless, and entirely too resilient to our slugs. I emptied half my feeder on a single enemy, missing the charging beast as much as not. It hit the pavement only to be trampled by the two charging behind it. A few stray slugs punched into my armor skin like miniature raknoth fists. I tried to raise a barrier. Turned to jam my booted heel into a charging hybrid's knee just as the leg planted. It hyperextended with a wet cracking sound, but the hybrid was sturdier than I'd expected. It crashed into me, shrieking.

I silenced it with a dagger to the under chin, pivoting past—and straight into its charging companion. My dagger leapt for its eye by almost subconscious telekinesis, but the hybrid tucked its head, took the blade to the scalp instead, and caught my wrist with frightening strength. Something popped, liquid fire coursing up my arm. With a wordless cry, I jammed my sidearm into the hybrid's eye and pulled the trigger three times.

I turned from the falling hybrid, arm on fire and head ringing. Less than a dozen rifles remained at my back, firing steadily into the night. The rest were already dead. I saw one wounded legionnaire on the ground beside them, feebly trying to draw his sidearm. Then a hybrid slammed down on him from one of the rooftops and tore into the group until there were only eight standing. And more hybrids were coming.

We weren't making it out of there.

I sighted on the closest hybrid anyway. Fired once, twice, and—

My senses screamed a warning. I spun, too late. A hybrid slammed into my back, driving me to the pavement. Something smacked against my shoulder—its helmet, I realized. So excited for its first bite that it'd forgotten to lift its faceplate.

I reached out and caught its head with telekinesis as it yanked the helmet loose, aiming to try again. I twisted, pointing my nearly empty sidearm far too close to my own head, and was about to shoot the bastard off my back when it gave a jerk, went limp, and was promptly rolled off my back. A second later, strong, slender arms yanked me to my feet, and I found myself face to face with Talia.

There were only five of us left between the cargo transports. And even more hybrids around the lot. Dozens of them. But there were legionnaires too, now, sweeping in from multiple directions, driving the hybrids before them.

"I'm going in," I cried to Talia, trying not to think about the number of bodies I left behind as I whirled for the lab.

Talia shoved me from behind before I could take a step. I thudded into the side of the skimmer just as a hybrid landed right where I'd been standing. Talia shot it neatly in the forehead. I drew my remaining dagger and caught it in the underjaw as it staggered into my range. Then I turned and ran for the lab.

The lot was pure chaos—full scale war between multiple squads of legionnaires and what must've been all the hybrids left on base at that point. My senses were too muddled from panic and exhaustion to make sense of it all. And as I rounded the transport and saw the lab doors bursting open and the pack of hybrids darting out, everything else ceased to matter.

They had Elise.

I screamed her name, reaching out and smashing two of her assailants into the side of the building with telekinesis. At that range, it cost me. But Elise was fighting too, twisting free of one hybrid, driving a brutal kick into another's head. I reached out to yank another away from her—

And cried out as something bit into my neck and arced through my body with electric fury. The next I knew, I was hitting the pavement, and someone was laying a hand on my shoulder. Sliding it down the front.

Plucking the cloaking pendant from my chest.

"I'm sorry, Haldin," came a voice as the pendant floated past my face on thin air, its chain sliding free of my helmet and neck.

Siren.

I shakily tried to look around, but I could barely move my head. There was nothing. For a brief second, I managed to focus enough to feel her there, but then she vanished from my senses, and the electric bite was back at my neck, digging in longer this time, ripping through my rigid muscles until the world receded to a dull, distant buzz I couldn't seem to make any sense of.

Shouts and gunfire were all around me now. Curses and heavy boots stomping past. I was going to be sick.

"Get her back!" someone was screaming. "Stop them!"

Elise.

The world wavered, pulling closer into focus, just enough for me to vaguely register Phineas staggering out of the lab building and thudding to his knees, his chest soaked with blood. He shot the nearest hybrid. Tried to aim at the next and collapsed. James and Franco came after him, screaming Elise's name.

Elise.

I tried to turn my head and look for her, but my body barely responded. I tried harder, and my head twitched around just in time for one last glimpse.

Elise was fighting furiously, bleeding from multiple wounds, clothes torn, and barely slowing for any of it. But the hybrids kept coming. Dropping down. Sweeping in. Carrying her away in a tide of dark armor and green hides until two managed to catch her in a secure grip and haul her around the corner and out of sight.

I howled her name, but barely managed more than a mournful groan. I tried to roll over and stand, but my muscles and nerves were too fried to listen. I flopped weakly on the ground, nausea sweeping through me, helpless panic clamping at my chest.

The need to follow after her burned so deeply that I found myself hoping when a hybrid rose from a nearby legionnaire, licking the blood from its lips and fixing its crimson eyes on me. If the hybrid came for me... if it took me with Elise...

I didn't care anymore. Didn't care about anything but Elise being dragged off on a writhing mass of hybrids. But a hail of gunfire cut the hybrid down to ribbons before it could lunge.

I pushed to my knees on shaky, spasmodic limbs, my head spinning wildly with the motion, and my stomach threatening to void its contents. It was more than exhaustion and the shock, I realized. Siren must've hit me with some of the stun rod's sedative too. Warm honey crept through my limbs, begging me to lay back down.

It's already too late, it whispered.

I closed my eyes, focusing on the thought of Elise, thinking of the time Carlisle had given me some kind of arcane stim to keep me moving, forming everything I had left behind a single prayer.

"Lise..."

I couldn't feel her out there. Alpha, why was it so hard to reach out? I let the panic fuel me, welcomed the adrenaline pulsing through veins. I drew energy without clear thought or form—only willing myself to get the scud up.

Odd tingles washed through me, and I was almost surprised when I opened my eyes to find myself standing on shaky feet. I lurched forward and almost fell over. I reached out with my drunken senses, desperate to feel a glimpse of her presence, to know there was still hope.

But she was gone. And I was empty, drifting in a dull sea of shouts and screams and gunfire, all unimportant, all miles away from my mind. I started forward again and tripped. Found myself falling. Someone caught me, but I hardly cared.

"...okay, buddy. Just take it easy."

Johnny's voice.

"We're gonna... We're gonna get her b—"

Explosions rocked the night, chaining across the distant reaches of Haven in a string of flashing infernos and deep booms I felt right in my heart.

"Scud," Johnny whispered beside me.

Like a buzzing insect in my ear, the reports came in on the main battle channel. Serious damage had been dealt at almost every major landing pad in Haven. Entire fleets of transports and skimmers wrecked in the space of seconds. But I couldn't bring myself to care about that either. Couldn't bring myself to care about anything but the only thing that mattered.

She was gone.

"Find her," I croaked. "Get her back, Johnny. Please."

He was already steering me down to the ground. Kneeling beside me to give me a quick once over.

"Just stay here, Hal. Don't move."

Then he was gone too.

35

LOW

I sat there, rocking on the pavement, numbly watching legionnaires rush by. All I could do was cling to the image of Johnny running off in the direction they'd taken Elise. That, and to pray that he would manage where I'd failed. And to curse my own battered body for giving up.

I couldn't understand why I couldn't just get to my worthless feet and keep moving. My brain felt stewed, like it had reached some agreement with the desperation and the sedatives and whatever else was pumping through my system, and like I wasn't really conscious at all so much as simply passed out with my eyes still open and my brain still receiving the meaningless inputs.

A few legionnaires stopped to check me for major wounds. I hardly noticed. It was only when one of them took my wrists—particularly the one that was still throbbing from the hybrid's iron grip—that my attention actually stirred.

When I saw that they'd fitted me with shackles, I came fully back to reality.

"Did you hear me, Citizen Raish?"

I looked up and into the severe frown of an ordo I didn't recognize. *Haga Company,* my mind dully noted. *323rd.*

"I said you need to come with us," said the ordo—Ordo Silvers, according to my helmet—as he gestured to the men beside him.

They stepped forward, hauled me to my feet, and only begrudgingly held on when my legs buckled beneath me. Ordo Silvers gave me a disgusted look and beckoned his men to bring me along.

I didn't understand what was happening. Somehow, I couldn't bring myself to care. My feet moved along mechanically as they half-dragged, half-carried me from the place of my failure and on to Alpha knew what.

"Hey!" someone was calling sharply behind us.

Johnny.

A shot of awareness sparked through me, and I jerked my head around, much to the startlement of the legionnaires dragging me along. Awareness spiked to tremulous hope as I saw Johnny wasn't alone... and deflated completely when I realized it wasn't Elise beside him, but Talia of the 122nd Wolves.

I sagged against my escorts as Johnny and Talia jogged up to Ordo Silvers of the 323rd Hagas, both looking ready for a fight.

"Where is she?" I tried to ask Johnny, but I didn't manage more than a hoarse, burning whisper. And Johnny was too occupied with Silvers.

"Hey!" he snapped again. "What the scud do you think you're doing?"

"Step aside, servitor."

"Where are you taking my charge, sir?" Talia asked, her tone decidedly calmer than Johnny's.

"*Your* charge?" Silvers sneered. "You mean the prisoner whom you and your squad allowed to escape during the incursion? He's—"

"Where is she, Johnny?" My voice was louder this time, enough to draw their attention. It sounded awful. Broken. But far, far worse, was the look on Johnny's face. That look was all the answer I needed.

That look broke something in me.

"Let go of me," I whispered, jerking my arms free of the legionnaires' grips. They caught roughly back on, another stepping forward to help.

"I SAID LET GO!" I screamed, lashing blindly out as the rage took over.

A low boom shook the air, jarring my brain, and the next I knew, I was staring at a ring of dazed legionnaires sprawled out all around me, my head was spinning, and every member of the 323rd Hagas who was still standing had their rifles leveled in my direction.

"Don't!" Johnny yelled, stepping in front of me, arms splayed wide as he faced the shooters. I was surprised to feel Talia likewise covering my back.

"Don't you gropping dare," Johnny growled.

But I saw the look on Ordo Silver's face. He wasn't going to listen. I gathered more energy, preparing to hurl that sneering face through the closest permacrete wall. Then Johnny spun to me, arms still held wide, and the pain in his voice stopped me dead.

"Hal…"

His eyes were brimming with tears.

I don't think I'd ever seen Johnny cry.

"Just… just breathe, buddy. Just think for a second."

Behind him, Silvers hesitated. He wasn't sneering anymore.

I let some of the energy trickle off.

"She's still alive," Johnny said. "She has to be. They carried her over the wall with them. Just her. No one else."

I looked that way as if I expected I might see them right there. My head was starting to clear a little now. If they'd gone over the wall… if they'd tried to carry her off on foot…

My shackles fell off without me hardly even having to think about releasing the mechanisms. Legionnaires cursed all around us.

Johnny grabbed me by the shoulders. "Hal…"

"I'm going after them."

He shook his head. "She's gone. They blew our rides and scattered."

"Then I'll follow them on foot."

"And what? Storm Oasis by yourself?"

"If I have to," I growled, reaching to knock his hands away only to be reminded of my injured wrist by a blinding lance of pain.

"You're hurt." His grip loosened on my shoulders.

"I have to get her back, Johnny."

"We will, buddy. Together. You can bet Alpha's shiny ass on that."

I looked around and realized we were drawing a crowd now. Legionnaires looked on from all sides, Haga trigger fingers tensing wherever my gaze landed. They were watching me like I was a wild animal.

"How?" I asked quietly.

"We'll take back Oasis," Johnny said, equally quietly. "You're close on…" He stopped himself before he said *the cloaks* for anyone in the crowd to hear. "I know you are. We'll find a way, man. But first, we need to get you patched up."

Something shifted in me, desperation and anger giving way to exhaustion and a deep, sickened despair that settled firmly in my stomach. I couldn't think about the cloaks and how much I wasn't even close to cracking them, or about how strong the hybrids were growing, and what they might be doing to Elise right then. I could barely even stand on my own two feet.

I nodded.

Johnny let out a heavy breath, nodding to himself and giving Talia a pointed look before he turned to the watching ordo of the 323rd Hagas.

"We'll see him to the medica, sir," Johnny said, his tone adding a heavily implied *you gropping beardsplitter* to the promise. "And back to his quarters after that."

His words brought forth another swell of guilt and shame. For me to be alive and standing there and even thinking about allowing myself to lay down in a medica bed when she was out there... It was almost more than I could take.

But it turned out not to matter. Because none of the legionnaires moved from our path when Johnny started us forward.

"He's to be taken to the brig," Ordo Silvers said, "to await proper trial."

Somehow, I wasn't all that surprised by the statement—or to realize the slick bastard had only been waiting for Johnny to talk me down. Johnny, on the other hand, was clearly as surprised as he was unhappy.

"Like scud he is," he spat. "Trial for what? And on whose authority?"

It was Silvers' turn to look confused, whether it was genuine or not. "Citizen Raish staged a violent escape from his house arrest."

"That's not true," Talia said beside me. "The hybrids attacked us at the barracks. Citizen Raish merely suggested our chances of survival were better if we relocated. Given that our own ordo had just been killed in the ambush, we agreed."

The flicker of hesitation in Silvers' expression was the first suggestion I'd seen that maybe he wasn't a sadistic bastard. "All the same, I have my orders," he said, turning to me. "You're going to have to come with us, Citizen Raish."

Honestly, I barely even cared if they wanted to lock me up. Unless they'd somehow found the scorcher pendant I'd had Franco hide after the White Tower, there wasn't a brig on Enochia that would hold me when I was ready to leave. All I cared about was getting at Oasis. That meant figuring out the Alpha-damned runes, and I was ready to do that whether it was in my quarters or with a stick in the dirt.

Johnny, though, still wasn't having it. He put a hand to my chest, indicating I should stay put. "On whose authority?" He asked again, speaking slowly and with an edge that was flirting with the line of insubordination.

"It's okay, Johnny," I said, stepping forward and nodding to Silvers before he could get any ideas about flexing his authority.

Johnny looked at me like I'd sprouted an extra eye, but I paid it little mind as something passed through me—a fleeting glimpse of subconscious intuition that told me now wasn't the time to fight. Not yet.

At a gesture from Ordo Silvers, a legionnaire cautiously stepped forward to clamp a fresh set of shackles on me.

"Yeah, good thinking," Johnny said. "That should definitely work this time. Did any of you happen to notice his gropping wrist is injured?"

The legionnaire paused, looking back to Silvers, who rolled his eyes and gestured for him to continue. So maybe he was a little sadistic.

"I'm sorry," I said quietly to Talia, trying not to wince as the legionnaire fastened the shackles. "About your squad. About everything."

After the initial fitting, the legionnaire at least refrained from clamping the restraints down too tight.

Talia was studying me in a way that made me think she'd been wondering if I'd say something like that. "You didn't ask to be targeted by those things."

I shook my head. "No. But I…"

I trailed off, not wanting to contradict her statement to Silvers with an apology for having forced the Wolves into following me to Therese's lab. She seemed to understand what I meant anyway. Emotions warred on her face—so many I didn't know what to expect. Finally, though, she just gave me a stiff nod and stepped back into the crowd.

"Good luck, Raish."

I nodded in silent thanks.

"Great," Johnny muttered under his breath, watching her go and looking around at the 323rd Hagas like he was sizing up our chances. *We have to help him,* she says. *They can't just haul him away like that.* Thanks a lot, lady."

"Johnny. It's okay."

"Like scud it is," he growled, swiping furiously at his palmlight. "Not until we know why… Oh gropping scud buckets."

I didn't need to ask what it was he'd just discovered on his palmlight. Because that's what had been bouncing around in the back of my head, I realized now. The pieces were all there. The attempt on my life. The last thing Siren had said to me before she'd climbed out my window. Her unexpected arrival and unsurprising betrayal tonight. The shackles on my wrist, and the squad itching to get me to the brig even as half of Haven burned around them.

I wasn't sure how deep the treachery went, only that it all seemed to trace back to the name on the ID line of the detainment order Johnny held out for my inspection.

General Gregor Aucuks – Haven High Command.

3 6

RECIPROCITY

"We don't have any proof," Johnny said, glancing surreptitiously at the closed cell door and then suspiciously at the cameras in the corners.

"Which is why I need to talk to Glenbark," I said for the third time, knowing full well it wasn't Johnny I needed to convince. I shook my head and sank down to the hard floor beside the cell's single cot. "I should just go rip the answers out of his head."

Johnny cringed, glancing at the cameras again, but I hardly cared if anyone was listening.

If it hadn't been for my battered body, the fractured wrist, the squad of trigger happy Hagas, and the generous hit of sedative I could still feel my body confusedly trying to burn off, I might've done the sensible thing before Ordo Silvers' squad had brought me here. The sensible thing being, of course, to have escaped them, stormed central command, tore General Auckus bodily from whatever hole the wormy bastard called an office, and ripped every thought and secret from his sad old mind until I'd had the full truth of what he'd done.

But I hadn't. I'd done what I'd thought had been right. And now I was sitting in a feeble Legion cell, playing prisoner and starting to wonder why I'd ever thought this was the smart choice.

"He could be behind all of it, Johnny. He could be..."

I didn't finish the sentence, *could be one of them,* but Johnny winced as if I had. He came and sat beside me before saying in a low, low voice, "He could be listening right now."

I said nothing. I didn't particularly care anymore if General Auckus or anyone else heard me out there. I was sure now that he'd helped Siren into the medica the night she'd tried to kill me. Or pretended to try. Before she'd stunned me in the back tonight, I'd actually been half-inclined to believe her when she'd said she'd spared me on purpose. Now, I couldn't even pretend to fathom her motivations. But whatever they were, I was pretty sure Auckus was somehow involved.

How had the hybrids even known where to find my quarters? I couldn't help but keep wondering. Why take Elise at all? They'd spoken of a master. Originally, I'd assumed that meant Alton Parker, or maybe even Frosty. But why not the man who'd quite possibly released a telepathic assassin to steal my cloaking pendant tonight? Why not the man who'd been more worried about drafting up detainment orders for me than tending to his base when it was literally burning around him?

Why couldn't Gregor Auckus be a raknoth?

I didn't have a compelling answer to that troubling question—only a long stream of self-directed curses for not having checked his mind the first time we'd ever met.

Of course, it might not be quite that sinister. Auckus might simply be working for the Sanctum. But either way, I was sure he needed to be stopped.

I looked at Johnny. "Where's Glenbark?"

He checked his palmlight for what must've been the thousandth time and came away disappointed. "She'll come through soon. There're a lot of fires that need her attention right now, and as much of a beardsplitter as he may be"—Johnny cringed up at the cameras, remembering himself—"I'm sure she's not in any rush to throw fuel on Auckus' whole *down with Glenbark* fire by blindly dismissing potentially legitimate charges against her pet demon."

I stared at him.

"What?" He shrugged. "I said *potentially*, broto. Hey, who's sitting here in the brig with you right now?"

I just shook my head and turned my attention to the bland permacrete wall. "It was a mistake, coming here, trusting any of them."

I felt more than saw Johnny's stare.

"You think you could've done better on your own?"

I shrugged.

"They have thousands of hybrids Hal," he said, his gaze shifting pointedly to the hard splint on my wrist. "And you're not exactly unbreakable."

I scowled at the splint, my mind drifting momentarily to Melanie, who'd made a special trip just to come treat me in the brig's rudimentary medical room when she'd seen my name enter the system, pending medical care.

I hadn't been good company, and certainly not deserving of her care. I hadn't even bothered to ask why she'd wept silently as she worked. Probably wouldn't have even noticed that she was if she hadn't stopped at one point to dab the tears away. Dazed and devastated as I'd been, I'd half-thought she'd already left when she'd come to my side, laid a gentle hand on my head, and planted a warm kiss on my forehead.

"Don't give up," she'd whispered.

Then she'd been gone too.

Don't give up, her voice whispered to me again as I sat staring at the splint, only to be followed by Carlisle's, *You are the best I have to offer this world, Haldin.*

Over and over, the two circled in my head, taunting me with their vague directives to fix this, solve this, make it better. But I didn't know where to start. Didn't even know where Elise was. Oasis was the obvious answer, but the scaly bastards had been clever enough to cover their tracks. From what little Johnny had been able to gather on the channels, once the hybrids had cleared the wall, they'd scattered every which way and ran like demons, some reportedly for miles, before the transports had swept in to collect them. The scouts were working through a scudstorm, trying to track it all in the dark out there with half of Haven's skimmer fleet lying in cinders.

Oasis might've been the likely choice, but by now, the hybrids could've been halfway across the world in any direction. Maybe farther.

The only thing that gave me any hope at all was that Franco was looking too. He and James had both sustained a few bruises and breaks in the fight, but neither was as bad off as Phineas, who'd nearly had his heart torn out by a hybrid. I was half-surprised the bear of a man had let even that slow him down, but for Franco, there was no question—he'd work his info until he found his daughter, broken bones or no, and he and the scouts would do a better job than I ever could.

Which left only two things in my arena: getting to the bottom of Gregor Auckus' treachery, and making damn well sure we were ready to open the doors to demons' depths right beneath the raknoth's clawed feet when we found Elise.

Seeing as I couldn't really do much about Auckus without either speaking to Glenbark or causing a base-wide incident, that left me right back where I'd been stuck since coming to Haven.

The damned cloaking runes. The one thing I could do to help was the only thing I was absolutely positive I had no gropping idea how to do.

If there was an Alpha, he was unquestionably a sadist.

"Want me to see if I can get some of your practice pendants brought here?"

I looked at Johnny, surprised by his apparent mind-reading only to realize he was watching my fingers, which were absentmindedly tracing the pattern of one of the runes from my pendant. My stolen pendant.

I sighed, not sure what to say. Not sure how I could possibly hope to suddenly solve the problem that'd been haunting my dreams. The runework itself would probably be doable enough. It relied on Expression, which relied on the power and conviction of a Shaper's will. To say my will was galvanized with Elise's life hanging in the balance would've been a gross understatement. I burned with the need to find her.

But I was missing a crucial piece of the puzzle. I knew I was. And no amount of brute willpower was going to change that.

"I'll see what I can do," Johnny was saying as he stood, brushing himself off. "It'll be good."

"Johnny…"

"Good to have something to keep your mind busy until Glenbark—"

"Johnny."

He hung there for a second, as if hoping he'd imagined the raw plea in my tone. The second passed, and he let out a long breath and turned to meet my eyes.

I made no attempt to mask the helplessness I felt inside.

"I can't do it, man." I shook my head. "I don't know if I'm even close. I don't know what the scud I'm doing. I never did. And she's out there, Johnny."

I gnashed my teeth, my hands curling into fists, unable to shut out the flood of images—Elise carried away on a writhing sea of eager hybrids. Crying for help, eyes wide, hands outstretched toward me. Bound and bloodied, surrounded by a horde of hungry hybrids, growling and harrying her from the dark. Rage flashed red behind my eyelids.

She needed me.

Elise needed me, and minute by minute, I was failing her. I was on the verge of lashing out when Johnny's hand found my shoulder and pulled me back down from the imminent explosion. He was watching me, waiting.

The rage bled out of me, sagging my shoulders. I was so tired. So tired of all of it.

"I can't keep doing this," I heard myself say. "Can't keep skirting by while the people I love take the fall for me. Carlisle, Elise. My mom and dad. All those legionnaires who came to pull me out of the White Tower. All the ones who've died next to me since. The Hounds. The Wolves." I looked up at him, more exhausted and empty than I'd ever felt. "Why do I keep going? Why me?"

He studied me for a while, his expression grave. Finally, he turned and sat back down beside me on the floor.

"I think this stuff has really gone to your head, man. Not that I blame you," he added quickly. "I mean, I get it, broto. Carlisle. Your parents. That scud can't be easy. But that doesn't mean it's your fault. It sure as scud doesn't mean you should've been the one to 'take the fall,' like you seem to think. And those legionnaires? I hate to break it to you, buddy, but they weren't fighting for you. You know that as much as I do. They were fighting for Enochia, and for duty, and their families, and just for what's gropping good and right in the world, man. And you're not what's threatening that. That's the raknoth. It's all the raknoth."

He turned to me, frustration in his eyes. "And the worst part is that I know you already know all this. Just like I know there's a bunch of scuddy little brain fairies flying around in there telling you that everything I'm saying is bullscud and that you're actually the Great Demon reborn."

I looked down at the floor, not wanting him to see in my eyes just how right he was.

"I love you, buddy," he said after a while, "so I'm gonna tell you something I feel like I should've said a long time ago. Here it is." He spread his hands in a grandiose manner. "This isn't all about you, you self-important beardsplitter."

I turned with an indignant scowl, but he silenced me with a raised finger.

"I said I love you, broto, so just shut up for a second. You need to see that this isn't all just Hal's World. You're not the only one who's lost people."

"I know that, you—"

"Ah, ah, ah," he said, waving his finger. "You *say* you know that, but you sure as scud don't act like it. Have you forgotten about Bells?"

His words hit me like a jab straight to the diaphragm. Consumed as I'd been in my own problems, I hadn't thought about Johnny's missing sister in days. I fumbled for words, but there was nothing to say. No excuse for what a scuddy friend I suddenly realized I'd been.

But Johnny wasn't even looking at me.

"Just because your abilities give you more pull than most of us in this fight doesn't mean the fight belongs to you any more than it belongs to the rest of us. It's not up to you to carry the weight of every bad thing that's happened."

A trace of his usual humor returned as he looked at me. "And as your friend and designated fairy swatter, it's my solemn duty to inform you that you don't get to pretend like it's all your fault anymore."

I dropped his gaze. "And what about Elise?"

"Elise is alive, Hal. We're going to get her back."

"I don't know how to do it, Johnny." My fingers drifted to the empty spot where my pendant no longer hung. "I'm missing a piece, here, and I… What if I'm just not capable of finding it?"

He clapped a hand on my shoulder. "Then I'll bust out of here and storm Oasis right beside you, buddy. We can drop down from the sky, guns-a-blazing. Scud, maybe Freya will even send an army with us, cloaks or no. But I don't think it's gonna come to that."

I met his gaze, waiting for some good explanation as to *why* he thought that.

He just shrugged. "C'mon, man. She needs you. And you need her. You'll pull it together. That's like your guys' entire thing, isn't it? One of you"—his finger pointed at me as if it had a life of its own—"falls apart. The other hoists 'em back up. Maybe there's touching involved. But, one way or another, you two always hold each other together, like a pair of…"

I'm pretty sure he kept talking, but I barely heard him.

I was frozen dumb, an intangible *something* crackling through my head in response to his words, racing around in blind, frantic circles. An answer, some deep part of me was suddenly certain. He'd just given me *the* answer. It hovered there at the very edge of my awareness like a silk fly ready to flutter off at any sudden movement.

"Hal?" Johnny was eyeing me uncertainly.

"Johnny, say that again. Quick."

He frowned. "The touching thing? Or…?"

"No, the… the holding together."

Johnny looked like he was trying to figure out if I'd just suffered a major brain hemorrhage. "You two always hold each other together?"

"That's it."

"That's it?" Understanding dawned in his eyes. "Wait, *that's* it? That's..." He looked hurriedly around the room. "Whatever's going through your head right now, hold on to it." Then he jumped to his feet, went straight to the cell door, and started pounding. "Hey! Hey, scudboots, we need an etcher in here, and we need it yesterday!"

The slit in the door slid open with a rasp, and Johnny began an animated discussion with the guards outside, who were clearly more than a little skeptical about how giving a prisoner a phase etcher was paramount to the survival of Enochia. I barely listened to the exchange. I was too busy staring off into space, trying to test the logic of my blossoming idea.

Without really thinking about it, I stood and turned to the wall, putting my back to Johnny and the guards. I conjured up the image of my cloaking pendant and its five interweaving runes, then changed my mind and went with Johnny's simpler four rune design instead. It wasn't hard to recall either in fine detail after the number of hours I'd spent staring.

One by one, I focused on each rune, channeled the requisite energy, and burned its likeness straight into the permacrete. A sharp, dusty odor wafted up on black tendrils of smoke, and I was vaguely aware of the conversation behind me gaining some urgency, but I shut that out and focused on my work, trying my best to push on without overthinking my admittedly abstract plan. Soon enough, I had a perfectly respectable replica of Johnny's pendant charred into the permacrete wall.

This time, I ignored the runes I'd always tried to empower before—the heat absorber and the actual cloaking field generator—and moved straight to the other two. Those two little etchings that had become the bane of my dreams and waking hours alike. Those magical marks that somehow held it all in place—four runes, operating in synchrony for months, years, Alpha knew how long.

They just needed to hold each other together.

How had I not seen it before?

I'd been embarrassingly close and yet laughably far from what now seemed so blindingly obvious. I'd toyed with the idea of a rune that would draw energy from the heat absorber rune in order to hold its fellow runes empowered. An empowerment rune. Simple. But then what would keep the empowerment rune empowered? Another empowerment rune? And what would keep that one going? Another empowerment rune, and another, and another after that. Runes all the way down to infinity.

Unless they reciprocated.

Then, feasibly, you'd only need the two. Two empowerment runes feeding on the energy of their shared heat absorber, all holding one another together in an infinite loop, as long as there was energy to be had.

I wanted to slap myself for not having seen it sooner.

The only question was whether I could properly Express these empowerment runes to start with. But that was hardly a question at all. This was the answer. I knew it was. Which meant it was only a matter of willpower now.

I stood there for a long while, adrift in a world of runes and energies, sinking into the Expression mindset, soaking in every detail of how I felt whenever I empowered a rune, and how I would pass that function on to another entity. It might've been a solid ten minutes of silence before I was ready to try. Maybe more. I couldn't have said. To his credit, Johnny seemed to have impressed the importance of the moment on the guards and was waiting patiently, offering his silent support.

Finally, when I was sure I had the headspace right and all the requisite links in order, I opened myself to the energy around me and poured my will into the first rune. Pleasant electric tingles buzzed through my head and chest. I waited until I was sure the first rune was set, holding the empowerment headspace firm all the while, then repeated the process for the second rune. Finally, apprehension thickening, I empowered the heat-absorbing power rune as I had a hundred times before.

Nothing happened.

For an awful second, my hope teetered, threatening to plunge. Then I remembered I still needed to empower the actual cloaking field rune. I allowed myself a minute to calm my mind. Assuming the empowerment runes worked, it wouldn't matter how long the next part took.

Finally, I finished and opened my eyes. "Okay."

Johnny let out a breath that sounded like it might've been pent up for the past half hour. "Holy scud, man. For the record, it's pretty damn creepy how still you get when you're doing your thing."

I turned and almost laughed at the gaping faces of the two guards peering through the door slit, heads bobbing in agreement. Then my attention shifted back to more important matters.

The wall was growing cool to the touch.

That alone didn't mean anything, I told myself as I reached out, heart thundering, sweeping my senses across the cell, through the wall, and—

There.

A blank edge.

A wall that even my extended senses couldn't pass.

"Did we win?" Johnny asked, watching me intently.

"I'm not…"

I reflexively reached to dial off my own cloaking pendant, thinking for a second that it must surely be the edge of my own cloak I was feeling. Then I remembered my cloaking pendant was gone.

With trembling fingers, I touched the cool permacrete wall and reached out again. Across the cell, through the wall, and…

Nothing.

"It… It's working."

Johnny clapped his hands and thrust them victoriously into the air. "Scud yeah, it's working, you magical bastard!" His eyes widened as he remembered something, and he woke his palmlight, swiping furiously. "We're telling Freya."

I shook my head. "No, wait. It's only been a minute. It might still…"

I didn't even want to say the words for some irrational fear they might send malignant ripples through the universe and bring about the undoing of my happy little runes. I just wanted it to be over. I needed to know that this was the answer and that moving forward from here was only a matter of repeating the familiar. But I couldn't be sure. Not yet.

Johnny opened his mouth. Closed it. Opened. Closed. Finally, he nodded and resigned himself to pacing around the room. I sat on the cot, going over and over what I'd done, making sure the feeling of the empowerment headspace was firmly lodged in my memory.

Five minutes passed.

"Hal…"

Ten minutes. Fifteen.

The cloak didn't fade.

I rose to my feet. "Call her. Tell her…"

Johnny clapped a hand on my shoulder. "I've got it, buddy. Give your brain a few minutes' rest."

I shook my head. "No, I need to keep going. Need to make sure I really have it." I looked around the cell, noting the supreme lack of materials available for getting started.

I needed to get out of there—back to my quarters, or at least to somewhere I could get the supplies I'd need. Forget Auckus and his bogus trials. It didn't matter anymore what he was playing at. He wasn't going to stop me. No one was going to stop me. Least of all a gropping locked door.

In hindsight, it would've been smart to wait to see what Johnny kicked up with Glenbark, or at least to inform him—and maybe even the guards outside—of my intentions.

Charged as I was in that moment, though, I was simply satisfied I managed to resist the urge to blast the cell door off its reinforced hinges. Not that my restraint meant much to the guards when I telekinetically killed the locking mechanisms and swung the door open. They both skittered back from the door, riot guns raised, one of them spewing a stream of alerts into his earpiece even as Johnny muttered a string of curses behind me.

"Stay right there!" one guard shouted, brandishing his riot gun.

"He just opened the door," the other was growling at whoever was on the receiving end. "Yes, send gropping backup!"

"No, he just popped the damn lock and went," Johnny was saying behind me. "Well he didn't ask my *permission*, sir!"

I held my hands up in peace, the ex-legionnaire part of my brain catching up to the part that was ready to do anything to save Elise and reminding it that breaking out of a brig cell was not just a casual misdemeanor.

"I'm not going to hurt anyone," I said, keeping my voice calm. "I just need to get back to my quarters, right now. I'm not exaggerating when I say it could be the turning point of this war."

The guards traded an uncertain look, but then the one who'd called for backup hardened his resolve when the sound of approaching boot steps filled the hallway. "I don't care if Alpha himself vouches for you. You're not leaving until I see that detainment order dismissed."

This time, it was putting the two guards through the wall that I had to resist. But restraint or not, I didn't have time for this. I fumed, teetering on the edge of making another less-than-advisable move.

Johnny slid past me before I could, no longer talking and hands clearly raised in surrender.

"Stand down, boys," he said, holding something on his palmlight out to each of them in turn. "We've got a gropping planet to save."

37

MINDSAFE

And like that, within the hour, Mission Mindsafe became a base-wide priority on Haven. Not that many people actually understood what we were really up to. I can't imagine what wild rumors would be circulating by morning—the High General herself, dismissing General Auckus' detainment order on the Demon of Divinity only to retreat with me, her servitor, and Alpha knew who else to my quarters under armed guard. All of us cooped up through the night, a full-service support staff sweeping in and out of the room with everything from meals to odd assortments of tools and supplies.

I was almost looking forward to hearing what stories they dreamt up.

Glenbark had suggested we move to a larger, more team-friendly space, but I'd resisted—in part because I hadn't wanted to waste the time in moving. But it was more than that. These quarters weren't much, but they were the closest thing I had to familiar. The closest link I had to time spent with Elise on Haven, twined in one another's arms. It helped. And given that I was the one who required absolute focus, no one had argued too much with my choice of locale.

The cloaking pendants themselves quickly evolved in design throughout the first several iterations. For one thing, they'd ceased being pendants once we'd discussed the most efficient way to produce the most cloaks in the shortest time. Now, they were simply small lightsteel disks whose runes were being etched and shuttled over from one of the engineering buildings orders of magnitude faster than I could actually empower them.

Also in the name of efficiency, we'd agreed there was no real need to worry about range adjustments, especially not when the men using them wouldn't be able to actually tell what the effective coverage was. Until we had the time and leisure to think of a way to calibrate some kind of range scale, we agreed a standard radius of roughly forty yards would suffice—large enough to cover a good number of legionnaires, and small enough to require an enemy to get fairly close to those legionnaires to wreak any telepathic havoc.

Once I'd actually gotten a feel for empowering the cloak to within a specific range, we realized a few additional details, the first and most dramatic being that a cloak with a forty yard radius required about eight times more energy than mine did when it was fully extended—and growing quite frosty—around twenty yards. Enough energy that we were worried the frigid lightsteel disks might become too brittle and that sticking them in pockets and packs might even lead to problems with frostbite and hypothermia. It would've been a risk we were willing to take, considering. But then Johnny asked why we didn't just stick a heater with each disk.

Hence the cloaking pack was born.

The only remaining problem, as far as I could see, was that the runework was draining me far more quickly than I'd expected. At first, there'd been thinking and talking from one cloak to the next. But now, with our assembly line more or less worked out, I was becoming the clear limiting step. By the time I'd finished my sixth cloaking pack, my head was already starting to spin.

There came a solution for that too, though I was hesitant to call the development lucky, or even favorable.

"What about the other Seekers?" Glenbark asked when it became apparent the pauses were growing longer and more frequent.

I looked at her, hesitant to even consider the idea. She already knew about Siren's betrayal—and apparent escape, given that no one had seen her on Haven since. Where that left Four's and Eight's allegiances, I honestly didn't know. But more importantly...

"I'm pretty sure they don't know the first thing about runework."

"How quickly could you teach them?"

I half-wanted to ask her how quickly she imagined *she* could teach a common legionnaire to exude her indomitable air of command and run a sprawling network of Legion bases, but I decided it might not be a fair comparison. I honestly had no idea if—and if so, how—Four and Eight might be able to accelerate our production. I was more worried about whether or not they were involved in whatever Siren and Auckus might be up to.

I looked warily around the living room, feeling a bit paranoid as I scanned over the few legionnaires and servitors who were sorting out our supplies and assembling more packs for empowerment. But grop it. Half the world was trying to kill me, and now they had Elise. There was no such thing as paranoia anymore.

I stood and gestured to the bedroom. Johnny and Glenbark followed me without argument.

"Aside from Franco," I said quietly when we were alone, "I'm not sure we can trust anyone outside of this room."

"I'm not asking you to trust them, Haldin."

"Asking me to even be in the same room with them is asking me to trust them. This is worse. This"—I waved the lightsteel disk I'd been toying with —"is exactly what those Seekers came here for. And once they have it…"

I trailed off, because even as I said it, I realized it didn't matter. If making enough cloaks to save Elise in time meant sharing dangerous secrets and exposing my throat to those who might want to slit it, I already knew what I'd do. But even so…

"What I told you about Siren attacking me earlier, sir… that wasn't the whole story. I think General Auckus sent her, and I'm worried the other two Seekers might still be involved somehow."

She studied me thoughtfully. "Why do you say that?"

"Auckus was the one who helped Siren access the medica the night she tried to kill me."

At first, I thought she was trying to process the accusation. But then she nodded. "I know."

"You…" I glanced at Johnny, wondering if maybe he'd filled her in from the brig or in the past hours, but he looked surprised as well. "You knew?"

Glenbark didn't shy away from it. "I did. And since coming to Haven, you've defied multiple direct orders, violated the conditions of your house arrest, and broke out of a brig cell simply because you felt it prudent in the moment. Do you blame me for expecting you might do something drastic if confronted with this information?"

I opened my mouth to argue, then decided that this, too, was inconsequential next to everything else at the moment. "Fine. You knew. Then you should also know that I think his treachery might run deeper than a few attempts on my life. I don't know what connections he might have with the other Seekers, and it's even occurred to me he could be…"

"You think he could be one of them," Glenbark said.

Hesitantly, I nodded.

To my surprise, she returned the gesture. "I understand. And rest assured, I've considered the possibilities quite exhaustively myself. Short of shooting him in the foot to be sure, though, I have no reason to believe Gregor Auckus is a raknoth, or one of their servants. Furthermore, I'm fairly certain he wasn't behind Siren's actions tonight."

"How do you know?"

"Suffice it to say, I've had my eye on him. And besides that, the circumstances surrounding her escape strongly point to the theory that she's working alone. The most likely explanation is that she simply wanted your cloaking pendant, and the attack just so happened to provide the distraction she was looking for."

I could tell from her tone that she wasn't any more blind than I was to the fact that her most likely explanation didn't exactly disprove that Siren might still be working with Four, Eight, and Alpha knew who else in any number of ways. Something told me it wasn't as simple as a snatch and grab, if for no other reason than that I didn't really think Four and Eight would've remained behind in that case.

"I need to start organizing for an assault," Glenbark said, shelving the discussion for the time being. "I'm going to have the two Seekers brought here. I urge you to consider employing their aid, assuming they're willing and capable. Let's end one war before we start another."

She seemed to take my silence as an affirmative.

To my surprise, she laid a hand on my shoulder. "Full disclosure? I'm truly sorry about Elise. More sorry than I know how to say. But there's still hope, Haldin. We're almost there. Keep at it, no matter what. Give me a hundred of these cloaks, and we'll do the rest."

I nodded, and she gave my shoulder a squeeze and turned to leave.

"Full disclosure, sir?"

She turned back to me, waiting.

"I *am* going to do whatever it takes to get her back. No matter what."

I didn't explicitly add that I'd even blast my way out of Haven and go fugitive again if it came to that, but the gravity of her expression told me she understood.

For a long moment, we held stares with uncomfortable intensity. Then she gave a small nod and turned to leave without another word.

Two cloaking packs and about a half hour after Glenbark had left, the ordo prime of our guards, the 51st Boar Company, came in to tell us we had two visitors—a swarthy-looking tall guy and some giant lady. Said their names were numbers. He looked surprised and wary when I told him to let them in, but not half as wary as Four looked stepping into the room.

The anger inside me wanted to pounce on that look, like his caution was solely intended to invite my wrath. I couldn't quite decide if the impassivity on Eight's face behind him made me more or less angry.

But there was work to be done.

"We heard whispers of sinister happenings in the Demon of Divinity's barracks," Four said, looking curiously around at the cloaking pack assembly line before finally meeting my eyes.

"Where's Six?" I asked.

"Right to business, then," he muttered, then held his hands up when he saw me tense. "We don't know where she is, Raish, or what she's doing. She didn't consult us before running off on whatever fool errand she's on. She never does."

"Convenient..." Johnny murmured from the couch.

"She attacked me while I was trying to save Elise," I said. "Stole my cloak. Left me stunned on the pavement while those things carried away the woman I love."

The words sounded oddly flat and emotionless to my ear, but they had their intended effect. Four paled a few shades, though he managed to keep his expression controlled. Eight's impassive mask broke into a momentary frown.

"Dammit," Four muttered.

"Where is she?" I asked, unable to keep the edge from my voice. "What would she do now that she has what she wanted?"

The two Seekers exchanged a thoughtful look, and probably a bit of telepathic communication.

"I'm not sure the cloak is what she wanted," Four finally said. "Not all of it, at least. It's possible she was even trying to save your girl."

"By dropping me cold with a cheap trick?" I growled.

"Six has a habit of trying to get cute and having it bite her in the ass. Which is why we're worried they might've taken her too. She's not responding to her palmlight."

On the couch, Johnny paused from his work assembling a cloaking pack.

"And you don't think it's possible the manipulative assassin lady might be ignoring your calls?"

Four tilted his head, not completely dismissing the point. "You don't know her like we do. She crosses lines, but…" He fingered the dark collar at his throat. "We're bound together by more than most. She wouldn't have left us here like that. Not without good reason. I'd like to get out there and try sweeping for her myself, but…" He shot a dark glance toward our hallway security, and his voice came to my mind this time. *I have a feeling when it's time to leave our courteous hosts, it'll be time to leave for good.*

I refrained from nodding, knowing all too well what he meant right just then.

When Four turned back, I couldn't tell if he looked more frustrated or worried. "As far as we know, helping you get Elise back might be our best bet to help Six too. So here we are."

"Well isn't that touching?" Johnny muttered over at the table where he was assembling a cloaking pack. "It's almost like you weren't escorted here by armed guard at all."

Four ignored him, but apparently the jab struck Eight right in her well-formed sense of nobility. She stirred, focusing on Johnny.

"Do not mistake the circumstances of our arrival as proof of anything but a desire to prevent additional conflict. It was your own Legion who bade us remain put throughout the attack. And we were both of us dismayed to hear of the fate of Elise Fields."

She remained fairly unexpressive throughout, but I got the feeling her words were sincere enough. Maybe it was just my desperation to get Elise back, but I found myself hardly caring what their motivations might be. Even if Auckus did have some kind of arrangement with them, which I was starting to doubt, I couldn't see any scenario in which their helping me with the cloaks would be a bad thing.

The question was whether they could help at all.

"I assume this isn't something you can teach in five minutes," Four said, seeming to read my mind as he studied the piles of practice runework scattered around me.

"Can you two help me manage the channeling fatigue like Six did back at the canyon?"

Four looked to Eight, who gave a solemn nod. He turned back to me and did the same.

That was something, at least. Even if they couldn't empower the runes themselves, I figured just having two more bodies to share the load with might as much as double the rate at which I could push on from rune to rune.

Of course, the tiny voice in the back of my mind couldn't help but point out that it was also wildly dangerous, letting them that close to my exhausted mind, and that this might in fact be exactly what they'd been after all along. But right then, none of that mattered.

"Fine, then," I said. "Let's get started."

3 8

STOWAWAY

Once, during the tyro years, rotating shifts of doceres had kept us awake and running drills for two straight days to impress upon us just how critically our performance could be affected by sleep deprivation. At the end of it, when I'd collapsed into my bed, fully delirious and somehow almost too tired to even fall asleep, I'd been sure there was no way I'd ever experience a deeper exhaustion than what I'd felt that day.

I'd been wrong.

It was mid-morning on Haven, and while I was only pushing a few hours past a full day of being awake, the long night of non-stop runework had left me on the stoop of complete incoherence.

"One hundred," I groaned, releasing my focus on the lightsteel disk at the center of our circle and letting go of Four's and Eight's hands in favor of slumping back against the wall.

The seemingly intimate contact had long since ceased to be awkward or strange. For the first couple hours, our telepathic meld had been sufficient without it. Then, as the fatigue had built, they'd realized it helped to lay their hands on my shoulders. Eventually, we'd all ended up in a ring on the floor, holding hands like we were attempting to summon spirits from beyond.

But we were finally done. For the moment, at least. One-hundred gropping cloaking packs in a night, and I could barely see straight anymore. Definitely couldn't think straight. By the last couple dozen, it had seemed a minor miracle I'd been able to conjure the focus to empower runes at all, but we'd been careful to check each and every one.

And by careful, I mean it had become a hardwired part of our mostly silent routine for the past several hours. How many hours? I looked at my left palm only to remember the wrist was splinted. I thought about checking my right palm instead, but then I caught sight of the half-empty caffa beside me and my stomach threatened mutiny. It had to be at least the tenth one.

"Praise Alpha," Johnny muttered, stumbling blearily over to collect our last cloaking disk. He nearly lost his balance when he bent to pick it up. "You all need to sleep," he declared, drawing himself up in a wobbly attempt at dignity.

We all shared a drunken smile. Even Eight's lips quirked by a sliver.

Nothing like the most grueling grind of your life to bring you and your natural enemies together.

I just hoped the hundred cloaking packs would be enough to enable a full strike on Oasis, immediately. The thought of waiting even one day with Elise out there in raknoth hands set my heart thudding so hard I could feel the pulse in my ears—though maybe that had something to do with the caffa and the sleep deprivation as well.

An hour ago, I'd been both encouraged and worried to learn that scouts had confirmed at least two of Franco and Therese's potential breeding facility locations to be accurate and active, with decommission operations pending and several more targets likely forthcoming. As good as the news was, I couldn't help but worry that the sudden perception of having strategic choices might distract the Legion from the urgent need to assault Oasis.

"Maybe we should do a few more," I half-said, half-slurred. "Just to be sure."

I'd be damned if I was going to see the Oasis campaign delayed for something as simple as not having sufficient cloaks. Maybe I was actually more worried about the fact that we still had no idea where Elise actually was. But I wasn't ready to stop. Not yet.

It was only then I noticed the Seekers were already standing.

"We require rest," Eight said.

"That's an understatement," Four added, fixing me with a serious dark-eyed stare. "You should get some sleep too. At least an hour or two. You probably don't need me to tell you you'll be of more use to everyone that way."

"Yeah, well maybe I'm just not equipped to walk away when people are counting on me."

The words, in all their tired snippiness, were out of my mouth before I'd even thought about saying them. Not that the Seekers didn't deserve far worse for everything they'd done in their lives. I was still pretty sure it had been unwise to let them sit front row to ninety-two iterations of everything I'd discovered about rune creation. But I'd been too tired to care properly. And after the night we'd just shared, despite whatever terrible things they'd done, I still felt just like just a little bit of a beardsplitter for letting my temper slip.

Johnny and Eight were both slightly tensed, apparently expecting a rapid and violent break in our momentary truce, but Four seemed to understand. He waved Eight on, something passing between them, and settled back on the floor with me as she turned her enormous frame hesitantly for the door. I watched him warily, in no mood to be preached to by a professional killer.

"I'm not going to pretend what we've done is right."

"Good."

The shadow of a grin touched his lips. *"Maybe I'm just tired, but for some reason..."* He shook his head, seeming to rethink his direction. *"How did you feel when you first realized you were... gifted?"*

"I'd just seen my parents murdered by the High General of the Legion. How do you think I felt?"

He inclined his head in a conciliatory fashion. *"But what did you do when you first glimpsed that something had changed in you?"*

"Carlisle taught me how to use it. And to be on the lookout for people like you."

He bobbed his head. *"Exactly. And what if Carlisle hadn't found you?*

"I imagine your friend Garrett would have killed me."

I could have hit him for the satisfied look on his face as he continued casually nodding along. *"At your age, it was a definite possibility. But while you're imagining, why don't you go a step farther? Why don't you imagine how things would've been if you'd lost your parents at twelve instead of seventeen. Imagine you hadn't had Carlisle to show you the way or teach you to control your gift. Imagine it was the clerics of the Sanctum who'd found you living in whatever alleyway hole you'd cobbled together for yourself."*

"I get the point."

"Imagine," he continued, shaking his head as if to say there were no worldly way I'd gotten the point yet, *"that those clerics took you off the streets and clothed you, fed you. Imagine they one day taught you, with the utmost solemnity, that the trauma you'd been through had bestowed you not with a gift, but with*

a gaping wound through which demons of all shapes and sizes might invade—already had *invaded, in fact."*

I said nothing.

"Imagine the holy authorities you'd been told all your life to listen to above all else one day told you that you were a monster and that the only way to ever find your way back into Alpha's grace was to use your curse to shield his blessed children from other monsters like you."

"Okay."

He shook his head. *"Imagine they stripped your cursed name from you, put a whip in your hand, and told you to cleanse yourself in the holy fire of pain until you were ready to accept that truth."*

My mind flashed to the impossibly dense network of scars on Siren's bare back. I felt sick. But Four was clearly not done.

"Imagine they outfitted you with a wearable death sentence," he sent, fingering the slender collar at his throat, *"and told you that, for your own safety, you and your fellow demons would all be killed at the press of a button if any one of you ever stepped too far out of line."*

"I can't help but notice you're still alive."

Maybe I was too tired to process everything he was telling me. Maybe I just didn't want to.

"We're not some band of evil murderers, Raish. No more than your Carlisle was the Great Demon our old High Cleric led us to believe."

"But you have *murdered."*

"Every bit as much as any legionnaire who's ever killed on command," he agreed. *"Though I'm fairly certain none of them have ever faced decapitation by explosive collar should they refuse to ob—"*

His mind and voice abruptly vanished from my senses, only to return again a few seconds later. We'd grown used to the telepathic flickers throughout the night—a quirk of having multiple cloaking fields shuffling about, spheres of influence intersecting, overlapping, and apparently forming discrete bubbles within bubbles where one cut into another. I looked around and confirmed this most recent telepathic pocket must've happened as the legionnaires carted out another load of the cloaking packs.

"Anyway," Four sent, rising to his feet with a slight groan of exhaustion. *"I think that's enough story time for now."*

That suited me just fine. I couldn't spare the brainpower right then to worry about what the Seekers might or might not have been through. I certainly couldn't spare the time to really think about how easily things might have ended up differently if Carlisle hadn't found me when he did. Still, I couldn't help but wonder…

"Do you still believe what they told you? That you're a monster?"

He was already halfway to the door, and I was thinking he wouldn't answer at all when he paused, not turning back.

"A decade's instruction is not easily forgotten."

I waited a few seconds, but he said nothing else.

"You and Eight could make a real difference in the coming fight, you know. If you weren't so set on making your escape."

He turned his dark-eyed stare on me, and I was surprised to see a faint grin tugging at his lips.

"You're a bit of a condescending beardsplitter, did you know that?"

For some reason, that put the beginnings of a smile on my face. *"I may have heard a rumor or two."*

"Eight and I have a lot to discuss about our plans moving forward," he sent, turning back for the door. *"For now, I'm going to ask these kind soldiers to guide me back to my bed, and I highly recommend you do the same."*

I watched him go, wondering if maybe—just maybe—the Seekers weren't all quite the evil demons I'd always believed. Probably, it was just the sleep deprivation talking. Probably.

"For the record, man," Johnny said, appearing in front of me and offering a hand up, "it's creepy as scud for us bystanders when you mind whisperers just sit there staring longingly into each other's eyes."

I scowled up at him. "Longingly? Seriously?"

He shrugged and tilted his head toward the legionnaires putting the finishing touches on the last of the cloaking packs. "Creepy either way." He waved his waiting hand. "Come on. Time for bed, young man."

"And you call me creepy," I muttered, ignoring the hand. "Just a few more. I need to be sure we have enough."

"Well, Glenbark already sent her compliments along with a request for the rest of the packs, so I'm thinking that's probably a good sign. Says she won't talk to you until you've had at least three hours' sleep, though."

"Well, thanks to Siren, I at least still need a new pendant. And what is it with everyone telling me to get some sleep?"

He scrunched his face. "I dunno, man. Probably has something to do with the fact that you look like I feel."

"Ginger?"

"Har har. But we both need to sleep before we think about entering an active warzone, mystical powers otherw—"

"Raish. She's back."

Four's voice cut in through Johnny's words a second before the ordo prime of the 51st Boars opened the door with a knock and stepped into the entryway. "Another one to see you, Citizen Raish."

"Siren," I hissed.

The ordo frowned at my apparent precognition. "I don't even wanna know what club these people are all hanging out in, but the names..." He trailed off at the look on my face. "You want her out of here? Raish?"

I was already on my feet, moving for the door.

"Hal?" Johnny said behind me. "What's going—Siren's back?"

"I need to speak with her," I growled at the ordo prime blocking my way. Pissed as I was, I barely restrained myself from fighting my way out until I had Siren's treacherous throat in my hands. But I needed the Legion behind me, now more than ever.

Arriving at some similar compromise, the ordo's stern scowl eased a fraction. "You stay in this hall. Understood?"

I nodded and moved past him as he relayed the command to his troops. Through the doorway, I turned, and there she was, held up at the end of the hallway by the two-fireteam security checkpoint right next to Four. She had a wild look I'd never seen on her—her clothes torn, her face scraped and dirty, and her golden-brown hair tangled and unkempt. Her eyes widened when she saw me stomping down the hall toward her, her hand tracing to the pendant at her breast. My pendant. She'd dialed it in to keep me from attacking her.

As if that would protect her.

I was reaching out to wrap her cloaked form in a telekinetic cage and yank her to me when Four's voice came to me again.

"She knows where Elise is."

I drew up short, fists clenched tight, trembling with rage.

At a command from the ordo behind, the legionnaires let the two Seekers past, and they approached me slowly, cautiously until they were within easy speaking distance. Siren refused to meet my eyes, keeping her gaze riveted to the carpet, looking pathetically guilty.

"She came back to tell you what she's found," Four said, glancing at Siren as if wondering what in demons' depths had compelled her to think that was a good idea. "Just hear her out."

"I should kill you for what you've done," I finally managed through a tight throat.

She just nodded softly, keeping her eyes down, looking on the brink of tears. "Maybe you should. But for what it's worth, I know where they took her, and it's not Oasis."

Somehow, her obvious guilt only made it worse. I wanted to scream. Wanted to tell her that they wouldn't have taken Elise anywhere if it hadn't been for her. But I was too tired, too desperate for this to just be over and done with.

"Where is she?"

"That bitch One, the one you call Frosty, she has her at a hybrid facility. A decommissioned hydroelectric plant north of New Amestown."

"How do you know?" I asked, stepping closer.

Four started to take a protective step forward, but Siren laid a hand on his arm. "I followed them over the wall and stowed aboard one of their transports. That's why I needed your cloak."

I tensed, anger swelling, but she pressed on, keeping her eyes averted.

"I laid low until we were there. I watched them take her inside. Followed them in and saw Frosty. And…" Her face fell at some memory.

"And what?"

"And I felt Garrett there too. I think. I couldn't—"

I silenced her with a raised hand, not caring one bit in that moment about Smirks or anything else besides Elise.

"What does Frosty want with her?"

"I don't know," she said, shaking her head, eyes still averted. "They were chaining her up when I had to run."

I was trembling again, my eyes drifting shut of their own accord, terrible images flashing behind my eyelids. "And why the scud," I growled quietly, "should I trust a single word you're saying right now?"

Slowly, carefully, she pulled my pendant off and held it out. "I'm not asking you to trust me. You don't have to trust any of this." She gave me a short, pleading look, then bowed her head as if she were offering me that as well.

"Take my mind, and I'll show you."

3 9

FAMILY

"You're absolutely certain she's not lying about any facet of this entire story?" Glenbark asked, watching me dubiously from my palmlight display.

I nodded. "Positive. It's not possible to directly lie to a telepath once they're inside your head."

Stepping into Siren's mind wasn't something I'd been happy about—no more than Four or Siren herself had been. But it had been necessary, the only way to know beyond doubt that she was telling the truth.

"And you're sure that's a universal law among your kind?"

"It's why I know she's planning to stow aboard if we don't allow her to come on whatever rescue mission we put together."

"You realize that's not exactly comforting."

"Elise is in that facility, sir. The only question is how we're gonna get her out."

"If we wait until after Oasis—"

"I can't do that." I shook my head. "I need to move on this. Now."

"You need a few hours' sleep to clear your head before—

"My head is clear. It's never been so clear about anything. Elise is all that matters."

On the other end of the call, Glenbark studied me, unstirred by my declaration. "Interrupt me again, and I might just have the 51st Boars come in and pelt you with stunners until one of them gets through."

"If you think that would work."

She let out a sigh and rubbed at her temples. "We're all tired here, Haldin. And you've done the Legion an incalculably valuable service. Get some rest and give us one more day. Allow us to repay you when we have the resources to do so."

I shook my head. "It has to be today, sir."

"And if I were to tell you that I want you at Oasis in case something goes wrong with the cloaks?"

"I'd tell you that I only ever wanted to help. Once Elise is safe."

"I see."

"Perhaps the Seekers could go in my place, sir."

"With the exception of Siren, who will be busy sneaking aboard your rescue mission?"

"I might be able to build a Seeker-proof prison cell for her with the cloaking runes. Except…"

"You think she might be a valuable asset."

I grimaced. "I don't like it, but she'd do just about anything to find Smirks. Garrett, I mean."

Anything like stun me in the back, steal my cloaking pendant, and let Elise get captured in the hopes that it would lead her to the high-priority prisoners, as I'd found during my brief dip in Siren's mind.

"That's precisely why I don't like it either," Glenbark said. "Not that I prefer the idea of you facing down that Frosty monstrosity alone."

"Maybe Siren and I could extract Elise without a fight."

"I think I like that idea even less." She drew her lips tight, considering something, then fixed me with a serious look. "I want you to wait a day and come to Oasis with us, Haldin."

I dropped her gaze, shaking my head in apology. "I could speak with Four and Eight for you," I offered instead.

"I don't think that will be necessary, thank you."

She didn't make any effort to hide her disappointment, but nor did she appear particularly angry or upset. I'm not sure if it was personal courtesy or professional wisdom that kept her from putting the matter to a direct order. Whatever it was, she seemed to understand that we'd reached the breaking point, and that we could either peacefully attempt to maximize both our chances of success, or violently split ways and limp into our separate battles on bad footing.

"The two of them should be able to handle more together than I could alone anyway," I added when the silence had stretched to an awkward length.

Glenbark returned from some thought with the faintest frown. "I'm not entirely sure either of us believes that."

She went silent again, thinking, and I resisted the urge to start begging. I was going after Elise either way—I'd already decided that much. The only question was whether I was going to be doing it with appreciable backup, and on the friendly side of the law.

The one thing that gave me hope on the latter point—aside from the lack of direct orders—was that Glenbark hadn't once yet mentioned the fact that I was technically still on house arrest, even if she *had* nixed Auckus' brig detainment order. Backup, on the other hand, would be immeasurably helpful either way. Especially since I, too, didn't love the idea of sneaking into a super-powered raknoth den with no one but a treacherous assassin watching my back.

On the other side of the call, Glenbark stirred. "I'm sorry, Haldin, but I don't have the resources or the political slack right now to sanction an official mission based solely on the hear-say of one rogue Sanctum operative who, by the records, barely even exists."

I stared at her, unbelieving, reeling with sudden betrayal—until I took in her continued thoughtful expression and realized she'd used the word, *official*.

"It'll have to be volunteer only," she added, the frown on her brow deepening. "And I'd prefer it be quiet. Or for it to at least look as if it were the first of our clandestine decommissioning operations."

Relief was flooding my chest. "I don't mind wrecking Frosty's facility, if that's what you're saying."

"All I'm saying is that, pending location confirmation from Citizen Fields, you have my permission to take a volunteer, off-duty force to reconnoiter the area in an unofficial capacity."

I almost could've grinned, but surprisingly, it wasn't all that hard to maintain a straight face right just then. "Understood, sir."

"In the meanwhile, I'll inform Ordo Baird that you are to have free reign of Haven, with armed escort, of course. I believe the 51st Hounds are on backup reserve after the losses they sustained this past cycle," she added. "Same for the 122nd Wolves after last night."

That sent the first flutter of hesitation through my gut. "You want me to ask companies that are half dead because of me to follow me into enemy territory?"

Her brow arched ever-so-slightly. "Would you prefer I ask them for you?"

I shook my head. "No, sir."

If I was going to ask them to lay their lives on the line for me again, or even just for Elise, I might as well do it right and ask them myself.

She gave a curt but approving nod. "Then good luck, Citizen Raish, and let me know if anything changes."

"Thank you, sir."

"Thank *you* for your service, Haldin. I know it hasn't been easy." She paused. "Your father would've been proud."

I swallowed against a suddenly tight throat, unsure what to say.

"Get some sleep," Glenbark added. "For Elise if nothing else."

And with that, she ended the call. I let out a long, steadying breath, feeling for the first time since they'd carried Elise away like the world might not actually be falling apart at the seams just yet.

It was cracked, certainly, and not far off from crumbling. But I knew where Elise was. And the Legion was finally poised to strike back at the raknoth in a major way.

We were going to do this.

But first, I needed to recruit some help.

***

"I'M IN," Johnny said as I stepped out of the bedroom, closing down my palmlight.

"You don't even know the plan yet."

"Storm the creepy enemy encampment, get the girl, quite possibly spring the trap, and fight our way out in a blaze of glory?"

I frowned, hoping only a quarter of his assessment would actually come true.

"I'm in," Johnny repeated. "I already told you, broto. Guns-a-blazing and all that."

"I'm not sure Glenbark would appreciate me commandeering her servitor for—"

He held up his palmlight and showed me an order, signed by Freya Glenbark, for one day's personal leave.

"Let's get her back, buddy."

I clapped him on the shoulder, not trusting myself to find the words of gratitude for my friend in that moment, and went to tell Ordo Baird of the 51ˢᵗ Boars that I needed to go see Dillard.

While they prepared to move, I made a quick call to Franco, who, having taken a plummeting hybrid to the leg outside the lab, was crutch-bound and bitterly resigned himself to assessing Siren's intel and running support. Phineas, though stable now, was going to be in the medica for at least half a cycle, and James wasn't much better off.

When I was done, Johnny offered to go talk to Dillard himself while I got some rest, but I refused to ask Dillard by proxy to put more of his men at risk. Judging by the look on the ordo's face when we'd finished filling him in, it was a good call.

"I don't like it," Dillard said, leaning back and crossing his arms at us over the kitchen table in his private Hound barracks quarters. "You've got next to no real plan, your one and only intel source has tried to kill you twice in the past half-cycle, and now you tell me she wants to tag along—probably so she can take crack number three."

"I mean, she only used a stun rod the second time," Johnny pointed out, as if that fundamentally changed the entire situation.

Dillard was less than amused. "Telepathic truth serum or not, I don't like it."

"I understand your hesitation," I cut in before Johnny could say any more. "And I truly apologize for even having to ask you for this, but I don't have any other choices here. I can't let them hurt Elise because of me. And if that means walking into a potential trap, the only option I see here is to try and make sure we're ready to beat that trap. Maybe we get lucky and take down a raknoth and a hybrid facility while we're at it. But I can't do it alone."

Dillard studied me, his frown deepening. "How long has it been since you last slept, Raish?"

"Eh," Johnny said, waving a hand at me. "He's just been sitting around all night, really. I'm not sure what all the fuss is about."

I took in Johnny's ragged appearance—his eyes sunken and captivatingly blood-shot, his jawline scruffy with amber stubble—and realized I probably looked even worse than he did.

"It doesn't matter. Not until Elise is safe."

"It matters if you expect any one of my people to follow you and your ginger mascot straight down into demons' depths," Dillard said, a sudden bite in his tone.

Johnny, thank merciful Alpha, was smart enough to not quip back. I waited at Dillard's mercy until the ordo let out a breath that was half-growl, half-sigh and thrust a finger at me.

"You stick to the orders this time. No wild flights of fancy. You let me do my job and keep us alive."

I bit down on my immediate urge to emphatically bob my head and cry, *Yes, Alpha yes!* I was asking Dillard to risk everything for me. He deserved complete sincerity.

"Can you trust me when I tell you what I can do to help?" I asked.

He might've narrowed his eyes a sliver, but after a moment's consideration, he nodded.

"Then I stick to the orders," I said. "I trust you and your Hounds."

"All right, then." He glanced at his palmlight. "Get some damn sleep, Raish. You too, Wingard. I'll talk to my people, but we're not going anywhere with you until you've had a solid three hours." He considered the palmlight again. "Five would be doable."

"Thank you, Dillard."

He held up a hand to stop me. "No thanks yet. It's volunteers only, like the High General said." He cocked his head. "That said, I doubt there's a single Hound in the 51st who won't be ready to step up after what you did back at that canyon. Crazy bastards. Might even be able to round out to a full company if I call in a few favors."

"I was going to talk with the 122nd Wolves next," I said. "They were with me last night when…"

"I know," Dillard said. "Their ordo prime was a friend of mine. Saw her name in the casualty reports." He shook his head, lost in some memory. "Told her you were a royal pain in the ass just a couple days ago when she found out they were rotating onto house arrest duty."

"She told me." I stared at the table, unable to meet his eyes. "I'm sorry, sir."

For a long time, he said nothing.

Finally, he pushed his chair back and stood. "Go get yourself together. I'll talk to the Wolves and anyone else I think of."

"Sir, if I'm gonna ask these people to risk their lives, I'd—"

He silenced me with a raised hand and a serious look.

"You made the right call, Raish, coming here to ask me yourself instead of hiding behind the general. But I'm not the High General. No one outside my own Hounds is gonna give half a damn about impressing me. There's no shame in letting me do this part, and I'll be damned if I can't tell them better than you can why they should be willing to risk their necks for you and the goodlady anyway."

Part of me wanted to ask him what he'd tell those legionnaires when they asked, but I was almost embarrassed by the conviction in his voice—thinking at first that it was on my behalf. But that wasn't it, I realized. It was the pain of the legionnaires we'd lost that I heard in his voice, and the smoldering belief that those sacrifices had meant something more than a few dead hybrids or a few civilian lives saved.

I paused from sliding my chair back under the table. "Sir, I never got the chance to ask... Mara..."

His face darkened to a new low, the pain evident in his eyes. "She's in bad shape. Might be out of commission for good with the amount of damage that Alpha-damned monster did to her leg and hip."

"All the more reason to hand Frosty her own ass on a platter," Johnny said, without a trace of his normal humor.

I left Dillard's with a gutful of sickening guilt, memories of Mara's tortured scream playing through my head on a loop. She'd been right all along, telling Edwards to keep away from me. Just one more life ruined because of me.

Maybe I really was cursed.

Either way, I didn't see what I could do about it other than make damn sure Frosty paid for all of this. With that goal held firmly in mind, I finally relented to return to my quarters and get some of this rest everyone kept insisting. When we passed by the medica, though, my guilty conscience got the best of me.

It wasn't going to change anything. I knew that.

But before I slept, I needed to at least atone for one small part of this scudstorm.

***

DILLARD HADN'T BEEN LYING. That much was abundantly clear.

Through the single polymer pane of the medica room door, Mara looked too thin and frail lying in her bed, her skin drawn, her leg and hip stabilized by so much external hardware that I could barely make out half of her body. Edwards sat motionless at her bedside, his giant shoulders slouched in defeat, her free hand engulfed in both of his.

I'd been lingering outside her room for a few minutes now, intermittently peering in at them, trying to work up the courage to knock and go in and say... Alpha, what was I going to say? What could I possibly say that would mean a damn thing to the adamantus-willed specter who might never walk again because of me?

There was nothing I could say, I realized. Even the idea of apologizing felt cheap somehow. I was starting to think it'd been a mistake, coming here at all, when I noticed someone approaching me from behind in my extended senses.

"He hasn't left her side since they brought her in yesterday," came Melanie's voice.

"He's a good guy," I murmured, not really sure what else to say. "They're both good. Good soldiers. Good people. The best."

When I finally glanced at her, she was watching me with that concerned caring look. "Are you doing okay?

"Not really."

She nodded, not surprised and not judging. "Do you want to talk?" She glanced at Mara's room. "Or are you going in?"

I swallowed. "I'm... not sure I should anymore."

She gave me an exasperated look. "Haldin. They've both been asking about you since they heard about... about Elise. I'm sorry, by the way. About last night." She took my left wrist in her hands and brought the splint up for her inspection. "About everything."

I'd nearly forgotten about our exchange—or lack thereof—as she'd patched me up and splinted my wrist last night. For the second time, I considered asking her why she'd been crying, but she was already lowering my arm back to the side and looking up to meet my eyes.

"You have more friends here than you know, Haldin. These people care about you, and they don't blame you even half as much as you blame yourself. You should go in."

I looked from her to the door and back again. Reluctantly nodded.

"You always seem to find me right when I need you to." I frowned at her. "You sure you're not a telepath?"

She might've blushed a shade or two. "Just well-connected, I'm afraid. It seems like my colleagues have gotten it in their heads that I'm your designated medic moving forward. They keep me posted."

"Thank Alpha for that," I said quietly, peering into Mara's room. Then, realizing that might've sounded sarcastic, I turned to her. "Really. Thank you. I couldn't have asked for better care..."

"Any of the five times I've patched you up in the past cycle?" she asked, arching a brow. "Or is it six? I'm starting to lose count now."

I grimaced. "Might be seven soon."

That killed what tiny bit of humor had crept into her eyes dead in its tracks. For a second, she almost looked angry. "Well mind that wrist, whatever you do. And get some rest, for the love of Alpha. You look—"

"Like a dead man walking, I know."

She searched my face, looking like she wanted to say something more, then she finally gave up and leaned over to knock gently on Mara's door.

"Go," she said. "Be with your friends. And don't even think about missing number seven."

I nodded, trying to conjure a reassuring smile. She turned and headed down the hall, moving quickly and not looking back. With a deep breath, I pushed into Mara's room... and straight into Edwards' and Mara's attentive stares.

For several seconds, none of us seemed quite sure where to start.

"I'm so sorry," I finally whispered, the warm weight of tears pressing at my eyes quite suddenly. She looked so broken this close up. It wasn't right, seeing her like this.

Edwards was unusually quiet, waiting for Mara to decide how she felt about my apology. And she took her time. I held her gaze, hating every second of it but refusing to shy away from the pain and suffering.

"Are you going after her?" she finally asked.

I wasn't sure whether she was talking about Frosty or Elise, so I started from the beginning of the attack and quickly explained what was about to happen.

"I'm going to make her pay for this," I promised at the end.

Mara considered it all for a little while. I couldn't help but feel like a criminal on trial. Couldn't help but wonder what I'd do with myself if she condemned me.

Instead, she beckoned Edwards closer, saying nothing to me. He stood and leaned over her like a titanic guardian. She murmured soft words to him, wrapping a hand behind his head and pulling him closer, nuzzling into him. I was caught off guard by the tender affections—so much so that I felt like I should step outside. I settled for turning to the window, trying not to watch out of the corner of my eye as they met for one long kiss.

Then, without a word, Edwards straightened and ushered me out of the room, Mara watching me with those hardsteel eyes every step of the way.

Out in the hall, when the door was closed behind us, I turned to Edwards, expecting him to send me off with a warning or to chide me for having come here at all. But he just hooked a thumb toward the nearest exit.

"Let's go, kid."

"You're coming with me?"

He frowned down at me. "Of course I'm coming with you. Who the scud else is gonna shove this thing in that Frosty lady's brainpan?" he asked, sliding a dagger from the back of his belt and giving it a surprisingly dexterous twirl on his massive hand.

When it stopped spinning, I recognized it as the dagger Mara had used to stab Frosty in the knee.

"Yeah," I said. "Good point, I guess."

"I'd better go to the barracks to get ready," Edwards said as we reached the atrium where my Boar Company guard detail was waiting. "You should probably—"

"Get some rest. I know."

He spread his hands in a mountain-sized shrug.

"Hey Edwards?" I asked, drawing up just short of the Boars. "What did she tell you at the end there, when she was giving me that look? The specter look."

"Well," he said, glancing around furtively, "she told me to give that raknoth bitch a knife in the brain from her. Or a good hard boot up the ass. Whichever came first."

"That was it?"

Edward made a face that almost looked… was it embarrassed?

"Never mind, man," I said quickly. "Sorry, I'm prying. I just…"

"No, no," he said, shaking his head as he sagely laid a huge hand on my shoulder. "It's fine. She actually wanted me to tell you."

"Tell me…?"

He scrunched his face up apologetically. "That she promised to personally wreak great—and most likely scrotal-related–pain and mutilation on you if you get her booga b—I mean her man—killed."

And with that, he cleared his throat, looked surreptitiously around, then gave me a mighty clap on the back and turned to leave.

"That's… That's a joke, right?" I called after him.

He just waved over his shoulder, lumbering on without looking back.

4 0

───────

BREACHED

The silence that filled the front transport cabin was as tense as it was thick, broken only by the odd whines and occasional coughs of the engines. After the hybrid assault had wrecked a sizable portion of Haven's fleet, they'd had to bring more than a few hunkers hastily out of retirement. Not that I was going to complain. We had a ride. And I had a team.

And on the bright side, Edwards had muttered to me during takeoff, *we might just crash and die on the way there.*

"That's it," Siren said from where she peering out over the pilots' shoulders. They both turned to her with irritated expressions, but neither of the men managed to hold up against her charms for long, even distracted as she was. One found himself murmuring thanks while the other gave her a healthily lecherous thrice-over.

"Take a seat, Siren," Dillard said. If he was affected by her looks or presence, it didn't show. Then again, he also had two transports full of legionnaires to worry about, and one of my newly-fashioned cloaking pendants at his breast.

Siren didn't pout or argue—just sat down beside me and Johnny. She'd been uncharacteristically cooperative and obedient since I'd agreed to let her come. It would've made me nervous if I hadn't understood the root cause. But I'd been in her head. I'd seen how desperately she burned to find Smirks—or Garrett, rather. Much as I'd tried to avoid delving into anything but the raw facts in her head, it had been hard to avoid. In some strange way, I was pretty sure she loved him.

That had actually been the hardest part for me to swallow—the part that'd nearly made me lose control when I'd dove into her mind back at Haven. Because, much as I wanted to hate Siren for what she'd done, I couldn't ignore the nagging voice that reminded me I would've done the same, and maybe worse, to get to Elise.

It didn't matter now.

Freed from their unintended distraction, the pilots brought the ship low, skimming right over the treetops as we descended into the lush valley at the southern extremity of the Auborean Mountains, headed toward the upper-most flight of the Red River, and the rust-tinged superstructure of the archaic hydroelectric facility that was our target.

Had I not been ready to scud myself with apprehension, I might have admired the sight of the structure, partially cantilevered over the roaring waters, with the river-facing side incorporating several long, curved sections of duraglass to permit a view of the river below and the rising, heavily-forested bank on the far side of the valley.

Beside me, Johnny glanced at his palmlight for maybe the hundredth time, equally unenthused by the sight ahead. I felt his worry in my own chest, amplified by yet another wave of guilt. The assault on Oasis would be starting soon, if it hadn't already.

But I couldn't worry about that now. I'd made my choice, and the Legion was… well, the Legion. The cloaking packs would protect their minds. The rest was up to them.

It felt scuddy even thinking it, but the mournful groan of age-kissed engines and the tug of deceleration firmly reminded me that that was a moral conundrum to wrestle with later. We had our own assault to worry about.

"Place looks dead, sir," one of the pilots said.

"Yeah, but at least it's not creepy as all scud," Johnny muttered beside me, craning his neck to look down at the dilapidated facility.

"I doubt the whole hybrid company I rode in with just vanished overnight," Siren said.

Dillard frowned at her then looked to me. I nodded, confirming that I'd seen the same in her memories.

"Guess we'll find out," he said. "We stick to the plan. Hard and fast. Let's get below."

It spoke volumes about the gravity of the situation that neither Siren nor

Johnny gave so much as an amused smirk at that. In the main cabin, surrounded by the most loyal of legionnaires and hovering half a mile from Alpha knew what terrors, Dillard kept his words simple.

"You all know the plan. You all know what might be waiting for us down there. Get in, do your jobs, and watch each other's backs." He looked around the cabin, taking in the sea of determined faces. "Get your asses back to Haven alive, and I might even tell you I'm proud to serve with each and every one of you."

"Scud, Ordo," someone called, "you're gonna make us cry."

That started the chuckles, which quickly led to the chest-thumping and back-clapping and name-calling that quickly grew through the cabin like a rising tide until the legionnaires were half crazed with war lust.

"Lock it down, Hounds," Dillard cried, and they all snapped to like a cracking whip, finely-tuned death machines that were ready to bleed and fight and die until Dillard said otherwise.

I prayed to Alpha they wouldn't have to.

"Take us in, pilot," Dillard said to his palmlight. "Hard."

I tightened my grip on the support ring overhead. The transport lurched forward with an indignant whine of strained engines, the pilots shedding what little altitude we had and bringing us around for a lightning-fast deployment. The hatch was already half open by the time we stopped rotating, and half the Hounds were on the ground and fanning out before we'd stabilized into a steady hover.

A kind of nauseated exhilaration gripped me as I moved into the exit stream and jumped with Johnny, Siren, and Edwards. As many fights and training drills as I'd been through, this somehow still felt new. And terrifying.

The pilots didn't bother landing. The instant Dillard's boots hit the permacrete behind us, the transport was pulling off, sweeping around to watch the facility for activity and keep ready for a hasty pickup anywhere it might be needed.

Behind us, the other transport was disgorging the second half of our forces with similar efficiency, but I was already busy sweeping the landing area with my senses. Nothing in the immediate vicinity. I dialed my cloak off completely to extend my scan to the larger field of our squad's cloaking pack and found myself caught in a pocket between our pack and the one I'd crafted for Second Squad.

Prowling forward, I found the edge of the pocket and felt the world in front of me pop back into existence in my senses. It was disorienting, but not as much as the lack of raging hybrids storming our location. I felt nothing but legionnaires and subtle thrum of some of the facilities subsystems running ahead.

The leading edge of First Squad was already across the series of metal walkways ahead, breaching the main entrance and sweeping in with military precision. Double checking I hadn't lost Johnny, Siren, and Edwards, I hurried along to catch up.

Inside, the signs of abandonment continued. The main floor appeared just as it had in Siren's memories of last night—the entrance atrium empty but for a few overturned pieces of furniture gathering dust just like the rest of the chic metallic floors and the duraglass walls that separated the atrium from what might've once been meeting rooms. The nuts and bolts of the hydroelectric plant, when it had been running, had likely been housed in the floors below, where I knew from Siren's scouting there were now at least several dozen hybrid breeding chambers.

I reached down to the few I could sense through the floor within the boundary of First Squad's cloaking pack. They felt full, but didn't seem to be drawing much power. And there was something else, too. I saw my own uncertainty mirrored on Siren's tense face as Dillard drew up beside us, glancing warily around the atrium.

"You got anything?"

"No live hostiles yet," I told him. "There are definitely breeding chambers down there, but… something's wrong."

"An ambush?" he asked. Then, with a slightly hopeful expression, "Are they empty?"

"Not empty," Siren said.

"No," I agreed, focusing in on a single hybrid floating inside its chamber, deep in… No. Not hibernation. "They're… I think they're dead."

"They weren't like that last night," Siren said, looking worried.

She didn't need to tell me. I'd seen in her memories.

Something was wrong.

Dillard was frowning, opening his mouth to ask something, when something else caught his attention. He put his hand to his ear to indicate he had reports incoming.

"Main floor's all clear," he said a few seconds later. "Dead hybrids? What about Elise?"

I shook my head, trying to control the building panic.

If they'd figured out Siren had been here… if they'd put the pieces together and decided to scrap the facility and move on…

"She had her pendant on," Siren reminded me.

But it was scarcely a comfort, seeing as I didn't feel Frosty or Garrett or any other living hybrids down there.

"We keep moving," Dillard said. "Let me know the moment either of you feels anything."

"They're still here," Siren told me quietly as Dillard marched off, but I could hear the note of desperate prayer in her voice.

I clenched my jaw, resisting the urge to snap at her. If Elise was gone... then, I could explode on Siren. Until we'd swept this entire facility, though, it was a waste of time to worry about anything else.

We lined up tight with First Squad and funneled down a dark stairwell that was much more utilitarian than the stylish atrium above. The room we filed into at the bottom was much more expansive than the floor above, an open, high-ceilinged space that had probably once been home to a host of generators and energy cells and transmission equipment.

Now, it was filled with hybrid chambers wall to wall—or at least as far as we could see in the feeble glow of the few dim lights and the weak daylight that filtered in through some windows above.

The breeding chambers were laid out in tight, neat rows—more than I could quickly count—and separated into clusters that obscured the view of the far walls and made the room feel like some kind of demented maze. And it *was* demented.

After sensing the dead hybrid, I'd expected things might not be pretty down here. But it was far worse than I'd imagined.

The duraglass panels on most of the chambers I could see had been shattered. The permacrete floor was littered with the debris and slick with untold gallons of the ambiguous green fluid that had spilled from the destroyed chambers. Most of the tanks still held floating hybrids in their discolored fluid. Some of the creatures almost looked at rest. Others looked as if they'd died trying to claw their way out, the panels of their tanks smeared with crimson blood and some darker ichor I could only guess at.

Worse was the unmistakable smell of death—sickly and sweet and laced with a stomach-turning undertone of decay and...

Blood.

I nearly retched when we emerged from a row of tanks and saw the morose display. Siren did.

Bodies. More than I could count—most piled high in the center of the room, but plenty more scattered messily about the space. The majority were too torn and blood-soaked to make out much of anything, but on some, I saw the clear marks of fangs and claws.

"You always bring us to the nicest places, kid," Edwards grumbled, looking a bit green himself.

"Gropping scudbuckets," Johnny growled. "Did they get tired of dealing with blood racks, or is this just some sick side project?"

"What the scud happened here?" Dillard's voice crackled in my helmet earpiece before I could even try to guess. Around us, several Hounds were asking each other similar questions in hushed tones.

"I don't know," I told Dillard. "Maybe Frosty lost it here last night. Or maybe the older hybrids got smart enough to rebel after they hit Haven."

"Somehow, neither of those strikes me as good news."

"No."

"Heads on a swivel, people," Dillard said to the entire company battle channel this time. "Demo, get those charges planted. Everyone else, fan out and keep looking."

Wiping her mouth, Siren straightened and turned for the far end of the next tank cluster. "They took her this way last night."

Johnny and Edwards swept ahead of her, weapons at the ready. I followed after them, and was almost caught up when Johnny shot a closed-hand signal to freeze over his shoulder.

I complied, throwing my senses out ahead, suddenly scared to even breathe. But I felt no hybrids. No Frosty.

"Grop, that's creepy," Johnny murmured at the tank ahead, shaking his head and turning back to us. "Hal, it's..." He made an inarticulate gesture, then shook his head some more. "Scud, just come see, I guess."

I stepped carefully around the chamber and immediately felt my insides go cold.

There on the floor, written in what had to be blood, was a single word.
Raish.

A long, crimson trail stretched from my name, as if the body that'd donated the blood to write my name had been dragged off that way. Only it wasn't a body that waited at the end of the blood-smeared trail. It was a crude arrow, formed of severed human limbs.

It pointed down the next corridor.

"That's..." Siren whispered.

"The way they took her last night," I said. "I know."

I keyed my palmlight. "Dillard, I think we found our path."

It took the ordo less than a minute to reach us, and even less than that to make up his mind about the macabre directions. "All teams on my position, now," he sent over the battle channel. "Let's move it, Hounds. We're closing in on—"

He paused, staring hard at his palmlight, hand clamped to his ear. "Say again. Repeat, come in. Can you—Damnit!"

"Sir?" I asked.

"The transports," he growled. "They're under attack out there. Sounds like Frosty."

As one, we all turned from the corridor and the mutilated arrow back to the stairs we'd come from, all of us caught in a silent moment of indecision.

Dillard opened his mouth—

A fearsome roar shook the putrid air before he could say a word. I tracked the sound to somewhere above just as a choir of unholy calls joined it.

There, in the windows above, pair after pair of crimson eyes were lining up, staring down at us. They'd circled around somehow, I realized. Slipped out of the facility as we'd landed and come around to flank us. Maybe they'd been waiting out in the woods the whole time, expecting us.

As the darkest of the hybrids raised its fist and smashed through the duraglass window, it hardly mattered.

"Down the corridor, Hounds!" Dillard snapped, already raising his rifle. "Move it!"

The first gunshots joined the hybrids' roars, Dillard and those closest to us opening fire as we shuffled toward the corridor, buying time for those who hadn't yet reached our position.

The first hybrids practically landed on top of us, slamming to the permacrete in a shower of broken duraglass. Johnny and I opened fire with our rifles, staggering a pair of the beasts. The rushing thrum of Edwards' modified pulse cannon joined in, and one of their scaly heads all but exploded from its body. Johnny and I dropped the second with concentrated fire to the head, and then we all turned to move.

I sensed something was wrong just as I met Johnny's eyes and saw them widen with the same realization.

Siren was gone.

"That traitorous bitch!" he cried.

Edwards shoved into us before I could rightly process the development, forcing us toward the corridor as more hybrids rained down from above.

"Wait!" I snapped, rounding and casting my will out and above, forming a flat, solid barrier above Dillard and the two fireteams still trying to buy time for the Hound stragglers.

Hybrids continued to leap down from above—and straight onto my barrier, where they smacked to unexpected halts against thin air. The first few, I felt like solid punches to the torso. The next few came with unforgiving speed. Within seconds, the weight was too crushing for me to even breathe.

But then the last of the Hounds were sprinting beneath my impromptu hybrid trap, and Dillard was turning, chasing on their heels and shouting all the way.

I gratefully released my hold on the barrier, and the writhing, growling mass of dark green hybrids slammed to the permacrete with a round of angry shrieks, more dropping down from above in twos and threes.

We backed into the circular corridor, firing all the way. I was relieved to see the demo boys had already had the good sense to plant charges at the mouth of the passage. Not that we had time to celebrate.

Though they had the look and durability of the older, more sentient kind, the hybrids pursued us like wild animals thirsting for blood. With the exception of Edwards' pulse cannon, our gunfire barely seemed to slow them. When the first few closed, I hit them with a blast of telekinesis, giving us just enough time to shuffle back to what could only by the loosest definition be called a safe distance.

Dillard snapped the order.

Almost instantly, a thunderous boom tore through the corridor, punching me in the chest with concussive force and shaking me to the teeth. Our faceplates saved us from the worst of the dust and fine debris, but between the sloshing of my brain and the ringing in my ears, it took me a few seconds before the world around me started making sense again.

And the hybrids were already coming.

The corridor was clear for the moment, our forces aligned behind us, and a wall of hardsteel and permacrete rubble ahead. But we could hear them roaring on the other side, could hear them tearing through the rubble barrier like walking demolition machines.

Dillard was snapping orders and getting the Hounds into formation when a voice came to me.

"She's here, Haldin. Hurry before that crazy bitch gets back!"

Siren.

I felt her there at the very edge of our cloaking packs, just past the door at the end of the corridor. I stared dumbly for a second, having been too caught up in our escape to even process her disappearance, much less to imagine she might've been running ahead to find Elise.

"Siren found Elise ahead," I said to Dillard, not pausing to let myself register all the suspicion and doubts that should've come with the statement.

Dillard didn't pause either.

"Go," he said. "Get her free and find us a way out. We'll hold them here until we can clear out and blow the place."

I hesitated, not wanting to leave them behind to handle Alpha knew how many hybrids. But Dillard was right. The corridor was a fantastic pinch point. Until we had another way out, it would be stupid to abandon it.

Unless Frosty showed up.

There wasn't time to debate it. I turned and started for the far end of the corridor at a run, not pausing when Johnny and Edwards fell in behind me. Behind us, there was a sound of cracking stone and shifting rubble, and a hybrid roar tore down the corridor, raw and unobstructed. It was met by the combined fire of at least a dozen weapons.

I didn't look back. I just kept running, Johnny and Edwards thundering after me. It was time to get Elise back and get the scud out of here.

4 1

______

PUREBLOOD

I wasn't sure what I'd been expecting in the room at the end of the corridor, cut off from my extended senses as it was by the Hounds' cloaking packs. As I barreled through the door, Johnny and Edwards at my back, all I knew was that we must be approaching the eastern side of the superstructure.

When we stepped out onto a balcony of glossy black floor tiles and glass-paned railings, though, I was taken by surprise—first at the long, curving wall of unbroken duraglass looking down on the roaring Red River and the eastern bank of the valley, then at what was on the ground floor.

"Elise!" I cried.

Her eyes widened, snapping up at my voice, and for a moment, I was so damned relieved to see her alive that I forgot everything else. Then I took in the excessive cuts and bruises, and the gag, and the extensive network of chains by which she was suspended—several separate chains, I saw, actually tying her in place rather than feeding to shackles or any other locks that would've been easily manipulated with telekinesis.

Siren was beside her, one of those thick chains in hand, glowing red hot several links above where she gripped it. She gave a growl of effort, and it snapped in two.

"Come on, Hal," Johnny shouted, heading for the curving stairs to the right. "Move your ass!"

I started after him, cursing myself for having wasted precious seconds.

There were at least three or four more separate chains tying Elise in place, and—

I stiffened, whipping around as a beacon of telepathic fury blazed into existence at the far edge of my extended cloak—just before a section of the duraglass wall exploded inward and a dark figure came shooting through like it'd been fired straight from a pulse cannon.

The thing that could only be Frosty skidded to a halt, rending long gouges in the tiles behind her, and looked up at us with burning red eyes just as a smoking transport roared past outside, careening wildly down toward the river.

"Good," she said, straightening herself and speaking as if they were simply picking back up after a minor distraction. "Now we can properly begin, if you'd—"

Her hand shot up just as I heard the rushing thrum of Edwards' pulse cannon behind me. The modified ten-inch armor-piercing bolt traveled so fast and stopped so abruptly that it appeared to simply wink into existence a few inches from Frosty's outstretched hand.

"Ah," she said, looking as if nothing had happened. "You finally managed to break a chain. How cute."

I was vaulting the railing, drawing off the energy from my fall to slow the descent and prepare to fight, so it took me a second to realize she was talking to Elise. The raknoth was watching her with narrowed eyes, and it was only then I noticed Siren had disappeared from Elise's side.

Disappeared—I realized as the razor-tipped bolt by Frosty's hand rotated to point Elise's direction—but not *moved*.

I threw my barrier into existence the moment before the bolt leapt forward from Frosty's hand. Even just deflecting the projectile instead of outright stopping it, it was frightening how hard the raknoth had flung it.

Unperturbed, Frosty casually waved a hand, apparently focusing directly on Siren this time. Siren reappeared, bouncing across the tile and away from Elise like a skipping stone until she hit the wall and sagged.

"Incessant ants," Frosty growled, looking to the staircase, where Johnny and Edwards were descending toward Siren, weapons at the ready. "All I wanted was Raish. I've found the answer, don't you *see* I've found the answer, you meddling, paltry…" Shaking with anger, she swung a backhand through empty air with an awful roar.

A transport-sized section of the duraglass wall exploded outward, and Frosty stood there, looking out at the water, shoulders heaving in rage.

She'd lost it. Gone mad.

I was about to blast her into the river below to buy us a minute when I noticed Johnny and Edwards prowling toward Elise, Edwards with a small phase torch in hand.

I laid my rifle down, figuring my slugs were worse than useless at this point anyway, dialed my cloak out, and started circling around to the left, away from Elise and the others.

"What's the answer, One?" I asked, approaching the breeding chambers I'd just noticed on the far side of the room—at first only feigning interest, then staring with a sickened jolt when I realized the figures inside were the size of children. But I couldn't worry about that now. "What did you find?"

To my relief, the raknoth turned my way instead of theirs, her face twisted in disgust.

"Do not call me by this vessel's pathetic numeral, Raish. I am Nan'Reylor," she said, stalking toward me now. "And you would do well to remember the name, pet."

Pet?

It didn't matter. Just a little closer.

"Okay, Nan'Reylor," I said, straining with every fiber not to let my gaze flick over her shoulder to where Edwards was silently starting the first cut. Above, the sounds of fighting had grown to a steady, distant roar in the corridor. I did my best to breathe, to keep it together.

"You have me here," I said, drawing up to the tanks and feeling a combination of relieved and exposed as I felt the edge of my cloaking field envelop Frosty, cutting us off from the others. "Can I ask what you want with me?"

"Al'Braka has been a fool, hoping to turn such weak creatures into anything of value," she said, not seeming to notice or mind the shift. "That our mighty Zar actually believed the fool bright…" She shook her head in disgust. "None of them saw the obvious."

"But you have?"

She drew herself up with a satisfied smirk. "Of course, I have. Of course. Of c—Agh!" She gave her head a violent shake, fangs bared in a snarl, then focused back on me as if nothing had happened.

She'd definitely lost it.

"While the other fools play at war and fret about their degenerating children," she continued, spreading her hands wide, "I will begin building from the proper stock." She smiled then—pure, demented bliss—and held her hands out to me. "The only stock that's proved itself worthy of anything more than my claws in its throat."

"And that's..."

Was she talking about me? I held her madly smiling eyes, trying not to betray the storm of apprehension raging through me. Any second, she'd turn, or the chains would rattle, or the hybrids would overwhelm the Hounds above.

"Tell me, Nan'Reylor. Tell me how you'll build."

Her smile grew, baring fangs as she traced her hands down her body. "You will plant your seed in this vessel, Haldin Raish, and from that seed I will fashion a race of true warriors, gifted and pure of blood, not given to the pathetic degradation of those, those... those sacks of worthless flesh above."

I was rooted in place, desperately trying to keep the revulsion from my face, thinking of what she was proposing, and of the hybrids floating dead in their chambers above.

"Is that why you killed them all?"

"Killed them?" She looked confused. "Good as dead already. All of us good as dead," she said, her head beginning to twitch again. "Dead. Good as dead, good as... Unless..."

Alpha be damned, I slipped—my eyes stealing a glance over her shaking shoulder by their own accord, barely long enough to register Johnny lowering a cut chain to the tile. And the mad raknoth didn't miss it.

I didn't know what else to do. As she turned to have a look herself, I drew a dagger and flung it at her eye with as much telekinetic juice as I could muster.

Not fast enough.

She roared as the speeding dagger struck her raised hand. I felt a moment's surprise that I'd actually driven the blade hard enough to punch the point through her palm and clear out the back of her hand. Then I realized what I'd just done.

"So disappointing," Frosty growled, sliding the weapon slowly from her hand and tossing it aside. "Very well." She must've reached for something outside our shared bubble then, because her brow furrowed, and she looked confusedly around until her eyes settled on my pendant.

"Clever ant," she muttered. Then, at a yell, "Garrett!"

Surprised as I was to hear the Seeker's name, I didn't wait to see what came next. I pulled the energy and blasted Frosty right back out the hole she'd smashed through the duraglass on entry.

"We've gotta go!" I shouted, calling my dagger back to hand and turning for Elise and the others.

"Oh really?!" Johnny shouted back, reaching for the gag in Elise's mouth. "Tell me something I—"

"Behind you, Johnny!" Elise cried as soon as the gag was free—right as Garrett the Seeker thudded down to the ground floor from the balcony, his usual smirk firmly in place.

His irises were a disturbingly pale shade of red.

For a second, I hesitated, remembering the raw desperation I'd felt in Siren's memories—her need to save Garrett. Johnny, having missed that experience and now seeing the red-eyed Seeker eyeing him like a meal, was already pulling the trigger.

A stream of softsteel slugs pelted the wall behind Garrett, deflected by whatever defenses he'd raised.

"Worth a shot," Johnny muttered, right before Garrett hit him with a telekinetic sucker punch and charged.

I came to my senses, swept Garrett's legs out with telekinesis, and was reaching for one of my secret weapons when Frosty flew back into the room and nearly took my head off with a wild fly-by punch.

I rolled back to my feet, reflecting that her harvesting my genetic material might not require me to be alive after all, and plucked a pair of lightsteel disks from my belt.

Ahead, Frosty was raising a hand my way as if to smite me down with telekinesis or worse. I dialed my cloak to mid-range, close enough to cut off direct attack and far enough to make indirect attack problematic. She snarled and ripped one of the breeding chambers into the air with telekinesis instead, intending to use it as a missile.

I flipped the switch on one of my disks and tossed it at her feet, and the chamber crashed back to the ground, cut off from her influence by the short-range cloaking field. I had a moment of grim satisfaction that my hare-brained contingency plan against the superpowered raknoth seemed to work. Then she lost it and leapt straight for me with a chest-shaking roar.

I dipped to the side, relying on telekinesis rather than my bum wrist to catch her by the arm and slam her to the tiles at my feet. Before she'd even hit, I was already falling on her with my dagger, but she caught the blade with telekinesis a full foot from her face.

I danced back before she could grab me, activating and dropping another cloaking disk as I went. Over by Elise, Edwards and Johnny were trading blows with red-eyed Garrett, who appeared to have disarmed both of them. I watched in horror as the smaller man caught one of

Edwards' titan-sized punches in an open palm and fired back with a straight kick that sent the bigger man sailing as Garrett rounded on Johnny.

I blasted the Seeker off his feet, caught a glimpse of Elise working on her chains with Edwards' torch, then dipped left as my extended senses cried a warning.

Frosty's blow was so fast I felt the gust of wind in its wake. She stomped after me in a rage, her face completely shifted to snouted green monster mode now. I fell into a kind of trance, giving myself over to my extended senses until I was twisting and dodging through a vicious series of blows almost without thought, feeling more than seeing the incoming strikes.

For a few seconds, I was untouchable.

Then an ocean of telekinetic force fell on me, slamming me to the dark tile before I could so much as take a breath. I was pinned too completely to even reach another cloaking disk from my belt. I reached my senses for my cloaking pendant instead, telekinetically dialing it in to break Frosty's hold.

Too late.

Frosty was already over me, stomping down with the killing blow.

I prayed for a barrier more than consciously summoning one, some desperate part of me reflexively pulling the energy. Her dark boot plummeted for my heart with the power of a speeding mag tram, and met thin air bare inches from my chest.

She might as well have landed the hit for the surge of channeled power that ripped through my body. It darkened my vision, blurred my hearing to dull background. I felt more than heard the tiles crumble beneath my telekinetic cocoon.

It seemed a rather large miracle I was alive at all.

And she was raising her foot to stomp again.

I had nothing. No more tricks, no more energy. Just a desperate prayer that Elise and the others would somehow make it out of here, and that Glenbark and the Legion would use my cloaks to eradicate every last one of these scaly bastards from our planet.

I snarled up at Frosty, preparing to attack her mind with my dying breaths.

Something blasted her clean across the room before I could.

"Get away from him, you crazy bitch," growled a voice that filled me with relief.

Elise.

I sat up, blinking the darkness from my vision, and found her limping over to me, the remnants of one of the dark chains dangling from her forearm like a weapon.

Behind her, Johnny and Edwards were both down, Johnny crawling feebly for his rifle. Garrett was standing between them, trembling like an enraged beast, caught in place by…

By Siren, I realized, just before she materialized in front of him, her hands planted to the sides of his face, her eyes wide and pleading as she looked into his.

"Hal," Elise groaned, reaching down for me.

I took her hand and climbed back to my feet, my insides catching fire at just how battered she looked up close.

Frosty's roar reminded me just where I could place that rising anger.

I slid one of the last two lightsteel disks from my belt, activated it, and dropped it just as the raknoth charged and Elise and I split apart.

I dialed my cloak out, stepping clear of the disk, found Edwards' pulse cannon on the floor, and called it to me as Frosty crashed down where we'd just been. With my splinted wrist, I fumbled the catch, and Frosty, having been debating her next target, decided that was her opening.

At least until Elise's dark chain smashed into the side of her head from behind.

The blow probably would've killed a human. Frosty just staggered to the side, throwing a blind backhand to cover her tracks. Elise easily dodged the strike and caught Frosty with a savage chain uppercut, followed immediately by a diagonal down slash across the face.

Frosty gave an infuriated snarl, swiping blindly as she pushed toward Elise, who danced backward, pivoting into a horizontal slash that caught straight on Frosty's hardsteel-strong forearm and yanked Elise off balance.

By then, I had the pulse cannon ready. What I didn't have was a clear shot, but as Frosty pulled Elise in, I didn't have a choice.

I drove a telekinetic wedge between them and put an armor piercing bolt right through Frosty's left thigh, then followed up with another through her stomach as Elise broke free and dove away.

I was aiming for Frosty's shrieking face when the raknoth whirled on me and hurled Elise's chain at me so fast that I fell over dodging it. The chain whooshed by and buried itself in the smooth permacrete wall behind the breeding chambers. I hit the tile and started rolling, thinking to draw another shot on Frosty—until she ripped the pulse cannon from my hands with telekinesis. I rolled over onto one of my disks, buying a moment's protection as I scrambled back to my feet.

This had to end before Elise and I were too tired and beaten to move.

So this time, when Frosty started forward, I didn't run. I drew my remaining dagger and charged in. Elise's presence surrounded mine as I cleared the disk's field, and I let her in, trusting us to guide one another just as my extended senses guided me.

I caught Frosty high with a telekinetic shove just as Elise darted forward and kicked her knee in from behind. The raknoth stumbled, and I dropped everything I could on her, driving her down as Elise kicked her other knee in. We held her there, Elise's strength flowing through me as I grabbed Frosty's short dark hair and thrust the dagger forward with all my strength.

She caught it with her mind, and we struggled there bitterly, each second costing us precious energy. Then Frosty cocked her head back and, with a blood-curdling scream, blasted us apart with an eruption of force. I hit the tiles hard and was still sliding when a faded green shape blurred in and slammed into Frosty, carrying her halfway to the wall before they hit the ground, tumbling until I recognized Garrett's faded green jacket coming to a stop on top, cocking his fist back to strike.

I forced myself to my feet, every inch of me protesting, and winced as Frosty caught Garrett with an open hand chest strike that sent him flying back the way he'd come. Battered and wounded but seemingly still full of that frighteningly endless energy, Frosty bounced back to her feet—

And sprayed the wall behind her with dark ichor as two shots punched through her chest, accompanied by the rushing thrum of the pulse cannon. I turned and saw Johnny attempting a third shot from his prone position before he and the cannon were both blasted across the room.

Seeing Garrett brushing himself off, looking hungry for more, hearing the gunfire bark from where Elise had found my rifle, I rounded on Frosty and charged.

The raknoth waded forward, deflecting a stream of softsteel slugs.

I gathered what I had and hurled her back against the wall, pinning her there. Elise was on her feet, still shooting as she stalked in, only letting up when Garrett came flying in on an inhuman leap and crashed into Frosty's face, boot-first. I kept up the telekinetic pressure as he landed in front of her and proceeded to unload, pounding her face into the wall until she actually seemed to feel it.

She fought to break free, but I held firm, leaning into Elise's strength as well as what little I had left. And not just hers, I realized as the burden shifted again, but Siren's and Garrett's too—the four of us pressing into her with everything we had, holding nothing back.

I closed on Frosty and caught her left wrist just as Elise caught her right. Without looking, Garrett paused from his onslaught of bare knuckle punching long enough to summon my other dagger from the floor.

"You don't know what you're doing," Frosty groaned as he took her hair in hand, her crimson eyes looking pale and feeble after the pummeling. "Kill these pitiful creatures, Garrett. Kill them now."

Hesitation flashed in his pale red eyes.

"Garrett…" I said.

Frosty's face hardened.

"OBEY ME, YOU WORTHLESS INSECT!"

Garrett tensed, and for a second, I saw it all unraveling.

Then Siren was there, laying her hands on his back, whispering his name, her eyes closed in concentration, and it was as if new life flowed into him from her touch.

"Say hi to One for me, you miserable bitch," he growled.

And with that, Garrett jammed Carlisle's dagger into Frosty's underjaw with every bit of his unnatural strength.

The blade sank to the hilt, drawing an oozing stream of dark ichor and an awful wet gurgling sound. I held tight anyway, not trusting it was enough until I felt her body go limp and her mind fade from my senses.

Then I stepped back, mustering what defenses I could and giving Elise a silent look to do the same.

"Relax, Raish," Garrett said, not looking at either of us as he yanked the dagger free and let Frosty's body crumple to the ground. As an afterthought, he tossed the blade down as well. "I'm not killing anyone else today."

"That sounds like good news, then," Dillard's voice crackled in my earpiece. I looked up and saw him on the balcony, looking grimy and scuffed up but otherwise unharmed. "Sweet Alpha…" he added, surveying the wreckage of our fight.

When his gaze fell on Johnny and Edwards, he turned back to the corridor and shouted for the combat medics. I was about to ask him if the coast was clear up there when wet slurping noises drew my attention back down to where Siren and Garrett were, for lack of a better phrase, suddenly and unapologetically making out.

Between the unexpectedness of the sight and the light jittery feeling of decisively having not died, I almost could've laughed as I scooted around them, ready to wrap Elise in my arms and to never let go. Then I saw Elise, swaying in place, looking more battered than ever, her eyes unfocused and her mouth half open. I rushed to close the distance between us before she could fall.

"So we can all agree," she said weakly, "no one's killing anyone anymore?"

"No more killing today, my love," I said, wrapping her in a hug. "You're safe now."

She teetered in my arms, her head lolling back, a kind of gentle, content smile on her lips. "Okay, then."

And with that she collapsed in my arms.

4 2

DEPARTURE

"I think my concussions have concussions," Johnny murmured, blinking at the field medic's light and then frowning up at the woman herself. "Are *you* a concussion?"

"Just relax, buddy," I said as the medic shot me an exasperated look.

Squinting past me, he pointed a finger instead. "Hey, isn't that that guy? The punchy one?"

I glanced back and saw Garrett standing behind me.

"It's okay now, buddy," I said, guiding his hand back to his torso and giving him a reassuring pat. "He's real sorry about all that punching."

"Good round, Red," Garrett added, smirking quite unapologetically.

"Look who's talking, Eyes," Johnny murmured, then let out a groan. "Sorry, I think that's the concussions talking. I can do better."

"I'll look forward to that," Garrett said.

Shaking my head, I moved over to check on Elise, who'd already been looked over by the field medic who was now tending a grumbling but seemingly stable Edwards.

Astoundingly, we'd made it through the ordeal with only a single casualty—one of the pilots who'd gone down in Frosty's initial attack. Most of the legionnaires who'd been on the ground were beaten to scud, and almost half had suffered serious wounds, including a few who were most likely going to be losing limbs, one who'd lost an eye, and at least five or six who were going to be in serious trouble if the med transport they'd called in didn't hurry.

But considering what we'd just been through, it almost felt like we'd been lucky.

I stroked Elise's cheek, careful to avoid the bruises, and immediately felt scuddy for calling anything about this lucky when she roused a little and winced as if the slight movement had caused her significant pain.

Maybe not lucky, then. But we were alive. Elise was alive. And as much as it hurt me to see her like this, I knew she was going to be okay with some rest and care.

I felt Dillard hovering behind me for a few seconds before he spoke.

"She's one tough lady. Would've made a fine legionnaire."

I stood to face him, smiling a little at the thought of how things might've played out if Elise had been a tyro with me and Johnny back in Sanctuary. "I dunno, sir. Something tells me she might've gotten into some trouble."

"Hmm," Dillard said, looking faintly amused. "Can't imagine how you'd know much about that, standup ex-legionnaire like you."

"Ex-tyro, sir."

He grinned. "Even better."

"Dillard, sir, I…"

He cocked his head, clearly happy to let me squirm.

"Thank you," I finally said. "For everything."

He studied me for a stretch, then shrugged. "The way I see it, I'm just paying it forward after your father saved my life." He looked around at his Hounds all licking their respective wounds. "These crazy bastards, on the other hand…"

"I'll be sure to thank them all as best I can," I promised.

That seemed to amuse him for some reason. "I think they might just turn around and thank you right back."

At my quizzical look, he held up his palmlight. "That's why I came over here. Reports are still preliminary, but Glenbark just put out the word on Legion channels. Oasis is ours, Raish. Your cloaking packs worked."

For a second, I just stared, feeling like I should have been ecstatic but apparently too beaten and drained to feel anything more than a slightly different kind of exhausted.

"Losses?"

He just shook his head. "Not sure yet. But what say we focus on the good news for once? We won today, Raish. All of us."

"That's right, boys and girls," he added at the few heads that'd turned our way, raising his voice loud enough for everyone to hear. "While we were busy beating down boots with asses, our brothers and sisters took Oasis back from those alien bastards!"

A round of cheers rocked through the room.

"That's probably 'cause they forgot their asses back at base, sir!" one of the Hounds called from over on the stairs, which earned a round of chuckles.

"Oasis is ours," Dillard repeated, pumping the air with his hands to calm the rowdy celebration. "You know what this means, right?"

"What's it mean, sir?" a legionnaire called from the balcony.

"It means drinks are on me tonight for every one of you crazy bastards that manages to not die on the way home! You hear that Coopski?" he added, kneeling down beside a few of the legionnaires who were in critical condition. "You hear that Trells? Hollis? No dying until you're all good and drunk on my coin."

"Wouldn't dream of it, sir," one woman groaned, spawning another round of cheers and laughs.

"They pay you too much anyway, sir," another added with a pained smile.

Shaking my head at the undying spirit of legionnaires, and satisfied that Elise and Johnny were stable and that maybe, in fact, the day had been a true win on all fronts, I turned to confront the last potential problem lingering on the edge of my mind.

I found Siren and Garrett separated from the legionnaires over by the hybrid breeding chambers on the far side of the room, once again with their tongues safely tucked away in one another's mouths.

I thought about clearing my throat or coughing as I drew close, but they finally broke apart and favored me with the kind of mutual stare that made me think they must be conversing about me telepathically.

"Sounds like celebration is in order over there," Siren finally said.

"Looks like you two are on top of it."

Garrett looped an arm around Siren's waist and pulled her closer. "Lock yourself in chaste slavery for eight years and then come talk to me, kid."

"Oh, he's just squeamish about lust," Siren said, stroking Garrett's chest even as she eyed me with a mischievous grin.

Garrett frowned back and forth between us. "You didn't... Not with *him*... Not with—"

"I'm just teasing," she promised, giving him a light kiss—or not so light, it turned out.

This time, I did clear my throat.

"Look," I said, "I just…"

They stared, waiting for me to continue. But I'd forgotten about them completely. I was too busy staring at the hybrid tanks behind them, with their too-small victims floating in pseudo-peaceful rest.

I distantly heard Garrett's voice, asking me what was wrong, but I was too busy staring at the one whose auburn curls, discernible even through the greenish hue of the transition fluid, nearly brought me to my knees.

The one who looked too much like a young hybrid replica of Annabelle Wingard.

"Johnny," I whispered.

The world spun. My knees hit hard tile floor.

Something touched my shoulder.

"Did you know her?" Siren asked softly.

"JOHNNY!" I shouted.

I couldn't look away. Couldn't seem to do anything but keep muttering, "Bring Johnny," over and over again.

Siren or someone must've listened, because it wasn't long after that the sound of Johnny's approaching voice broke through the thick malaise permeating my brain.

"—thing he's been through, it's no wonder he—he—Bells?"

I finally tore my eyes away from Annabelle's still form in time to see the life drain from her brother's face.

"Bells?" he whispered again, his eyes filling with tears. "No. No…" He looked at me, his eyes pleading. "Hal, what… what's…"

I was on my feet and moving to him when he collapsed. I sank to the floor with him, embracing my friend as he shook in my arms, dazedly muttering on.

"Hal, tell me that's not… Tell me… Why…" He broke into quiet sobs like I'd never heard from him, whimpering her name over and over. "Bells…"

"She's alive, Johnny," I said when he'd finally gone silent. "I can feel her in there. We can… We'll…"

"Get her to Therese," Johnny whispered. "Bells…"

"We'll get her to Therese," I repeated, nodding, trying to sound confident about it. "She told me back at Vantage. Was appalled we were destroying the place. She said they were just people in those tanks. Just people caught in the wrong place. She'll figure this out, make it right."

"Transports are arriving, people," Dillard was calling on the other side of the room. "Let's get moving."

When I looked up, he was eyeing me and Johnny with a concerned frown, but he quickly turned back to the task of getting his legionnaires packed and ready to move. Judging him stable enough, I finally let Johnny go and shifted to sit beside him, both of us facing Annabelle side-by-side. When I glanced back at the exit procession, Dillard was hovering nearby, looking to me for some sign.

"You should get back to Haven, Johnny," I said.

"No." He shook his head. "No, I can't… can't—"

"I'll stay," I said quickly. "I'll stay right here with her until Therese can get her team over here. You go. You need the medica more than I do for once. I'll stay right here."

"Promise?"

"I promise, buddy."

He just stared at his sister until one of Dillard's men stepped in and hoisted him to his feet, guiding him away with a stream of soothing words.

"We need to blow this facility, Raish," Dillard said quietly when Johnny was out of earshot.

With a heavy breath, I pulled myself to my feet and faced him. "Maybe so. But not before we talk to Therese Brown."

"It's command I'm worried about."

"But if we have Oasis, if this war is turning… They've already found other breeding facilities. We might—"

He cut me off with a raised hand. "You don't have to convince me, Raish. Alpha only knows how many like these we'll find in the coming cycles. I'm in no more hurry than you are to write them all off as collateral damage if there's even a shot at turning them back."

He looked around the room, clearly debating our options. "It's gonna have to go through command sooner than later. But for now, I'll leave two fireteams until we can send backup and get the lab types out here to figure it out properly. You don't have to stay yourself," he added, running an assessing eye over my battered body.

I shrugged. "I promised."

He seemed to approve of the answer. "That, you did. I'll put in the official requisition for a specialist consult out here, but you should call Brown yourself. Probably faster that way."

I nodded my understanding, and Dillard went to arrange my vigil companions. It was only when he'd left that I realized Siren and Garrett were nowhere to be seen.

"Son of a…"

I dialed my cloak out, sweeping my senses all around. Nothing. It was only when I clicked the cloak completely off that I felt them somewhere on the opposite bank of the river, nestled under the cover of the trees.

"Going somewhere?" I sent.

"You all seemed busy," came Siren's voice.

"And considering the circumstances," Garrett added, *"I got the feeling you might get your unders in a twist about the whole thing."*

"Considering you might go red-eyes and start eating people, you mean?" I sent, striding over to the larger of the two gaping holes in the duraglass wall and peering into the woods across the river. I couldn't see them, but I felt them out there.

"I'm not planning on causing any trouble," Garrett sent.

"None?" Siren asked playfully, obviously for my benefit as well, seeing as she could've just said it to him in private.

I ignored her.

"I doubt any of the hybrids were planning on causing trouble either."

"I'm not a gropping hybrid," Garrett growled.

I thought about his pale red eyes and the uncanny strength and wasn't sure what else he could be. Yet he still seemed to be his usual smirky self, and his mind didn't have that strange touch of otherness I'd come to associate with the raknoth.

"What did they do to you, then?"

I wasn't sure he'd answer at all, and I also wasn't even remotely eager to try to chase them down out in the forest, so I was relieved, and then quickly confused when his reply came.

"Crazy bastard made me drink his spit."

"Spit?"

"Spit," he confirmed. *"Saliva. Sometimes he'd make me drink it. Sometimes he'd inject it. He also put me under a few times, when that bitch Nan'Reylor wasn't busy flaying my mind into submission, but I'm pretty sure all the stuff that made me... whatever I am, came from his saliva."*

"Okay," I sent, trying to process that. *"And who is he?"*

"That salt-and-pepper beardsplitter, Alton Parker."

My stomach fell. *"I think you should come back with me. You can't trust you're just gonna be okay now after he's had his... spit in you."*

"Eh, I think I'll be fine."

"You tried to kill us all less than an hour ago."

"You say that like you think it took convincing."

"I'm serious, Garrett."

"And I'm serious, Raish. I didn't go through eight years of slavery and all this alien abduction bullscud just to turn around and volunteer to be some lab rodent for the Legion and the Sanctum to poke and prod until they decide it's time to execute me. I'm done."

Alpha be damned, I didn't know what to say to that.

"He'll be safe with me," Siren added.

"So what?" I sent, feeling a bite of irritation creeping in. *"You want me to come chase you down? Is that it? Why stick around at all?"*

"Because I wanted to say thank you," Siren sent, catching me off guard once again. *"And because I wanted to apologize one last time."*

"From a safe distance?" I sent, stubbornly refusing to take her at her word, even if it did sound sincere.

"This is as sentimental as it gets. Take it or leave it."

I took a steadying breath, weighing my options, painfully aware that every minute I didn't call Therese was another minute I left Annabelle floating helplessly in that Alpha-damned tank.

"Okay. Look, I... I don't know how this is all gonna play out, but I'd rather you two not get yourselves caught by the raknoth after today. Let me at least give you cloaks before you go."

I turned to look for the disks I'd scattered around the room during our showdown, and frowned when I only spotted one.

"I think we're all set," came Siren's voice.

I looked back out over the Red River, understanding dawning like a brisk slap in the face, and there they were.

They stood together on the opposite bank, Garrett's arm looped around Siren's waist, and I could just make out Siren's guilty smile as she held out her hands to reveal the silver disks she held in each palm.

It was kind of embarrassing that I was even capable of being surprised by her sneakiness at this point.

"Goodbye, Demon," she sent.

Garrett just raised a middle finger.

Then they both vanished—from sight *and* from my extended senses.

"Assholes," I muttered. But for some reason, I actually found a little grin pulling at my lips.

Whatever else happened out there, I was pretty sure those two were going to do just fine.

43

ARRIVAL

"Much as I appreciate you bringing my daughter back alive, I'm fairly certain she'd sleep better without all the tactile stimulation."

I finished tucking the errant strand of dark hair behind Elise's ear and leaned back from her medica bed, smiling guiltily at Franco in the chair beside me.

"Guess I'm starting to understand how she felt all those times I put her through this. Not so fun from this side of the bed."

He arched a thick eyebrow. "Are you implying it was fun from the other side?"

I looked at the cuts and bruises on Elise's face, quickly healing thanks to the nanites, but still plainly visible. "This is definitely worse."

For a while, an easy silence passed between us. Then he took my shoulder and gave it a long squeeze.

"Thank you, Haldin."

When I met his gaze, I was taken aback by the warmth in his eyes.

"You know she never would've been involved in any of this if it weren't for me, right?"

He cocked his head. "Maybe not. Impossible to say, really. But what we can say with certainty is that you did everything in your power to bring her back. And here she is."

He pursed his lips, hesitating with his next thought. "When I lost Liandra..." He shook his head, his face pinched with pain. "Sometimes everything in our power simply isn't enough. I pray neither of you ever has to learn that as harshly as I did."

I searched for something to say to that but eventually surrendered to the silence. I couldn't recall having ever heard Franco talk about his wife. What little I knew about Elise's mother had come from Carlisle and from Elise herself.

"I don't know what I would do if I ever lost her," I said after a while.

He studied me with a sideward glance, and I half-expected him to feed me some line about how we were young and we'd be wise to keep our minds open and remember that life would go on. Instead, though, he said only one word.

"Don't."

I looked at him. "I don't intend to."

A low groan from Elise broke our gaze.

"Well this is awkward," she said, her voice hoarse. "You gonna throw in a swine with the dowry, Dad?"

We were both too busy rushing—or in Franco's case, hurriedly crutching —to her side and showering her in affections to produce any worthy comebacks.

"Okay, okay," she said raising her hands for space. "Sweet Alpha, who knew this was all it took to get your attention. I should get abducted more often."

"Please don't," I said.

"I should've implanted that tracking chip in you years ago," Franco said, shaking his head with a smile.

"I was so worried about you," I said quietly, cupping her cheek in my hand.

"How's that for a change?" she asked, laying her hand over mine.

"I'm not a fan," I admitted. "But it did give me the kick I needed to finish Mindsafe."

Understanding lit her eyes. "I thought I might've been hallucinating those new little toys of yours. You cracked the cloaking runes?"

"You were my inspiration."

"Oh yeah?"

I nodded and planted a kiss on her forehead. "Two stubborn-ass runes, holding each other together for all of eternity. That was all it took."

"Well if that doesn't ooze romance…" She lifted her head to look over at Franco, who'd backed away to give us a moment. "You see what you're handing me off to, here?"

Franco just smiled, looking perfectly content.

"Wait," Elise said, "so if you figured out the cloaks…"

"I made enough to share. The Legion retook Oasis yesterday."

"Oh… Oh, well that's…" She frowned. "How many days have I been out?"

"Just one," Franco said.

She looked at me. "You must've had a busy night after I left."

"I think it's safe to say we've both had better nights." Half-wincing at how insensitive I was pretty sure that sounded, I added, "Are you…?"

"I'll be okay." She considered her own words. "Psychologically scarred for life, maybe, but…"

I just held her hand, waiting to see if she'd say more.

"So, Oasis?" she asked, clearly not eager to delve into the memories right then.

Franco and I sat back down and willingly filled her in on the highlights. From what we'd heard, with the cloaking packs on hand and Four and Eight discreetly in tow, the Legion had actually rolled the raknoth forces at Oasis quite handily. So handily, in fact, that Legion command was speculating the raknoth might've been in the middle of some power struggle—possibly even civil war—when the assault had begun.

It had only been towards the end of the operation that things had gotten unexpectedly out of hand, when what sounded a lot like two Seeker-powered raknoth had blown through the Legion forces and escaped.

"Two more Frostys running around?" Elise asked, looking a bit ill. "Wonderful."

I said nothing, ruminating on my own dark memories of just how much it had taken to bring that monster down. I needed to talk to Four and Eight about what had actually happened at Oasis. Even with the hybrid army broken and the breeding facilities set to follow, I didn't want to think about how much damage two more Frostys could do out there.

"Were there any confirmed raknoth kills?" Elise asked.

"Maybe," I said. "One suspected kill, but it sounds like some of the hybrids were mature enough that they weren't sure it wasn't just one of them."

"Therese's crew is dissecting to confirm as we speak," Franco said.

"Which will hopefully just leave Alton Parker," I said. "Wherever he is."

Elise's face darkened. "He was at the facility."

"What?"

"He came to talk to me once they'd chained me up."

I hesitated, not wanting to press too hard too soon. "What did he want?"

She shook her head. "I don't know exactly. He wasn't making a whole lot of sense, but... well, for one thing, he told me he was going to send you word about where Frosty was keeping me."

"Why?"

She frowned at the memory. "I... don't know. Like I said, he wasn't making much sense. Speaking in riddles, that kind of thing."

"Well he didn't send any word, for whatever that's worth."

"Maybe Siren just beat him to it." She shook her head in disbelief. "She was the last person I expected to show up and start cutting my chains."

"I wouldn't give her too much credit, seeing as it was at least partly her fault you were taken at all."

"Duly noted," she said, frowning down at the IV line in her hand. "Speaking of which, what happened after I—"

A knock drew our collective attention to the door.

"And to think," came Johnny's voice as he hobbled into the room, escorted by Melanie, who had her arm around his waist and his arm wrapped over her shoulders. "I woke up without anyone even holding my hand." He shook his head, heaving a heavy sigh. "Where's the love, broto?"

Alpha help me, I tried to dish the banter right back, but he'd caught me by surprise, and looking at him, all I could think about was Annabelle, lying sedated in a reinforced cell here on Haven, and the sound of Johnny sobbing into my shoulder back at the facility.

"It's only because she's cuter, buddy," I forced out, tilting my head at Elise.

He smiled, but I knew it was equally forced.

Thankfully, Franco broke the tension by pulling himself up on his crutch and offering Johnny his seat. "Please," he said. "I need to get back to the lab and finish our report on potential breeding facility locations anyway."

Even the mention of breeding facilities felt like another emotional pit trap waiting to swallow us all whole, but Johnny simply thanked Franco and moved to take the seat. I rose to help him, but Melanie shooed me away, and Johnny just shrugged.

"She's cuter too, fly-boy."

"Well aren't you two just a pair of charmers," Elise said

"Aren't they?" Melanie said, stepping back

"Alpha only knows how we could ever resist."

"Astonishes the mind," Melanie agreed.

"Befuddling, through and through," Elise added.

"Perplexing, even."

Elise smiled at her. "I think I like you, Medic Mills."

Johnny gave me a wide-eyed look. "If I'd known I was walking into this, I might've just stayed in bed. Or dying on the floor."

I scrunched my face at him. "I'm not sure you were actually *dying*."

"Yeah, tell that to my internal bleeding and all eight of my concussions, broto. I didn't see you getting pummeled by a superpowered asshole."

"You mean you didn't see me get stomped *through the floor* by a super-powered asshole?"

"Okay, boys," Elise said. "I think we can all agree you both got your asses kicked really good and hard."

"*Thank you*, Lise," Johnny said, before shooting me a look. "At least *she* gets me."

Melanie, watching this all unfold with a warm smile, shook her head in wonder. "I can't tell you how relieved I am to see the three of you pull through all this madness safe and sound."

"Well, pull up a seat, goodlady," Johnny said, thumping the empty corner table beside him. "Stay a while and let us regale you with tales of our spec-tacular manliness."

Whether it was just to humor Johnny or out of genuine desire, Melanie did sit and stay for a while. And for that little while, we pretended like there weren't still Seeker-powered raknoth on the loose, and like the Sanctum wasn't still out there watching me with noose in hand. For that little while, we pretended like Johnny's sister wasn't lying comatose in some unknown stasis between human and raknoth, and like Elise hadn't just been through the worst trauma of her life.

And for that little while, it almost felt like everything was okay again.

ONE DAY. That was about all we managed before reality caught up. For what it was worth—and it felt like it was worth quite a bit—it was a damn good day. I spent the night cuddled up next to Elise in her medica bed, sleeping the sleep of the dead and waking to the wonderful revelation of her warmth in my arms.

In the morning, once Elise had been cleared to leave the medica, we stopped by our quarters long enough to bathe and change, then we went out for a walk and decided we might just never go back. Not when we could simply keep walking, hand in hand, on such a perfect sunny day. It was so nice I almost forgot we were stuck on a Legion base. But at least Glenbark had seen fit to leave me that much freedom, and under only two fireteams of guard detail now, instead of a full squad.

Perks of saving the day.

Or so I thought, until Four found us in one of the Haven gardens early that afternoon and informed us exactly how the Sanctum felt about our demonic heroics.

"Can you repeat that?" I asked, staring up at the dark-eyed Seeker who'd just decidedly ruined what had been shaping up to be a lovely day.

"The High Cleric tried to kill us all this morning."

It was only then that I noticed the pale tan line where his collar no longer rested.

"The detonation signal was triggered," Four confirmed, noticing my gaze.

"But…" I said, scrambling to remember if Siren had still been wearing hers when I'd last seen her. Or Garrett. Or Eight. "The others?"

"They're okay," Four said.

"Uh, detonation signal?" Elise asked.

"The Sanctum fitted them all with explosive collars to keep them in line," I explained.

"Oh." Elise considered that. "Oh. Holy scud, that's messed up."

"That's one way of putting it," Four muttered.

"But how did you know he was going to do it?"

"We didn't. We didn't risk abandoning our posts at all until we were sure the system had been disarmed. Even then, we left the collars on until we knew all our people were clear, just to be sure."

"So this exodus has been a long time in the making?" I asked.

"Two years, give or take," Four said. "It started with Garrett, actually. He and One were some of the first to be made aware of the previous High Cleric's impending revolution. Of course, they didn't realize what the High Cleric actually was. They thought they were fighting for the freedom of people like us, not for a gropping alien invasion. Thankfully, it got Garrett started on disabling the collar system anyway. The rest of us only came into his plan recently, right before he was taken."

I traded a look with Elise.

"He's still kind of a beardsplitter," I grumbled.

Four smiled. "I won't argue with that."

"So why did the High Cleric pull the trigger today?" Elise asked.

Four shrugged. "I'm assuming they've caught on that we're up to something by now. Scud, they might have even caught wind that Eight and I were there for the Oasis invasion. They've definitely caught on that the Legion was packing your arcane gear for the assault."

"Do you think they realize you're all still alive?" I asked.

"I sure as scud hope not," he said. "But I kind of doubt we're going to make it out of here without them finding out. Especially with Eight in the medica."

"I hadn't realized she was…" I started. "Is she okay?"

"She'll be fine," Four said. "She traded fisticuffs with Seven, or the thing that used to be Seven, when it was trying to make a break for it. Thing got ahold of her and broke a few bones."

"So those raknoth that escaped did take over more of your people?" Elise asked.

Four gave a grim nod. "Looks that way. Five was no great surprise. He might've even volunteered for this bullscud. But Seven… she always seemed all right. Makes me nervous for the rest of our people."

"Well," Elise said, "for what it's worth, there may only be one other raknoth out there without a gifted body now."

"Alton Parker," I agreed. Then, to Four, I added, "I can help you with cloaks for your people if you'd still like."

He looked a little surprised, but mostly just relieved. "That would be appreciated. We get the basic idea, but I have a feeling the execution might take a while to grasp."

He gave me an odd look as he said the last part, like he was wondering just how in demons' depths I'd managed to figure it out in the first place.

"We can work on it together," I said.

"Where are you headed after that?" Elise asked. "You said something about making it out of here with Eight?"

"You do realize you're probably on the Sanctum's kill list too now, right?" I added.

He smirked. "I'm familiar with how they do business. Our people will be waiting for us in a safe place. We'd like to join them."

I wanted to ask for more details, but it was pretty clear he'd said all he wanted to say on the matter.

"No more fighting the good fight?" I asked instead.

He shrugged. "As far as I can tell, there's more than a few good fights to be fought out there. We don't wish to incur the Sanctum's wrath any more than we already have."

I couldn't really blame them for that. Especially not when I'd spent all morning wishing I could somehow escape it all myself. But I couldn't. And even as we said our farewells with Four and made plans for a cloaking rune session that evening, I had the distinct feeling that he and Eight might well yet find themselves pulled into this scudstorm as inexorably as I seemed to be. But maybe that was just wishful thinking.

I was kind of conflicted on the matter.

"What are you thinking about?" Elise asked some time later when we'd been sitting together in the garden for a good while, lost in our own thoughts.

I paused and realized I'd been toying with Carlisle's holodisk. "Guess I'm just wondering if maybe the Seekers don't have the right idea, running for the hills and not looking back."

"Sounds like Four and Eight did look back. Pretty hard."

"Yeah, I guess they did. It's just… I can't stop wondering how many more Shapers are out there, living in the shadows, either ignorant of their power or terrified of it. I mean, can you imagine how much quicker the raknoth invasion could've been shut down if people like us were… I don't know, common? Accepted?"

Elise arched an eyebrow at me. "Can you imagine how frightened everyone *else* would be if they understood how easily someone could walk by and steal their darkest secrets, or make them do anything they wanted?"

I frowned. "We don't really have to imagine. We're already looking at what happens when the fear wins."

"Hey," she said, holding her hands up, "I'm not arguing with you. Just pointing out the first of many prominent roadblocks to that world."

I sighed. "We need to find Burton Kovaks and his pasty little friend."

She didn't argue, or even ask what I might hope to learn out of the endeavor. Probably because she knew that I had no idea what we might find. Only that Kovaks and Pasty had too many arcane secrets stashed away down there with their elaborate rune devices and their ancient Emmútari records.

"You ever wonder what our relationship would be like if we were just normal civilian kids?" she asked after a thoughtful silence. "Like, if our biggest concern was where we could sneak a swive instead of whether or not we could win a war or survive being hunted by aliens and the entire Sanctum?"

I scrunched my face up. "Ehhh, I don't think it would've worked out between us."

She shot me a dramatically affronted look. "Oh, no?"

I shook my head. "Nah. I think you would've realized pretty quickly that I'm actually a breathtakingly boring guy when no one's trying to kill m—"

An alarm blared so loud that it almost seemed to be coming from inside my head.

"You've gotta be gropping kidding me," I growled, jumping to my feet and clamping my hands over my ears as the alarm amp fired up again.

I looked around, noting an immediate spike in activity all around us—legionnaires gathering, shouting to one another, and pointing toward... what, exactly? I followed the stares, squinting, and spotted a dark speck in the eastern sky.

A dark speck that was getting closer. Fast.

Too fast.

No sooner had I seen it growing closer than it seemed to be rushing by overhead, so fast I could barely make out more than a dark purplish hue and an elongated hull.

"Well," Elise said breathlessly beside me. "Nothing boring about that."

We exchanged a look, and set off after the ship without another word.

We were halfway to the western edge of Haven, about ten minutes into the trek, when my palmlight buzzed with a call from Glenbark herself.

"That can't be good," Elise said.

I slid my earpiece in and answered.

"Sir?"

"Haldin." She hesitated more than I was used to. Probably, she was just addressing someone on the other end. "I need you at the western gate, immediately."

"On my way already. This doesn't happen to have anything to do with the thing that just zipped past Haven, does it?"

"Just hurry, please."

She killed the connection.

I shot Elise an uneasy look.

"I've got a bad feeling about this," she said.

"And here I was thinking that was my line."

Somehow, neither of us smiled.

Quickening our pace, we arrived about five minutes later to a growing crowd of onlookers. Several companies' worth of heavily-armed legionnaires were piled on the western walls and towers, all clearly ready to blow whatever was on the other side of the wall straight to demon's depths.

I had a decent guess where the unidentified purple blur had landed.

I clicked my pendant off and tried to reach my senses ahead only to find there were at least a few cloaking packs nearby—more than a few, actually, judging by how many odd little cloaking field pockets I found myself passing through in just the next ten yards alone.

I decided I might have to do something about that at some point, but now clearly wasn't the time to worry about such things.

Finding Glenbark, at least, wasn't much of a challenge. We pushed our way toward her, the crowd parting to admit us more readily the closer we got. Johnny found us just before we reached her, dressed in a tunic and no armor, which reminded me that I was equally unprotected in my civilian clothes.

The one day I decide to go without the armor skin.

"Had a feeling I'd find you guys here," Johnny said, pushing over to us. "Any idea what's going on?"

"We were about to ask you," I admitted.

Ahead, Glenbark waved down a captain who was talking rather animatedly with his hands and disengaged from her officers to come join us. My insides clenched when I saw the murderous glare General Auckus aimed at her retreating back. His gaze shifted from Glenbark to me and back again, only darkening. Traitor or no, that look left little question about it. He wasn't done with either of us.

But the gravity in Glenbark's expression suggested we had more pressing problems at the moment.

"It's Alton Parker's ship," she said without preamble as she drew close, speaking just loud enough to be heard over the commotion around us.

"As in, his *ship* ship?" Johnny asked. "His… alien ship?"

"We've never seen anything like it," she admitted, turning to me. "And he's made it clear he'll talk to you and you only, Haldin."

"What? Why?"

She shook her head. "I can only assume for the same reason he's seen fit to target you in the past, whatever that might be. He wouldn't say more than that. Only that it has to be you and that, if we try anything, it will take no more than his death or a single telepathic thought to trigger his ship to destroy the entire planet."

"And you believe that?" Elise asked.

"I wouldn't go that far." Glenbark glanced toward the gate. "But given that I've also never seen a ship like that, I'm disinclined to casually dismiss a planetary threat." She looked at me. "Are you willing to speak with him?"

I looked to Elise.

"I don't like it," We both sent at the same time.

"They're not going to let me go with you, are they?"

"You're one day out of the medica."

"That's rich, coming from you."

"I don't like it either, for what it's worth," Glenbark said, guessing the gist of our exchange.

"But hey," Johnny said, "on the bright side, we finally found the ship, right?"

"Yeah, Praise Alpha," Elise muttered.

Glenbark ignored their comments, still fixed on me. "We have over twenty snipers on him, and you won't have to leave our sight. He's waiting out in the open."

I half-thought about asking her to clear the cloaking packs out of the area so I could commune with him from that very spot, but on top of that being a dangerous idea, it probably didn't matter anyway. If Alton Parker wanted a face-to-face, he probably wouldn't be happy until we played his little game. That alone made me want to refuse. But there had to be a damn good reason he'd decided to make such a drastic move.

We needed to know what he was up to.

"Hal, I really don't like this," Elise sent.

"I know." I held her gaze until I felt the shift between us and knew that we'd come to the same decision.

"Just please don't get on that ship," she said quietly.

"I'll second that," Glenbark said. "No matter what threats he might make."

I nodded, kissed Elise's forehead, touched Johnny's shoulder, and started for the gate. At an order from Glenbark, the massive doors began to open with a ponderous groan.

It was embarrassing, seeing doors that enormous opening just to let one man through. Even more so when some of the legionnaires lining the way decided to turn and throw me salutes. I walked on, trying not to blush, trying not to let it show just how much I did not want to march through that gate.

The gargantuan doors halted in their tracks when the opening was no wider than a few shoulder widths. I paused at the threshold, fighting the urge to look back. The doors loomed over me, pressing in like the dark jaws of some colossal beast.

I stepped into the gap.

Halfway through, I caught sight of Alton Parker. He stood a hundred yards from the wall in a crisp dark suit, watching me with crimson eyes.

The ship parked behind him was of alien origin—I was almost positive about that the moment I laid eyes on it. Tracing the long, oddly flowing shape of the hull as I emerged from the gate doors, I could see it was larger than five or six transports combined, but probably smaller than a legion carrier. As to what the hull was made from, I didn't have the faintest idea. It seemed to have a deep, dark purple hue to it, but it shimmered with a kind of iridescence that made it hard to tell for sure.

I shifted my focus back to Alton Parker, remaining vigilant, but he seemed content just watching, waiting. I drew my mental defenses tighter and continued out to meet him.

"Haldin Raish," he finally said when I was within easy speaking distance. "Demon. Savior. Bastard son of Enochia."

"What do you want with me, Parker?"

Instead of answering, he just studied me for a long while. Too long. I pulled a telekinetic barrier in place, suddenly sure he must be waiting for some trap to spring—for hybrids to come pouring out of his ship, or for one of Frosty's peers to telekinetically yank me in.

The silence stretched.

Then he came to some decision, took a short step forward, and offered his wrists out to me with a smile, as if courteously inviting himself to be shackled.

"I think it's time we had ourselves a proper talk."

END BOOK TWO

AUTHOR'S NOTE

THE "META NOTE" EDITION (UPDATED SEPTEMBER 7TH, 2020)

Let me ask you something, Dear Reader: Do you remember the worst nightmare you've ever had?

It's probably a rhetorical question here, given that it's kinda hard to reply via book back matter. But, if you're like me, you probably have a few (thousand) you'll never forget.

Truth be told, when I was a wee little lad, it was actually a rare occasion I *didn't* jolt awake at least once to go running and crying to dear ol' Mom about the nightmare flavor of the night. It was pretty bad.

There were the running-from-monsters dreams *(legs like Jello in quicksand)*. There were the random falling dreams *(I never woke up in time to avoid impact)*. There were the midnight murder castle sagas *(embarrassingly gratuitous for the mind of a five-year-old child)*.

There was even a gang of persistent mobsters who'd often chase me from one shifting dreamscape to the next, beating me bloody whenever they caught me *(my guidance counselor recommended I try sprouting wings and flying away from them—those cheeky pricks sprouted handguns and shot me down)*.

(In hindsight, it's *possible* I was wound a bit tight for a child.)

Through it all, though, there was one nightmare that I'll always remember above all the rest. The one that struck me straight to the core.

See, by that point, the nightmares had become so frequent and multilayered (a nightmare within a nightmare, Inception-style) that I could never really trust that I was *actually* safe until I'd made it to dear ol' Ma's arms.

Expanding on the Inception metaphor, she was basically the totem *(bless her friggin' heart)* that anchored me back to the real world and convinced me that I was actually awake and everything was okay. (For real this time.)

Then came that fateful night.

That night, I was running from the red-eyed lizard people at the carnival *(you know, THAT old chestnut)*. Running straight to dear ol' Ma, in that particular dream.

I still remember the way she reached for me in that yellow pajama dress of hers, beckoning me into the safety of her embrace.

And I'll never forget the stomach-clenching horror I felt as she morphed into one of the monsters right before my eyes.

(We're talking full-on green, scaly Mama-monster in a friggin' yellow nightgown. Which, admittedly, sounds kinda comical nowadays. But back then…)

Imagine, little Momma's Boy waking from yet another terrible nightmare only to find, for the first time ever, that he had no one to run to. That he was in fact suddenly TERRIFIED of the one person who was always supposed to be there, no matter what.

That night, for the first time ever, I felt what it was like to lose my trusted totem. Reality was broken. Nowhere was safe.

Of course, I got over it in the light of day. But that feeling? It stuck with me. I'll never forget it. I'm pretty sure it was the first time I'd ever felt truly unsafe—my first naive little inkling that the world, for all its bubbly "rightness," could also be a dangerous place, and that even the people we trust the most can sometimes fail us without warning, sometimes for reasons beyond their control.

Momma couldn't protect me from everything, after all.

(How's *that* for a sobering tale of five-year-old disillusionment?!)

And while I'd totally be lying if I said I ever suspected back then that this experience had planted the seeds of what would eventually grow into an epic dystopian alien invasion trilogy...

Well, I guess it doesn't matter what I suspected. Because that's totally what happened. (Or so I tell myself now, looking back through narrative-colored glasses.)

It's often said that most writers' first novels end up being highly autobiographical, whether they like it or not (and even if that "autobiographical" nature ends up hidden beneath several layers of otherworldly magic powers and alien incursions and whatnot).

To that end, you probably won't be all that surprised to hear that this story—that of a young man finding his once-unshakeable world suddenly overturned by insidious alien invasion—was actually the first full-length novel I ever wrote.

(It probably also doesn't come as a surprise that the red-eyed lizard people made their triumphant return as the culprits of this shadowy planetary heist.)

What you might NOT have guessed (unless you happen to be quite the shrewd psychoanalyst) is that I also lost my father to pancreatic cancer in the middle of writing this book.

And while that's not something I just toss casually into discussion most days, in this case it seems particularly pertinent.

See, it's probably no coincidence that this story begins and ends with Hal losing father figures. I still remember the first night I sat down and started writing. I'd just gotten home from grad school to visit my father as he began chemo in the wake of his diagnosis.

Interestingly enough, the very first draft actually didn't even show Hal's life in Sanctuary before Kublich's attack. It opened (perhaps cringe-worthily) directly with Hal hearing his mother scream and racing out of the sim room to find a red-eyed monster laying into his parents.

That same draft made it about as far as Hal's trial at the White Tower before I finally realized the rather obvious fact that I had no clue how to finish the story.

It was only months after my father had passed that I finally came back to the manuscript and saw Carlisle's sacrifice sitting there clear as day, just waiting to be written. Once that was done, I returned to the opening chapter to add an *actual* opening and properly explore what it was Hal had had before that red-eyed monster came bursting in to take it all away.

The reader needed to better understand what Hal had lost, I told myself. Which was probably true. But in hindsight, I can't help but think now that the same thing was probably doubly true of myself.

The funniest part in all of this is that it took me well over a year to look back and realize what I'd actually done—how the pieces had fallen in such neat, predictable synchronicity with the events of my own life.

And if you're currently wondering why in the name of Alpha I'm telling you ANY of this overly personal mumbo jumbo... well, amongst other things, I guess it's because there's the stuff that we bumbling pen monkeys *mean* to say with our stories... and then there's the stuff that falls out of us whether we intend to let it or not.

In my limited experience, it's that latter bit that tends to scratch at the good stuff.

All of which to say, I sure hope you've found something of value in these pages—even if it was just a compelling read. This story has meant a lot to me for a lot of different reasons, and I truly do appreciate you coming along for the ride.

In fact, now that we're proper old chums, I'd love to give you something more than a simple *thank you*.

I'd love to give you the rest of the story.

See, the more I realized how much of me was tied up in this book, the more I was pulled to circle back and revisit the events surrounding Hal's journey in *Shadows of Divinity*.

I ended up writing two additional stories. (In addition to the next two books of the main trilogy, that is.)

The first was a kind of eulogy for Carlisle, written in the format of a short story called *Eye of the Storm*.

The second was a full-length novel called *Fallen*, which explored the events both leading up to and throughout *Shadows of Divinity* through the eyes of none other than Garrett (AKA Smirks) the Seeker.

I was pleasantly surprised by what I found in writing them both. And today, I'd like to share them with you, free of charge. All you have to do is tell me where to send them.

Interested? Just go to *lukermitchell.com/demons-of-divinity-signup*

There, you'll be able to join my mailing list and download your free copies of *Fallen* and *Eye of the Storm*.

Plus, in addition to occasional behind-the-scenes notes like the one above (which was actually adapted from a few of my Sunday newsletters), as a member of the list, you'll *also* get access to free books from all of my other fictional worlds—as well as discounts and short stories you won't find anywhere else. (Carlisle's *Eye of the Storm* story, for instance, is only available in the box set or to my mailing list readers.)

All you have to do is visit the link above to join the party and grab both Enochian War stories free today!

'Nuff said? Got it.

If newsletters and email shenanigans aren't your bag, no worries. You can also just go to *lukermitchell.com/books* to find the full list of my published works—including the trilogy finale, *Children of Enochia* (Enochian War

Book Three). Whichever way you go, I sure do hope you enjoy your next adventure!

Thanks so much for reading.

We'll see you on the other side.

Cheers,
Luke Mitchell

ABOUT THE AUTHOR

Not a llama. Mostly human.

Luke is a storyteller whose dreams include learning the ways of the Force, becoming a sentient robot, and maybe even one day growing up. Also, lots of zombies… Don't ask.

Oh, and that "growing up" bit? That was a lie.

After studying engineering science at Penn State and neuroengineering at Drexel, Luke finally decided to throw in the towel on building a working Iron Man suit and opted instead to simply make things up and write them down. Boy, is he having more fun now.

When he's not holed up in his writing cave trying to string words together, he can often be found powerlifting, video-gaming, reading, and/or drinking the darkest, most roasty beers he can get his mitts on. Sometimes all at once.

But you know what? That's enough about Luke. He's really not that interesting. Still, if you'd like to say hi to him for whatever reason, he'd probably be glad to hear from you!

Go to **lukermitchell.com/demons-of-divinity-signup** to join the mailing list and grab your free copies of *Fallen* and the list-exclusive, *Eye of the Storm*, today!

Additionally (as you wish)…

Follow me on BookBub for new release alerts
bookbub.com/authors/luke-r-mitchell

Browse the rest of my published titles
lukermitchell.com/books

Join the Patreon team for digital copies of ALL of my work (past, present, and future) — and much more!
patreon.com/lukermitchell

Thank you for reading!